KARA LEOPARD · KELLY & NICHOLE MATTHEWS

PANDORA'S LEGACY ™

kaboom! ™

PANDORA'S LEGACY, November 2018. Published by KaBOOM!, a division of Boom Entertainment, Inc. Pandora's Legacy is ™ & © 2018 Kara Leopard. All rights reserved. KaBOOM!™ and the KaBOOM! logo are trademarks of Boom Entertainment, Inc., registered in various countries and categories. All characters, events, and institutions depicted herein are fictional. Any similarity between any of the names, characters, persons, events, and/or institutions in this publication to actual names, characters, and persons, whether living or dead, events, and/or institutions is unintended and purely coincidental. KaBOOM! does not read or accept unsolicited submissions of ideas, stories, or artwork.

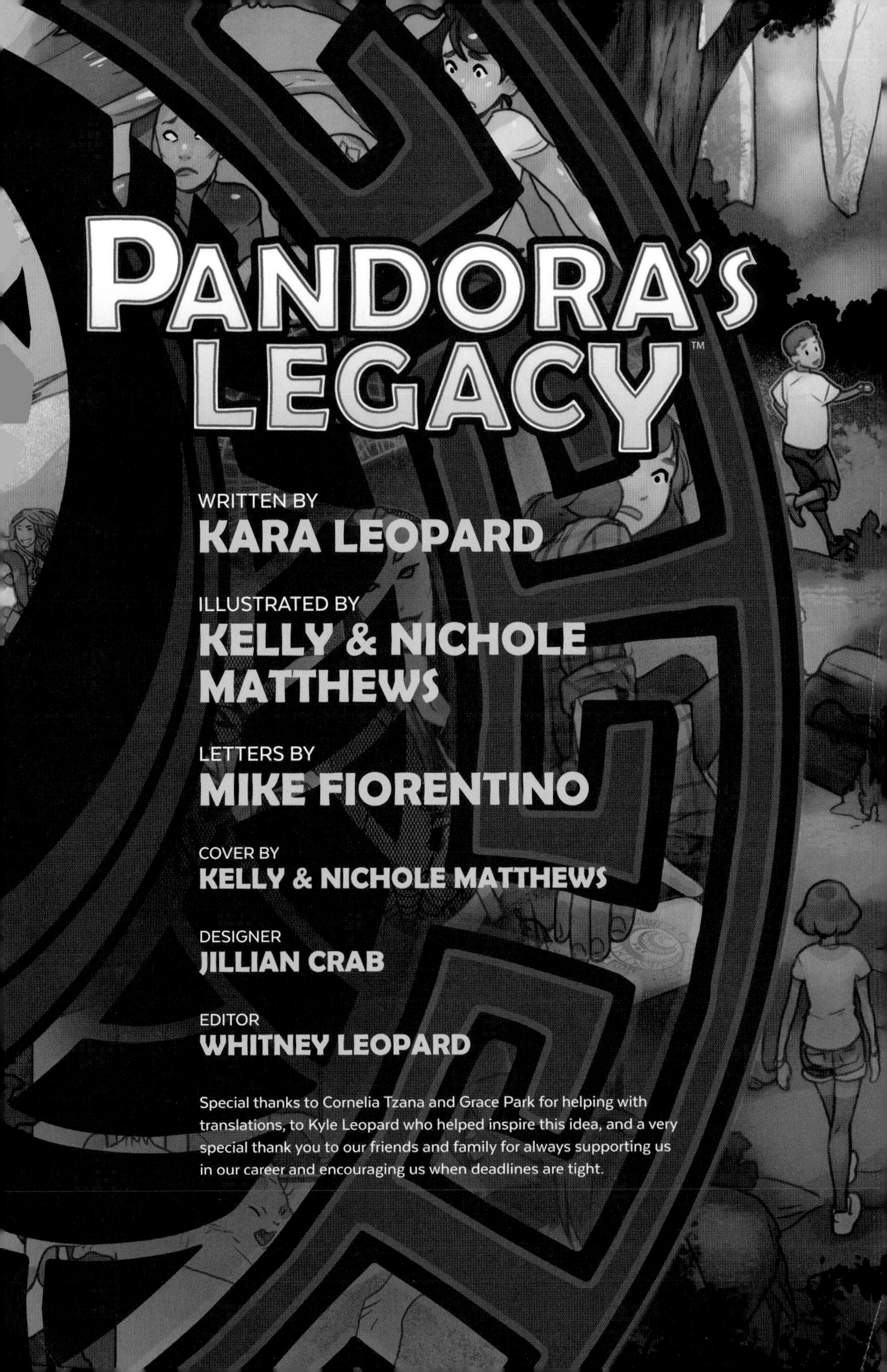

PANDORA'S LEGACY™

WRITTEN BY
KARA LEOPARD

ILLUSTRATED BY
KELLY & NICHOLE MATTHEWS

LETTERS BY
MIKE FIORENTINO

COVER BY
KELLY & NICHOLE MATTHEWS

DESIGNER
JILLIAN CRAB

EDITOR
WHITNEY LEOPARD

Special thanks to Cornelia Tzana and Grace Park for helping with translations, to Kyle Leopard who helped inspire this idea, and a very special thank you to our friends and family for always supporting us in our career and encouraging us when deadlines are tight.

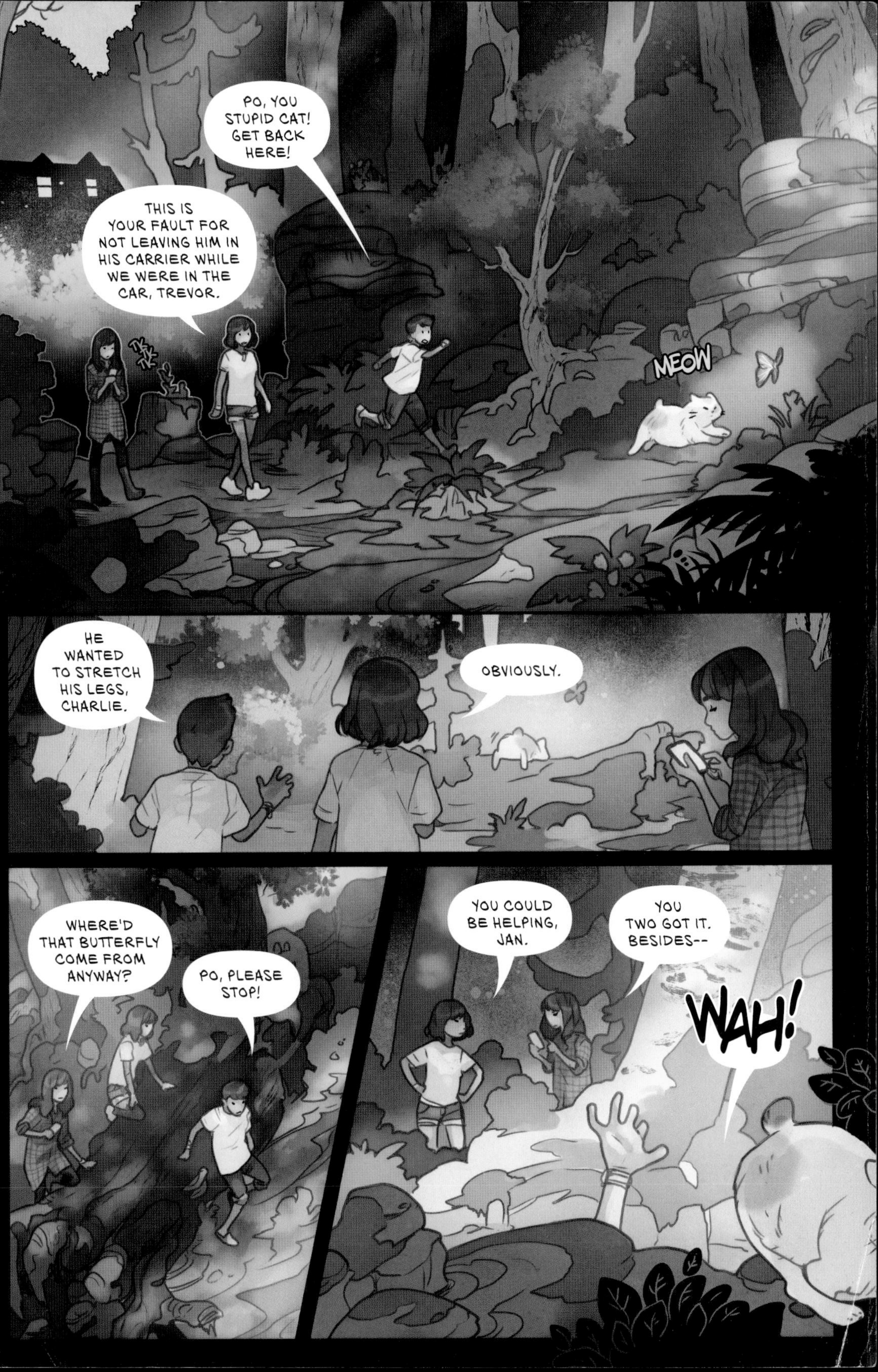
PO, YOU STUPID CAT! GET BACK HERE!
THIS IS YOUR FAULT FOR NOT LEAVING HIM IN HIS CARRIER WHILE WE WERE IN THE CAR, TREVOR.
TK TK TK
MEOW
HE WANTED TO STRETCH HIS LEGS, CHARLIE.
OBVIOUSLY.
WHERE'D THAT BUTTERFLY COME FROM ANYWAY?
PO, PLEASE STOP!
YOU COULD BE HELPING, JAN.
YOU TWO GOT IT. BESIDES--
WAH!

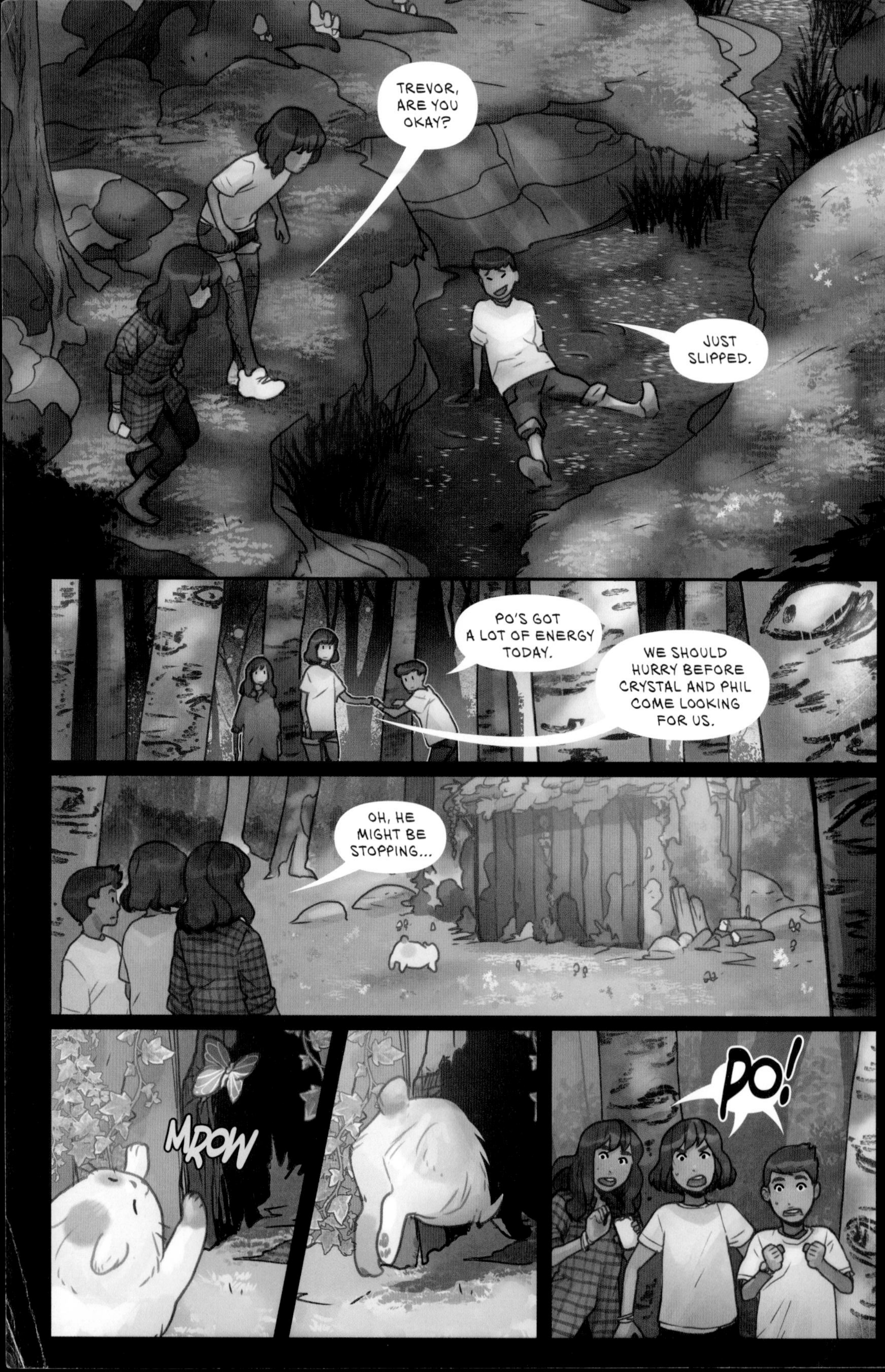

TREVOR, ARE YOU OKAY?
JUST SLIPPED.
PO'S GOT A LOT OF ENERGY TODAY.
WE SHOULD HURRY BEFORE CRYSTAL AND PHIL COME LOOKING FOR US.
OH, HE MIGHT BE STOPPING...
MROW
PO!

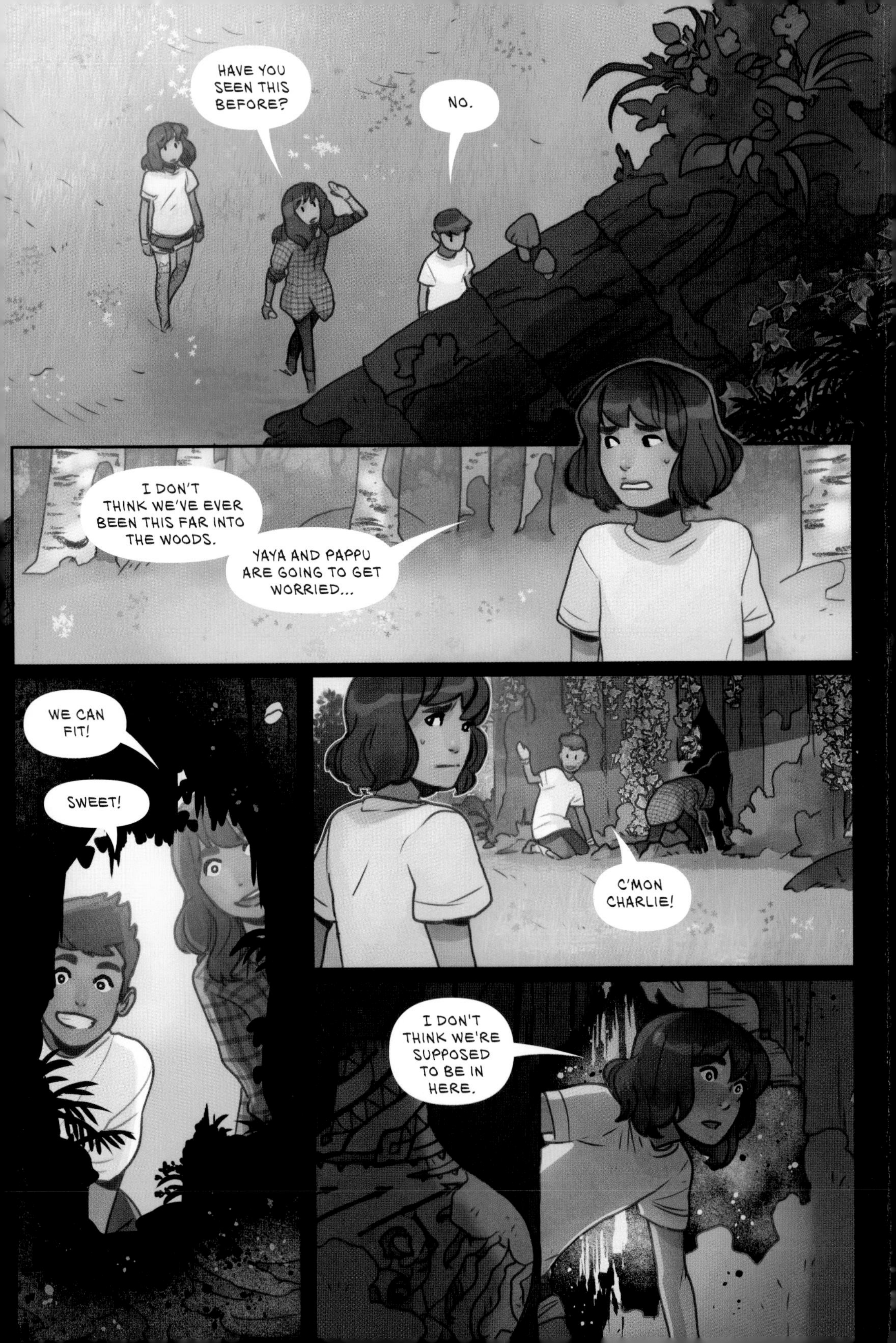
HAVE YOU SEEN THIS BEFORE?
NO.
I DON'T THINK WE'VE EVER BEEN THIS FAR INTO THE WOODS.
YAYA AND PAPPU ARE GOING TO GET WORRIED...
WE CAN FIT!
SWEET!
C'MON CHARLIE!
I DON'T THINK WE'RE SUPPOSED TO BE IN HERE.

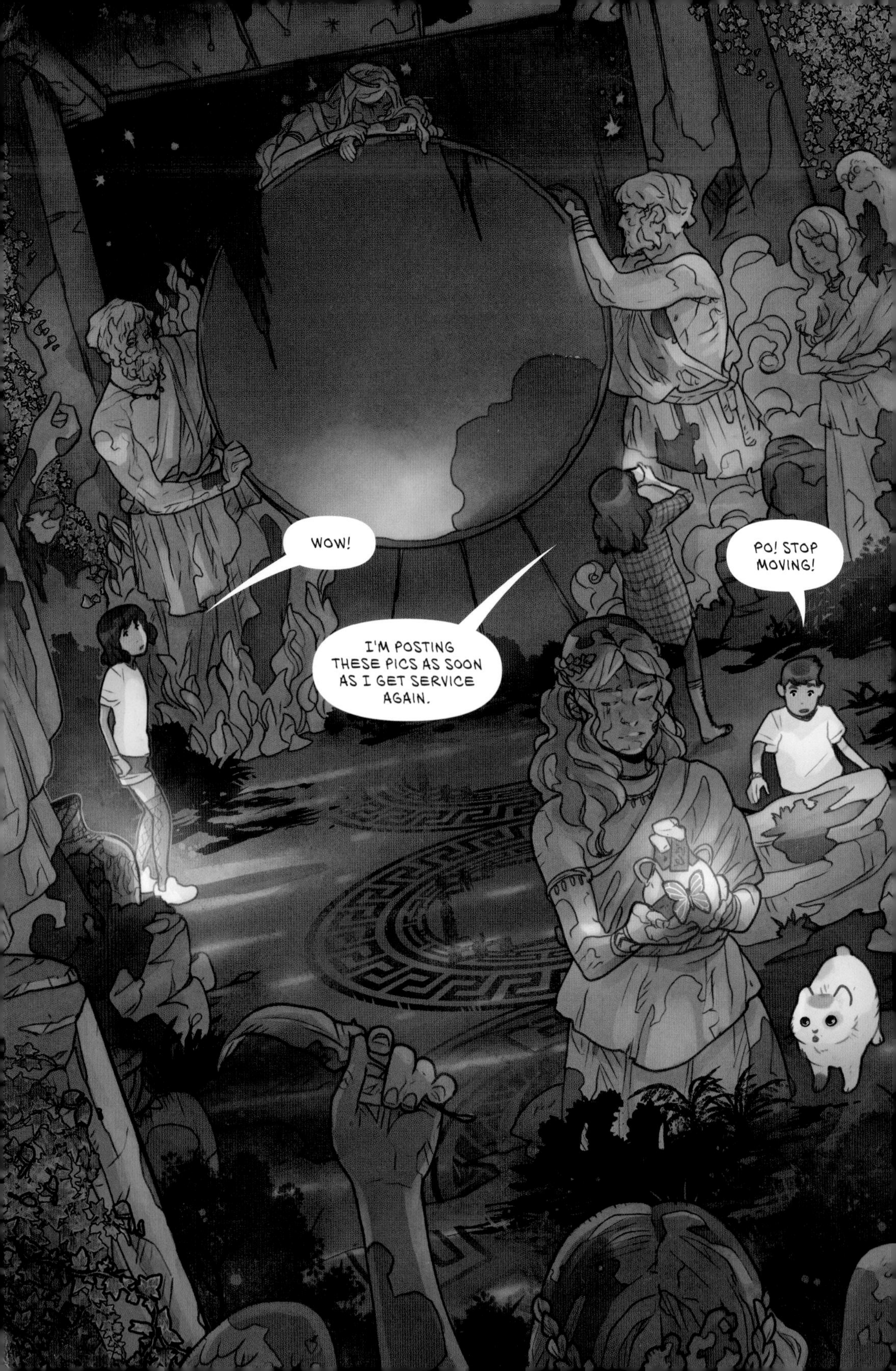
WOW!
I'M POSTING THESE PICS AS SOON AS I GET SERVICE AGAIN.
PO! STOP MOVING!

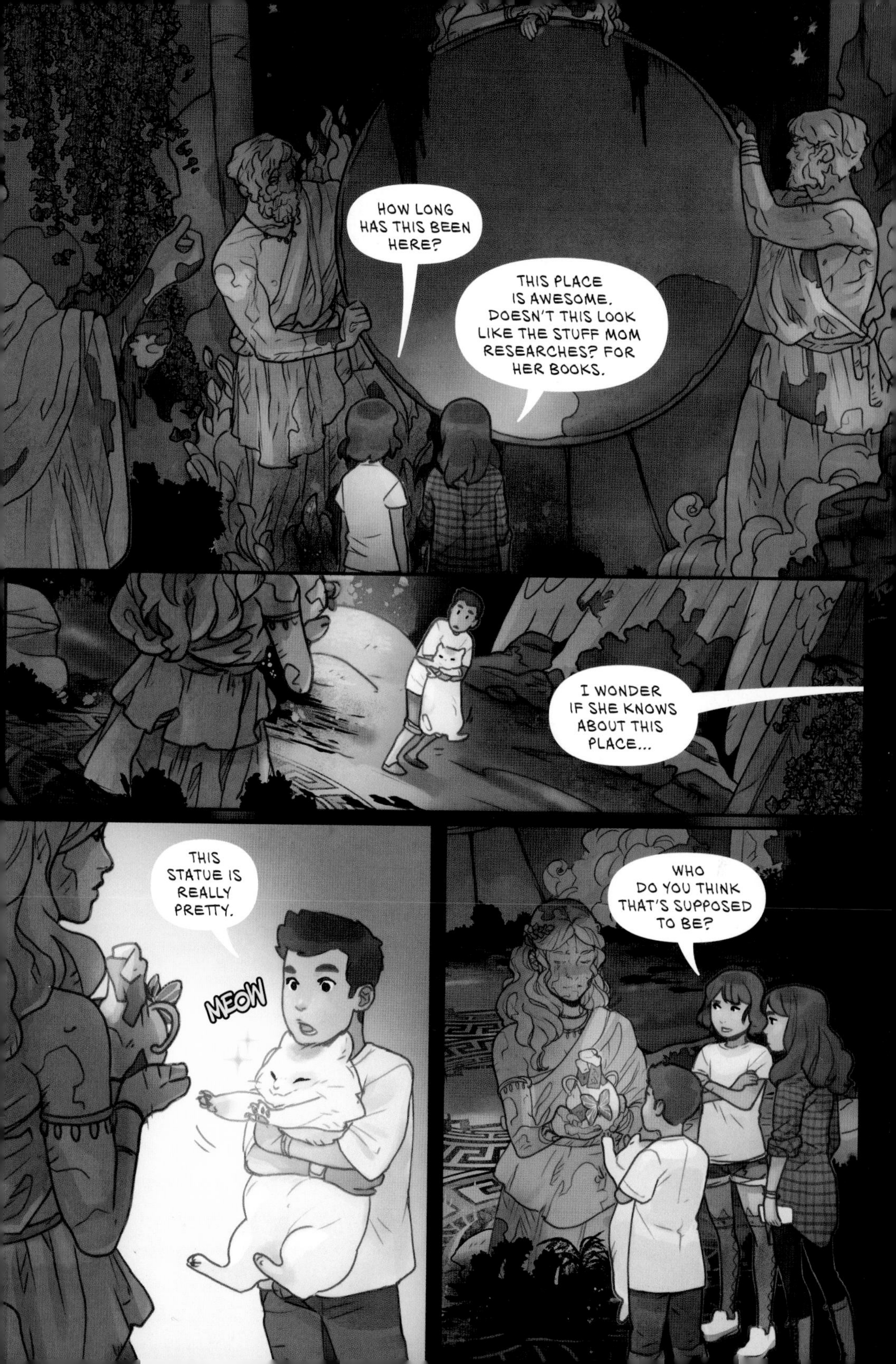
HOW LONG HAS THIS BEEN HERE?
THIS PLACE IS AWESOME. DOESN'T THIS LOOK LIKE THE STUFF MOM RESEARCHES? FOR HER BOOKS.
I WONDER IF SHE KNOWS ABOUT THIS PLACE...
THIS STATUE IS REALLY PRETTY.
MEOW
WHO DO YOU THINK THAT'S SUPPOSED TO BE?

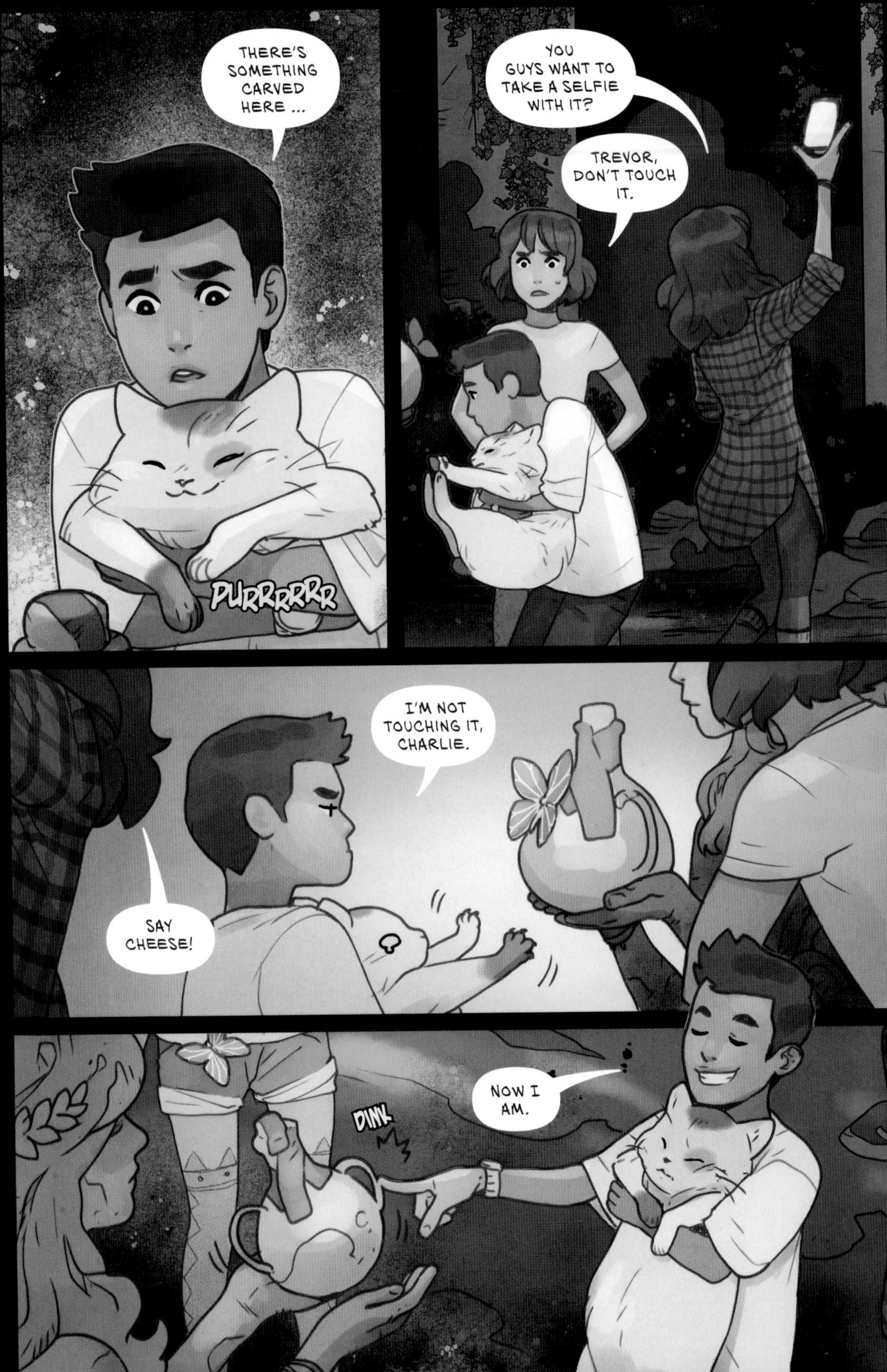
THERE'S SOMETHING CARVED HERE ...
PURRRRRR
YOU GUYS WANT TO TAKE A SELFIE WITH IT?
TREVOR, DON'T TOUCH IT.
I'M NOT TOUCHING IT, CHARLIE.
SAY CHEESE!
DINK
NOW I AM.

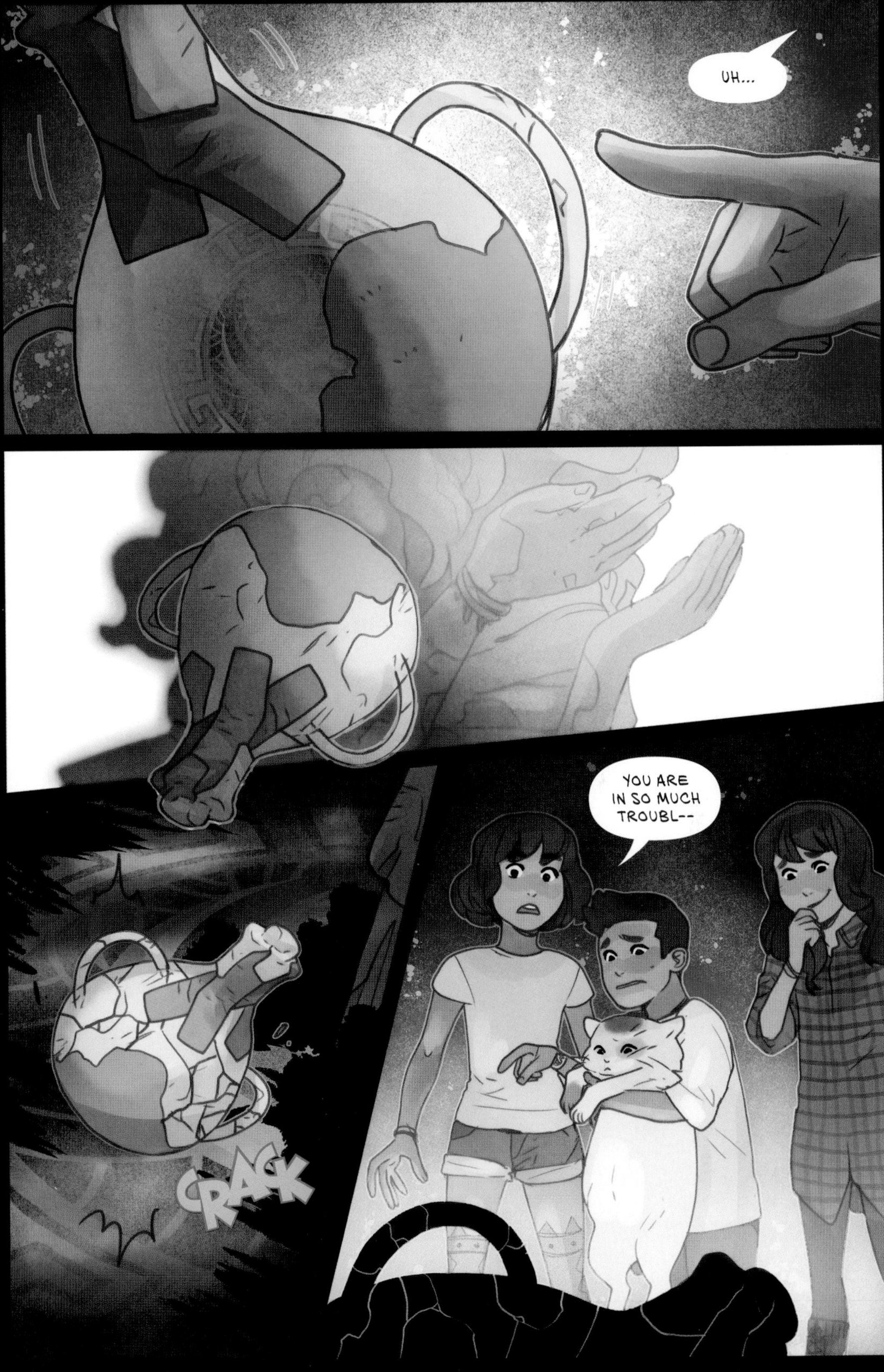
UH...
YOU ARE IN SO MUCH TROUBL--
CRACK

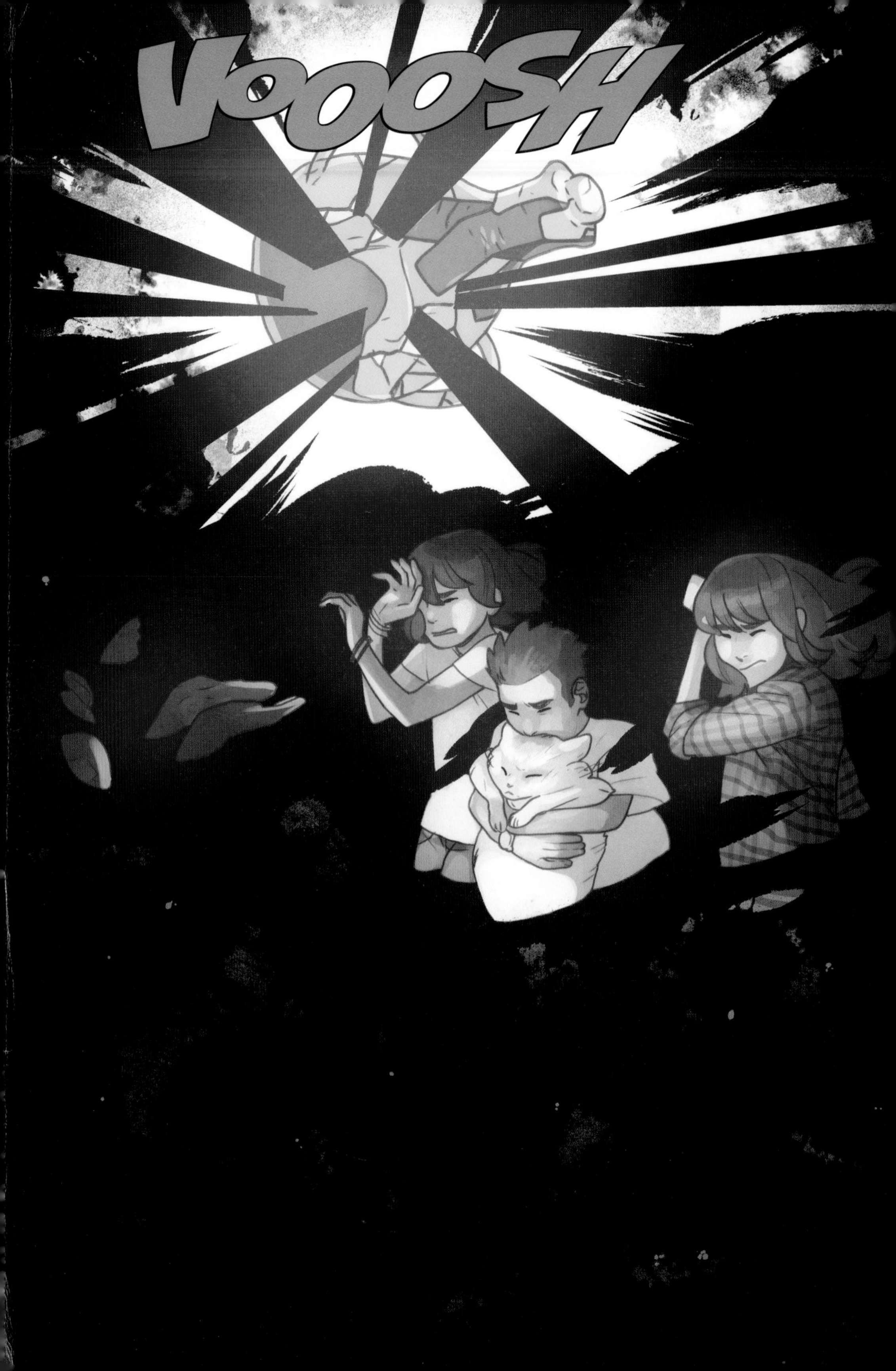
VOOOSH

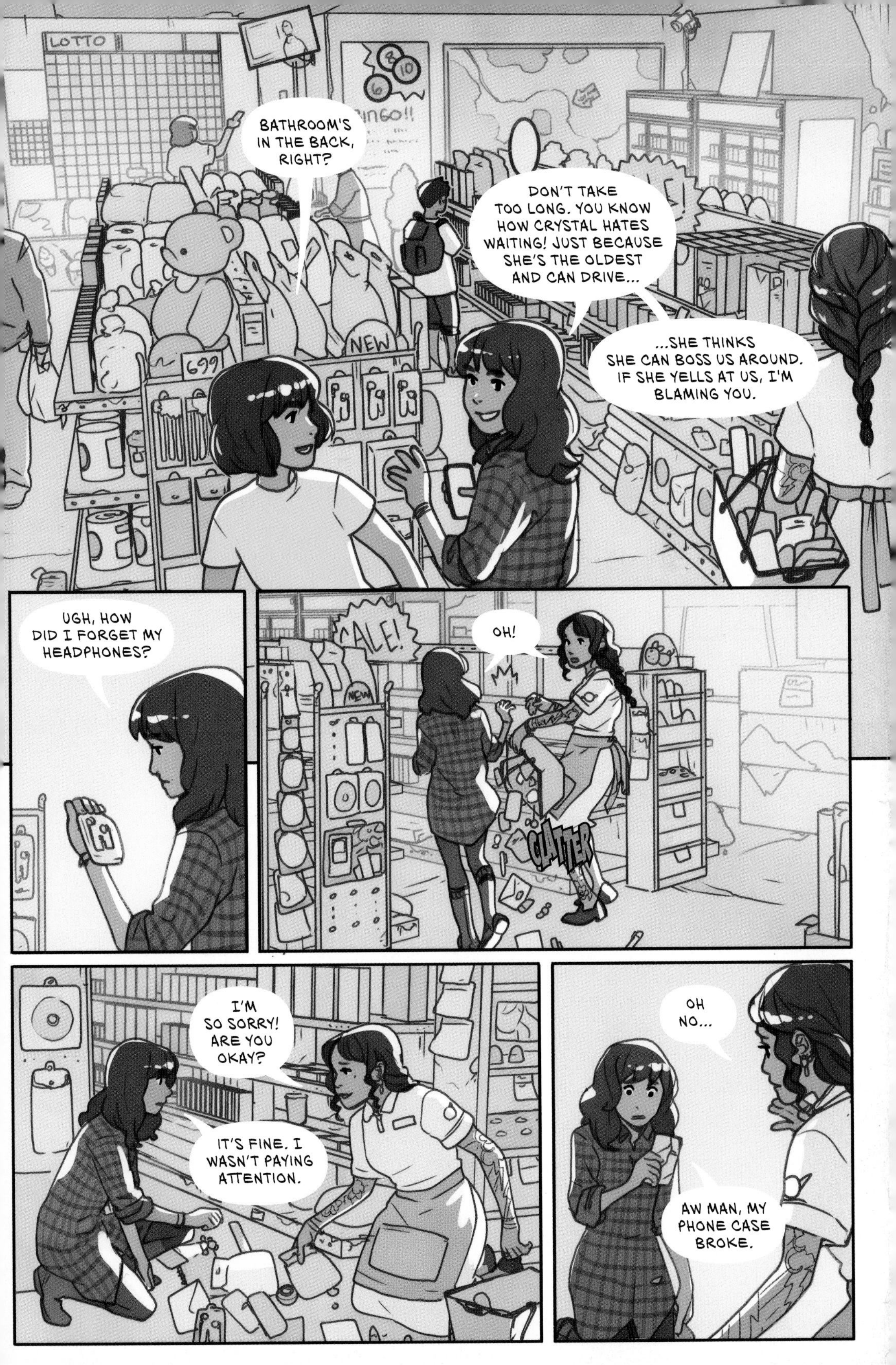
LOTTO
BINGO!!
BATHROOM'S IN THE BACK, RIGHT?
DON'T TAKE TOO LONG. YOU KNOW HOW CRYSTAL HATES WAITING! JUST BECAUSE SHE'S THE OLDEST AND CAN DRIVE...
...SHE THINKS SHE CAN BOSS US AROUND. IF SHE YELLS AT US, I'M BLAMING YOU.
NEW
699
UGH, HOW DID I FORGET MY HEADPHONES?
SALE!
OH!
CLATTER
I'M SO SORRY! ARE YOU OKAY?
IT'S FINE. I WASN'T PAYING ATTENTION.
OH NO...
AW MAN, MY PHONE CASE BROKE.

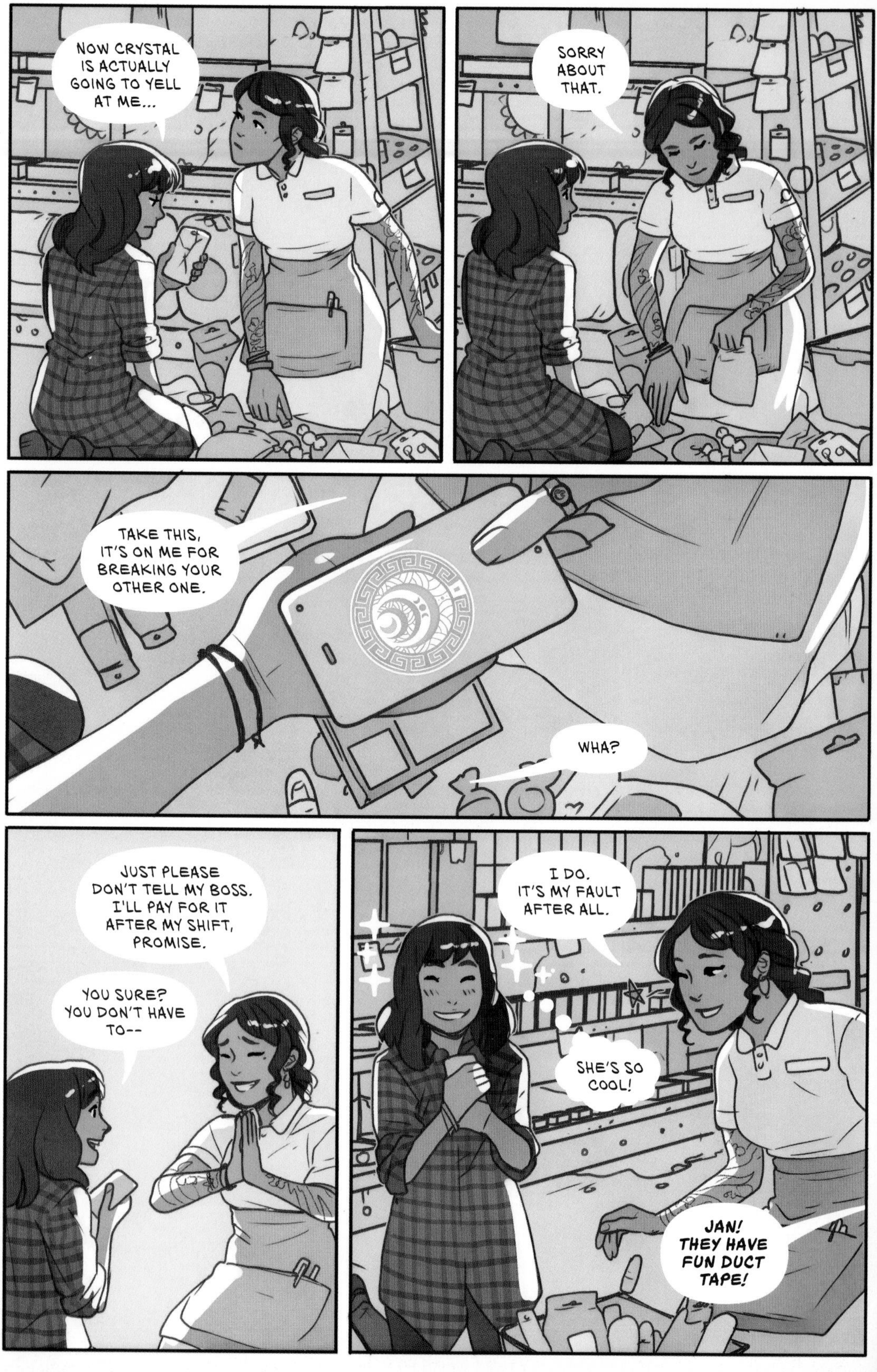
NOW CRYSTAL IS ACTUALLY GOING TO YELL AT ME...
SORRY ABOUT THAT.
TAKE THIS, IT'S ON ME FOR BREAKING YOUR OTHER ONE.
WHA?
JUST PLEASE DON'T TELL MY BOSS. I'LL PAY FOR IT AFTER MY SHIFT, PROMISE.
YOU SURE? YOU DON'T HAVE TO--
I DO. IT'S MY FAULT AFTER ALL.
SHE'S SO COOL!
JAN! THEY HAVE FUN DUCT TAPE!

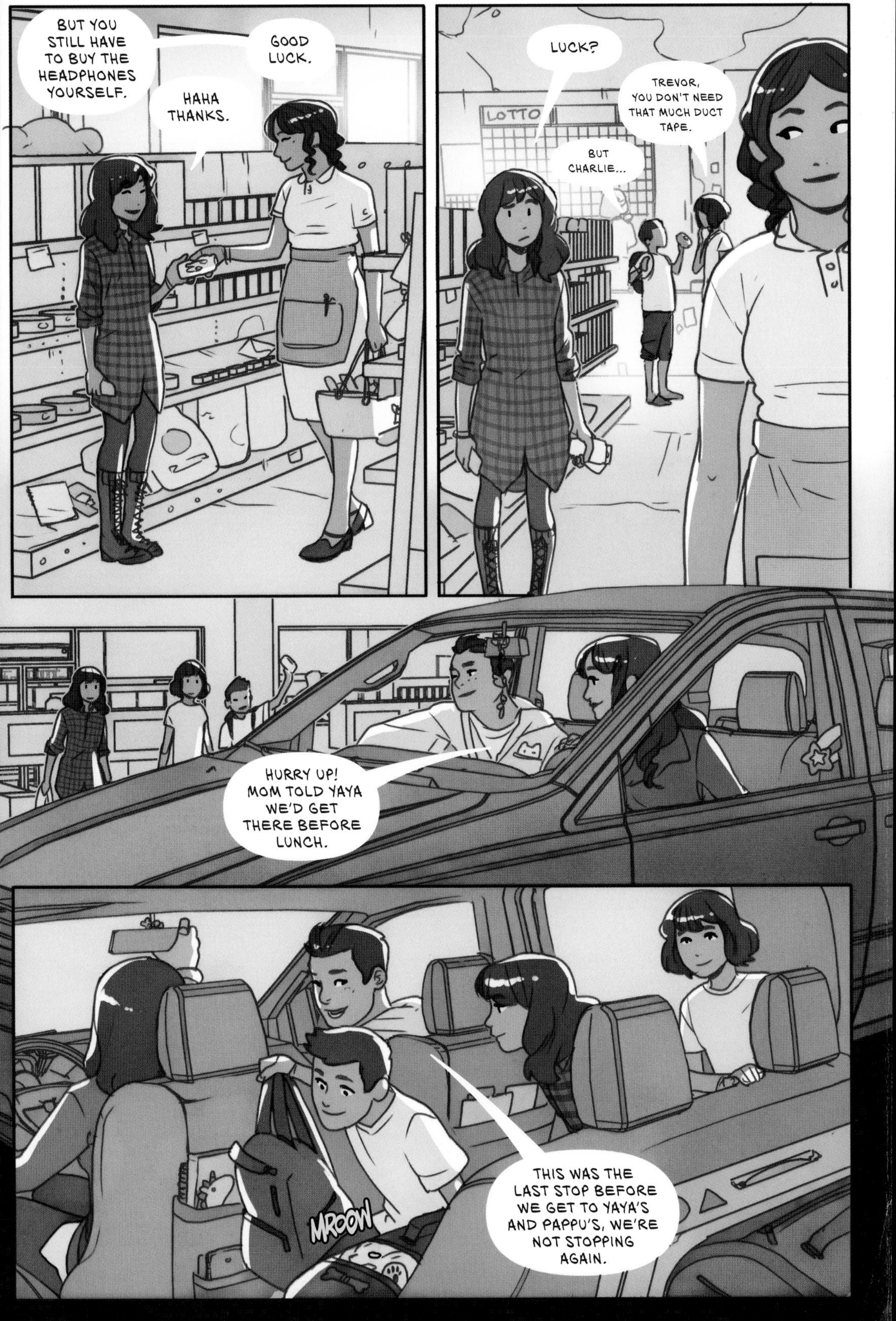
BUT YOU STILL HAVE TO BUY THE HEADPHONES YOURSELF.
GOOD LUCK.
HAHA THANKS.
LUCK?
LOTTO
TREVOR, YOU DON'T NEED THAT MUCH DUCT TAPE.
BUT CHARLIE...
HURRY UP! MOM TOLD YAYA WE'D GET THERE BEFORE LUNCH.
THIS WAS THE LAST STOP BEFORE WE GET TO YAYA'S AND PAPPU'S, WE'RE NOT STOPPING AGAIN.
MROOW

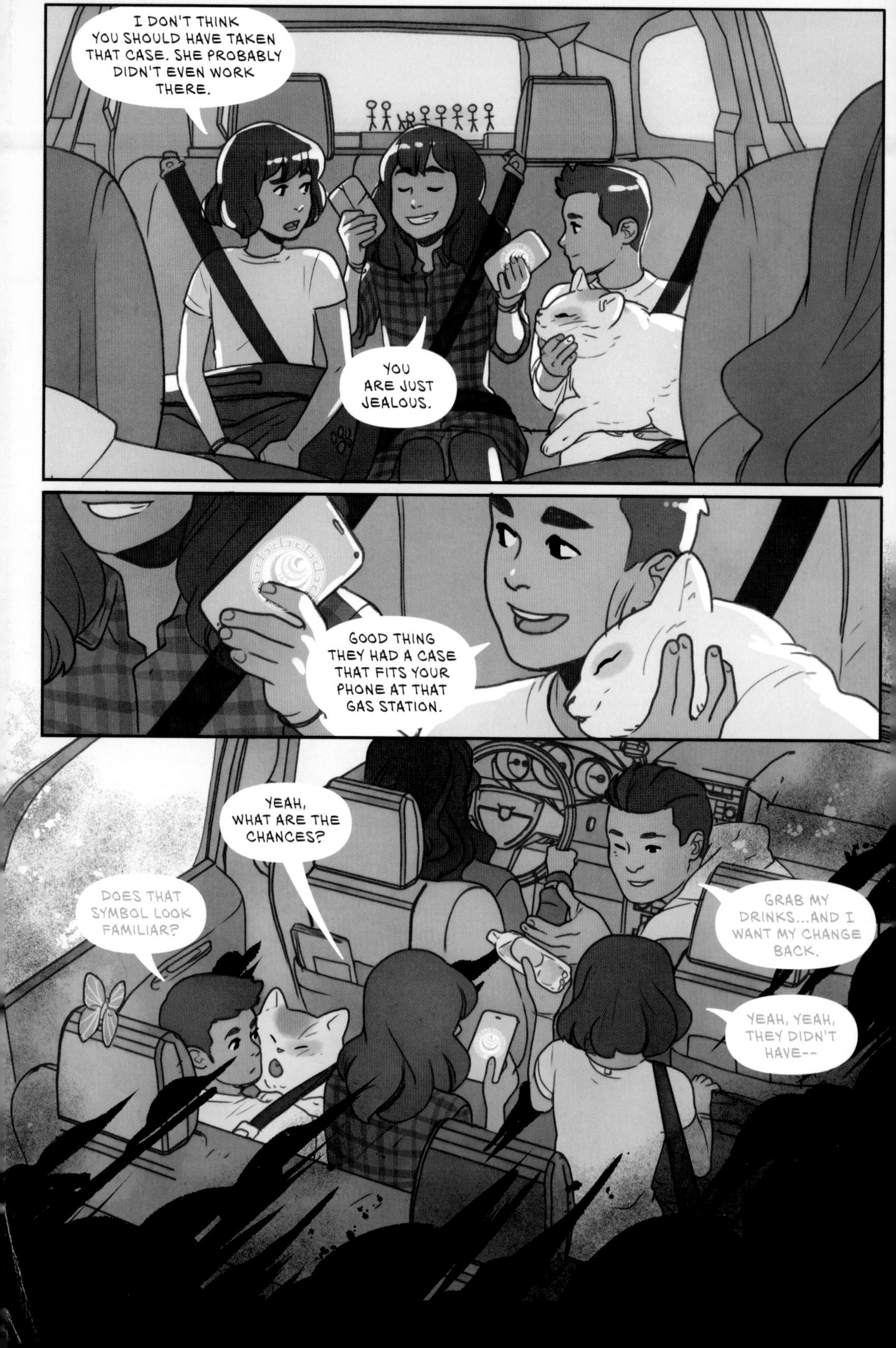
I DON'T THINK YOU SHOULD HAVE TAKEN THAT CASE. SHE PROBABLY DIDN'T EVEN WORK THERE.
YOU ARE JUST JEALOUS.
GOOD THING THEY HAD A CASE THAT FITS YOUR PHONE AT THAT GAS STATION.
YEAH, WHAT ARE THE CHANCES?
DOES THAT SYMBOL LOOK FAMILIAR?
GRAB MY DRINKS...AND I WANT MY CHANGE BACK.
YEAH, YEAH, THEY DIDN'T HAVE--

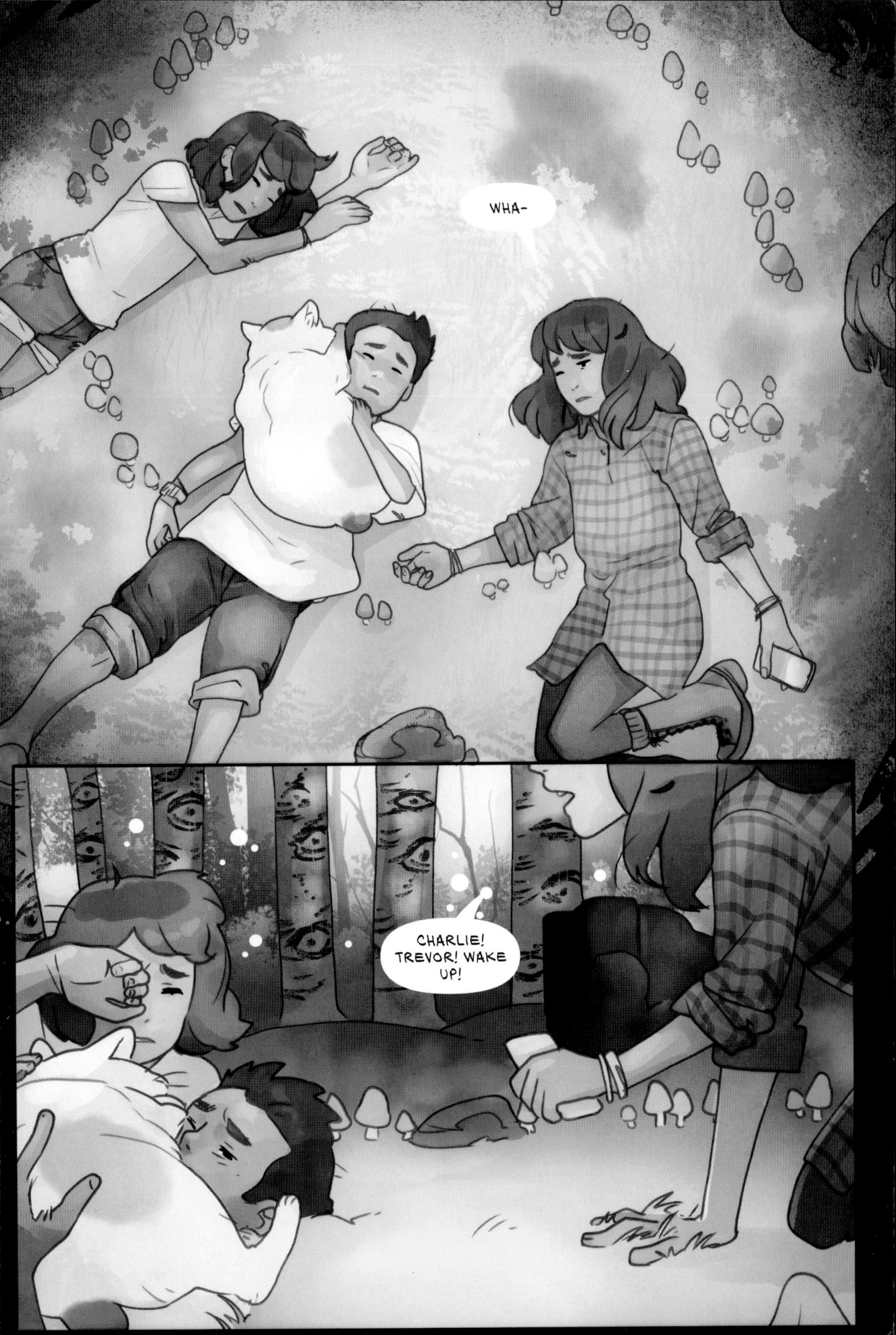
WHA-
CHARLIE! TREVOR! WAKE UP!

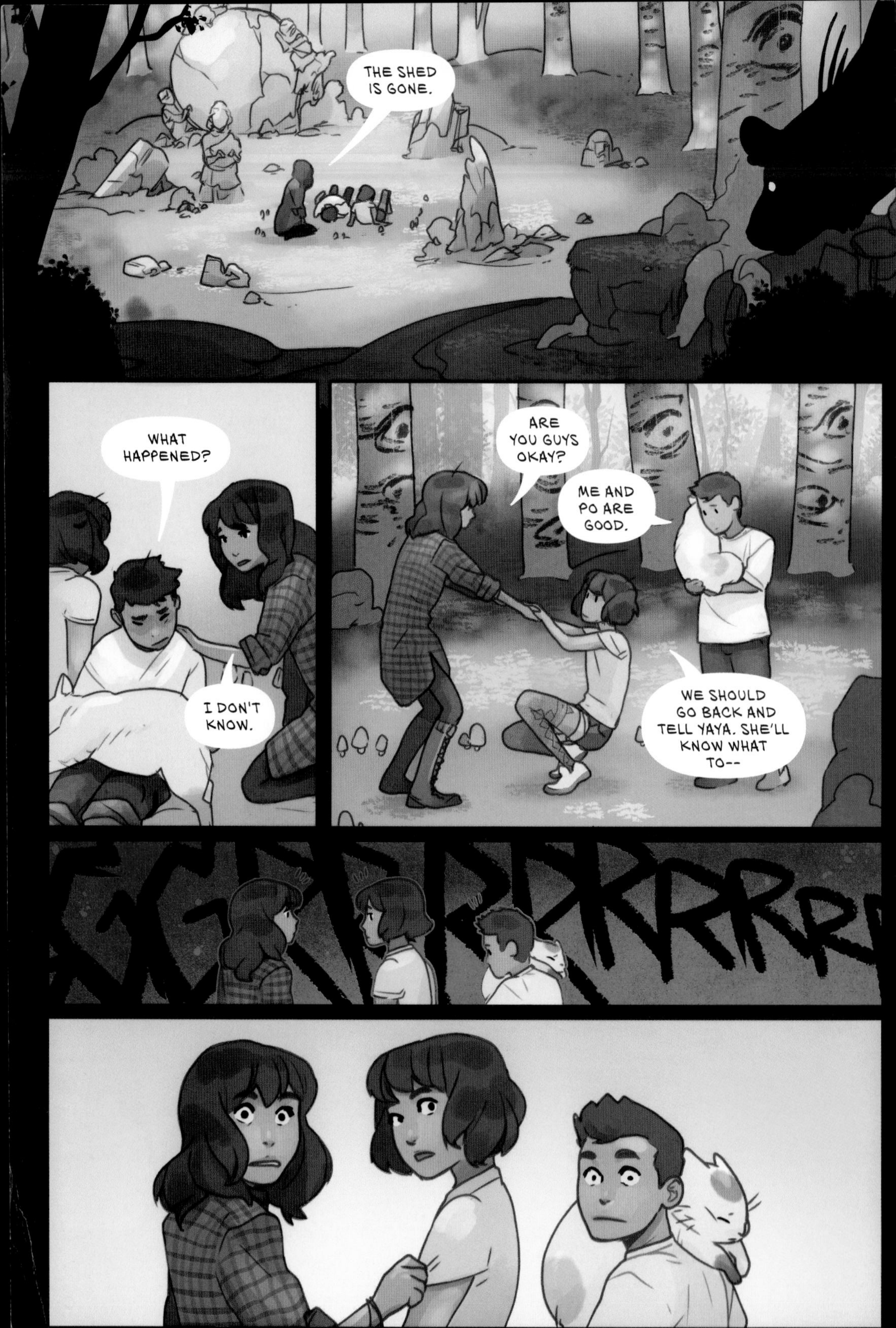
THE SHED IS GONE.
WHAT HAPPENED?
I DON'T KNOW.
ARE YOU GUYS OKAY?
ME AND PO ARE GOOD.
WE SHOULD GO BACK AND TELL YAYA. SHE'LL KNOW WHAT TO--
GRRRRRR

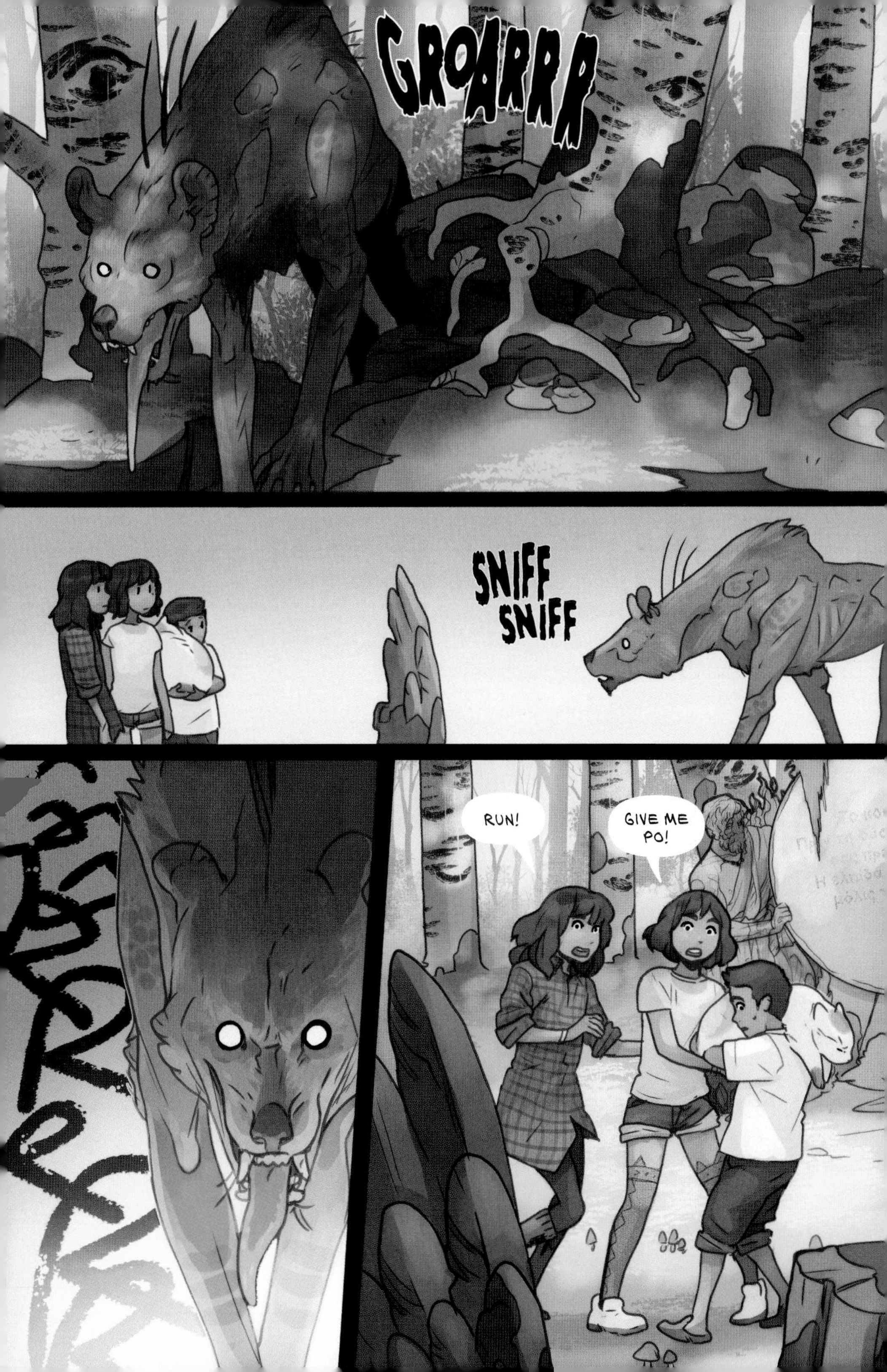
GROARRR
SNIFF
SNIFF
RUN!
GIVE ME
PO!

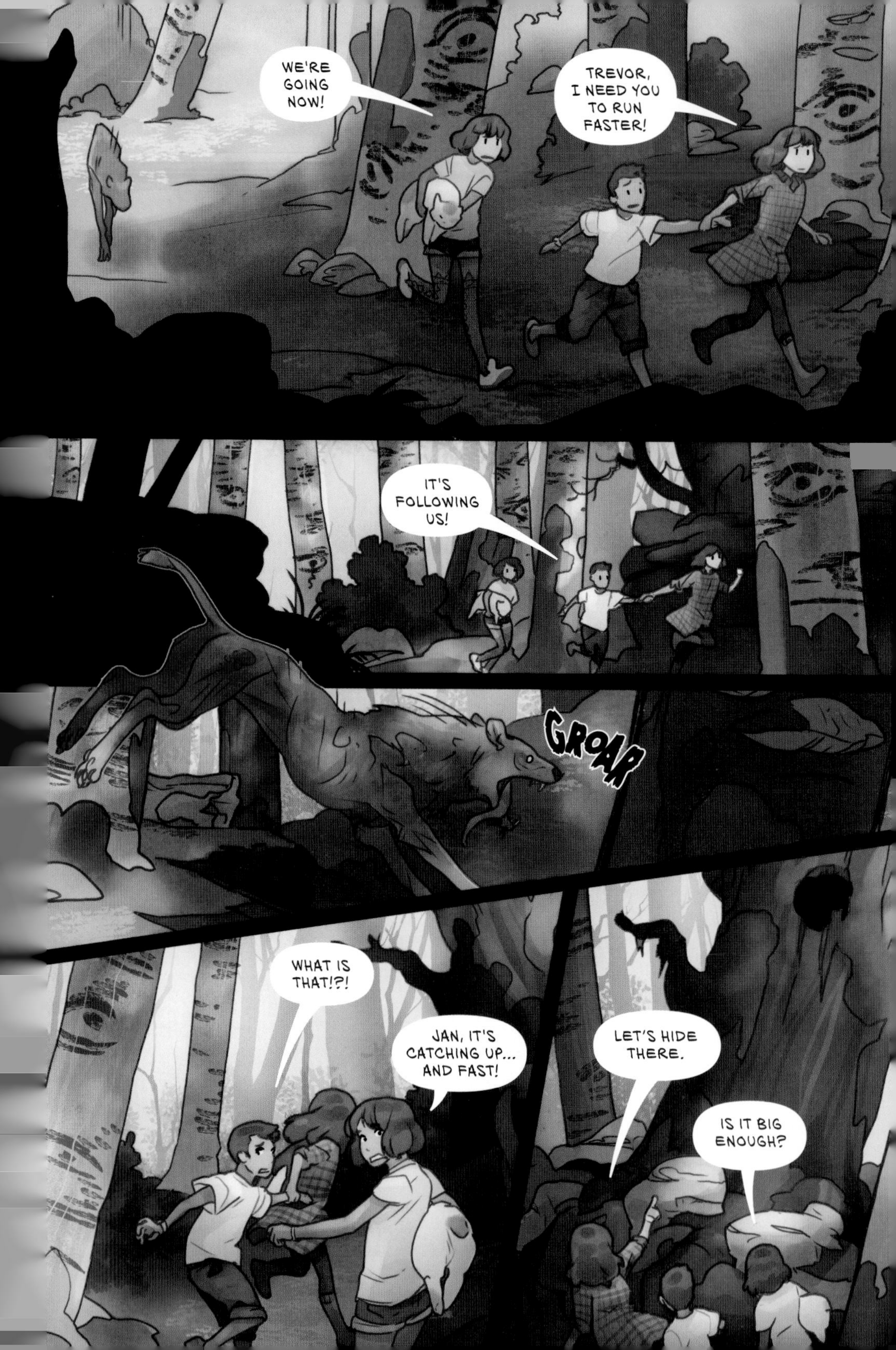
WE'RE GOING NOW!
TREVOR, I NEED YOU TO RUN FASTER!
IT'S FOLLOWING US!
GROAR
WHAT IS THAT!?!
JAN, IT'S CATCHING UP... AND FAST!
LET'S HIDE THERE.
IS IT BIG ENOUGH?

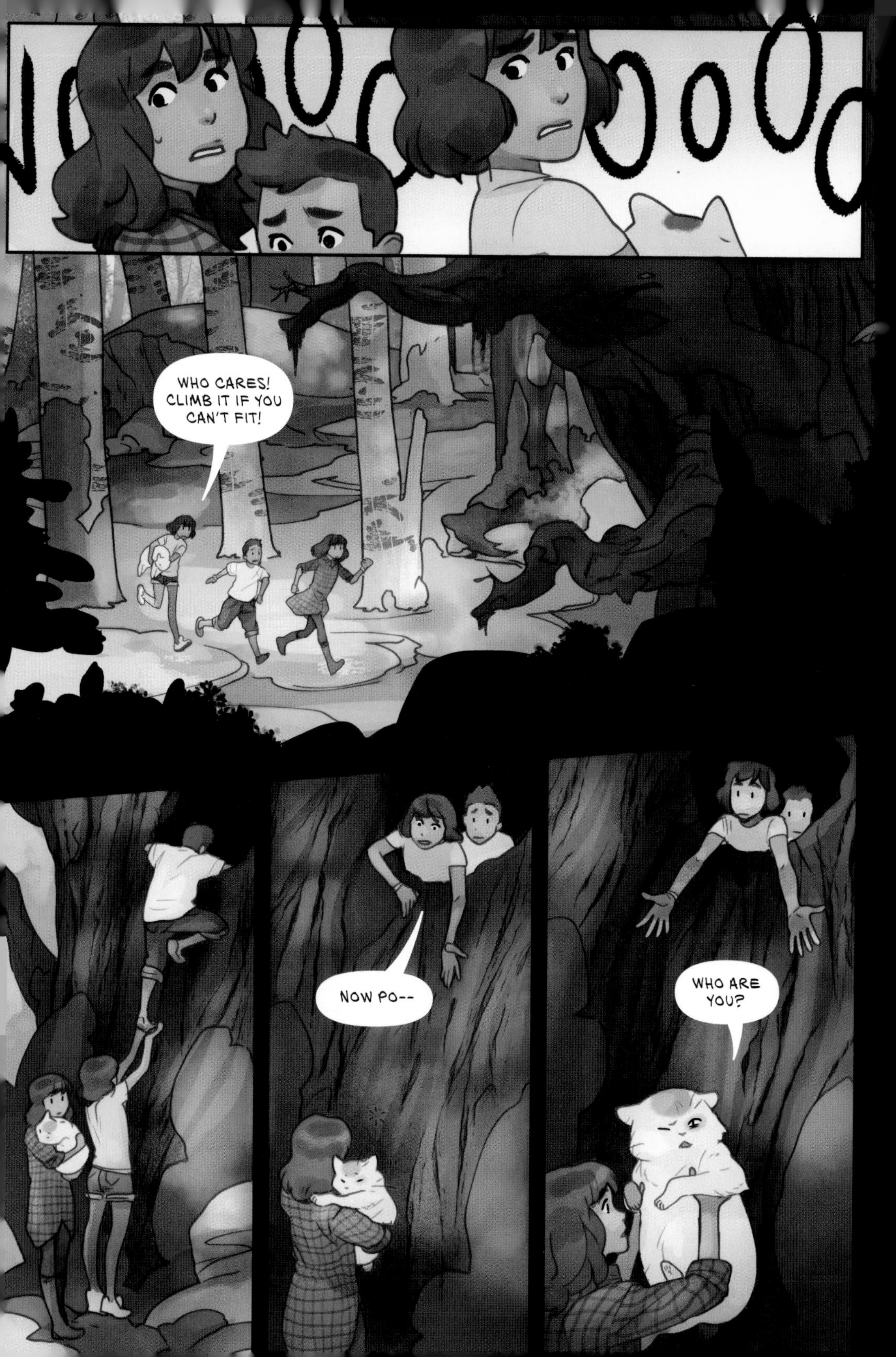
NOOOOOOOOOOOOO
WHO CARES! CLIMB IT IF YOU CAN'T FIT!
NOW PO--
WHO ARE YOU?

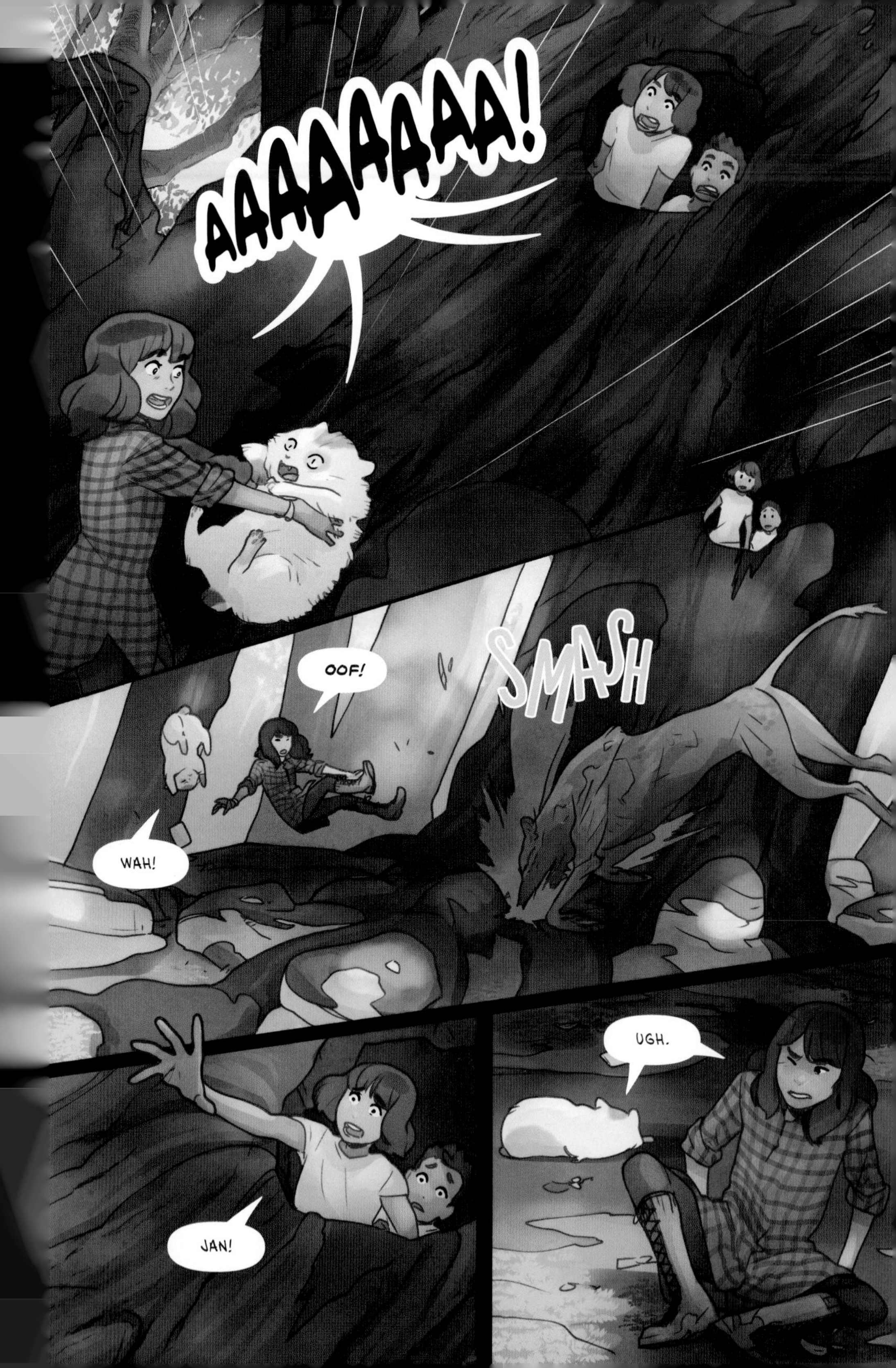
AAAAAAAA!
OOF!
SMASH
WAH!
JAN!
UGH.

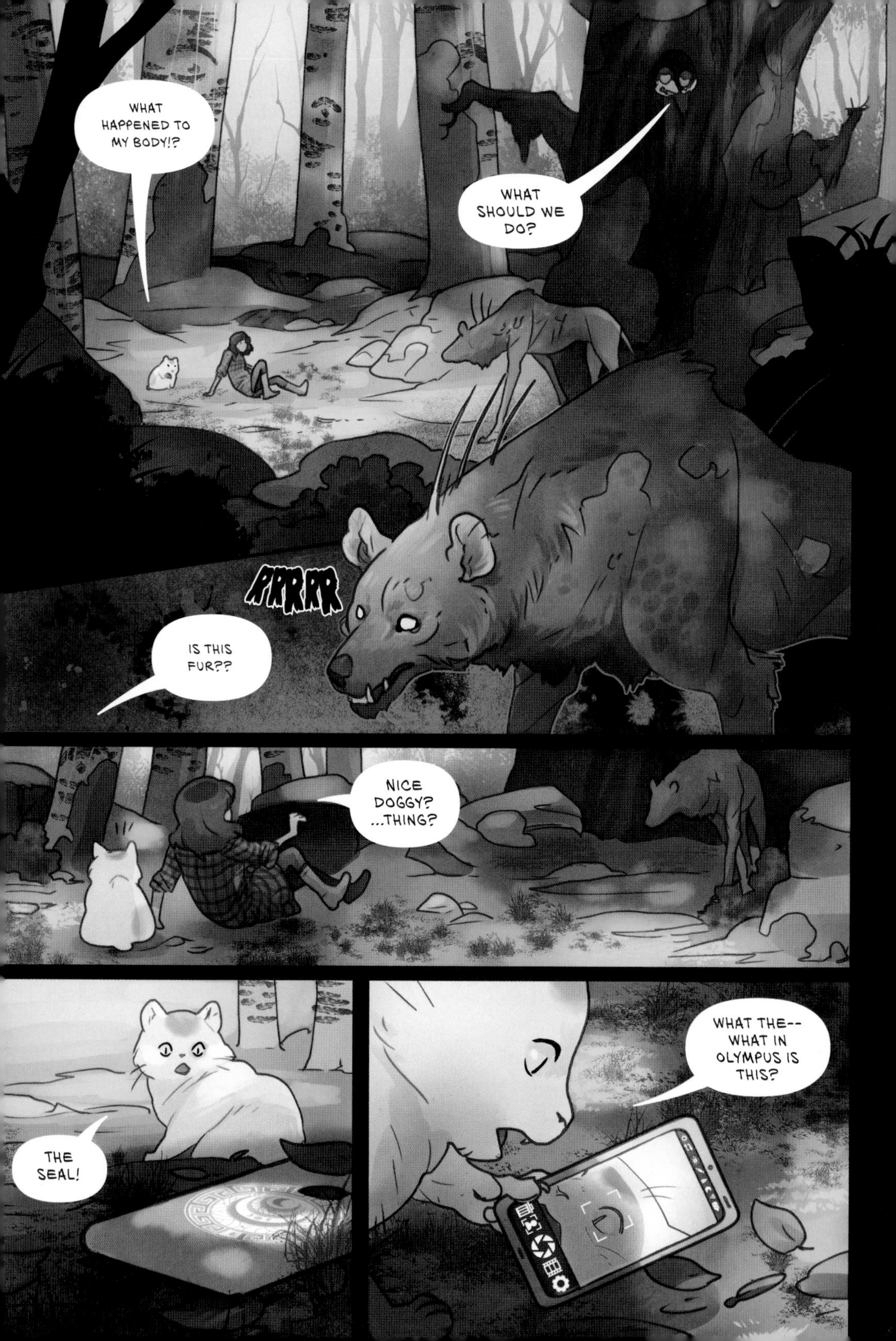
WHAT HAPPENED TO MY BODY!?
WHAT SHOULD WE DO?
RRRRR
IS THIS FUR??
NICE DOGGY? ...THING?
THE SEAL!
WHAT THE-- WHAT IN OLYMPUS IS THIS?

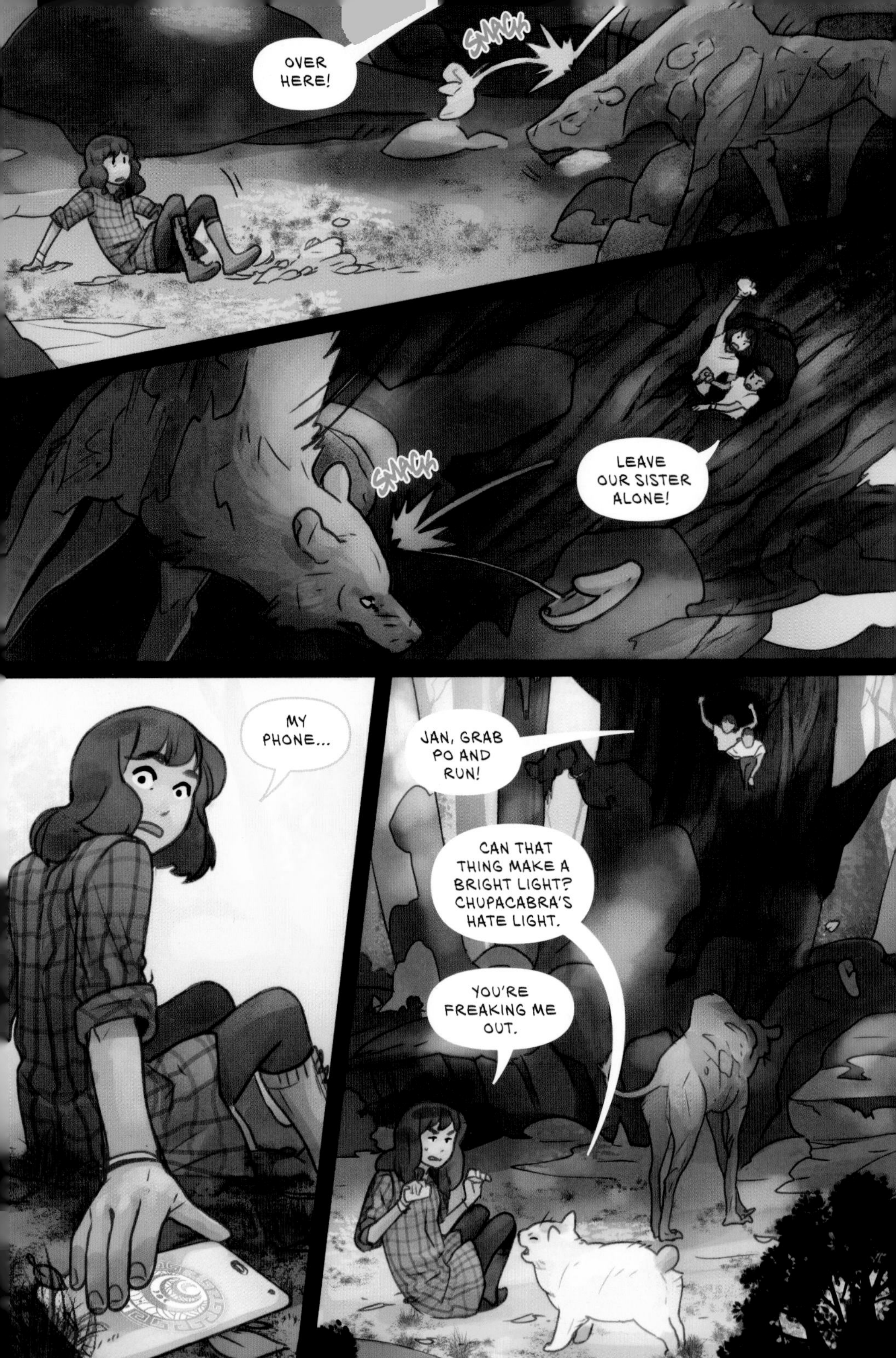
OVER HERE!
SMACK
SMACK
LEAVE OUR SISTER ALONE!
MY PHONE...
JAN, GRAB PO AND RUN!
CAN THAT THING MAKE A BRIGHT LIGHT? CHUPACABRA'S HATE LIGHT.
YOU'RE FREAKING ME OUT.

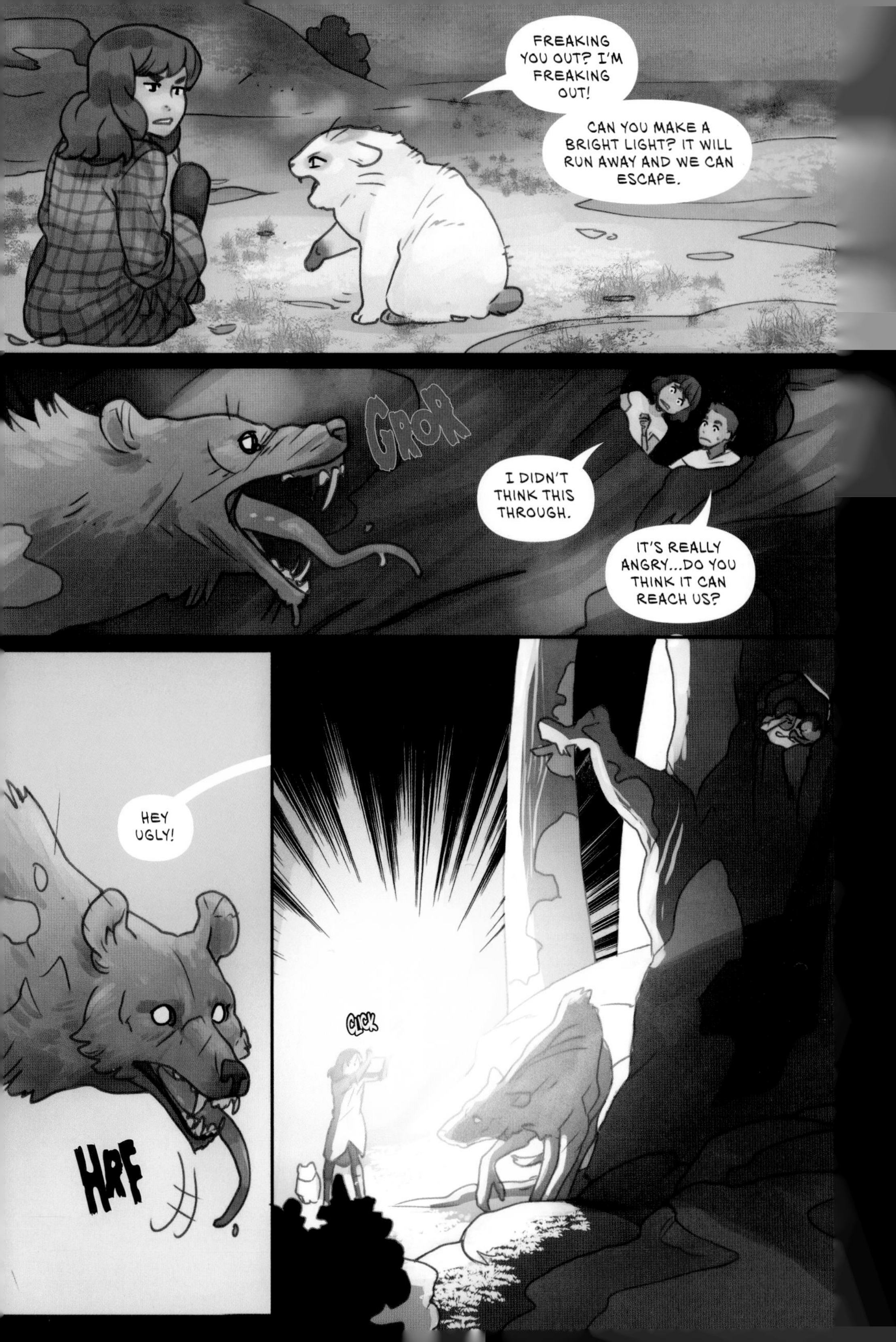
FREAKING YOU OUT? I'M FREAKING OUT!
CAN YOU MAKE A BRIGHT LIGHT? IT WILL RUN AWAY AND WE CAN ESCAPE.
GROR
I DIDN'T THINK THIS THROUGH.
IT'S REALLY ANGRY...DO YOU THINK IT CAN REACH US?
HEY UGLY!
HRF
CLICK

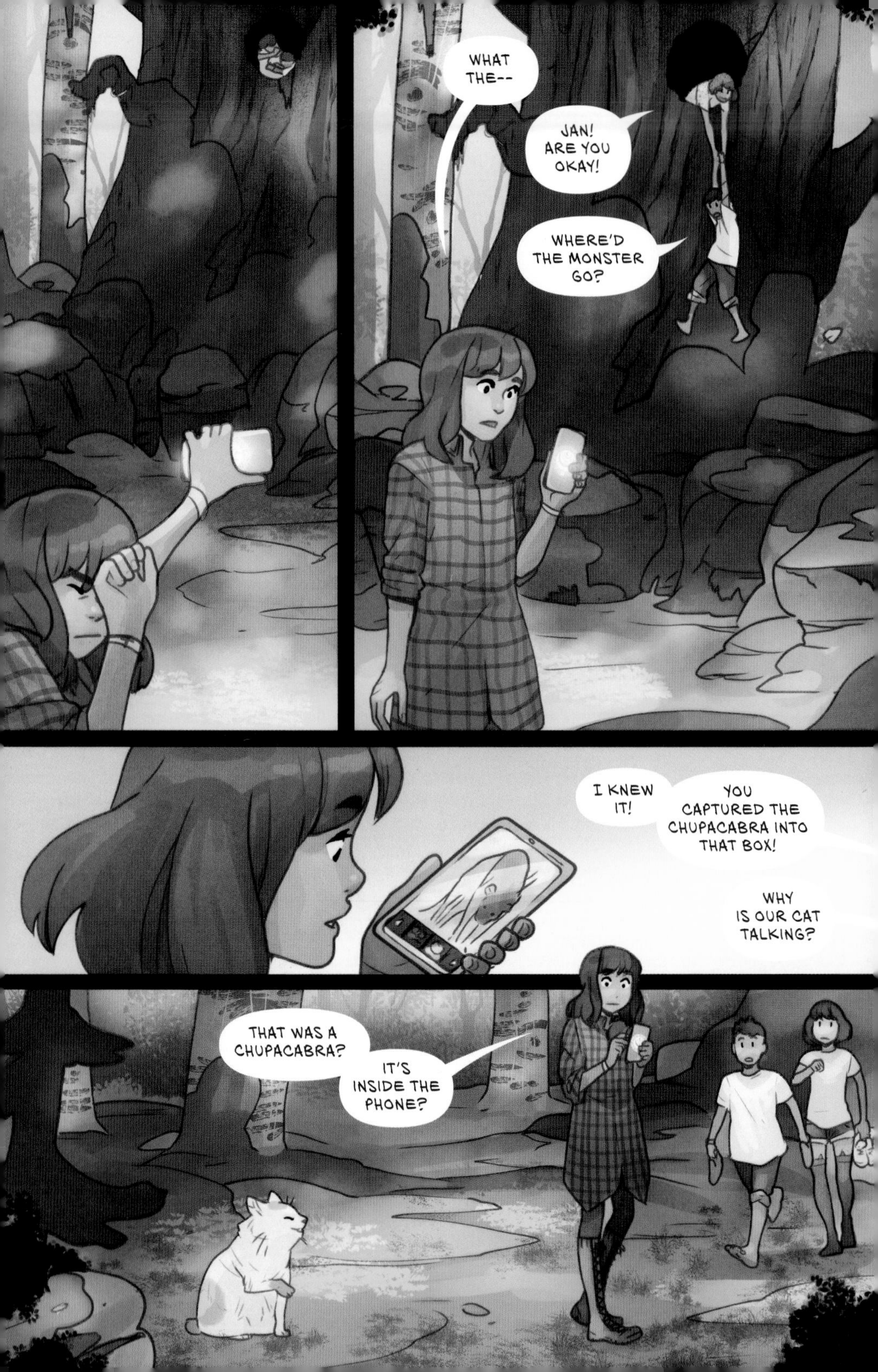
WHAT THE--
JAN! ARE YOU OKAY!
WHERE'D THE MONSTER GO?
I KNEW IT!
YOU CAPTURED THE CHUPACABRA INTO THAT BOX!
WHY IS OUR CAT TALKING?
THAT WAS A CHUPACABRA?
IT'S INSIDE THE PHONE?

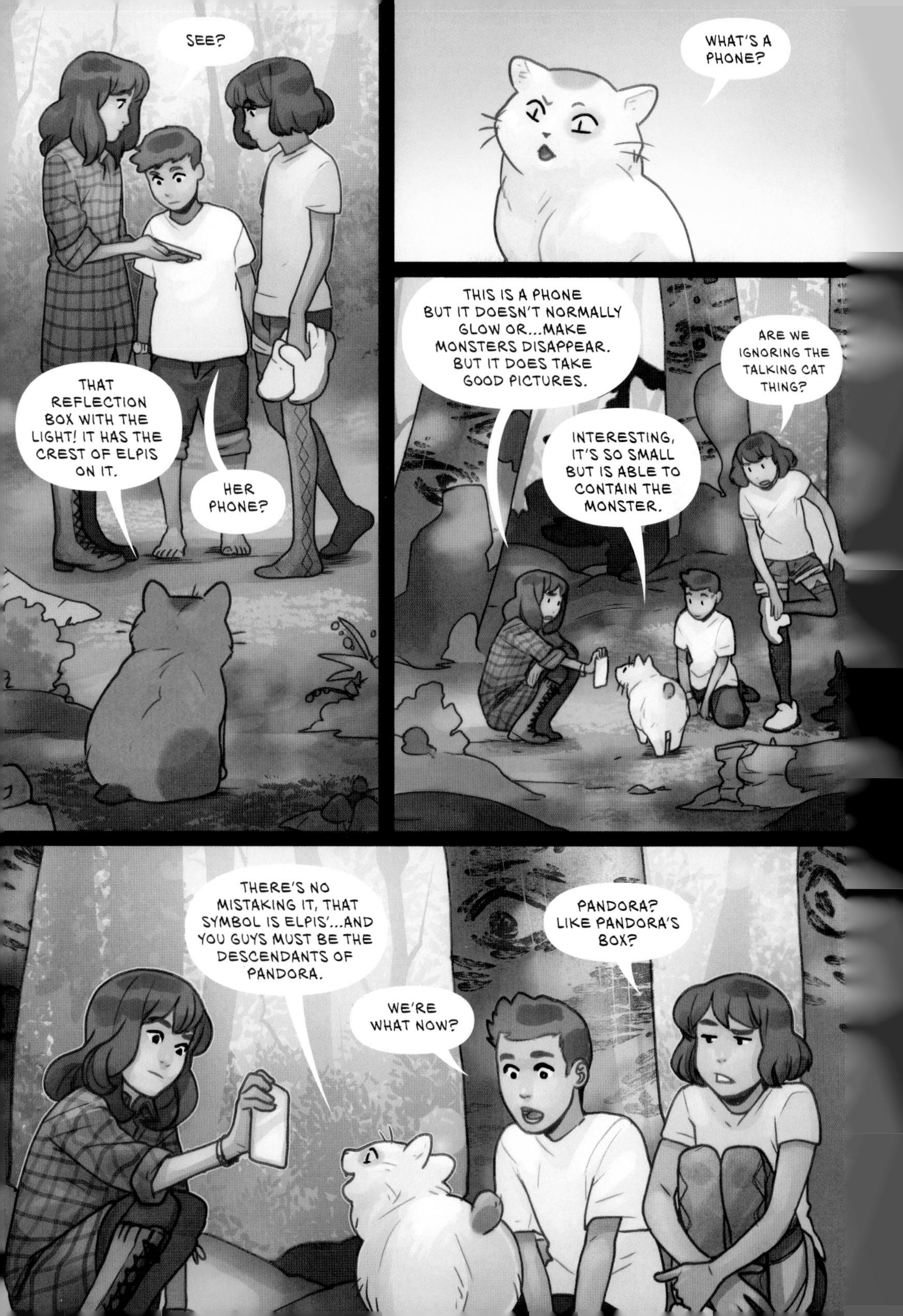
SEE?
THAT REFLECTION BOX WITH THE LIGHT! IT HAS THE CREST OF ELPIS ON IT.
HER PHONE?
WHAT'S A PHONE?
THIS IS A PHONE BUT IT DOESN'T NORMALLY GLOW OR...MAKE MONSTERS DISAPPEAR. BUT IT DOES TAKE GOOD PICTURES.
ARE WE IGNORING THE TALKING CAT THING?
INTERESTING, IT'S SO SMALL BUT IS ABLE TO CONTAIN THE MONSTER.
THERE'S NO MISTAKING IT, THAT SYMBOL IS ELPIS'...AND YOU GUYS MUST BE THE DESCENDANTS OF PANDORA.
PANDORA? LIKE PANDORA'S BOX?
WE'RE WHAT NOW?

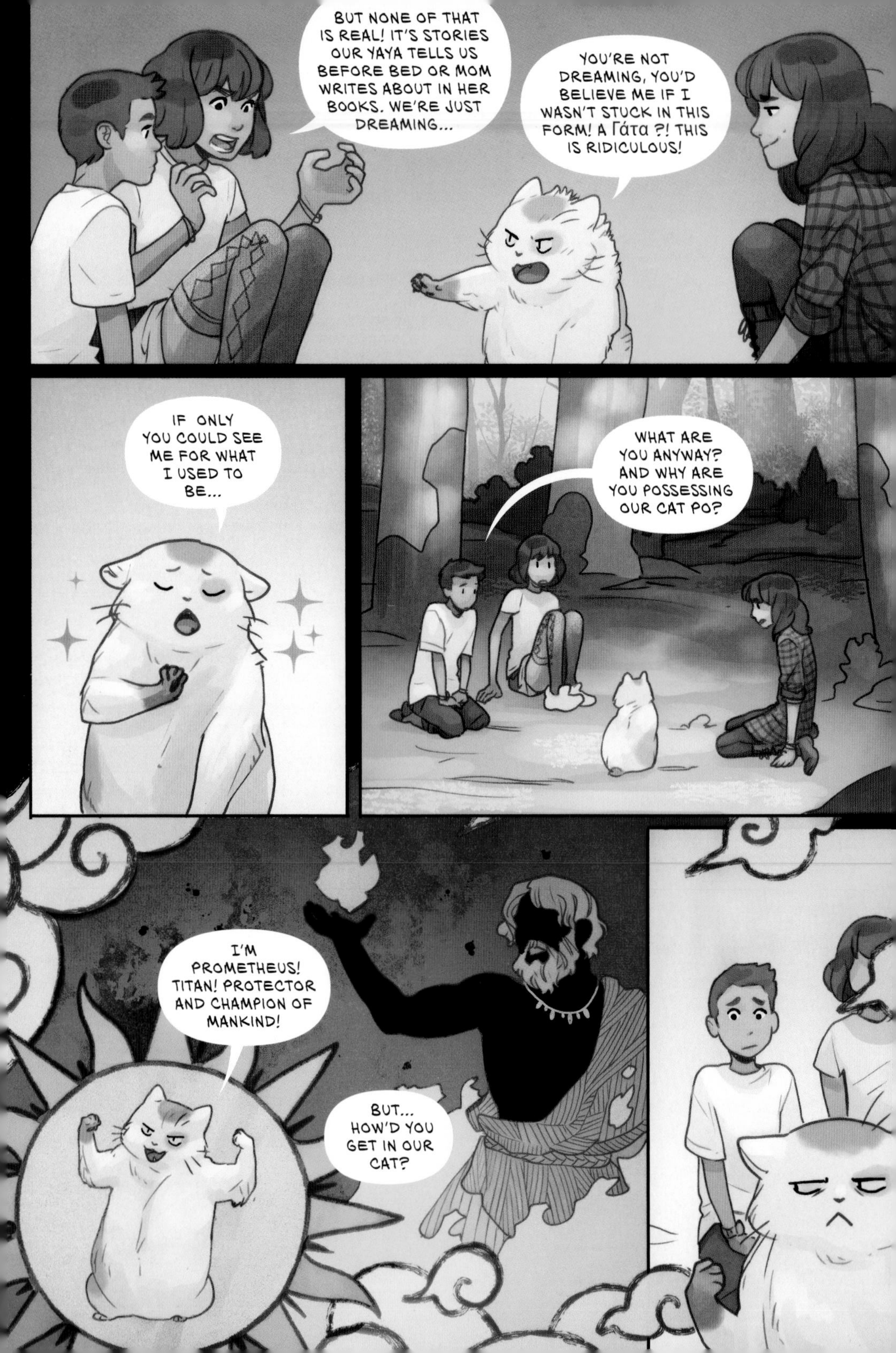
BUT NONE OF THAT IS REAL! IT'S STORIES OUR YAYA TELLS US BEFORE BED OR MOM WRITES ABOUT IN HER BOOKS. WE'RE JUST DREAMING...
YOU'RE NOT DREAMING, YOU'D BELIEVE ME IF I WASN'T STUCK IN THIS FORM! A Γάτα ?! THIS IS RIDICULOUS!
IF ONLY YOU COULD SEE ME FOR WHAT I USED TO BE...
WHAT ARE YOU ANYWAY? AND WHY ARE YOU POSSESSING OUR CAT PO?
I'M PROMETHEUS! TITAN! PROTECTOR AND CHAMPION OF MANKIND!
BUT... HOW'D YOU GET IN OUR CAT?

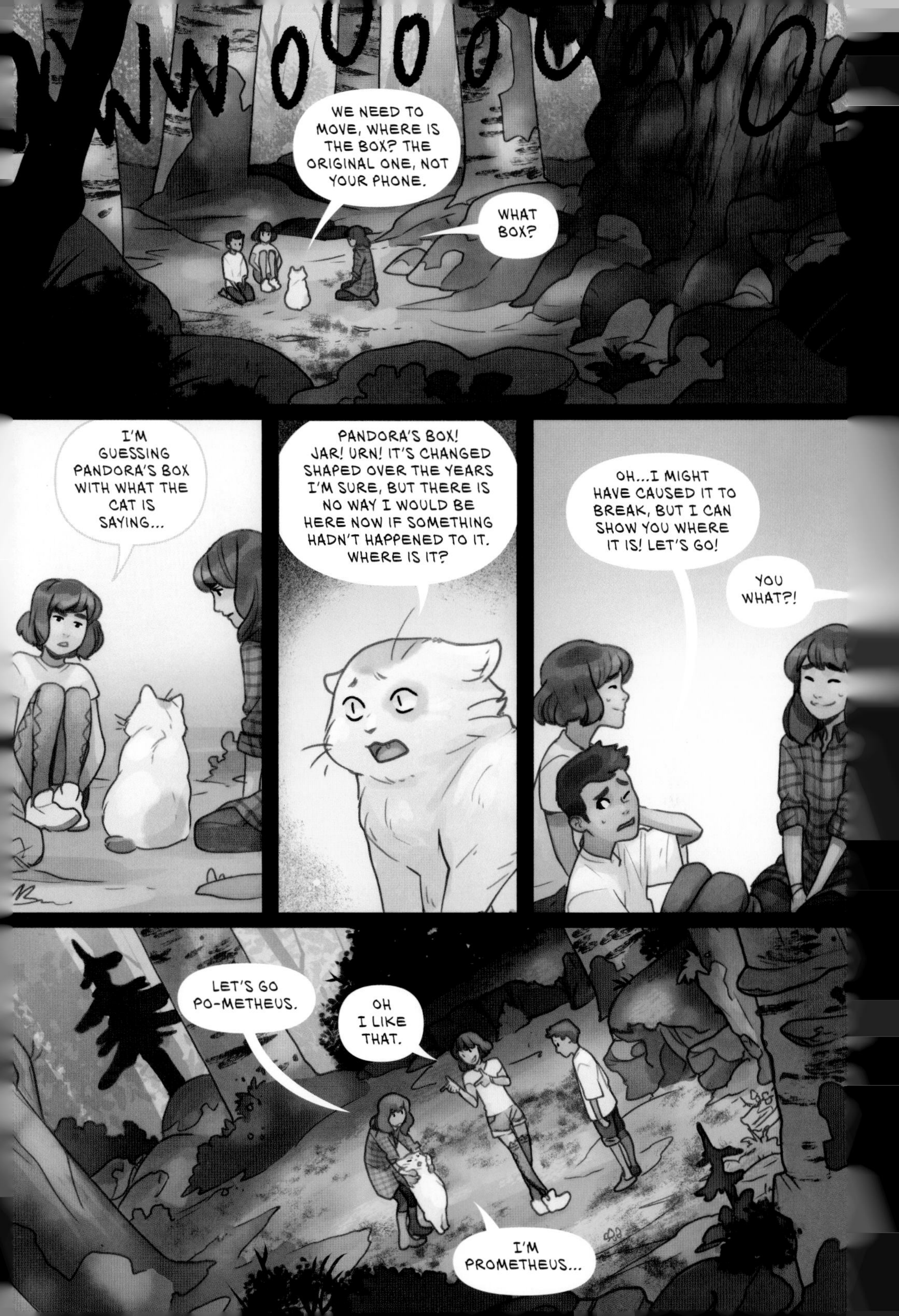
WWOOOOOOOOO
WE NEED TO MOVE, WHERE IS THE BOX? THE ORIGINAL ONE, NOT YOUR PHONE.
WHAT BOX?
I'M GUESSING PANDORA'S BOX WITH WHAT THE CAT IS SAYING...
PANDORA'S BOX! JAR! URN! IT'S CHANGED SHAPED OVER THE YEARS I'M SURE, BUT THERE IS NO WAY I WOULD BE HERE NOW IF SOMETHING HADN'T HAPPENED TO IT. WHERE IS IT?
OH...I MIGHT HAVE CAUSED IT TO BREAK, BUT I CAN SHOW YOU WHERE IT IS! LET'S GO!
YOU WHAT?!
LET'S GO PO-METHEUS.
OH I LIKE THAT.
I'M PROMETHEUS...

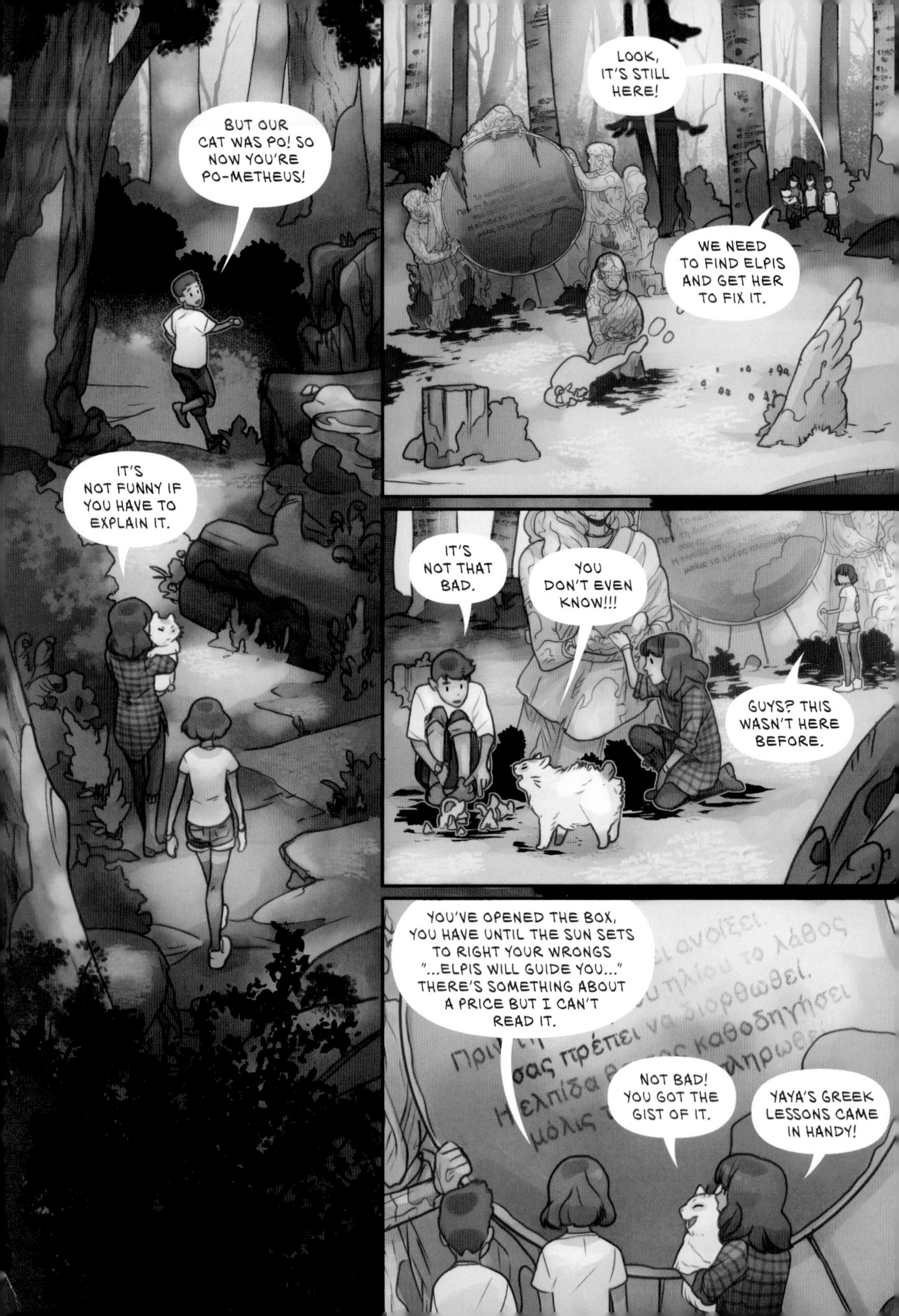

BUT OUR CAT WAS PO! SO NOW YOU'RE PO-METHEUS!
IT'S NOT FUNNY IF YOU HAVE TO EXPLAIN IT.
LOOK, IT'S STILL HERE!
WE NEED TO FIND ELPIS AND GET HER TO FIX IT.
IT'S NOT THAT BAD.
YOU DON'T EVEN KNOW!!!
GUYS? THIS WASN'T HERE BEFORE.
YOU'VE OPENED THE BOX, YOU HAVE UNTIL THE SUN SETS TO RIGHT YOUR WRONGS "...ELPIS WILL GUIDE YOU..." THERE'S SOMETHING ABOUT A PRICE BUT I CAN'T READ IT.
NOT BAD! YOU GOT THE GIST OF IT.
YAYA'S GREEK LESSONS CAME IN HANDY!

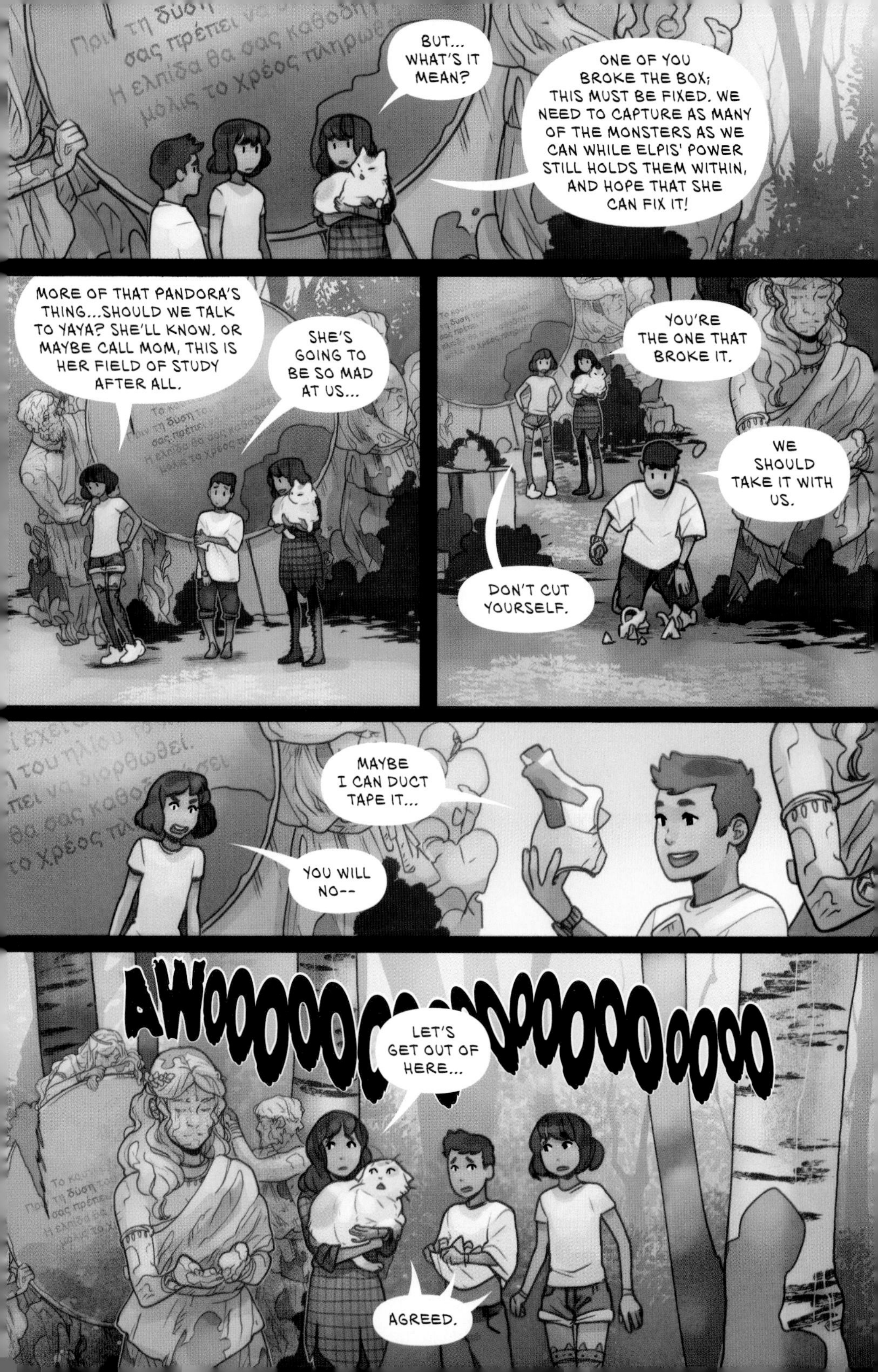
BUT... WHAT'S IT MEAN?
ONE OF YOU BROKE THE BOX; THIS MUST BE FIXED. WE NEED TO CAPTURE AS MANY OF THE MONSTERS AS WE CAN WHILE ELPIS' POWER STILL HOLDS THEM WITHIN, AND HOPE THAT SHE CAN FIX IT!
MORE OF THAT PANDORA'S THING...SHOULD WE TALK TO YAYA? SHE'LL KNOW. OR MAYBE CALL MOM, THIS IS HER FIELD OF STUDY AFTER ALL.
SHE'S GOING TO BE SO MAD AT US...
YOU'RE THE ONE THAT BROKE IT.
WE SHOULD TAKE IT WITH US.
DON'T CUT YOURSELF.
MAYBE I CAN DUCT TAPE IT...
YOU WILL NO--
AWOOOOO...OOOOOOOOOO
LET'S GET OUT OF HERE...
AGREED.

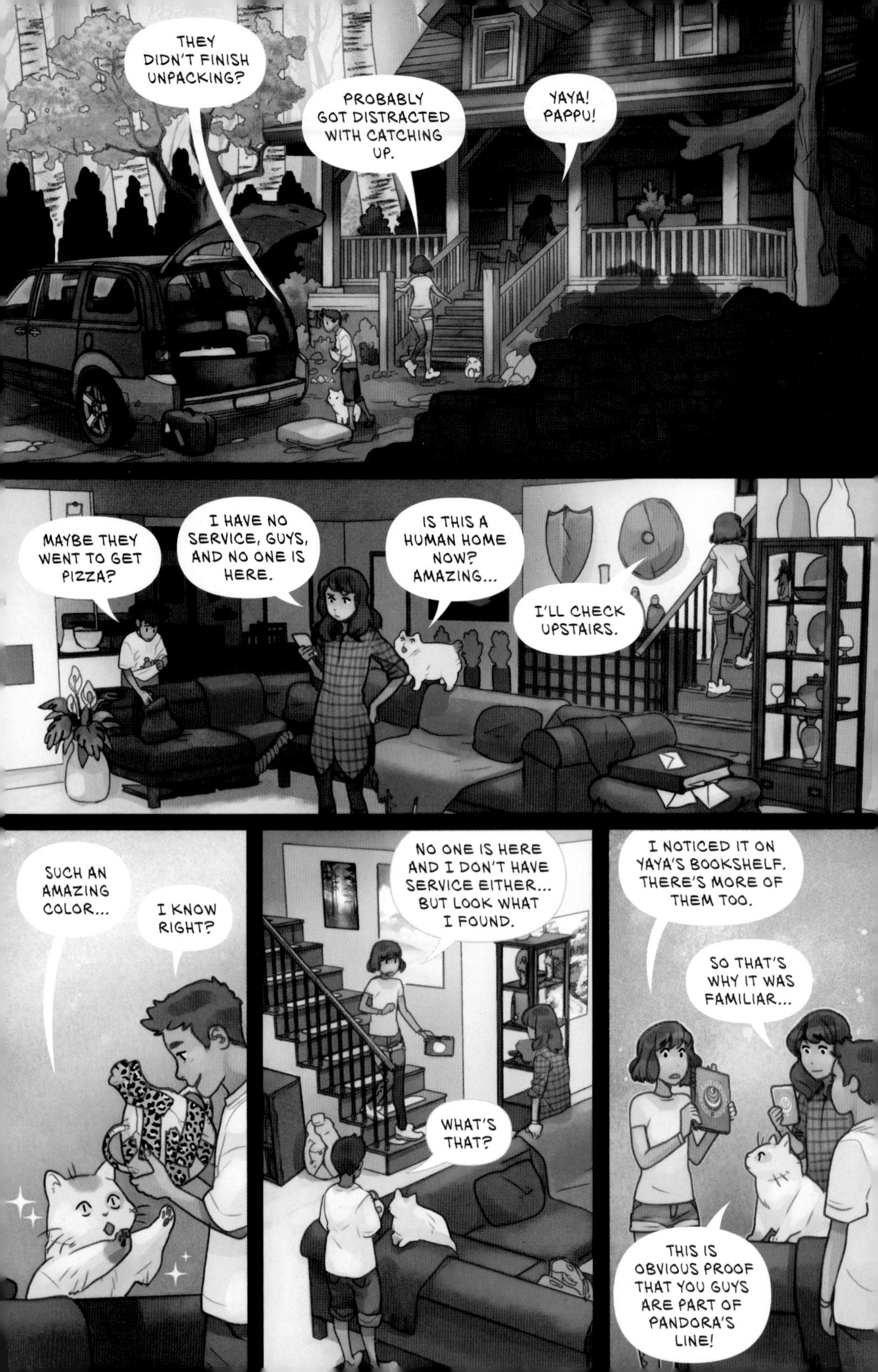
THEY DIDN'T FINISH UNPACKING?
PROBABLY GOT DISTRACTED WITH CATCHING UP.
YAYA! PAPPU!
MAYBE THEY WENT TO GET PIZZA?
I HAVE NO SERVICE, GUYS, AND NO ONE IS HERE.
IS THIS A HUMAN HOME NOW? AMAZING...
I'LL CHECK UPSTAIRS.
SUCH AN AMAZING COLOR...
I KNOW RIGHT?
NO ONE IS HERE AND I DON'T HAVE SERVICE EITHER... BUT LOOK WHAT I FOUND.
WHAT'S THAT?
I NOTICED IT ON YAYA'S BOOKSHELF. THERE'S MORE OF THEM TOO.
SO THAT'S WHY IT WAS FAMILIAR...
THIS IS OBVIOUS PROOF THAT YOU GUYS ARE PART OF PANDORA'S LINE!

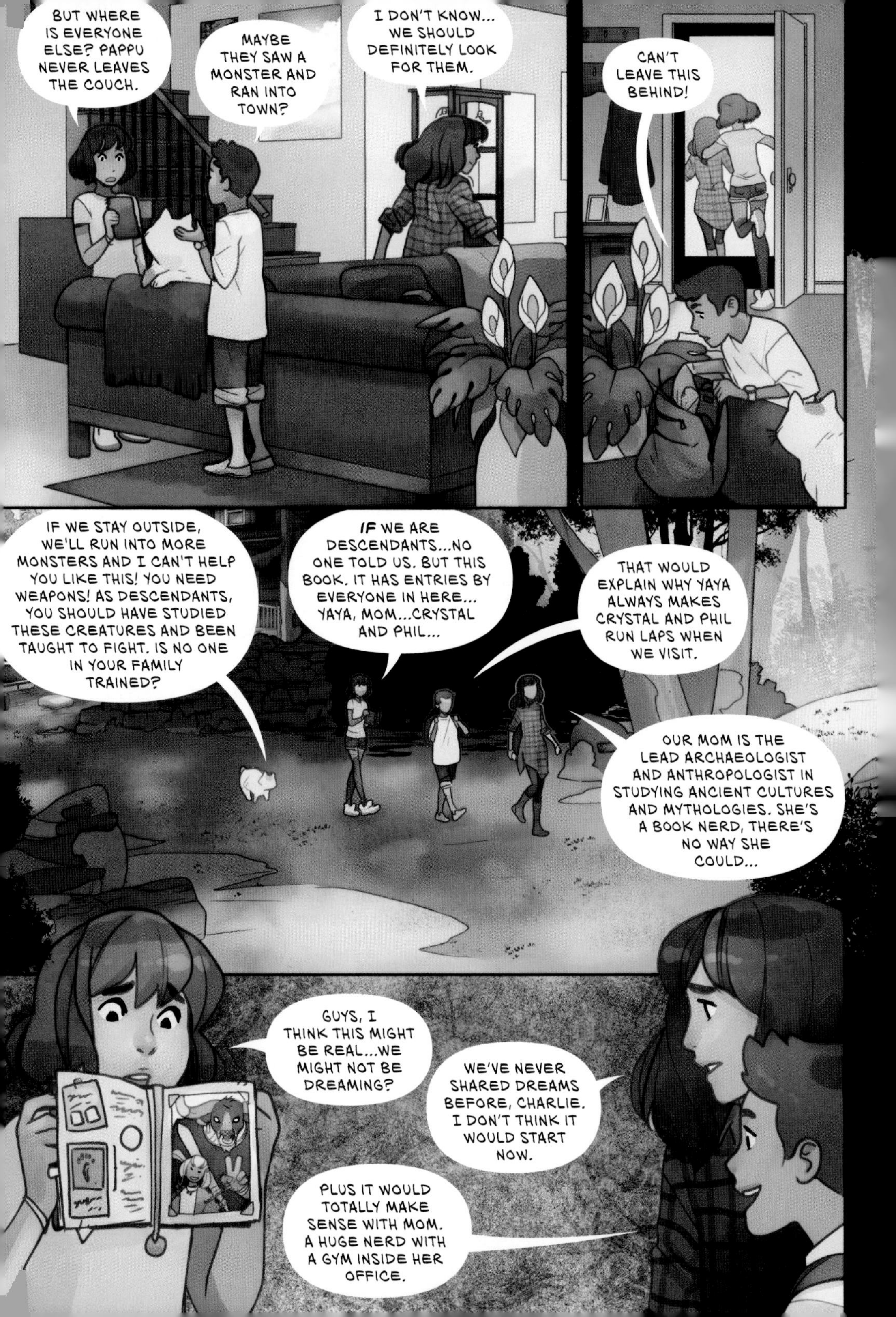

BUT WHERE IS EVERYONE ELSE? PAPPU NEVER LEAVES THE COUCH.
MAYBE THEY SAW A MONSTER AND RAN INTO TOWN?
I DON'T KNOW... WE SHOULD DEFINITELY LOOK FOR THEM.
CAN'T LEAVE THIS BEHIND!
IF WE STAY OUTSIDE, WE'LL RUN INTO MORE MONSTERS AND I CAN'T HELP YOU LIKE THIS! YOU NEED WEAPONS! AS DESCENDANTS, YOU SHOULD HAVE STUDIED THESE CREATURES AND BEEN TAUGHT TO FIGHT. IS NO ONE IN YOUR FAMILY TRAINED?
IF WE ARE DESCENDANTS...NO ONE TOLD US. BUT THIS BOOK. IT HAS ENTRIES BY EVERYONE IN HERE... YAYA, MOM...CRYSTAL AND PHIL...
THAT WOULD EXPLAIN WHY YAYA ALWAYS MAKES CRYSTAL AND PHIL RUN LAPS WHEN WE VISIT.
OUR MOM IS THE LEAD ARCHAEOLOGIST AND ANTHROPOLOGIST IN STUDYING ANCIENT CULTURES AND MYTHOLOGIES. SHE'S A BOOK NERD, THERE'S NO WAY SHE COULD...
GUYS, I THINK THIS MIGHT BE REAL...WE MIGHT NOT BE DREAMING?
WE'VE NEVER SHARED DREAMS BEFORE, CHARLIE. I DON'T THINK IT WOULD START NOW.
PLUS IT WOULD TOTALLY MAKE SENSE WITH MOM. A HUGE NERD WITH A GYM INSIDE HER OFFICE.

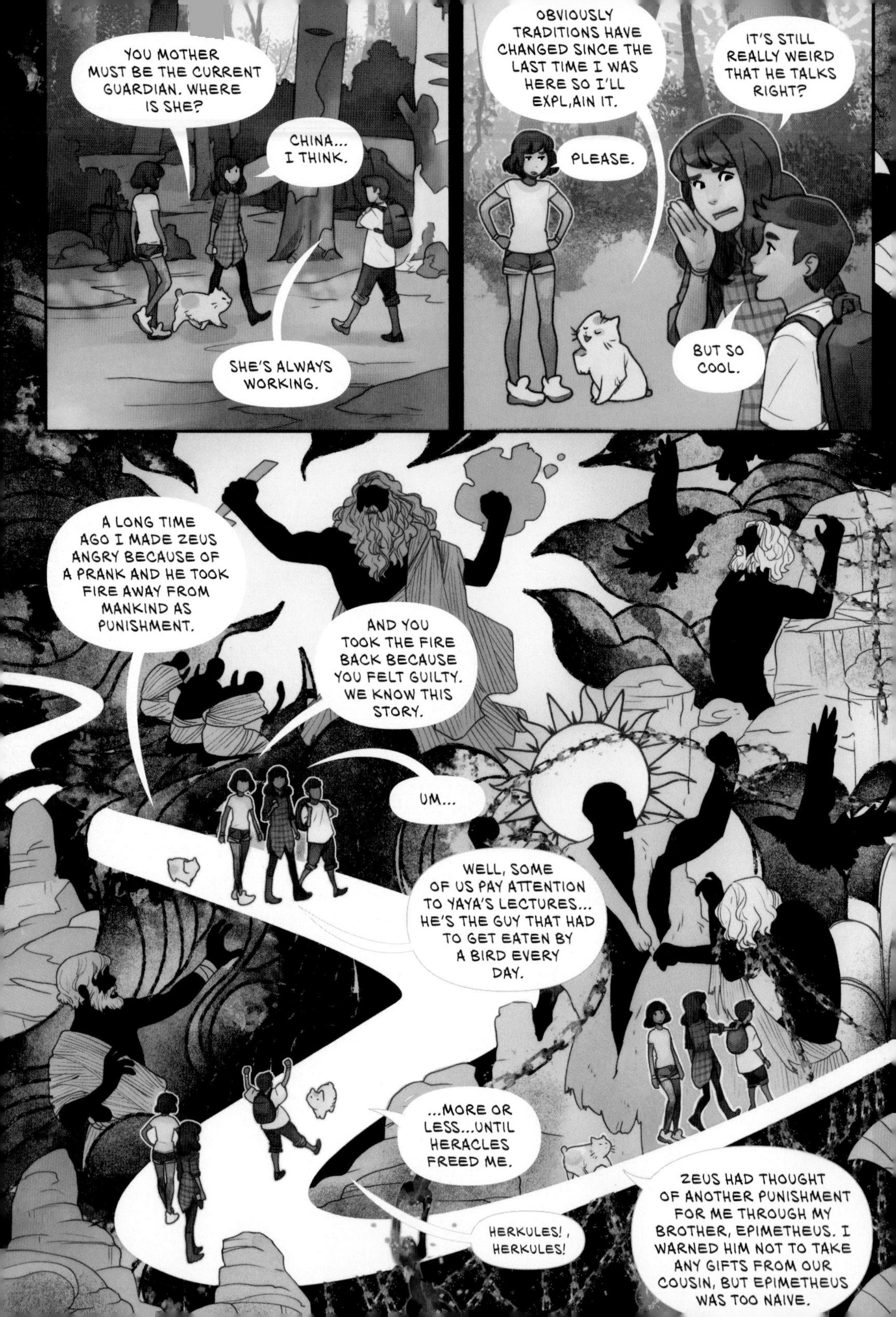
YOU MOTHER MUST BE THE CURRENT GUARDIAN. WHERE IS SHE?
CHINA... I THINK.
SHE'S ALWAYS WORKING.
OBVIOUSLY TRADITIONS HAVE CHANGED SINCE THE LAST TIME I WAS HERE SO I'LL EXPL,AIN IT.
PLEASE.
IT'S STILL REALLY WEIRD THAT HE TALKS RIGHT?
BUT SO COOL.
A LONG TIME AGO I MADE ZEUS ANGRY BECAUSE OF A PRANK AND HE TOOK FIRE AWAY FROM MANKIND AS PUNISHMENT.
AND YOU TOOK THE FIRE BACK BECAUSE YOU FELT GUILTY. WE KNOW THIS STORY.
UM...
WELL, SOME OF US PAY ATTENTION TO YAYA'S LECTURES... HE'S THE GUY THAT HAD TO GET EATEN BY A BIRD EVERY DAY.
...MORE OR LESS...UNTIL HERACLES FREED ME.
HERKULES! , HERKULES!
ZEUS HAD THOUGHT OF ANOTHER PUNISHMENT FOR ME THROUGH MY BROTHER, EPIMETHEUS. I WARNED HIM NOT TO TAKE ANY GIFTS FROM OUR COUSIN, BUT EPIMETHEUS WAS TOO NAIVE.

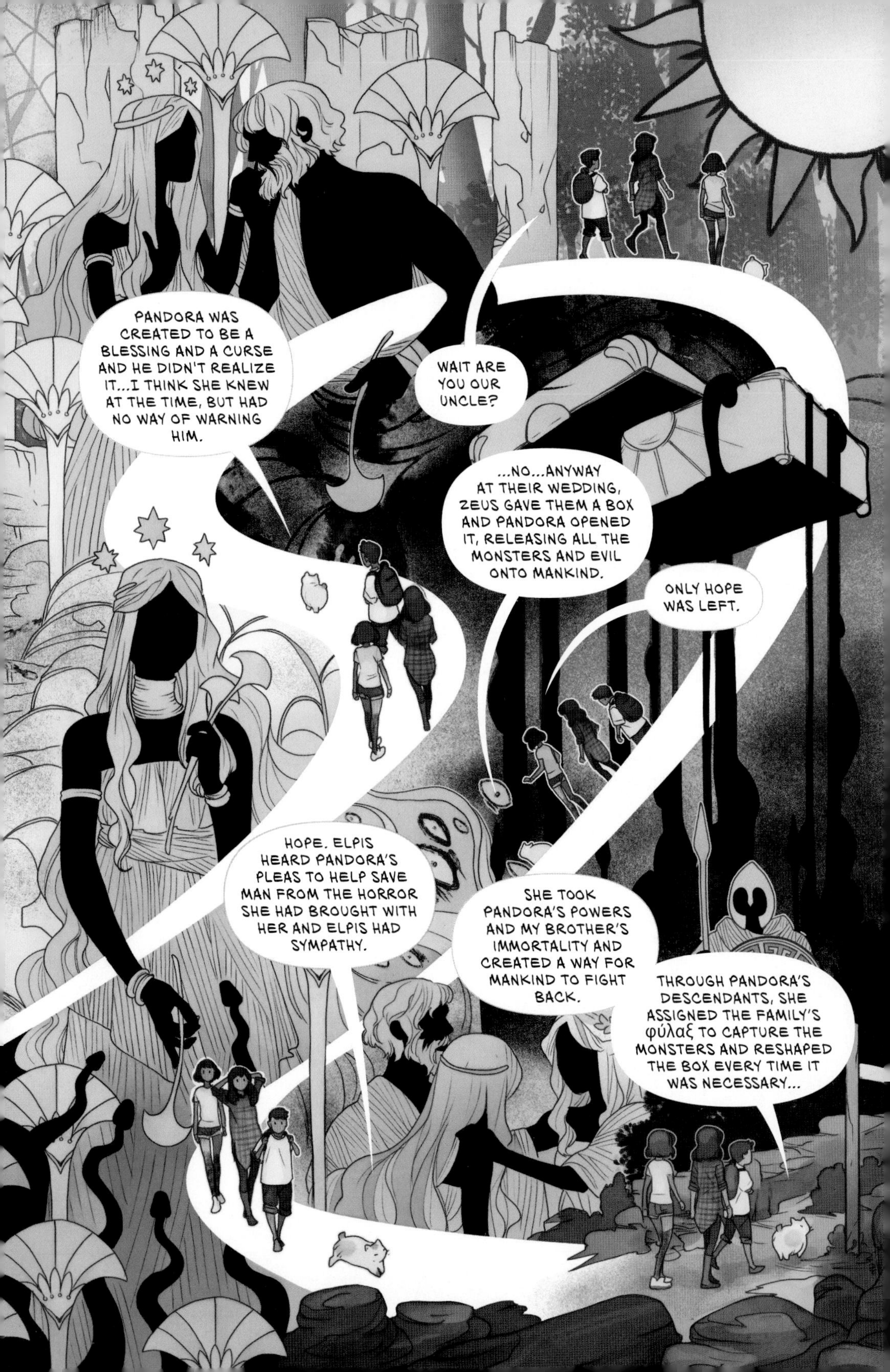
PANDORA WAS CREATED TO BE A BLESSING AND A CURSE AND HE DIDN'T REALIZE IT...I THINK SHE KNEW AT THE TIME, BUT HAD NO WAY OF WARNING HIM.
WAIT ARE YOU OUR UNCLE?
...NO...ANYWAY AT THEIR WEDDING, ZEUS GAVE THEM A BOX AND PANDORA OPENED IT, RELEASING ALL THE MONSTERS AND EVIL ONTO MANKIND.
ONLY HOPE WAS LEFT.
HOPE. ELPIS HEARD PANDORA'S PLEAS TO HELP SAVE MAN FROM THE HORROR SHE HAD BROUGHT WITH HER AND ELPIS HAD SYMPATHY.
SHE TOOK PANDORA'S POWERS AND MY BROTHER'S IMMORTALITY AND CREATED A WAY FOR MANKIND TO FIGHT BACK.
THROUGH PANDORA'S DESCENDANTS, SHE ASSIGNED THE FAMILY'S φύλαξ TO CAPTURE THE MONSTERS AND RESHAPED THE BOX EVERY TIME IT WAS NECESSARY...

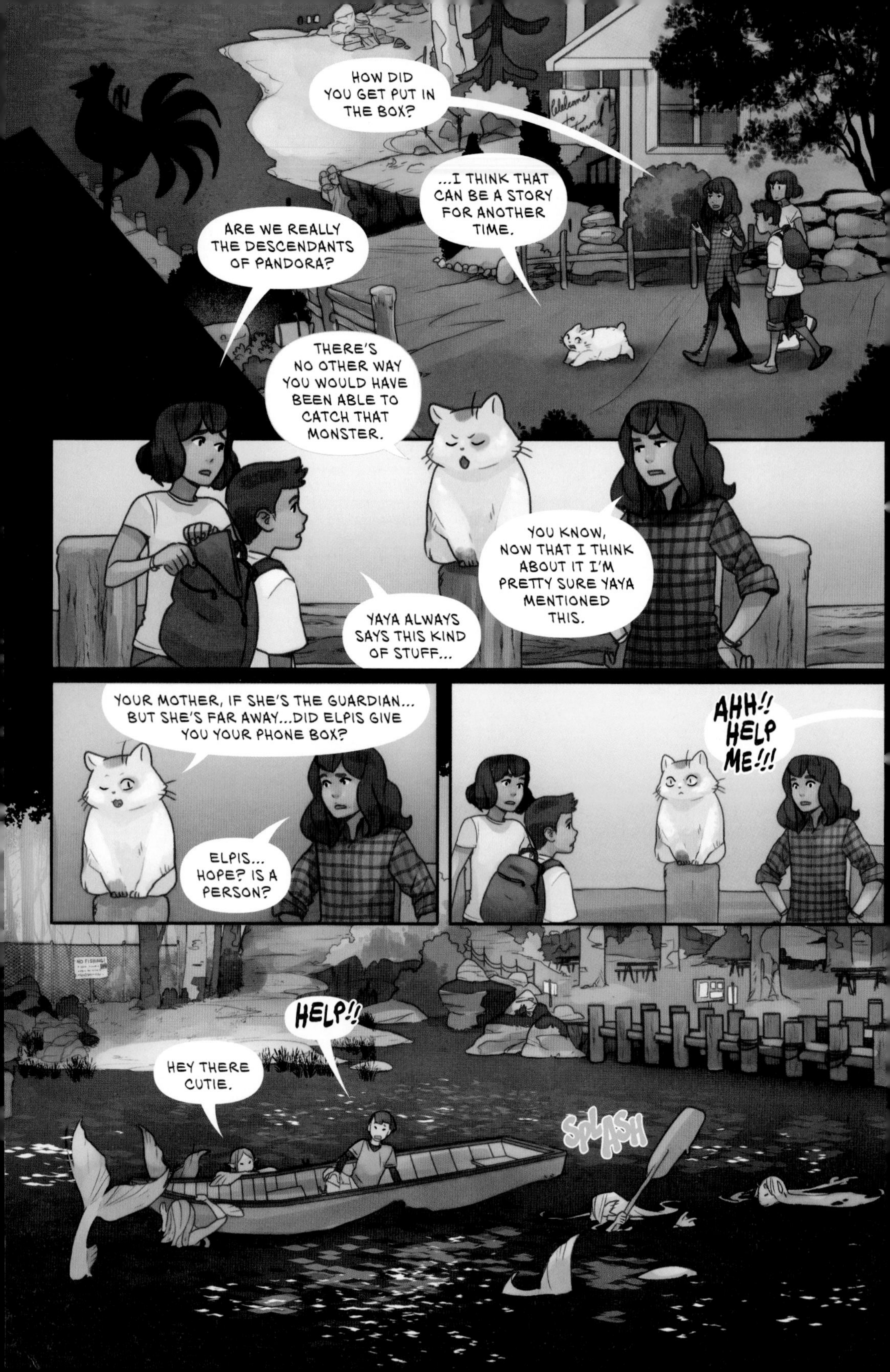
HOW DID YOU GET PUT IN THE BOX?
...I THINK THAT CAN BE A STORY FOR ANOTHER TIME.
ARE WE REALLY THE DESCENDANTS OF PANDORA?
THERE'S NO OTHER WAY YOU WOULD HAVE BEEN ABLE TO CATCH THAT MONSTER.
YOU KNOW, NOW THAT I THINK ABOUT IT I'M PRETTY SURE YAYA MENTIONED THIS.
YAYA ALWAYS SAYS THIS KIND OF STUFF...
YOUR MOTHER, IF SHE'S THE GUARDIAN... BUT SHE'S FAR AWAY...DID ELPIS GIVE YOU YOUR PHONE BOX?
ELPIS... HOPE? IS A PERSON?
AHH!! HELP ME!!!
NO FISHING!
HELP!!
HEY THERE CUTIE.
SPLASH

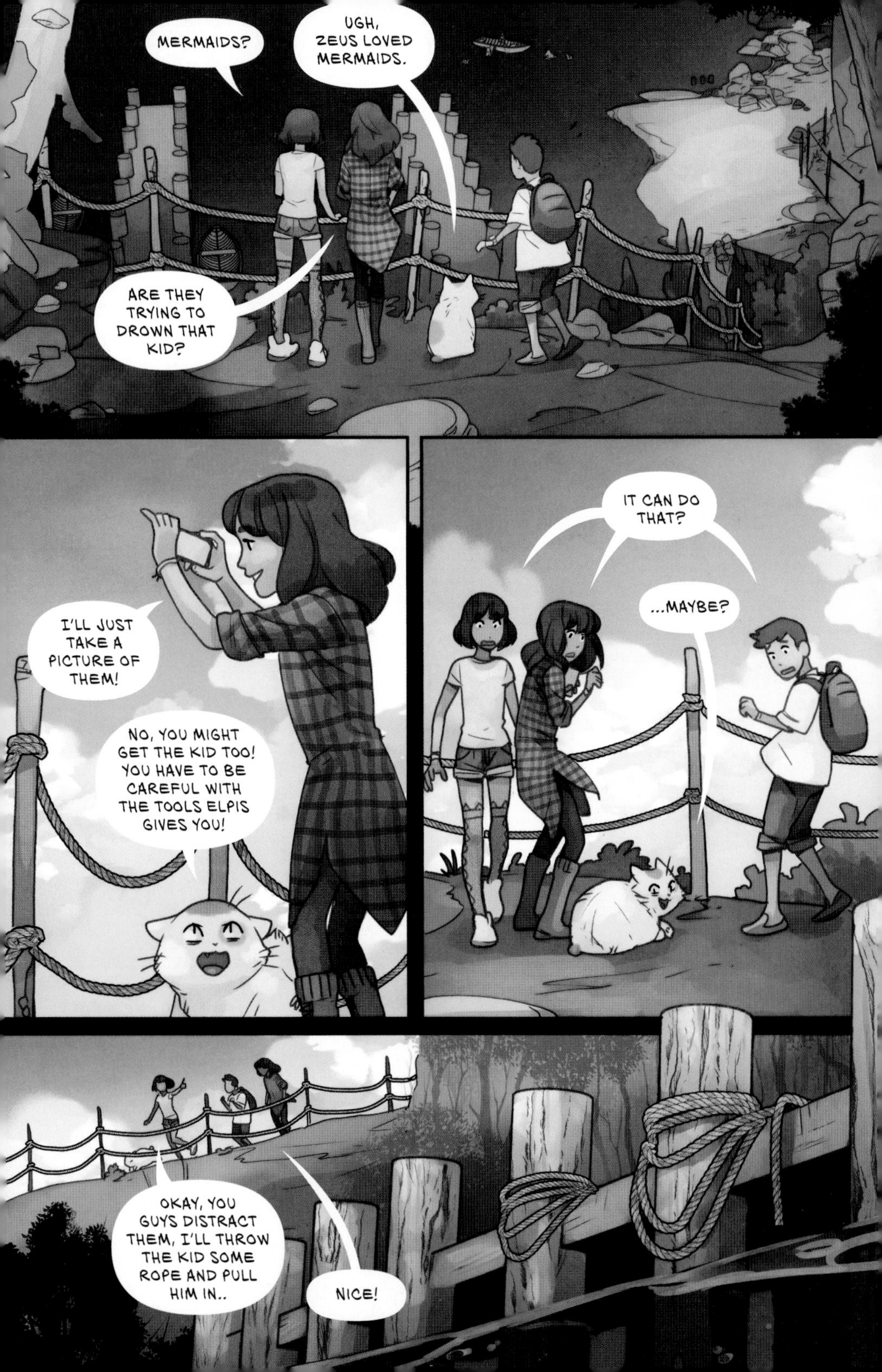
MERMAIDS?
UGH, ZEUS LOVED MERMAIDS.
ARE THEY TRYING TO DROWN THAT KID?
I'LL JUST TAKE A PICTURE OF THEM!
NO, YOU MIGHT GET THE KID TOO! YOU HAVE TO BE CAREFUL WITH THE TOOLS ELPIS GIVES YOU!
IT CAN DO THAT?
...MAYBE?
OKAY, YOU GUYS DISTRACT THEM, I'LL THROW THE KID SOME ROPE AND PULL HIM IN..
NICE!

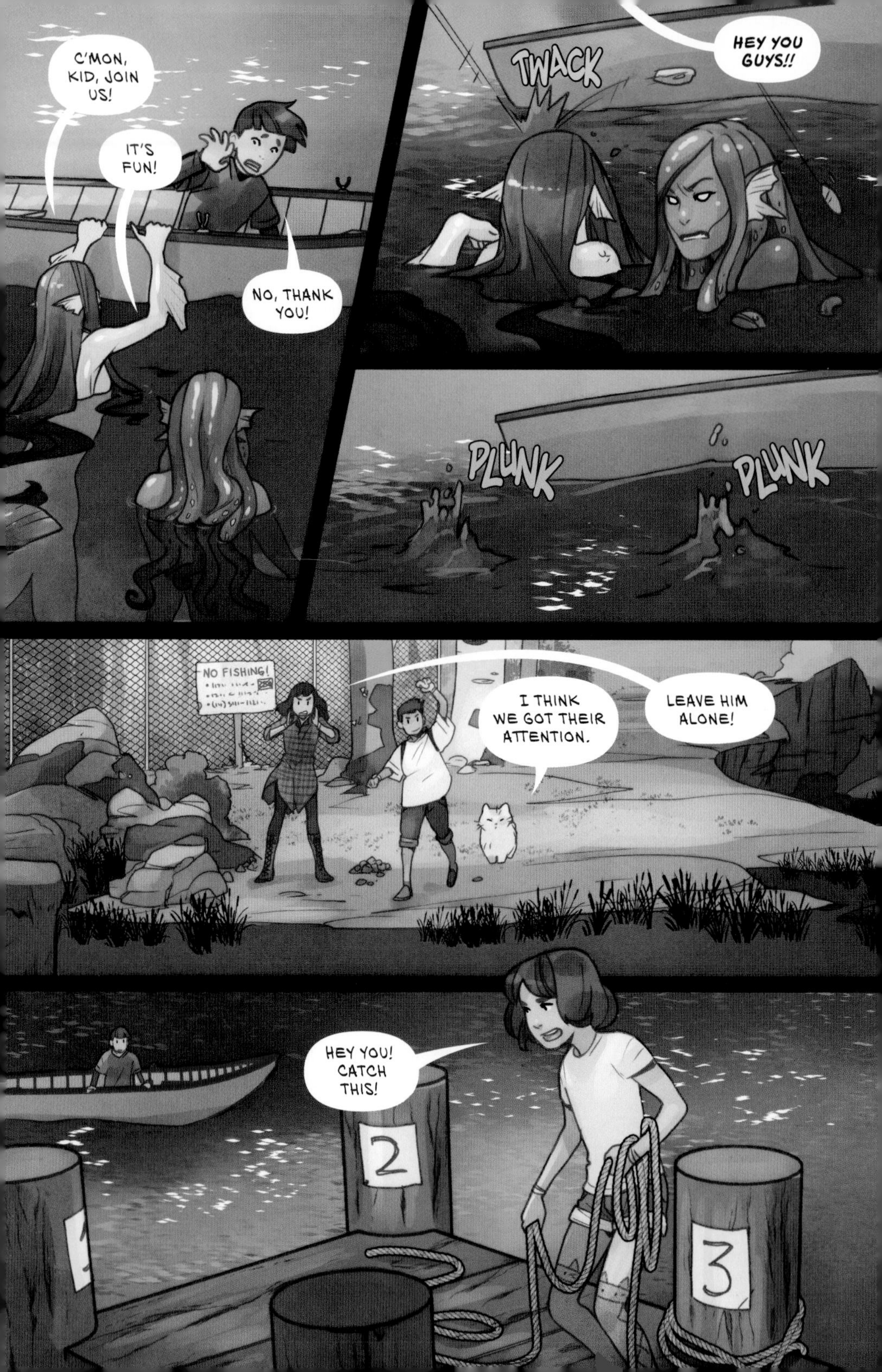
C'MON, KID, JOIN US!
IT'S FUN!
NO, THANK YOU!
HEY YOU GUYS!!
TWACK
PLUNK
PLUNK
NO FISHING!
I THINK WE GOT THEIR ATTENTION.
LEAVE HIM ALONE!
HEY YOU! CATCH THIS!
2
3

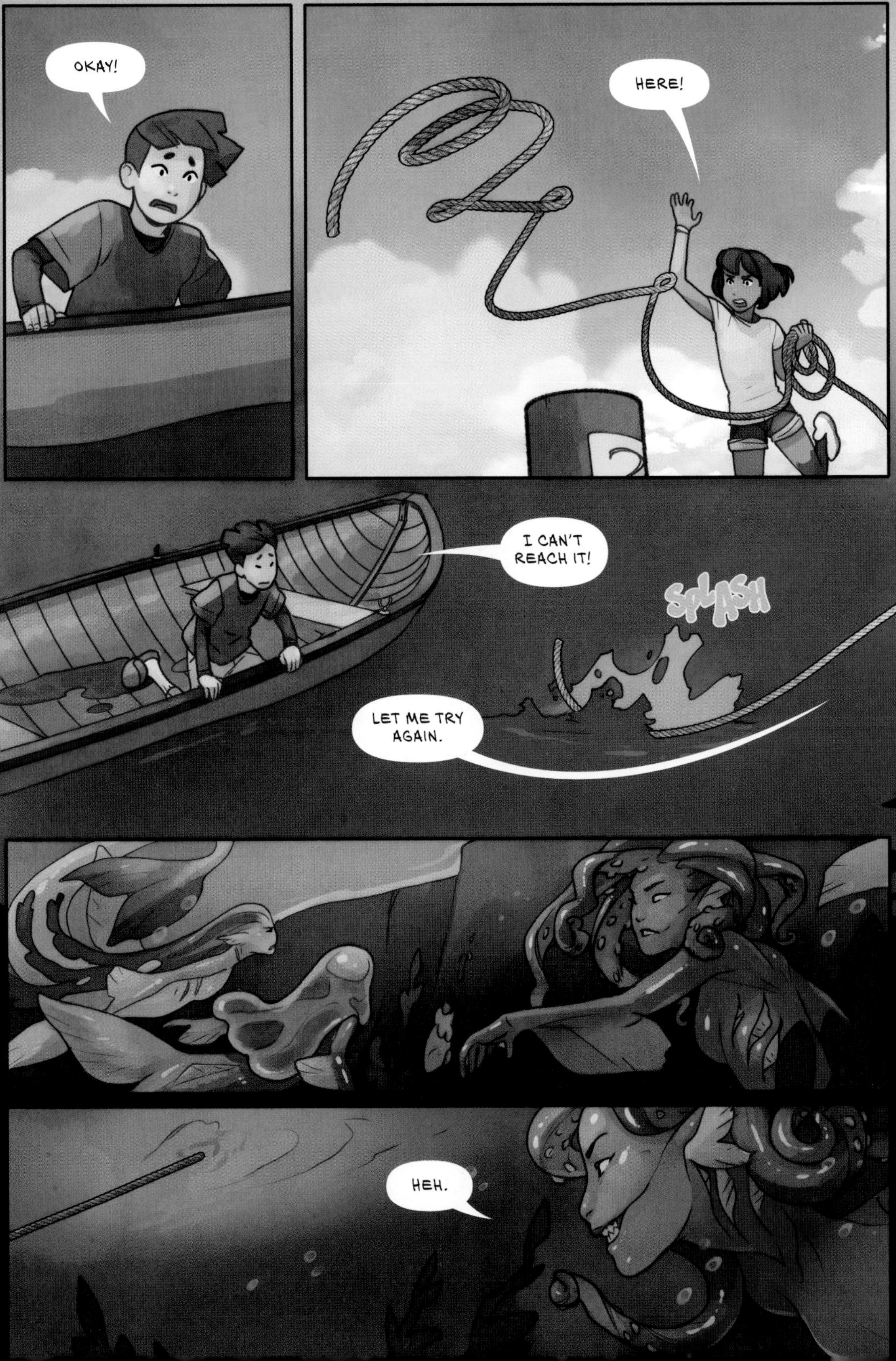
OKAY!
HERE!
I CAN'T REACH IT!
SPLASH
LET ME TRY AGAIN.
HEH.

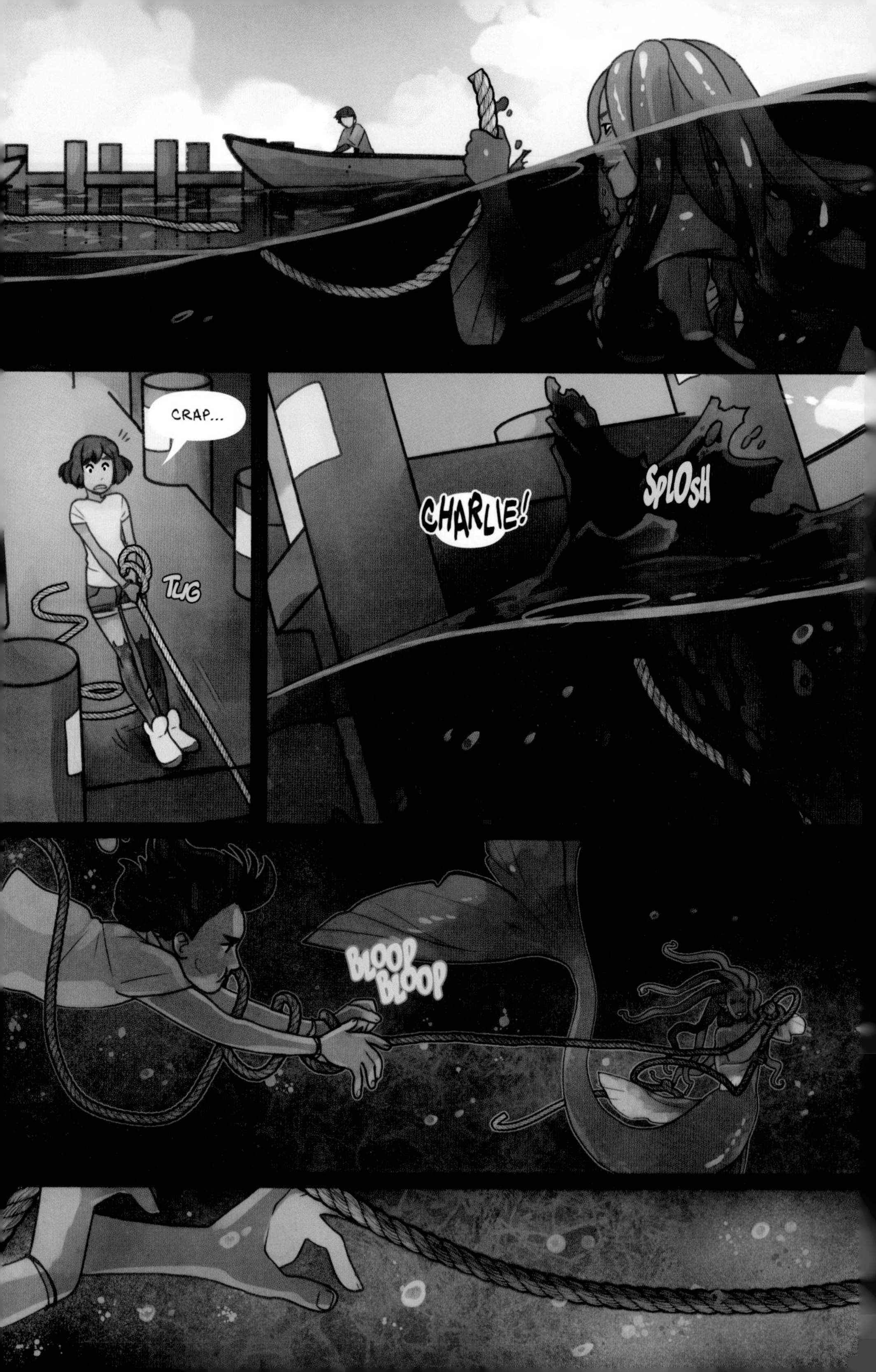
CRAP...
TUG
CHARLIE!
SPLOSH
BLOOP BLOOP

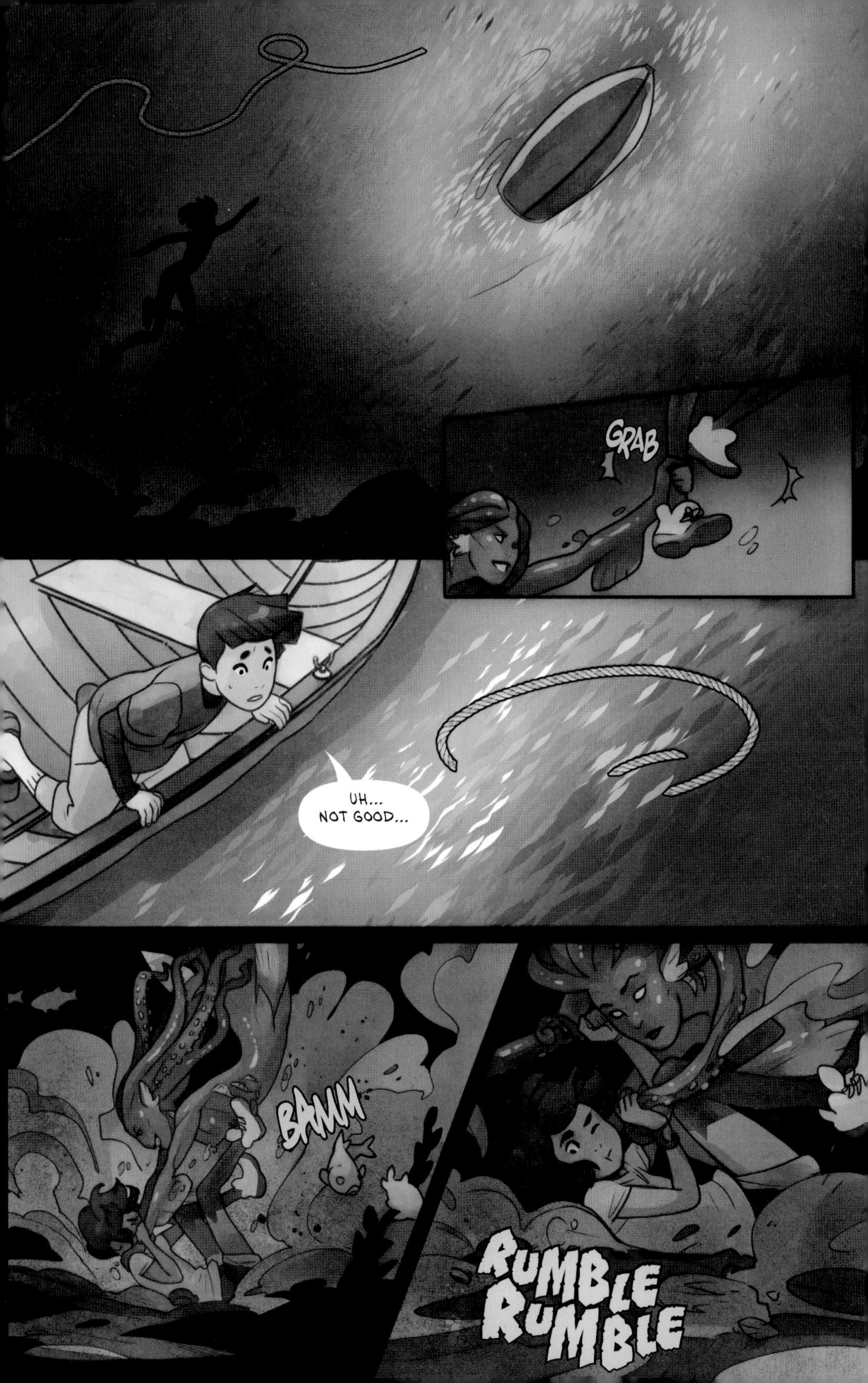
GRAB
UH... NOT GOOD...
BAMM
RUMBLE RUMBLE

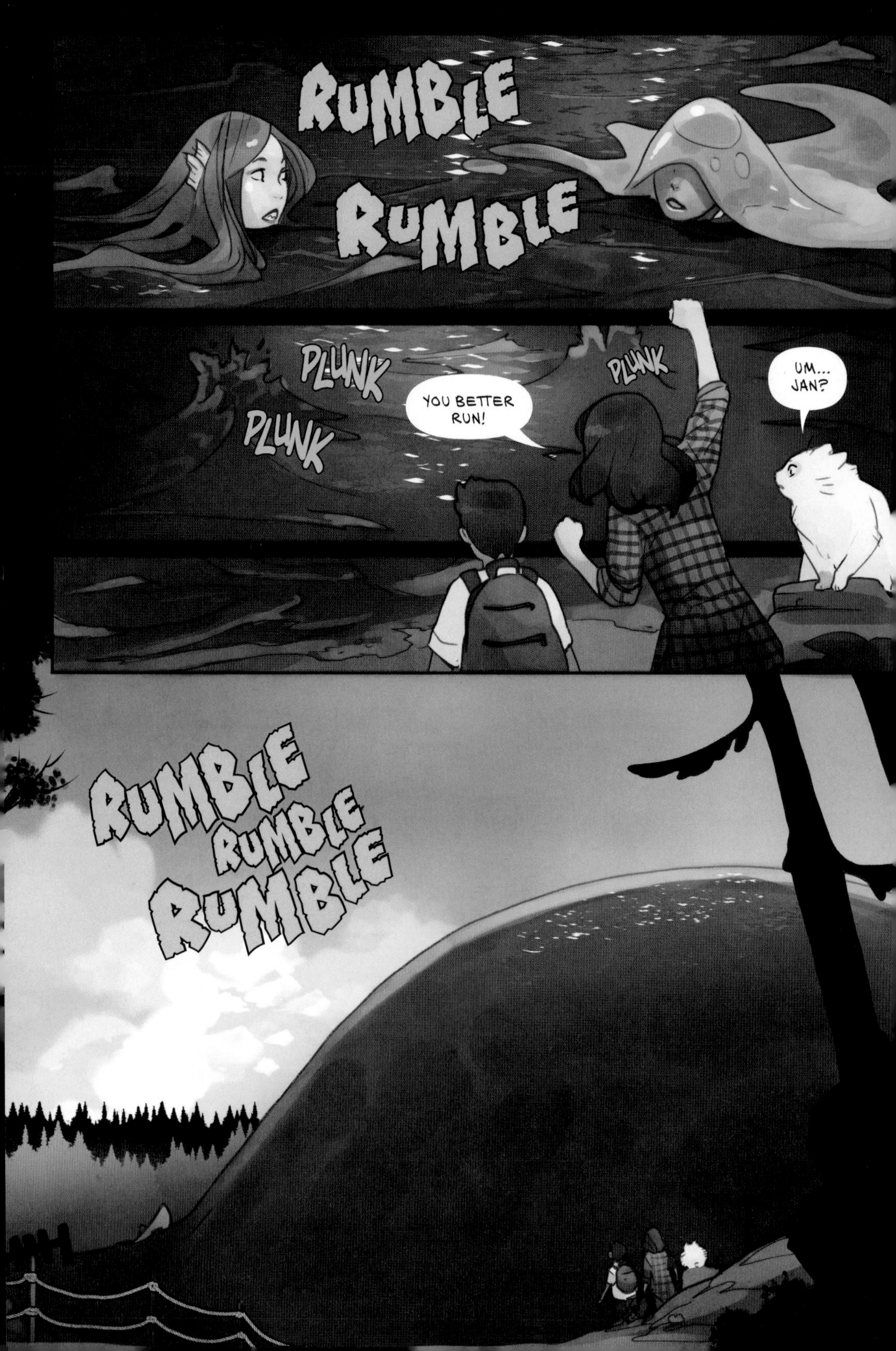
RUMBLE
RUMBLE
PLUNK
PLUNK
YOU BETTER RUN!
PLUNK
UM... JAN?
RUMBLE
RUMBLE
RUMBLE

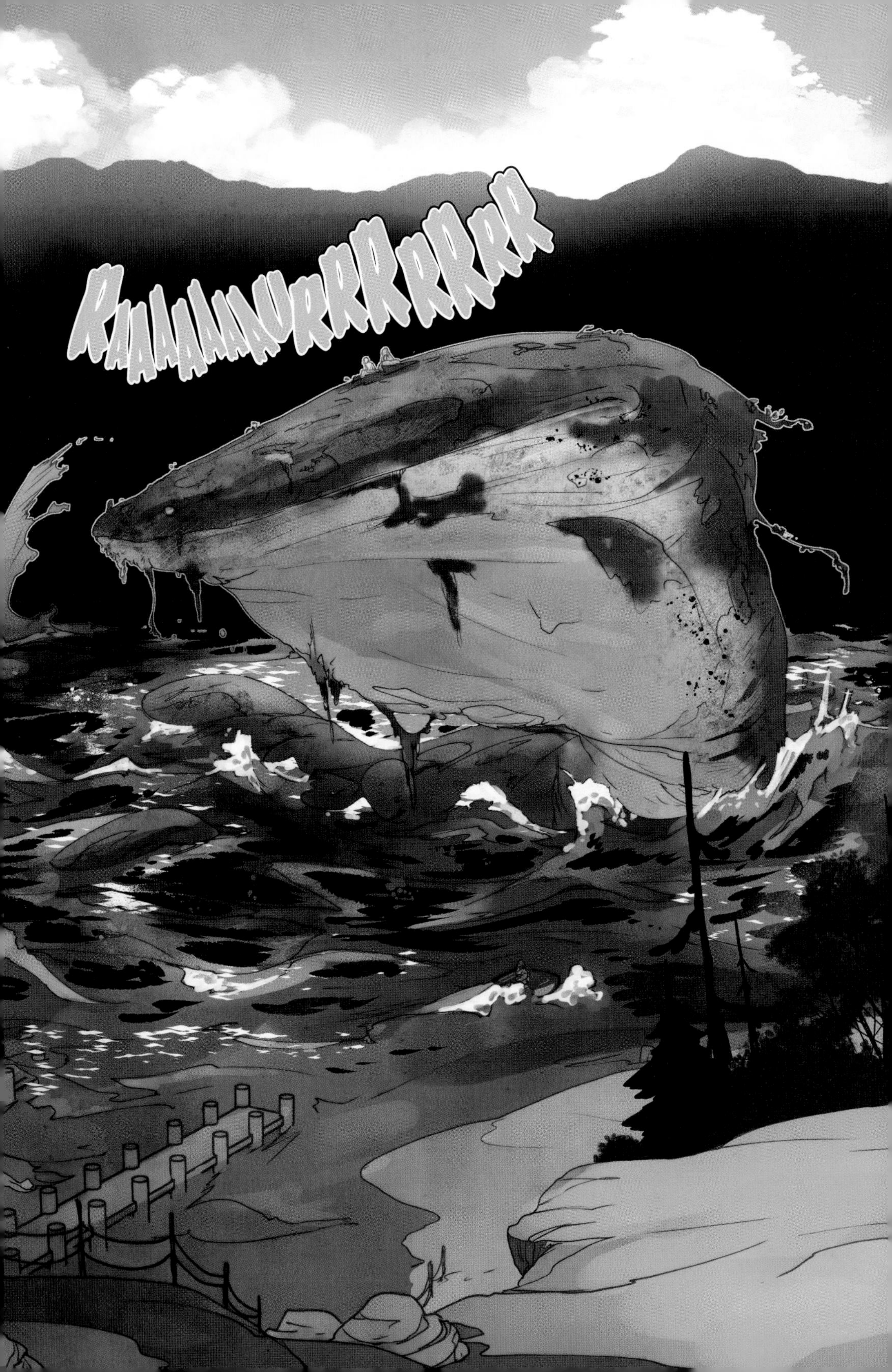
RAAAAAAAURRRRRRR

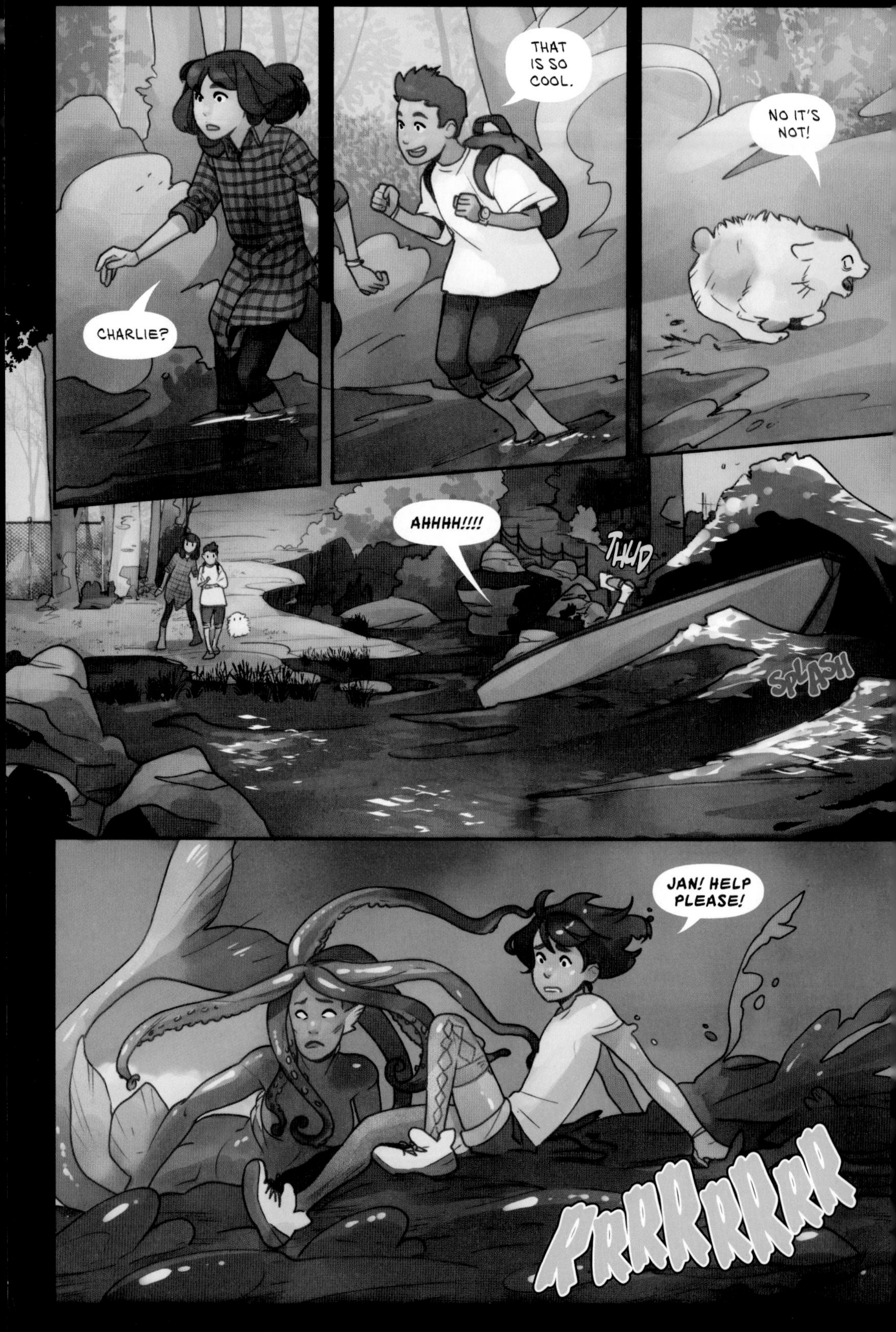
CHARLIE?
THAT IS SO COOL.
NO IT'S NOT!
AHHHH!!!!
THUD
SPLASH
JAN! HELP PLEASE!
PRRRRRRR

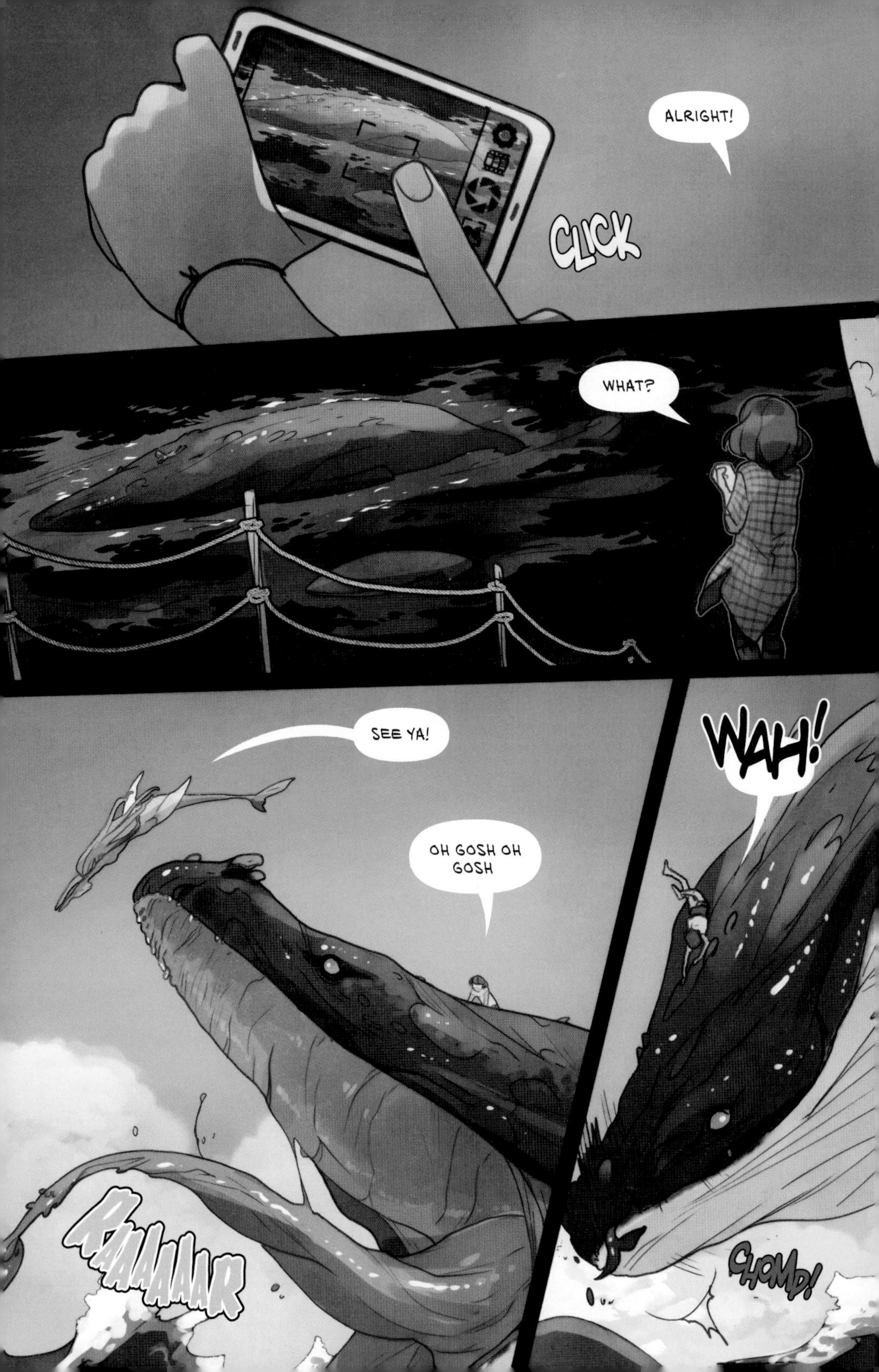
ALRIGHT!
CLICK
WHAT?
SEE YA!
OH GOSH OH GOSH
RAAAAAAAR
WAH!
CHOMP!

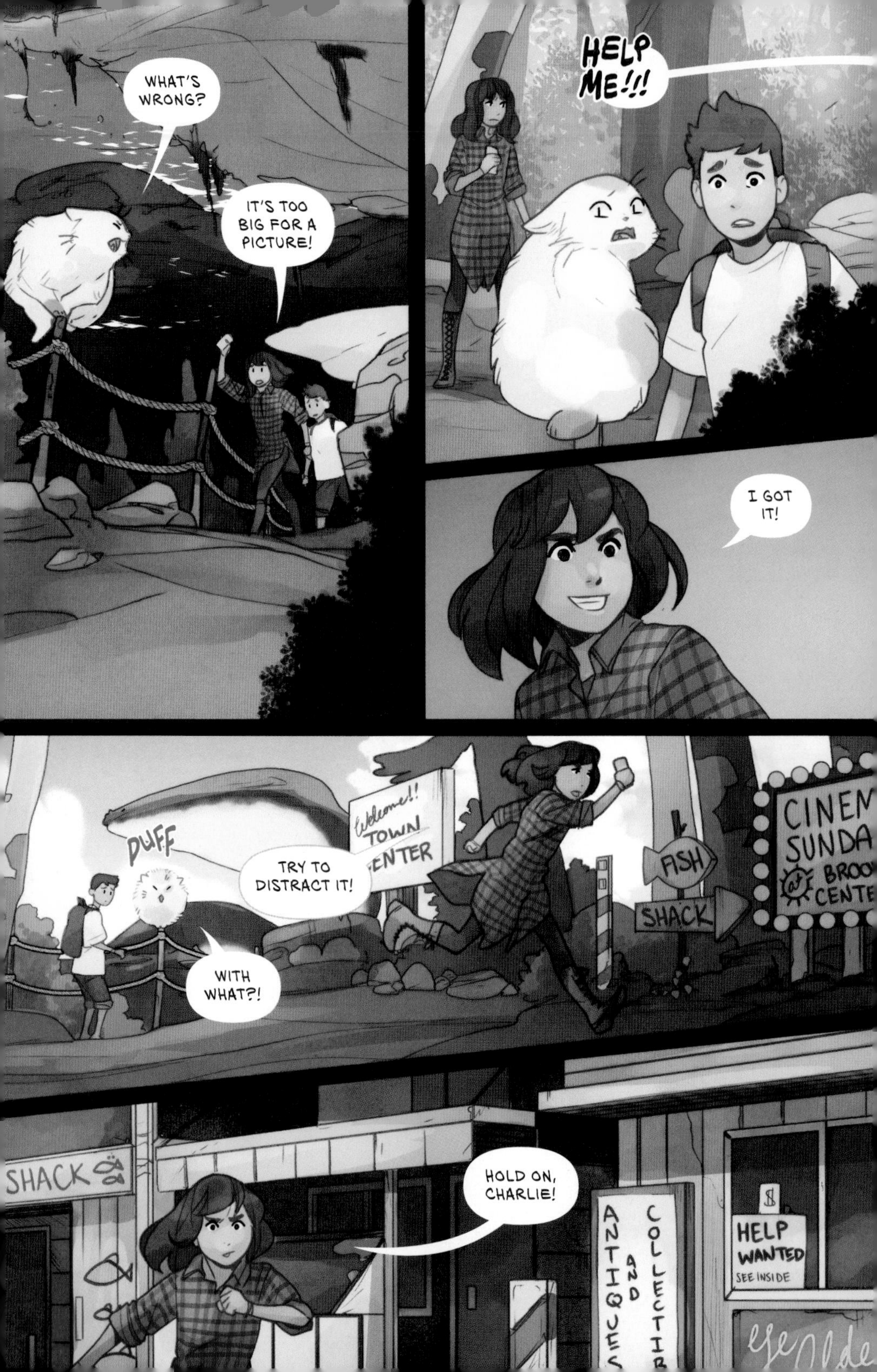
WHAT'S WRONG?
IT'S TOO BIG FOR A PICTURE!
HELP ME!!!
I GOT IT!
DUFF
Welcome!! TOWN CENTER
TRY TO DISTRACT IT!
FISH
SHACK
WITH WHAT?!
SHACK
HOLD ON, CHARLIE!
ANTIQUES AND COLLECTIB
HELP WANTED SEE INSIDE

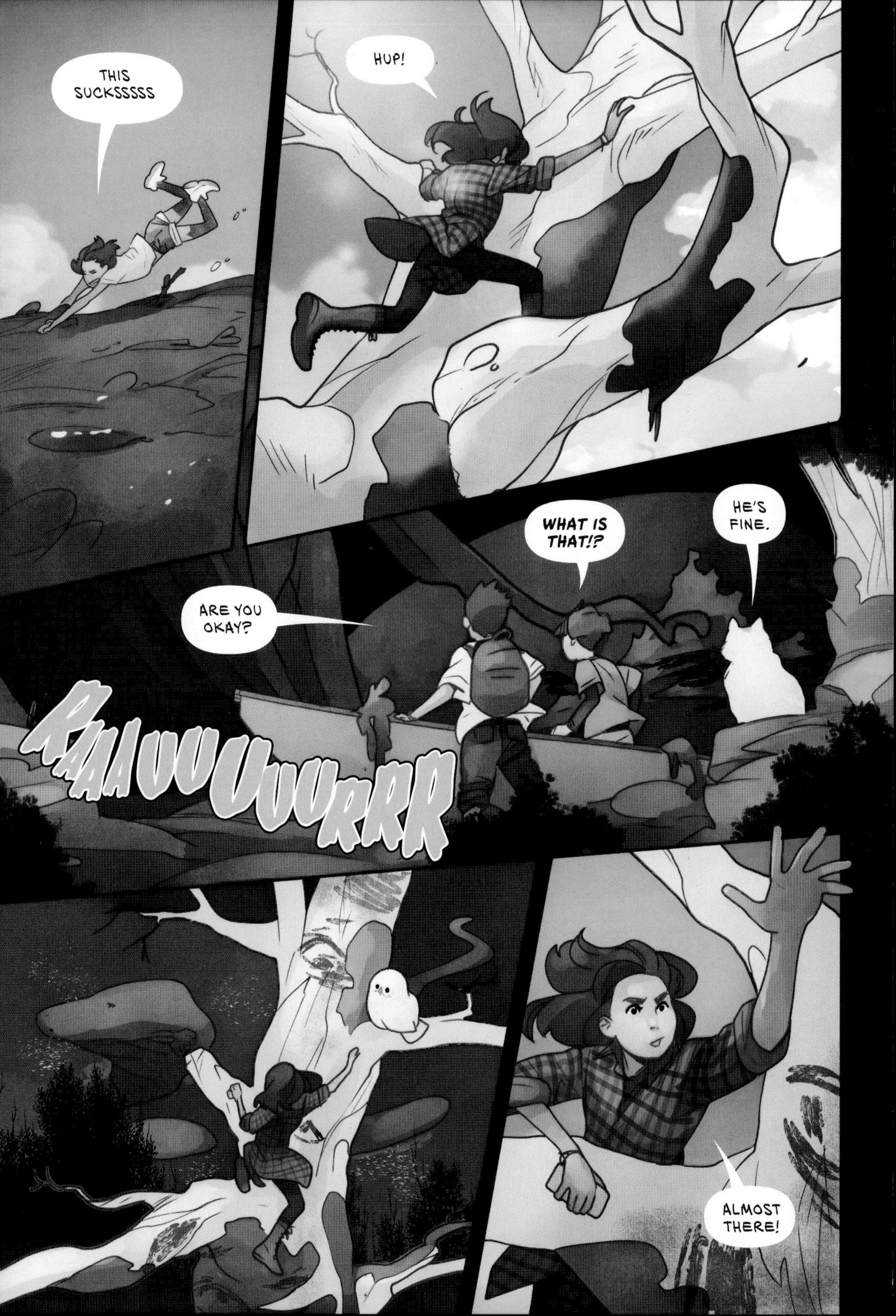
THIS SUCKSSSSS
HUP!
ARE YOU OKAY?
WHAT IS THAT!?
HE'S FINE.
RAAAUUUUUURRR
ALMOST THERE!

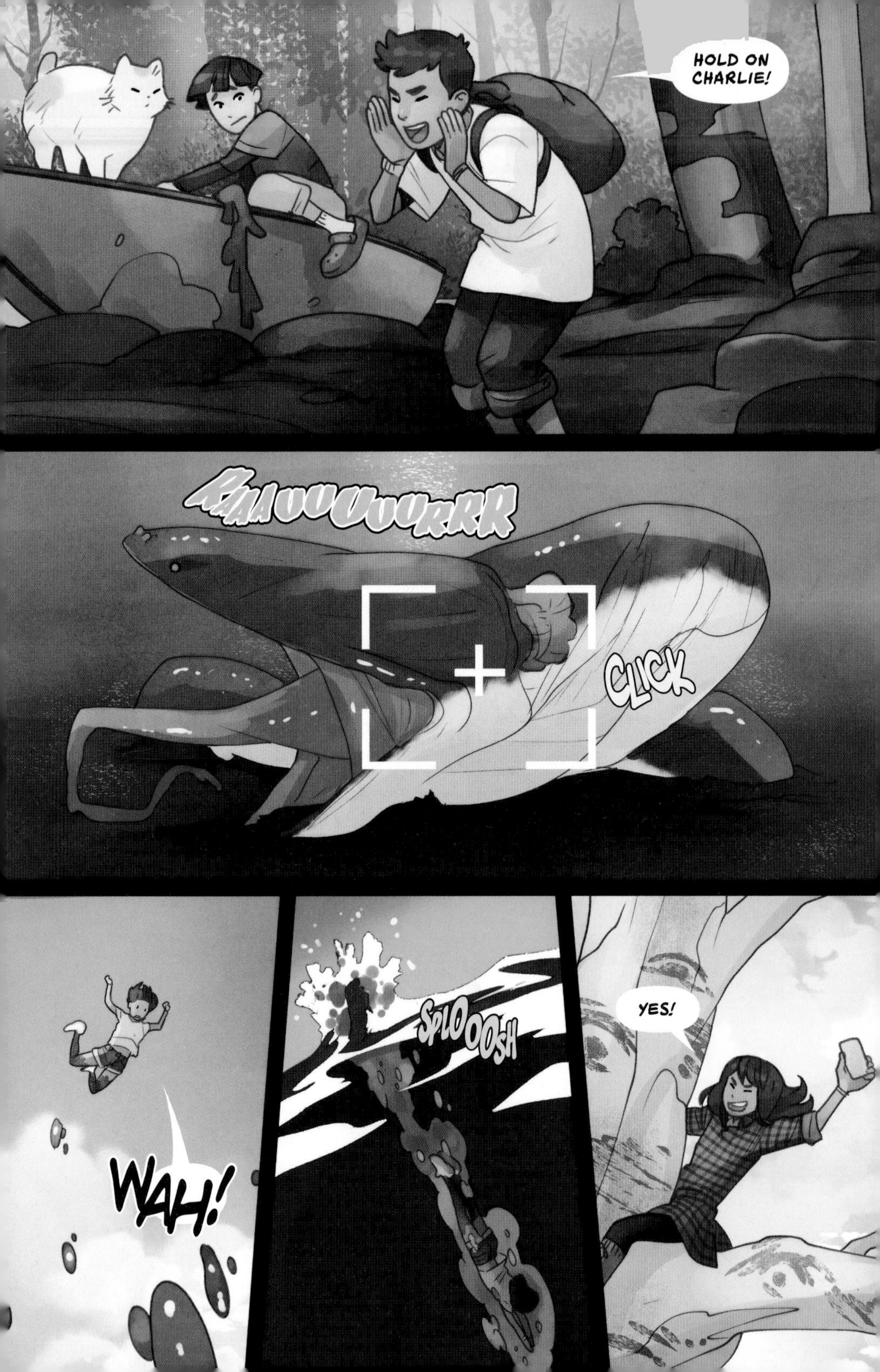
HOLD ON CHARLIE!
RAAAVUUVUUURRR
CLICK
WAH!
SPLOOOSH
YES!

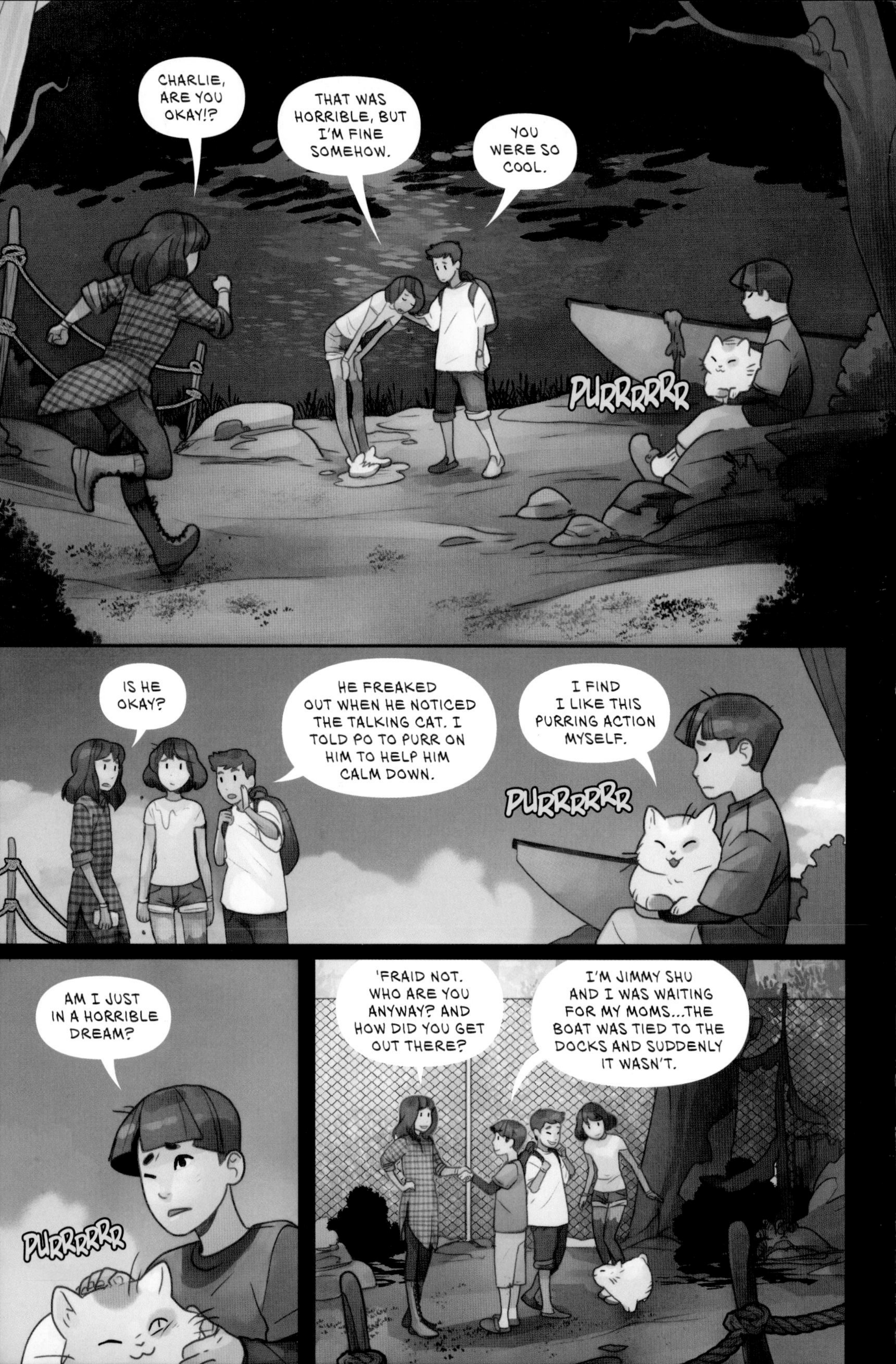
CHARLIE, ARE YOU OKAY!?
THAT WAS HORRIBLE, BUT I'M FINE SOMEHOW.
YOU WERE SO COOL.
PURRRRRR
IS HE OKAY?
HE FREAKED OUT WHEN HE NOTICED THE TALKING CAT. I TOLD PO TO PURR ON HIM TO HELP HIM CALM DOWN.
I FIND I LIKE THIS PURRING ACTION MYSELF.
PURRRRRR
AM I JUST IN A HORRIBLE DREAM?
PURRRRRR
'FRAID NOT. WHO ARE YOU ANYWAY? AND HOW DID YOU GET OUT THERE?
I'M JIMMY SHU AND I WAS WAITING FOR MY MOMS...THE BOAT WAS TIED TO THE DOCKS AND SUDDENLY IT WASN'T.

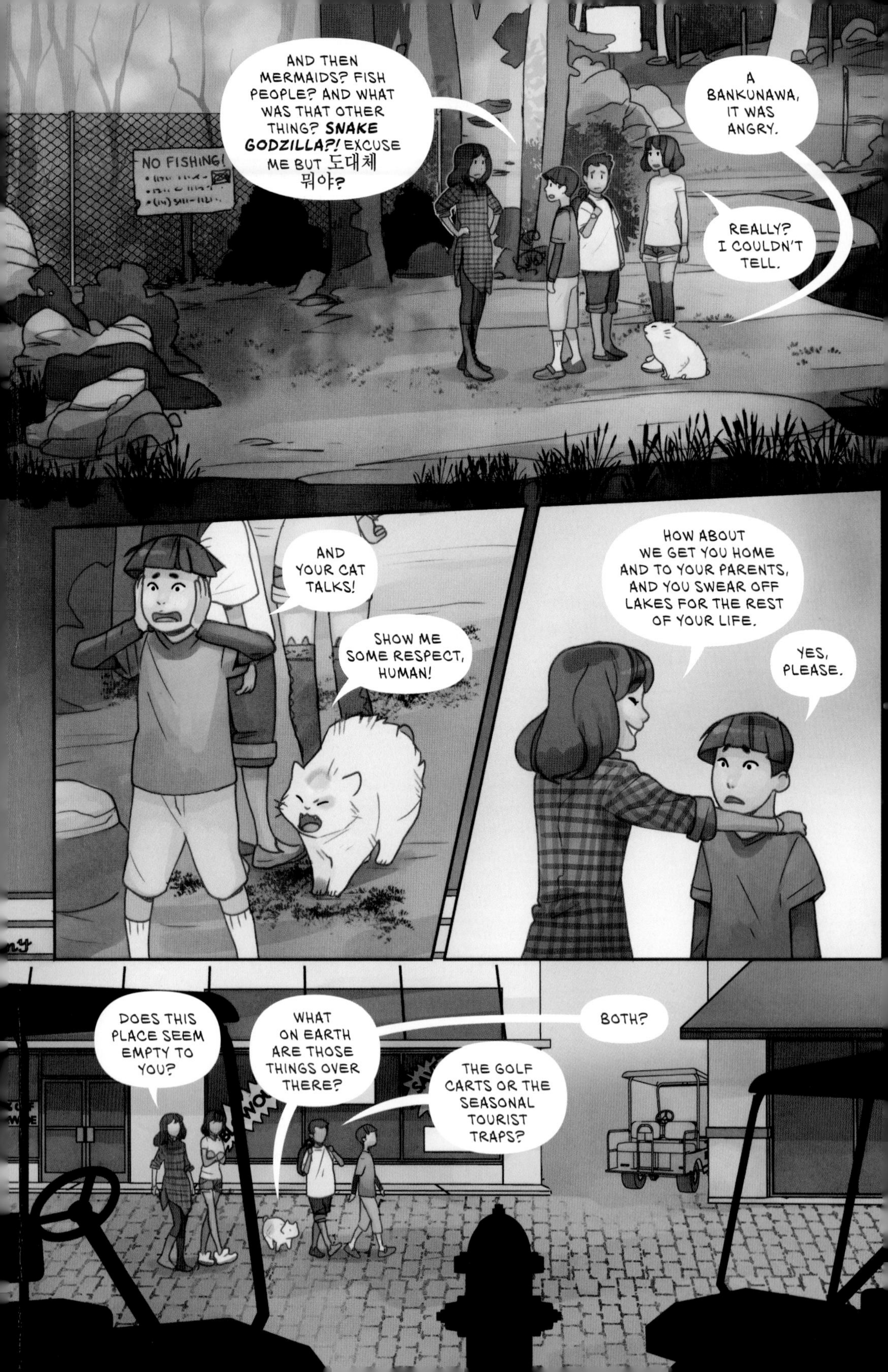
NO FISHING!
AND THEN MERMAIDS? FISH PEOPLE? AND WHAT WAS THAT OTHER THING? **SNAKE GODZILLA?!** EXCUSE ME BUT 도대체 뭐야?
A BANKUNAWA, IT WAS ANGRY.
REALLY? I COULDN'T TELL.
AND YOUR CAT TALKS!
SHOW ME SOME RESPECT, HUMAN!
HOW ABOUT WE GET YOU HOME AND TO YOUR PARENTS, AND YOU SWEAR OFF LAKES FOR THE REST OF YOUR LIFE.
YES, PLEASE.
DOES THIS PLACE SEEM EMPTY TO YOU?
WHAT ON EARTH ARE THOSE THINGS OVER THERE?
THE GOLF CARTS OR THE SEASONAL TOURIST TRAPS?
BOTH?

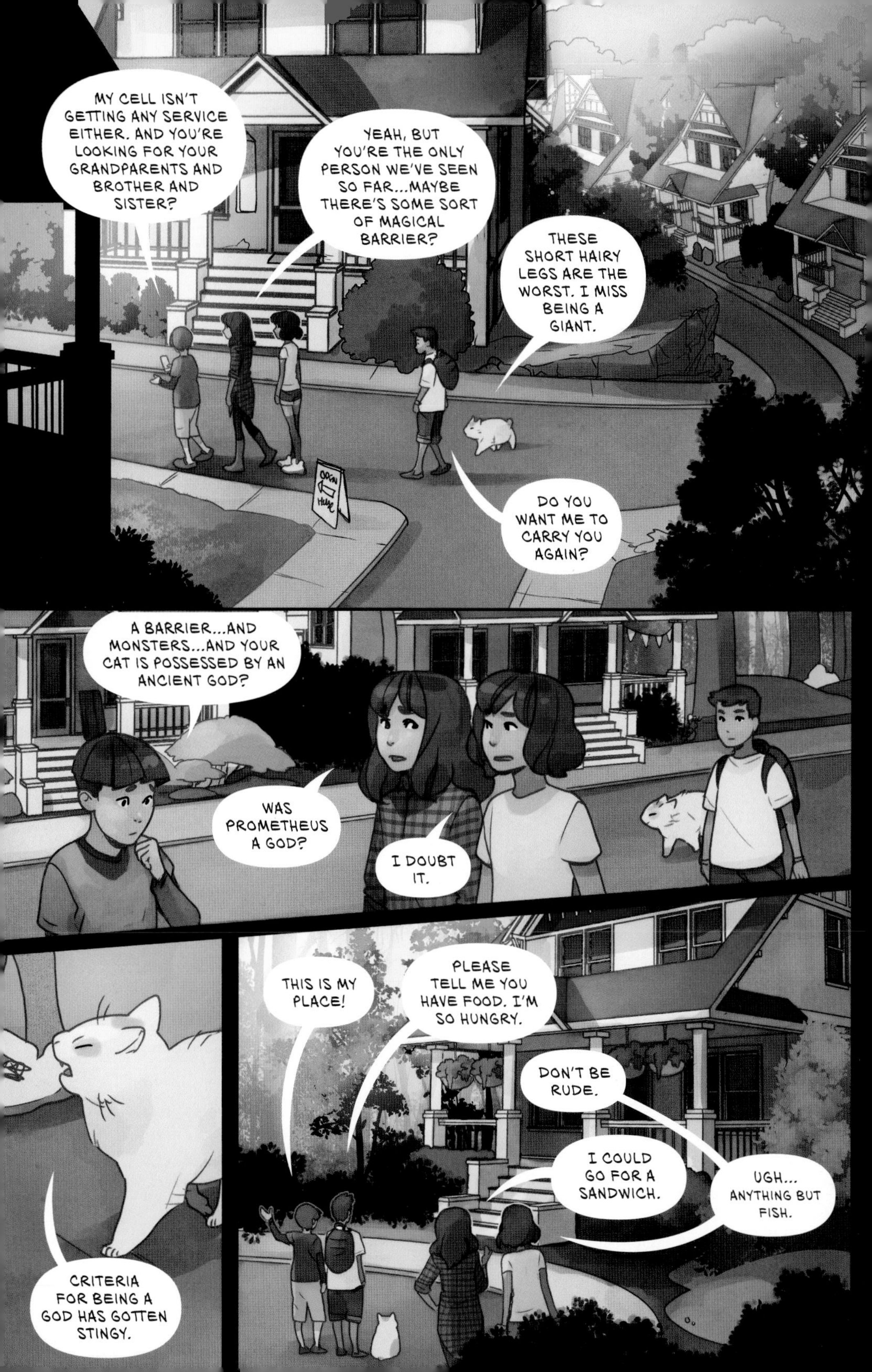
MY CELL ISN'T GETTING ANY SERVICE EITHER. AND YOU'RE LOOKING FOR YOUR GRANDPARENTS AND BROTHER AND SISTER?
YEAH, BUT YOU'RE THE ONLY PERSON WE'VE SEEN SO FAR...MAYBE THERE'S SOME SORT OF MAGICAL BARRIER?
THESE SHORT HAIRY LEGS ARE THE WORST. I MISS BEING A GIANT.
DO YOU WANT ME TO CARRY YOU AGAIN?
A BARRIER...AND MONSTERS...AND YOUR CAT IS POSSESSED BY AN ANCIENT GOD?
WAS PROMETHEUS A GOD?
I DOUBT IT.
CRITERIA FOR BEING A GOD HAS GOTTEN STINGY.
THIS IS MY PLACE!
PLEASE TELL ME YOU HAVE FOOD. I'M SO HUNGRY.
DON'T BE RUDE.
I COULD GO FOR A SANDWICH.
UGH... ANYTHING BUT FISH.

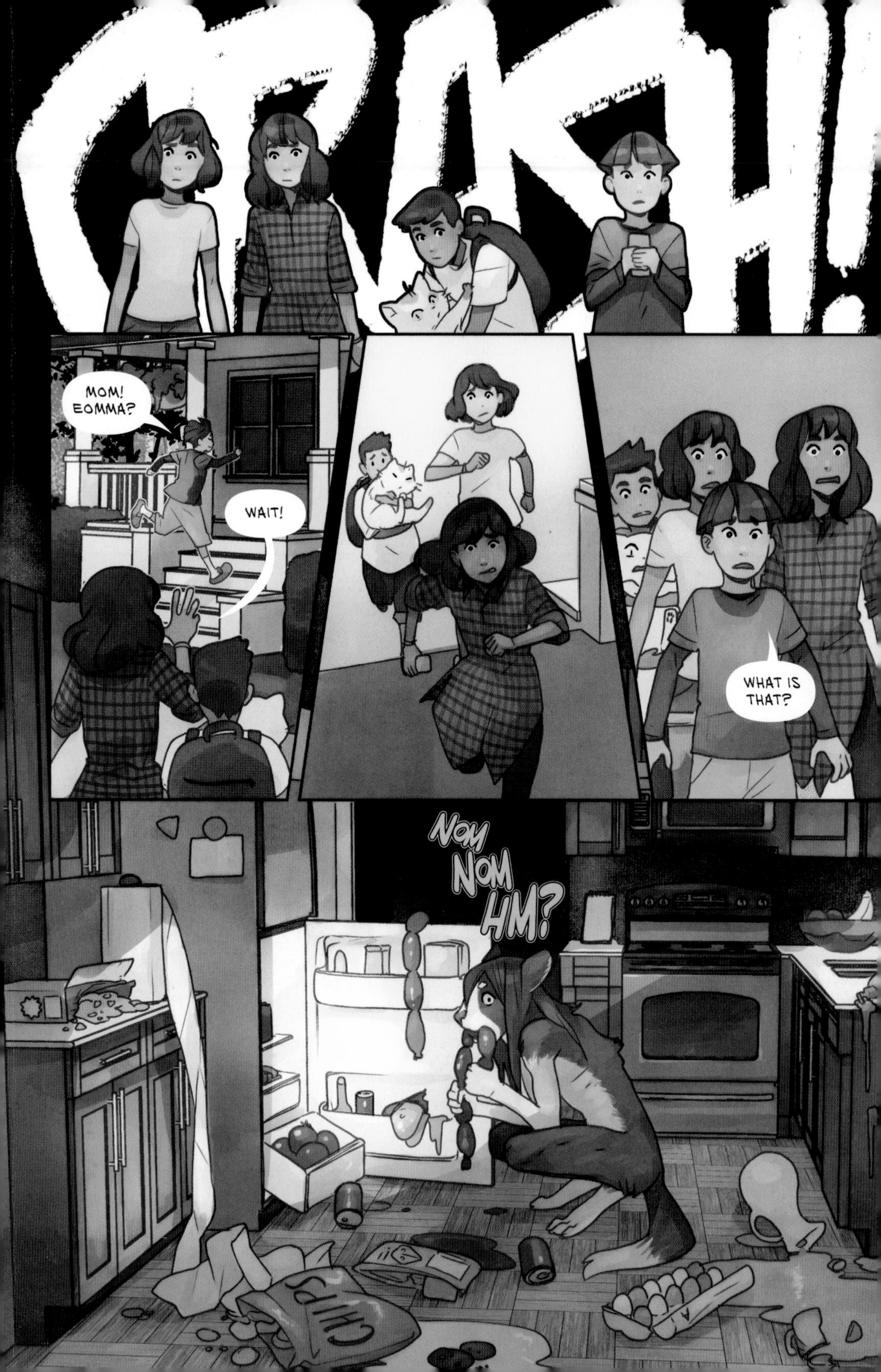
MOM! EOMMA?
WAIT!
WHAT IS THAT?
NOM
NOM
HM?

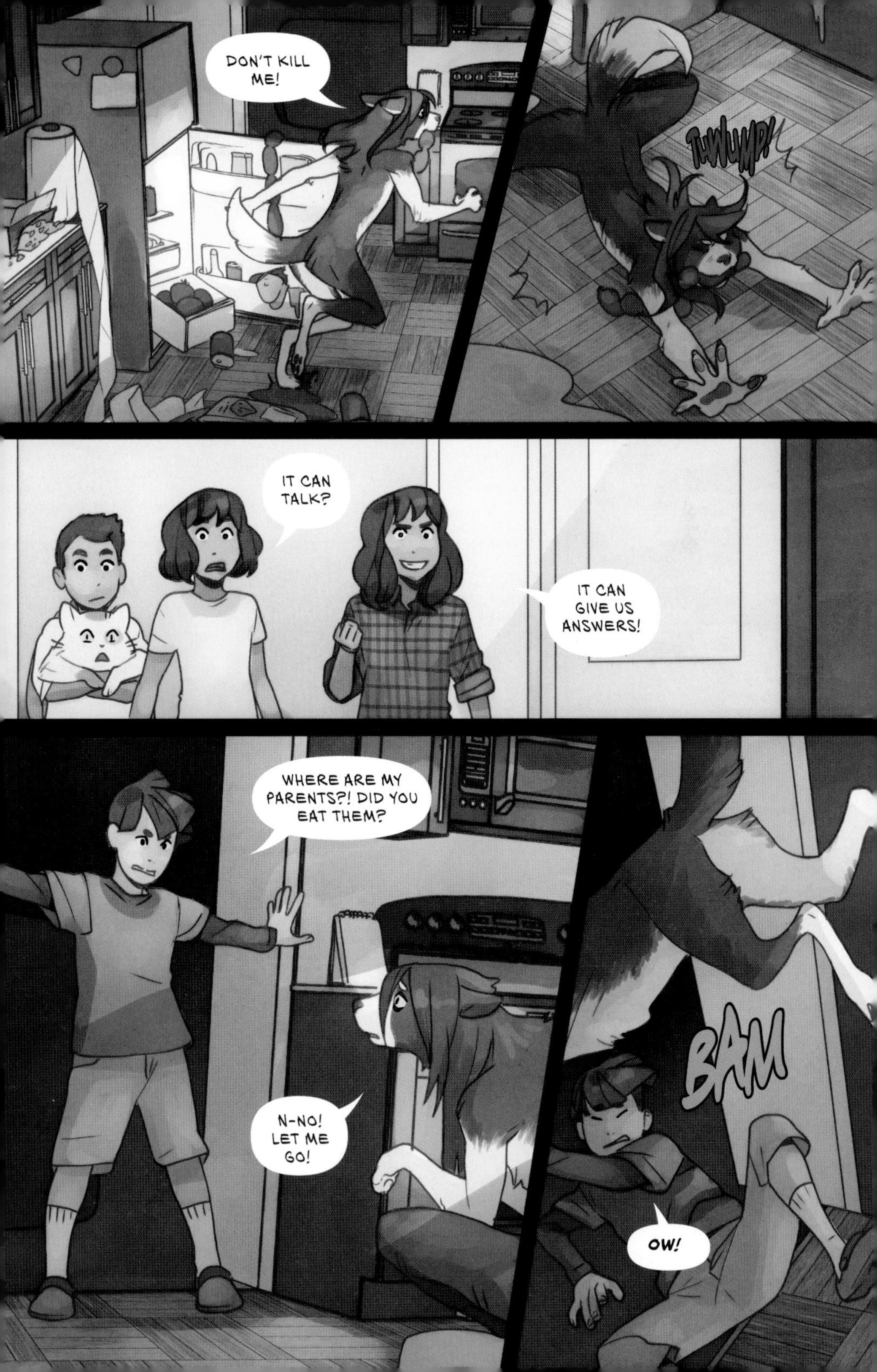
DON'T KILL ME!
THWUMP!
IT CAN TALK?
IT CAN GIVE US ANSWERS!
WHERE ARE MY PARENTS?! DID YOU EAT THEM?
N-NO! LET ME GO!
BAM
OW!

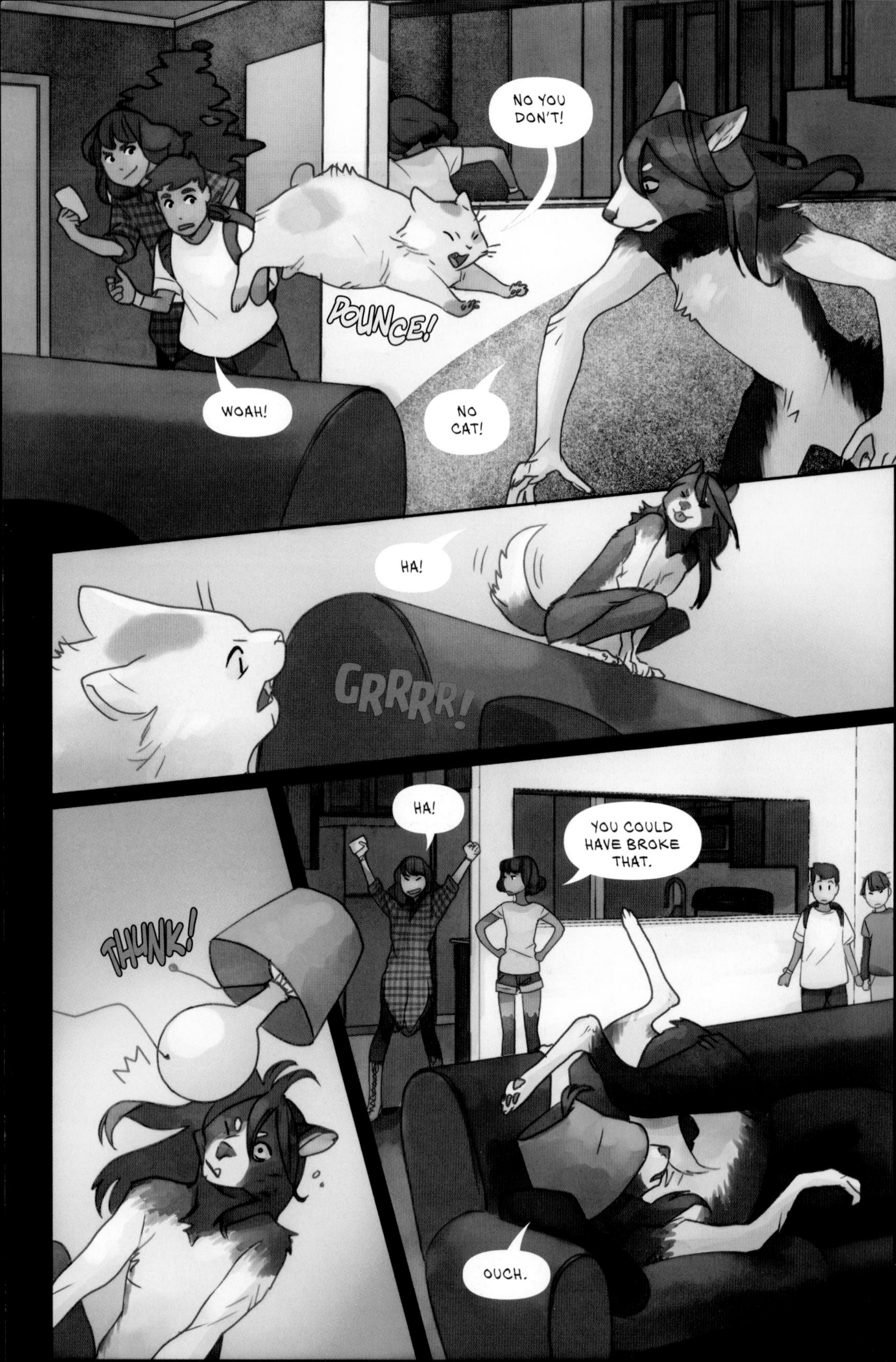
NO YOU DON'T!
POUNCE!
WOAH!
NO CAT!
HA!
GRRRR!
HA!
YOU COULD HAVE BROKE THAT.
THUNK!
OUCH.

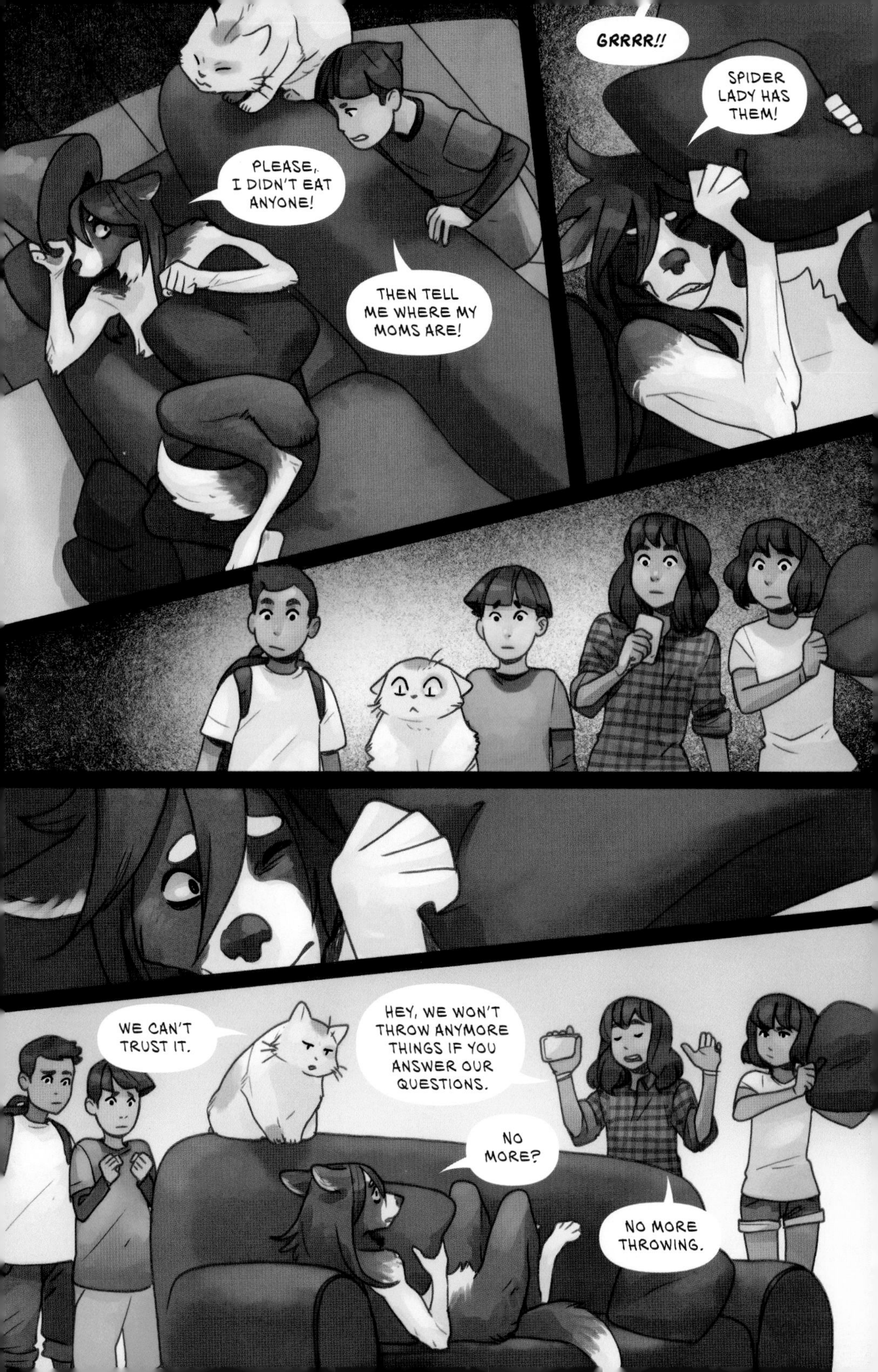
PLEASE, I DIDN'T EAT ANYONE!
THEN TELL ME WHERE MY MOMS ARE!
GRRRR!!
SPIDER LADY HAS THEM!
WE CAN'T TRUST IT.
HEY, WE WON'T THROW ANYMORE THINGS IF YOU ANSWER OUR QUESTIONS.
NO MORE?
NO MORE THROWING.

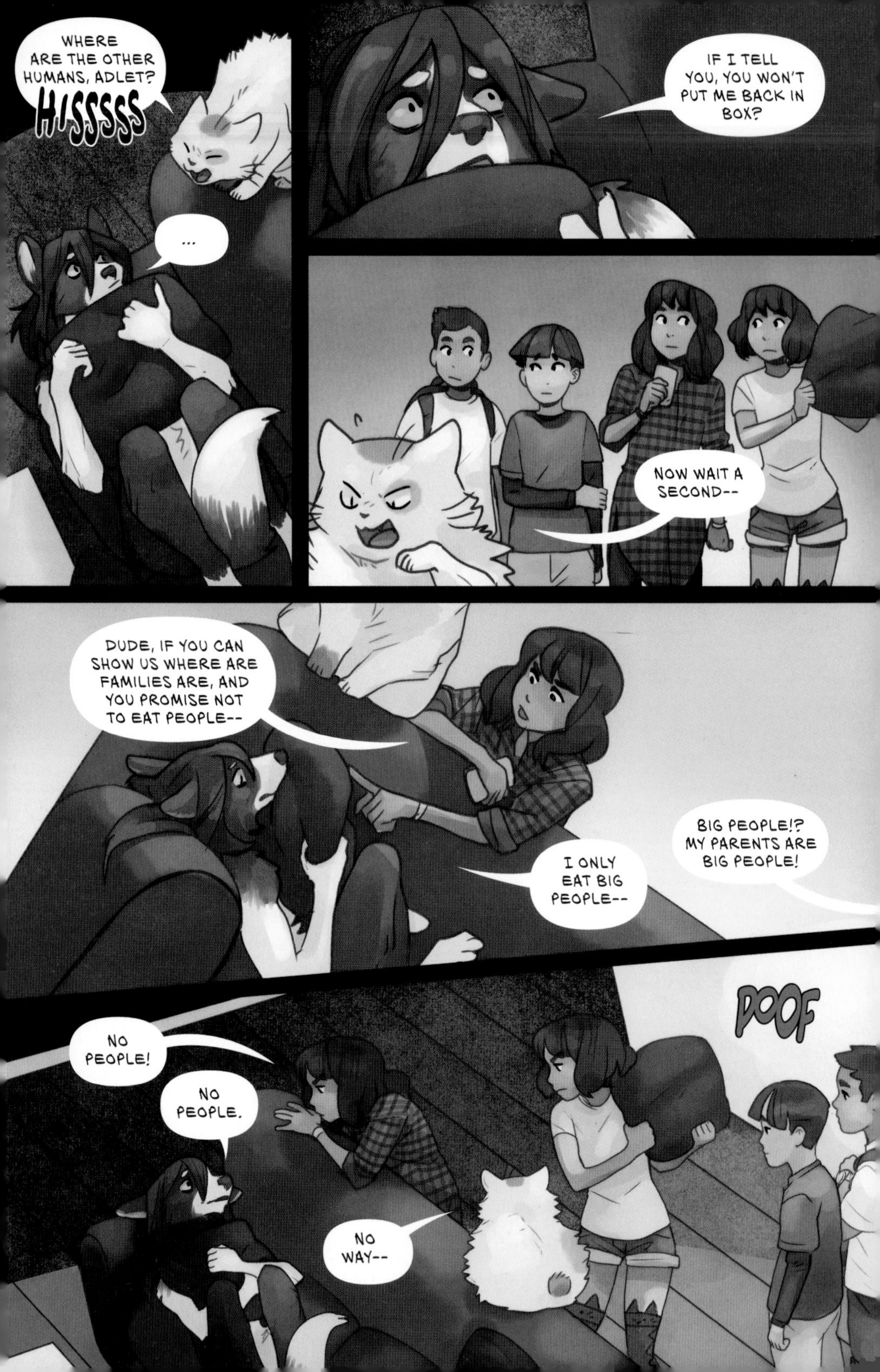
WHERE ARE THE OTHER HUMANS, ADLET?
HISSSSS
...
IF I TELL YOU, YOU WON'T PUT ME BACK IN BOX?
NOW WAIT A SECOND--
DUDE, IF YOU CAN SHOW US WHERE ARE FAMILIES ARE, AND YOU PROMISE NOT TO EAT PEOPLE--
I ONLY EAT BIG PEOPLE--
BIG PEOPLE!? MY PARENTS ARE BIG PEOPLE!
DOOF
NO PEOPLE!
NO PEOPLE.
NO WAY--

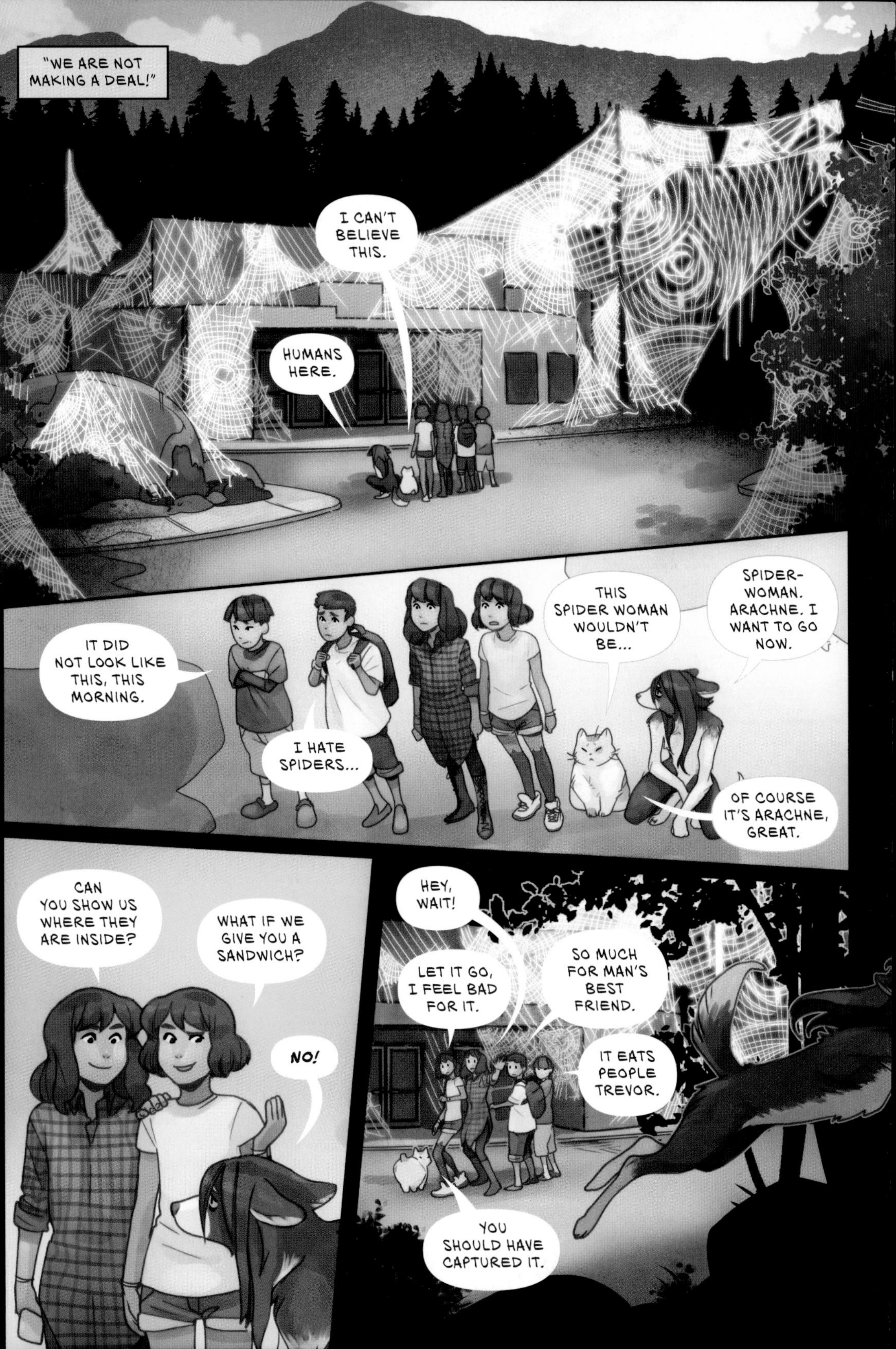
"WE ARE NOT MAKING A DEAL!"
I CAN'T BELIEVE THIS.
HUMANS HERE.
IT DID NOT LOOK LIKE THIS, THIS MORNING.
I HATE SPIDERS...
THIS SPIDER WOMAN WOULDN'T BE...
SPIDER-WOMAN. ARACHNE. I WANT TO GO NOW.
OF COURSE IT'S ARACHNE, GREAT.
CAN YOU SHOW US WHERE THEY ARE INSIDE?
WHAT IF WE GIVE YOU A SANDWICH?
NO!
HEY, WAIT!
LET IT GO, I FEEL BAD FOR IT.
SO MUCH FOR MAN'S BEST FRIEND.
IT EATS PEOPLE TREVOR.
YOU SHOULD HAVE CAPTURED IT.

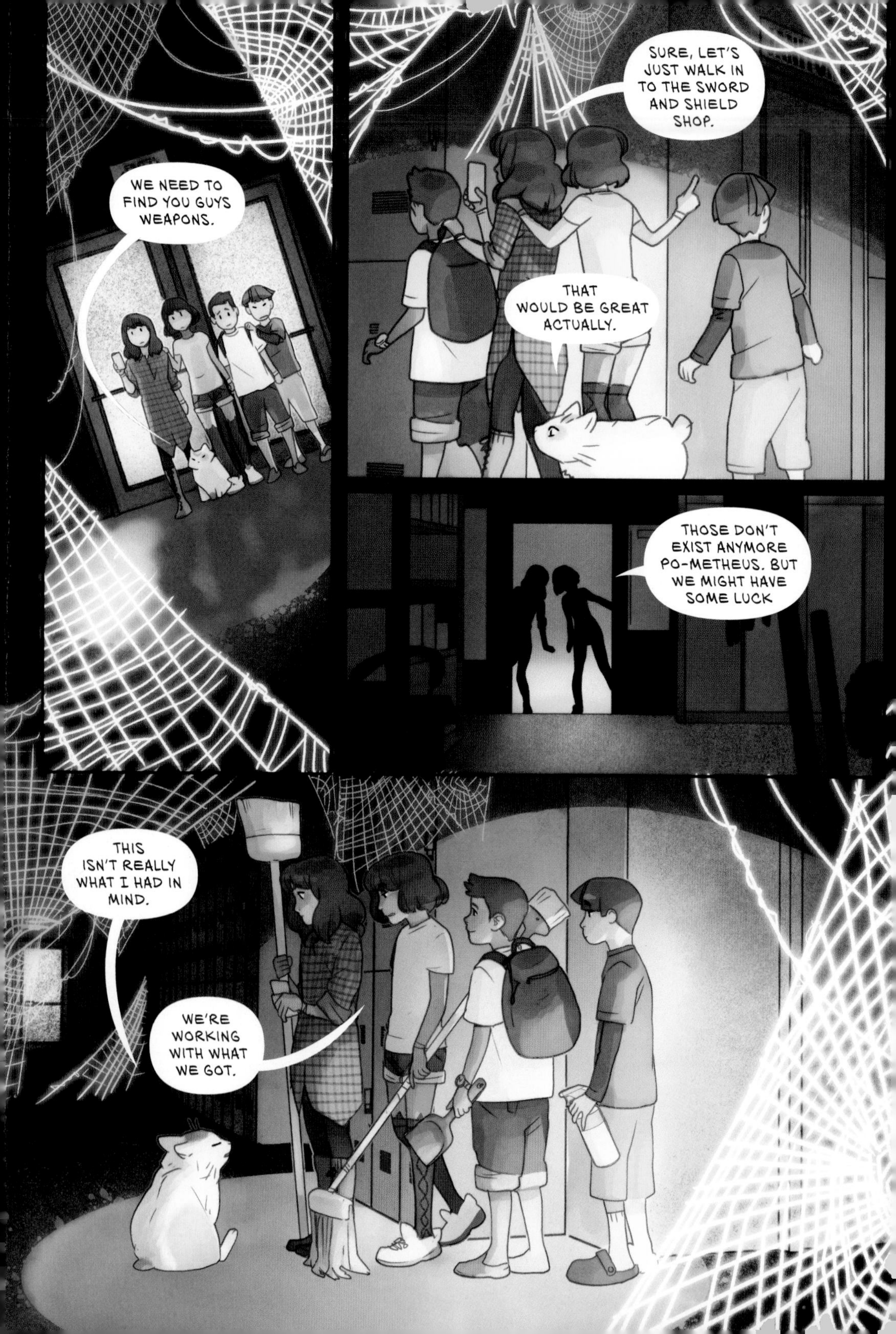
WE NEED TO FIND YOU GUYS WEAPONS.
SURE, LET'S JUST WALK IN TO THE SWORD AND SHIELD SHOP.
THAT WOULD BE GREAT ACTUALLY.
THOSE DON'T EXIST ANYMORE PO-METHEUS. BUT WE MIGHT HAVE SOME LUCK
THIS ISN'T REALLY WHAT I HAD IN MIND.
WE'RE WORKING WITH WHAT WE GOT.

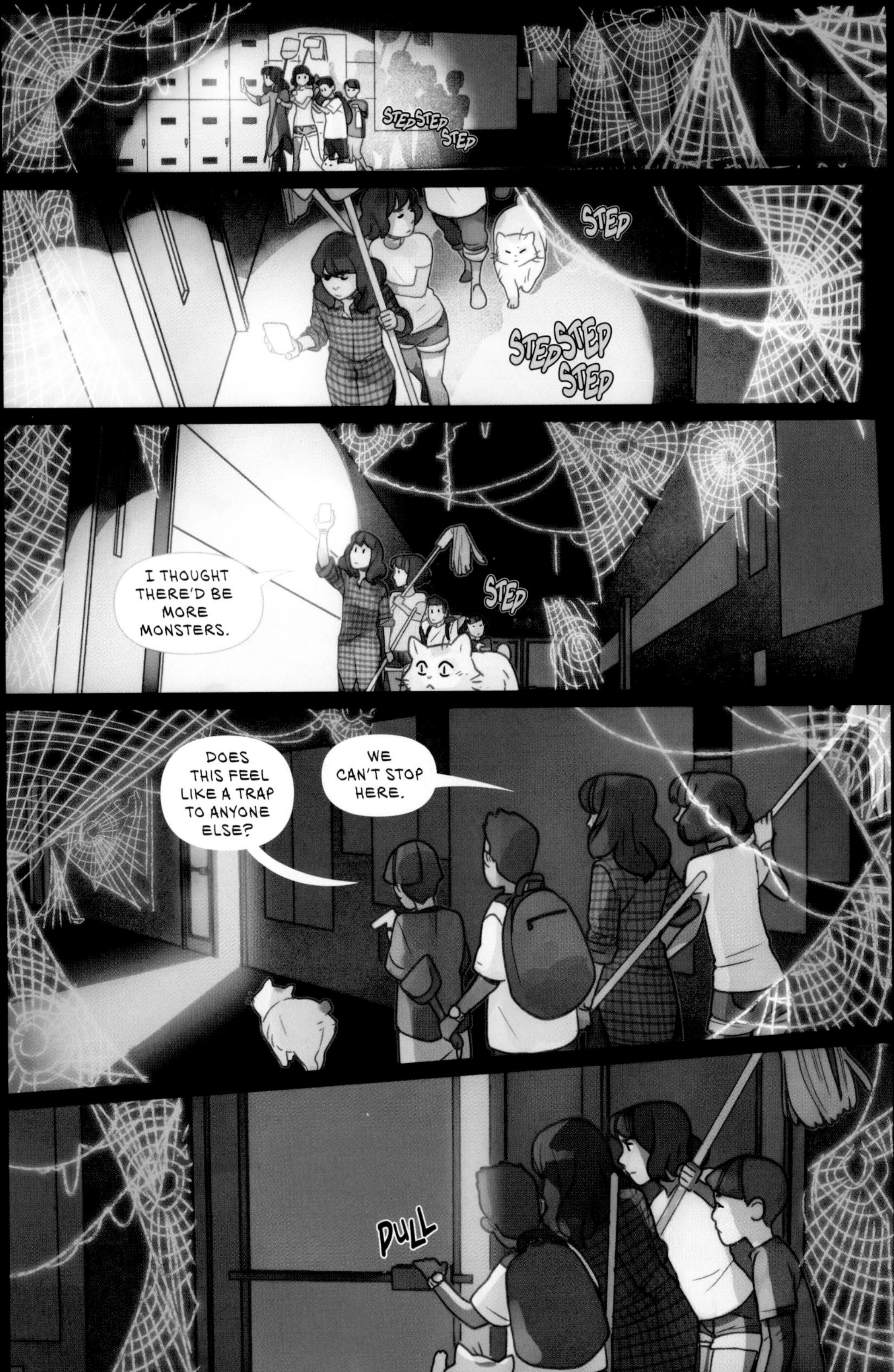
STEP STEP STEP
STEP
STEP STEP STEP
I THOUGHT THERE'D BE MORE MONSTERS.
STEP
DOES THIS FEEL LIKE A TRAP TO ANYONE ELSE?
WE CAN'T STOP HERE.
PULL

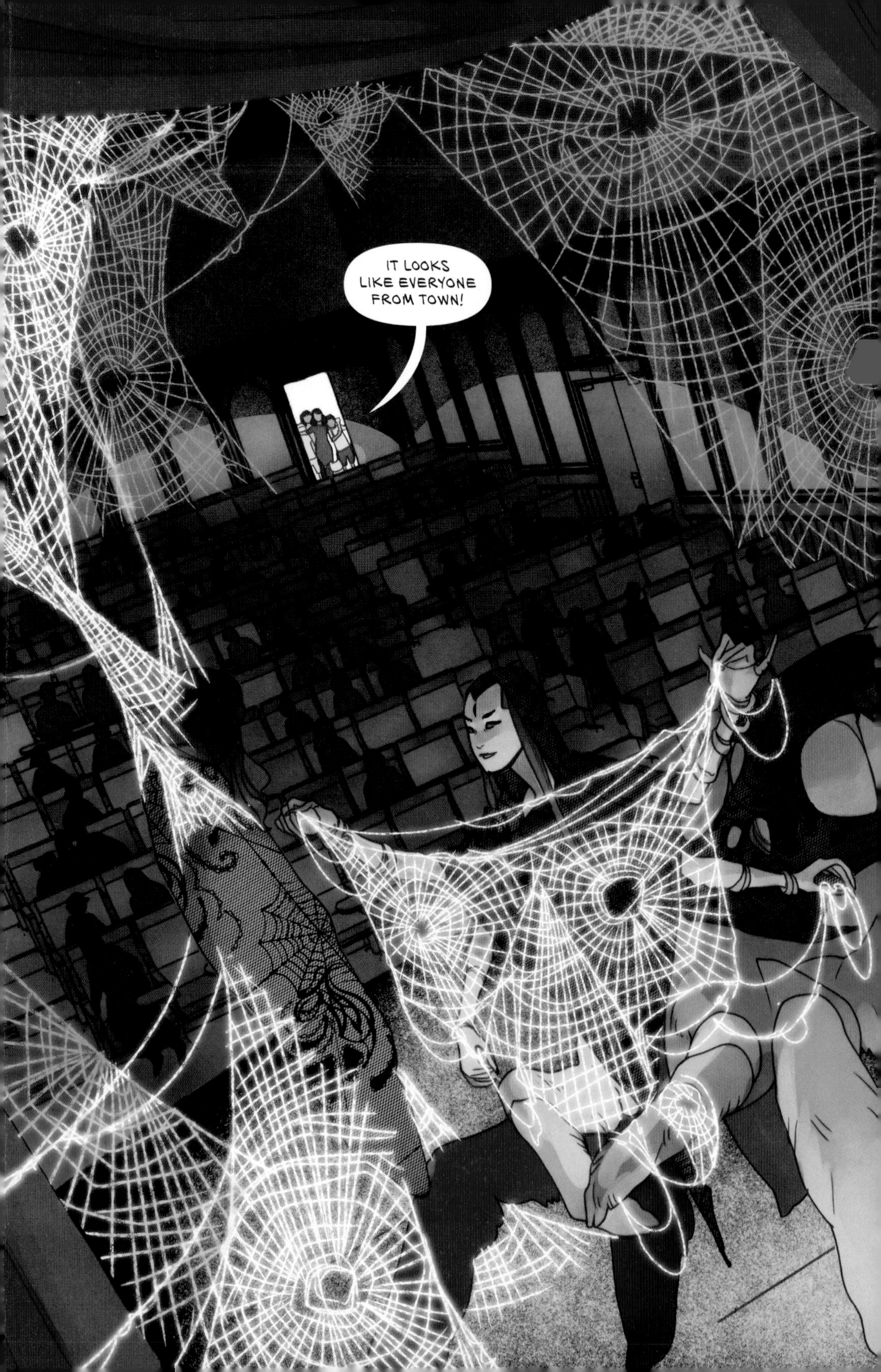
IT LOOKS LIKE EVERYONE FROM TOWN!

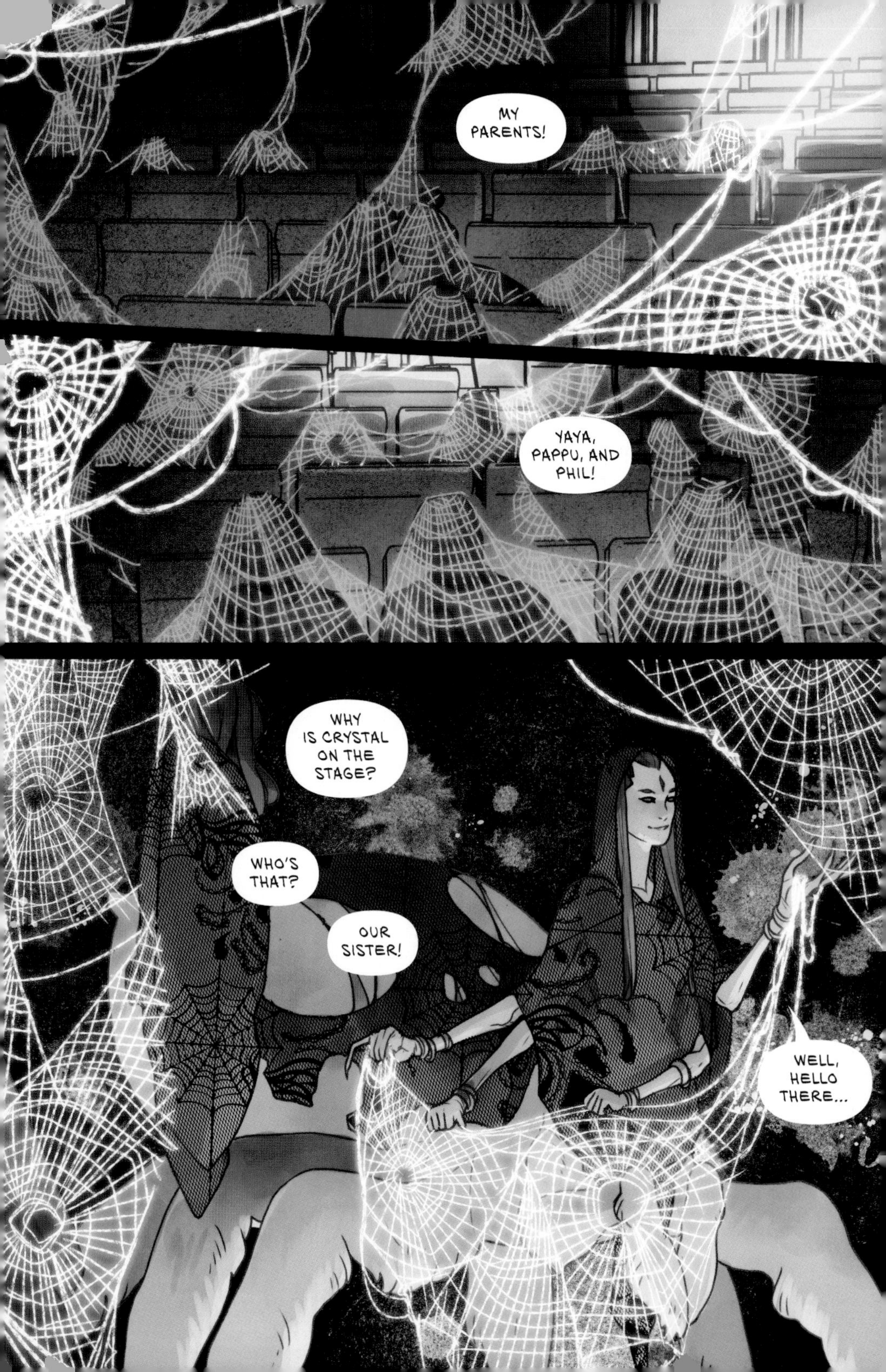
MY PARENTS!
YAYA, PAPPU, AND PHIL!
WHY IS CRYSTAL ON THE STAGE?
WHO'S THAT?
OUR SISTER!
WELL, HELLO THERE...

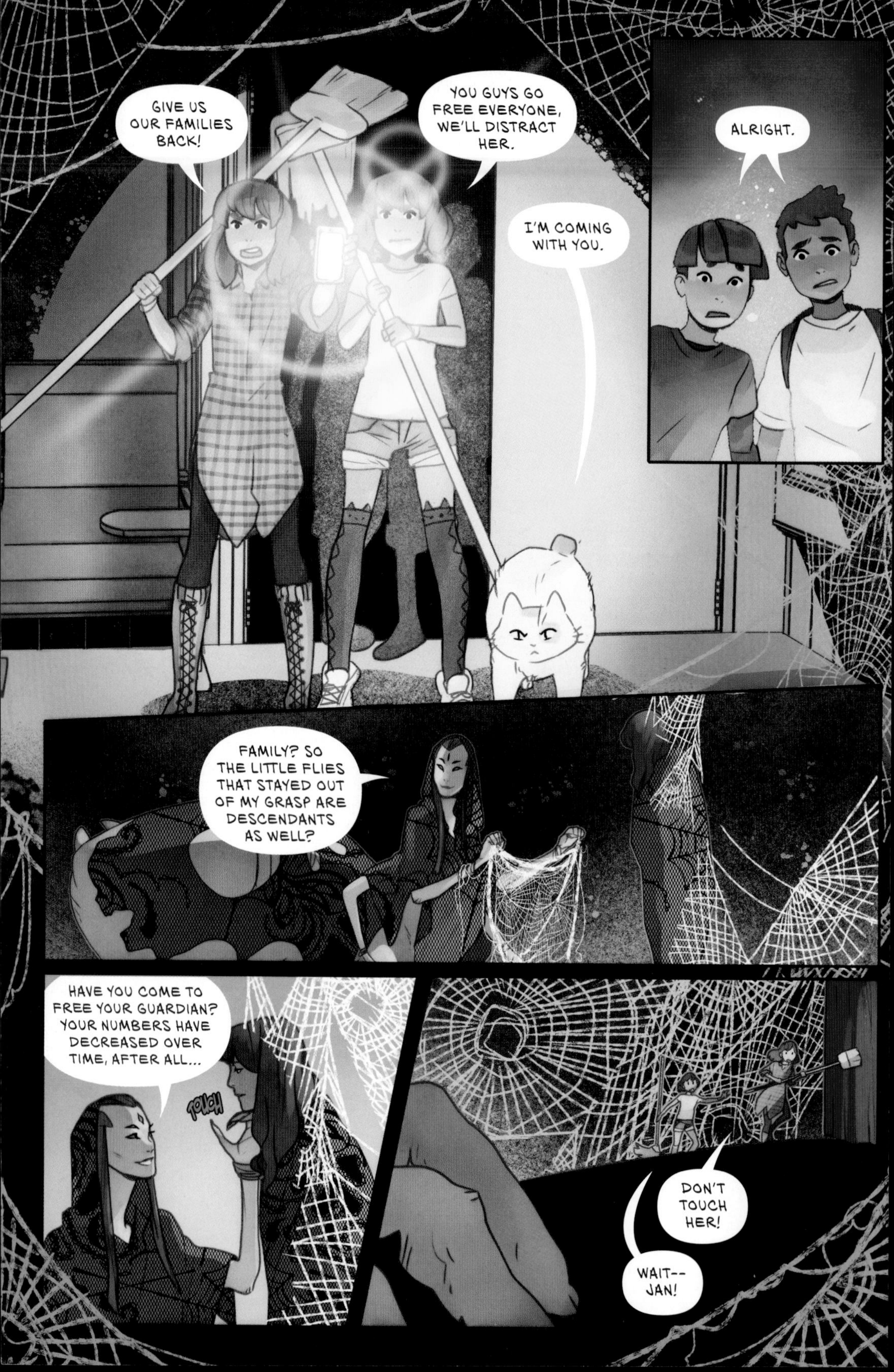
GIVE US OUR FAMILIES BACK!
YOU GUYS GO FREE EVERYONE, WE'LL DISTRACT HER.
I'M COMING WITH YOU.
ALRIGHT.
FAMILY? SO THE LITTLE FLIES THAT STAYED OUT OF MY GRASP ARE DESCENDANTS AS WELL?
HAVE YOU COME TO FREE YOUR GUARDIAN? YOUR NUMBERS HAVE DECREASED OVER TIME, AFTER ALL...
TOUCH
DON'T TOUCH HER!
WAIT-- JAN!

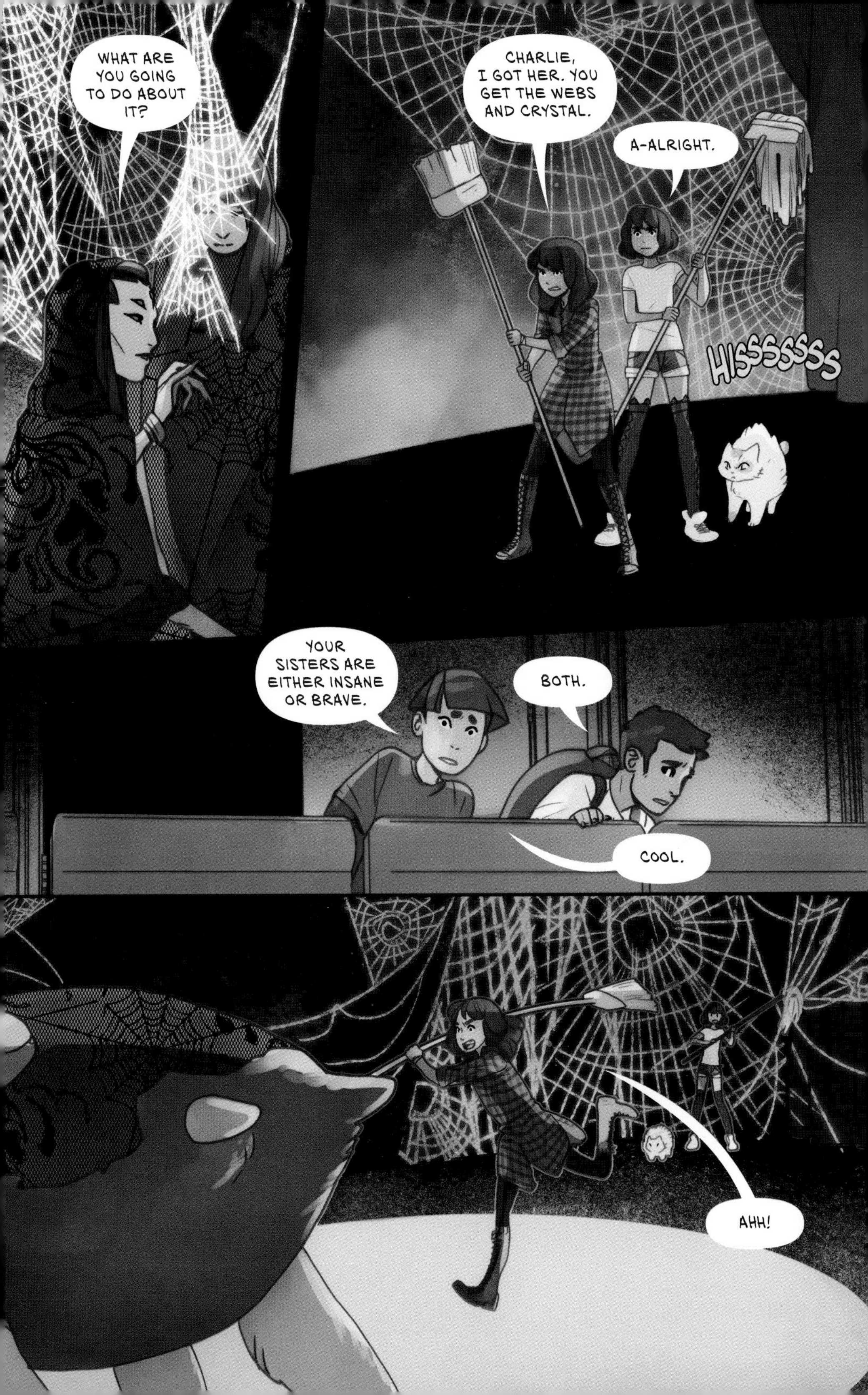
WHAT ARE YOU GOING TO DO ABOUT IT?
CHARLIE, I GOT HER. YOU GET THE WEBS AND CRYSTAL.
A-ALRIGHT.
HISSSSSSS
YOUR SISTERS ARE EITHER INSANE OR BRAVE.
BOTH.
COOL.
AHH!

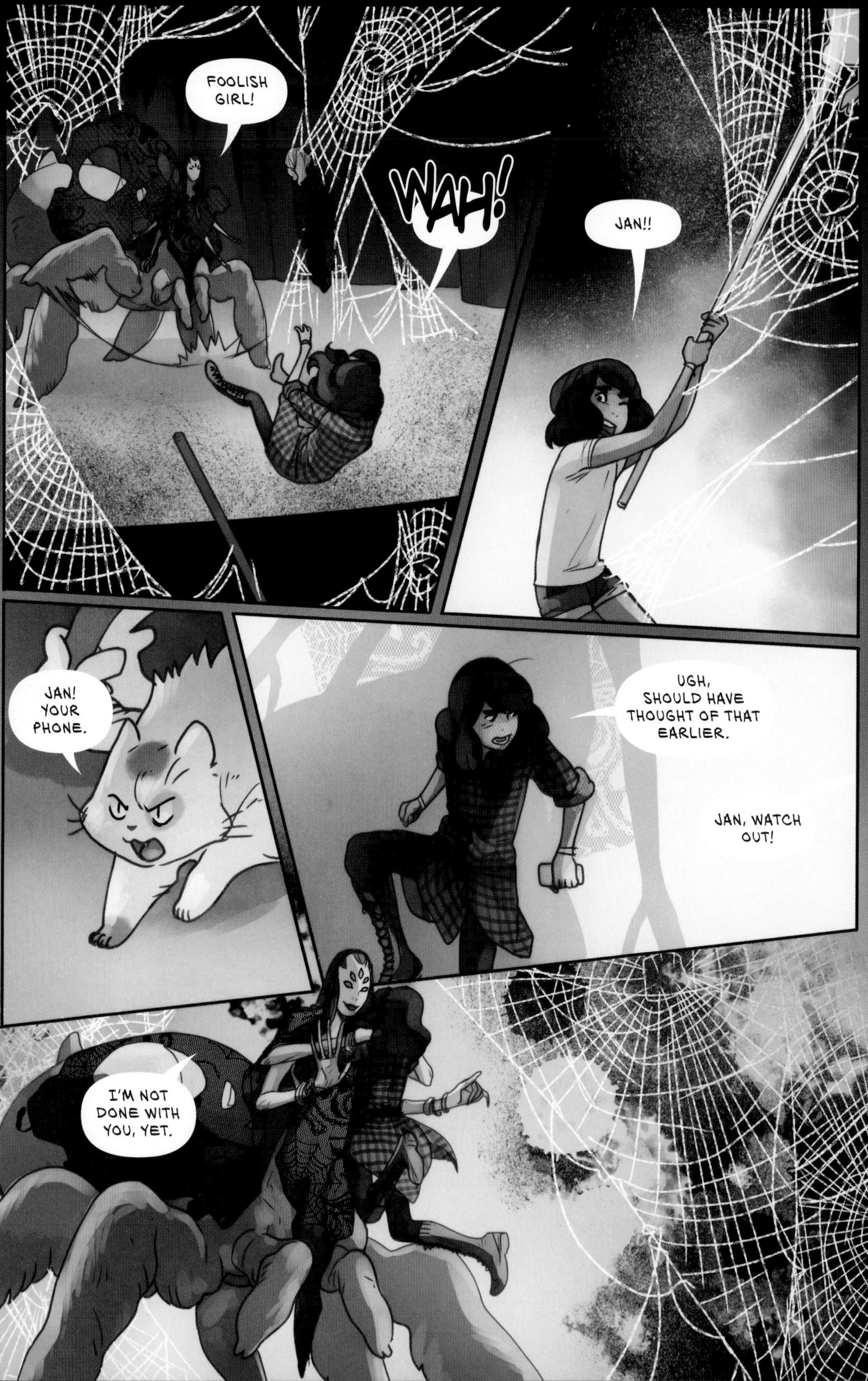
FOOLISH GIRL!
WAH!
JAN!!
JAN! YOUR PHONE.
UGH, SHOULD HAVE THOUGHT OF THAT EARLIER.
JAN, WATCH OUT!
I'M NOT DONE WITH YOU, YET.

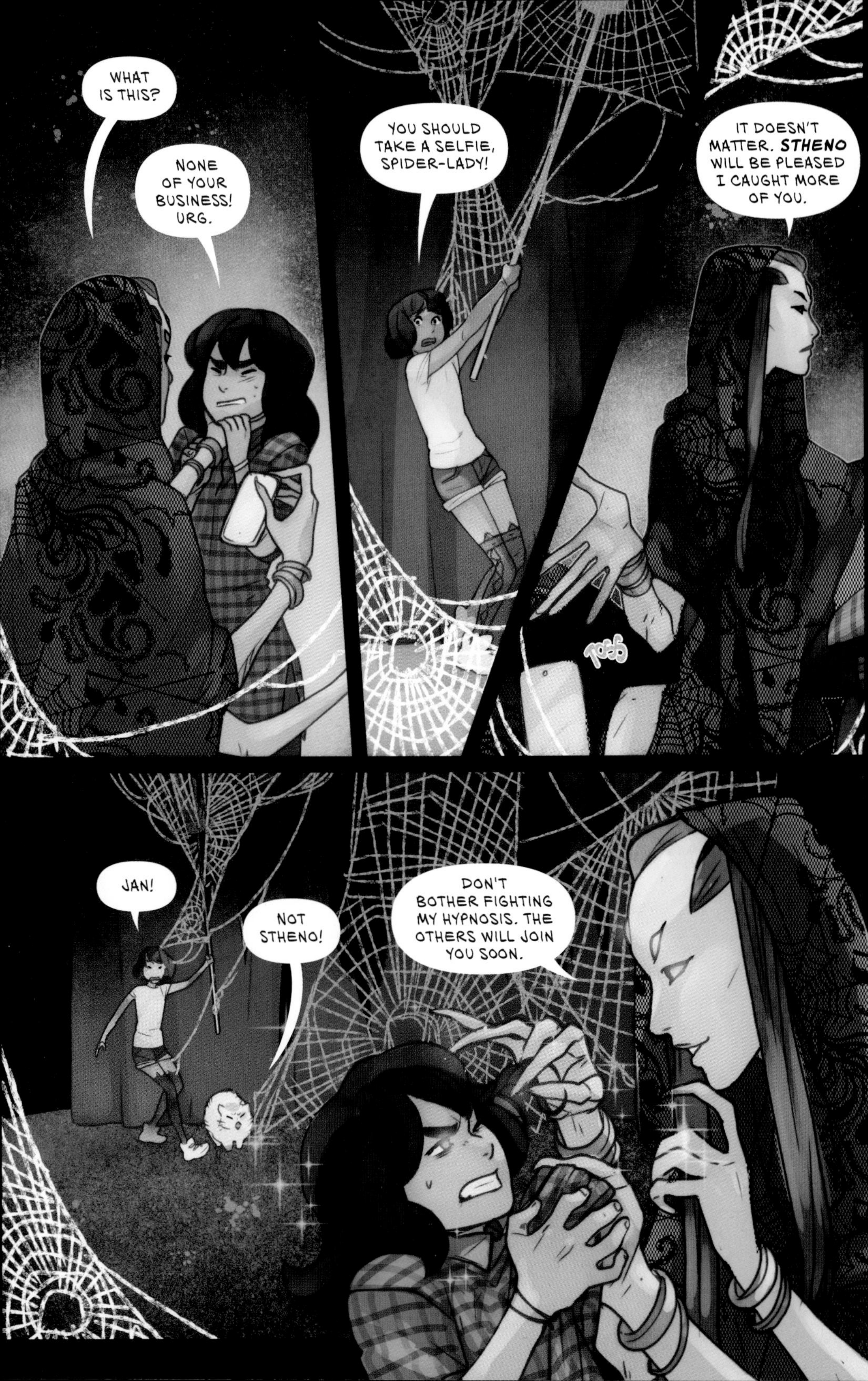

WHAT IS THIS?
NONE OF YOUR BUSINESS! URG.
YOU SHOULD TAKE A SELFIE, SPIDER-LADY!
IT DOESN'T MATTER. STHENO WILL BE PLEASED I CAUGHT MORE OF YOU.
TOSS
JAN!
NOT STHENO!
DON'T BOTHER FIGHTING MY HYPNOSIS. THE OTHERS WILL JOIN YOU SOON.

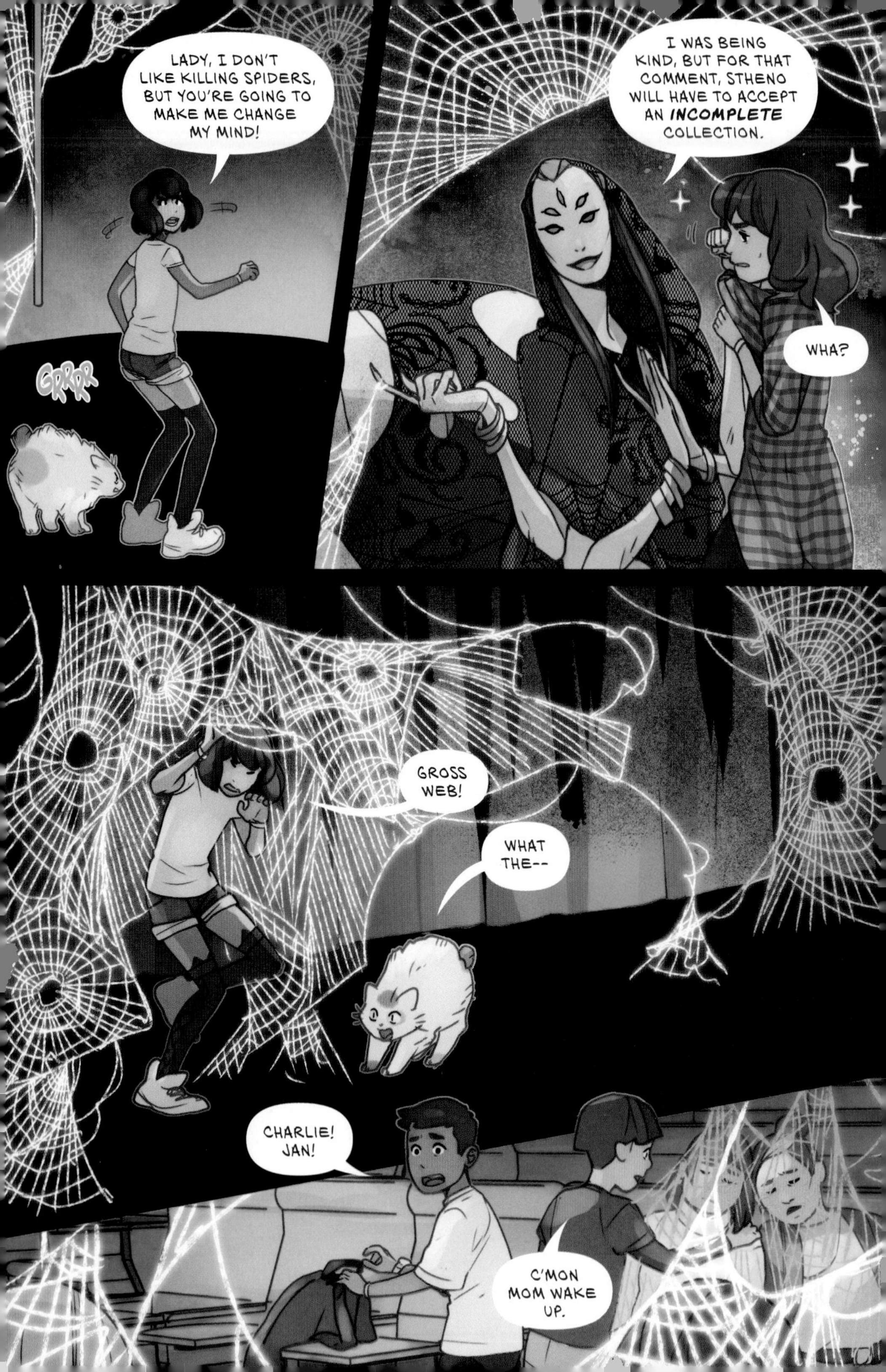

LADY, I DON'T LIKE KILLING SPIDERS, BUT YOU'RE GOING TO MAKE ME CHANGE MY MIND!
GRRRR
I WAS BEING KIND, BUT FOR THAT COMMENT, STHENO WILL HAVE TO ACCEPT AN **INCOMPLETE** COLLECTION.
WHA?
GROSS WEB!
WHAT THE--
CHARLIE! JAN!
C'MON MOM WAKE UP.

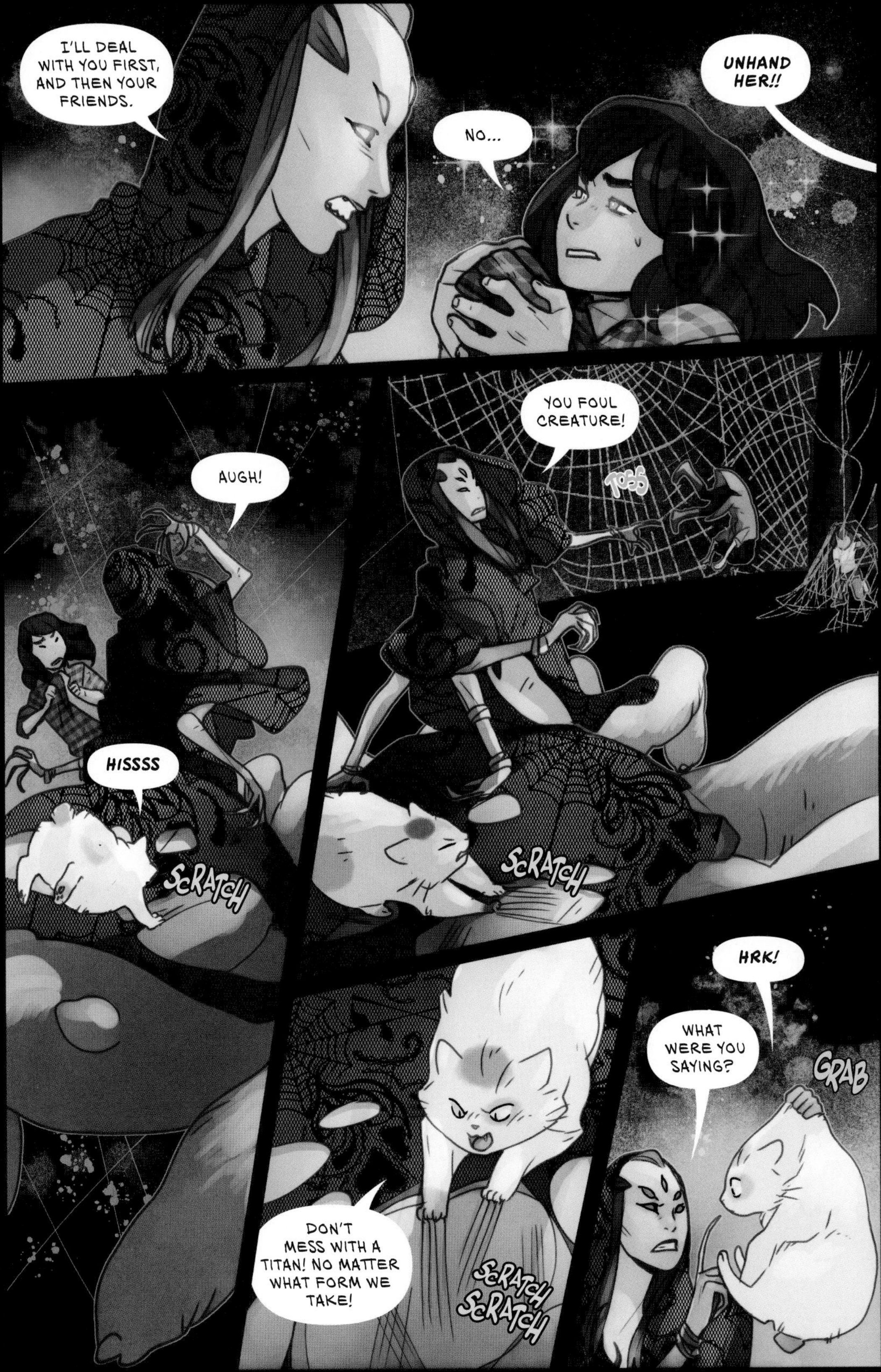
I'LL DEAL WITH YOU FIRST, AND THEN YOUR FRIENDS.
NO...
UNHAND HER!!
AUGH!
HISSSS
SCRATCH
YOU FOUL CREATURE!
TOSS
SCRATCH
DON'T MESS WITH A TITAN! NO MATTER WHAT FORM WE TAKE!
SCRATCH SCRATCH
HRK!
WHAT WERE YOU SAYING?
GRAB

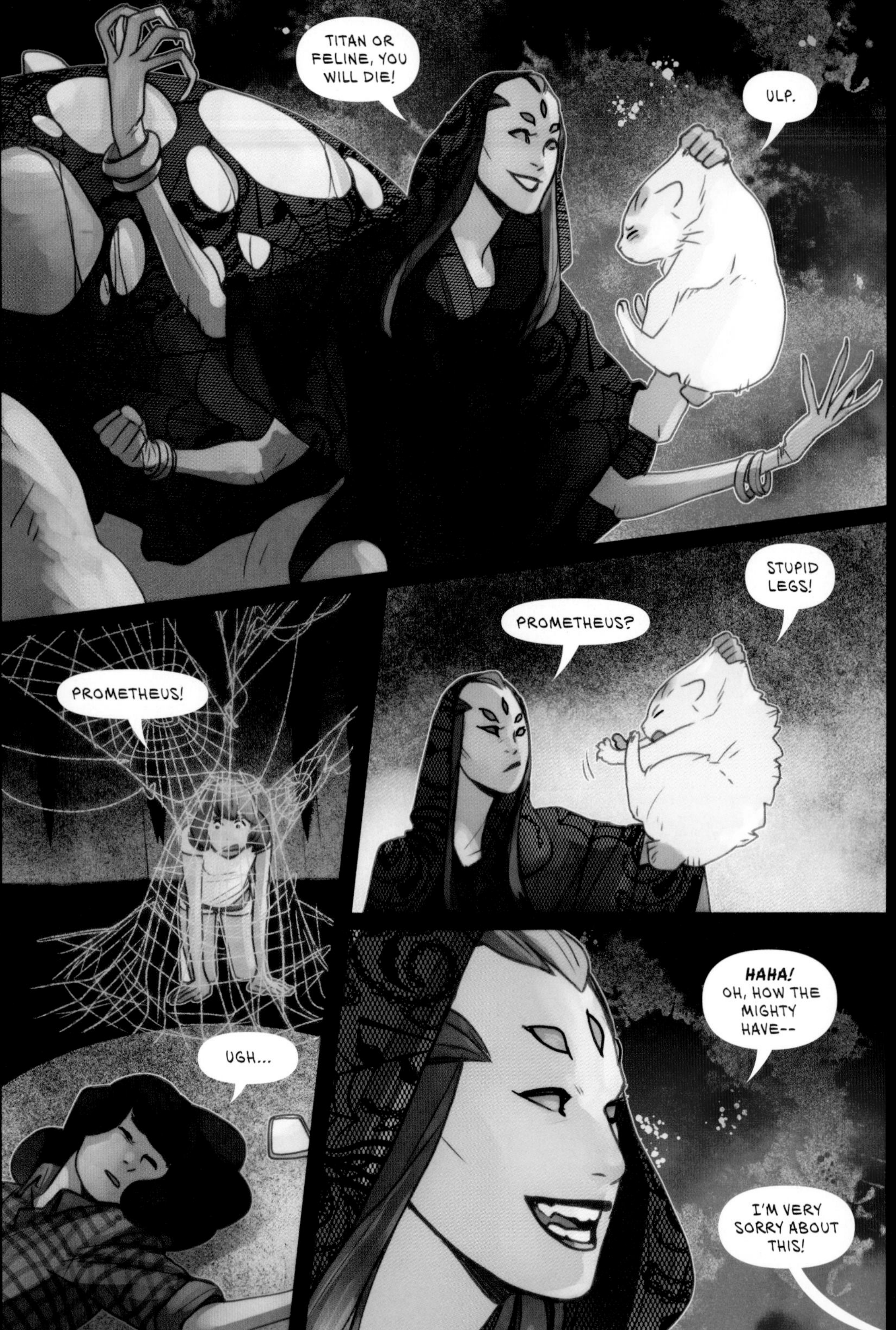
TITAN OR FELINE, YOU WILL DIE!
ULP.
STUPID LEGS!
PROMETHEUS?
PROMETHEUS!
HAHA! OH, HOW THE MIGHTY HAVE--
UGH...
I'M VERY SORRY ABOUT THIS!

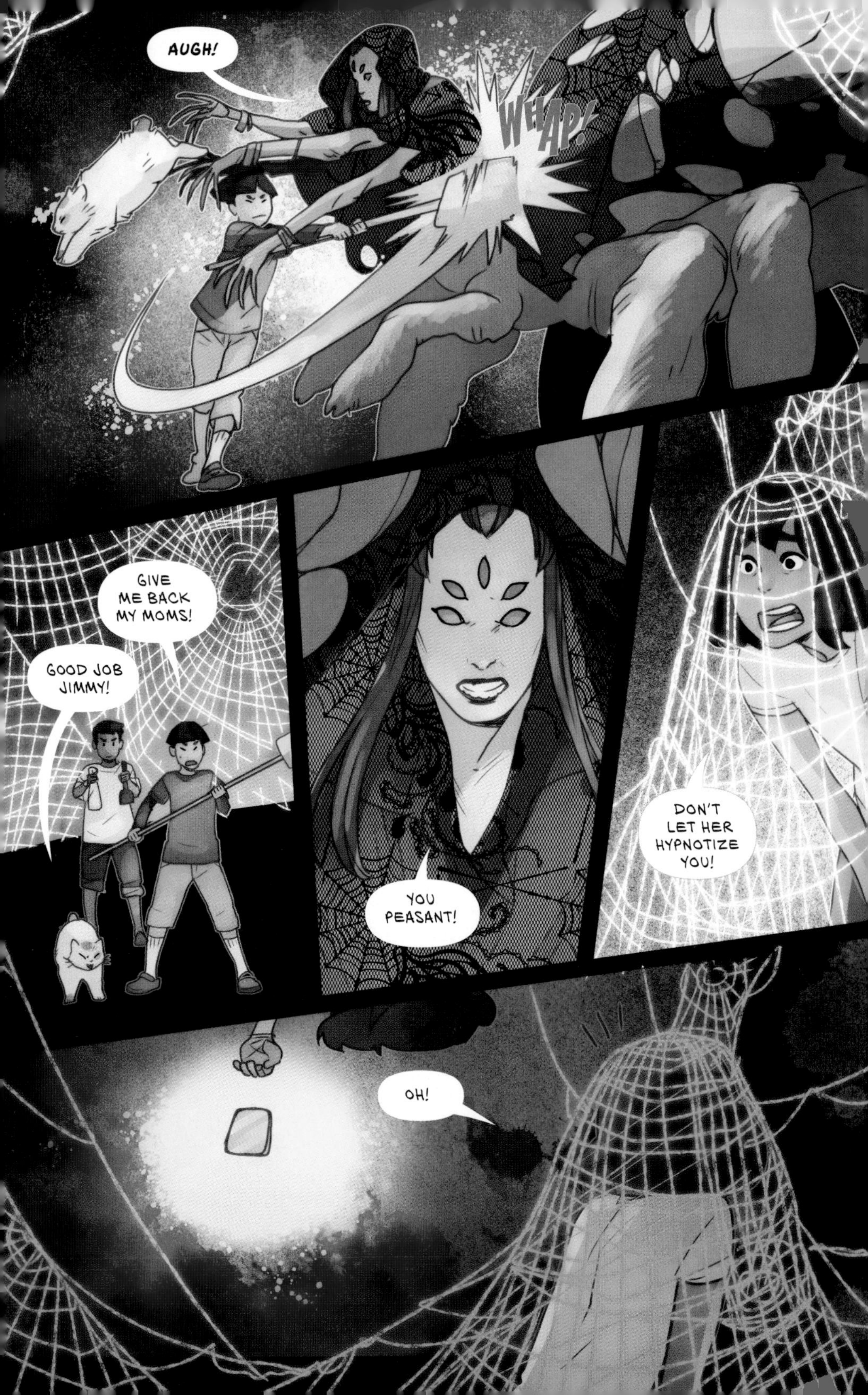
AUGH!
WHAP!
GIVE ME BACK MY MOMS!
GOOD JOB JIMMY!
YOU PEASANT!
DON'T LET HER HYPNOTIZE YOU!
OH!

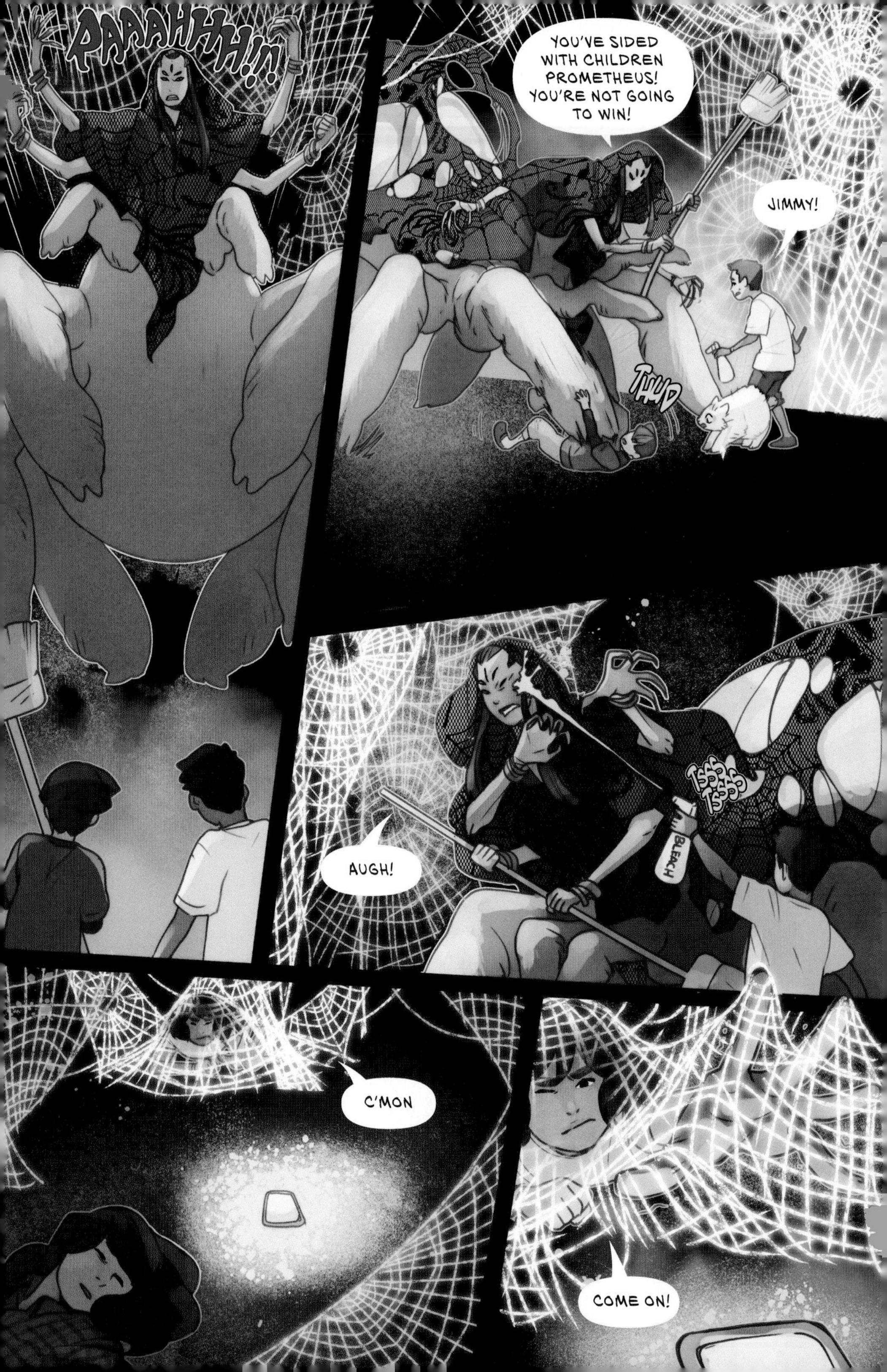
RAAAHHH!!!
YOU'VE SIDED WITH CHILDREN PROMETHEUS! YOU'RE NOT GOING TO WIN!
JIMMY!
THUD
TSSS TSSS
BLEACH
AUGH!
C'MON
COME ON!

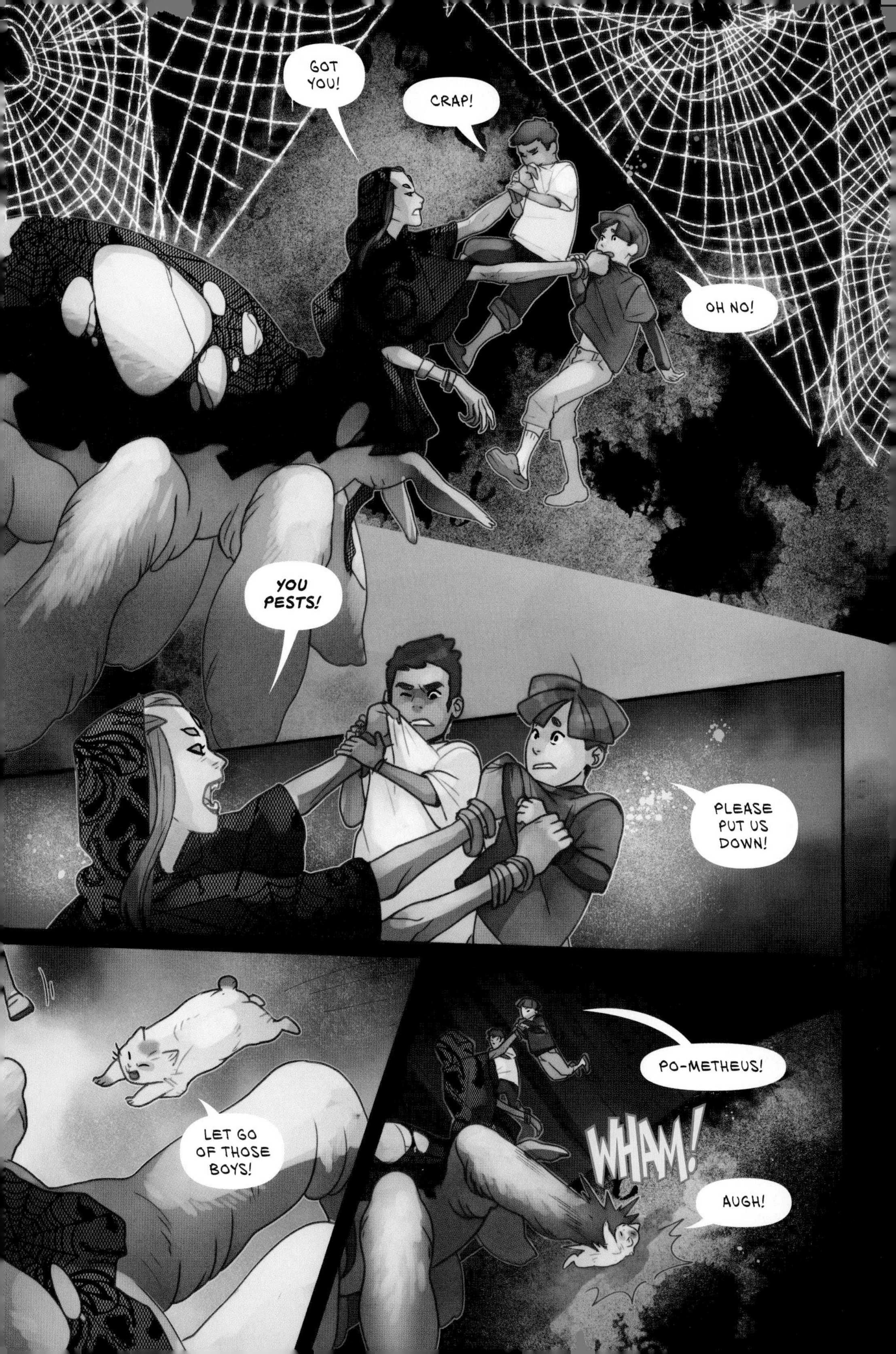
GOT YOU!
CRAP!
OH NO!
YOU PESTS!
PLEASE PUT US DOWN!
LET GO OF THOSE BOYS!
PO-METHEUS!
WHAM!
AUGH!

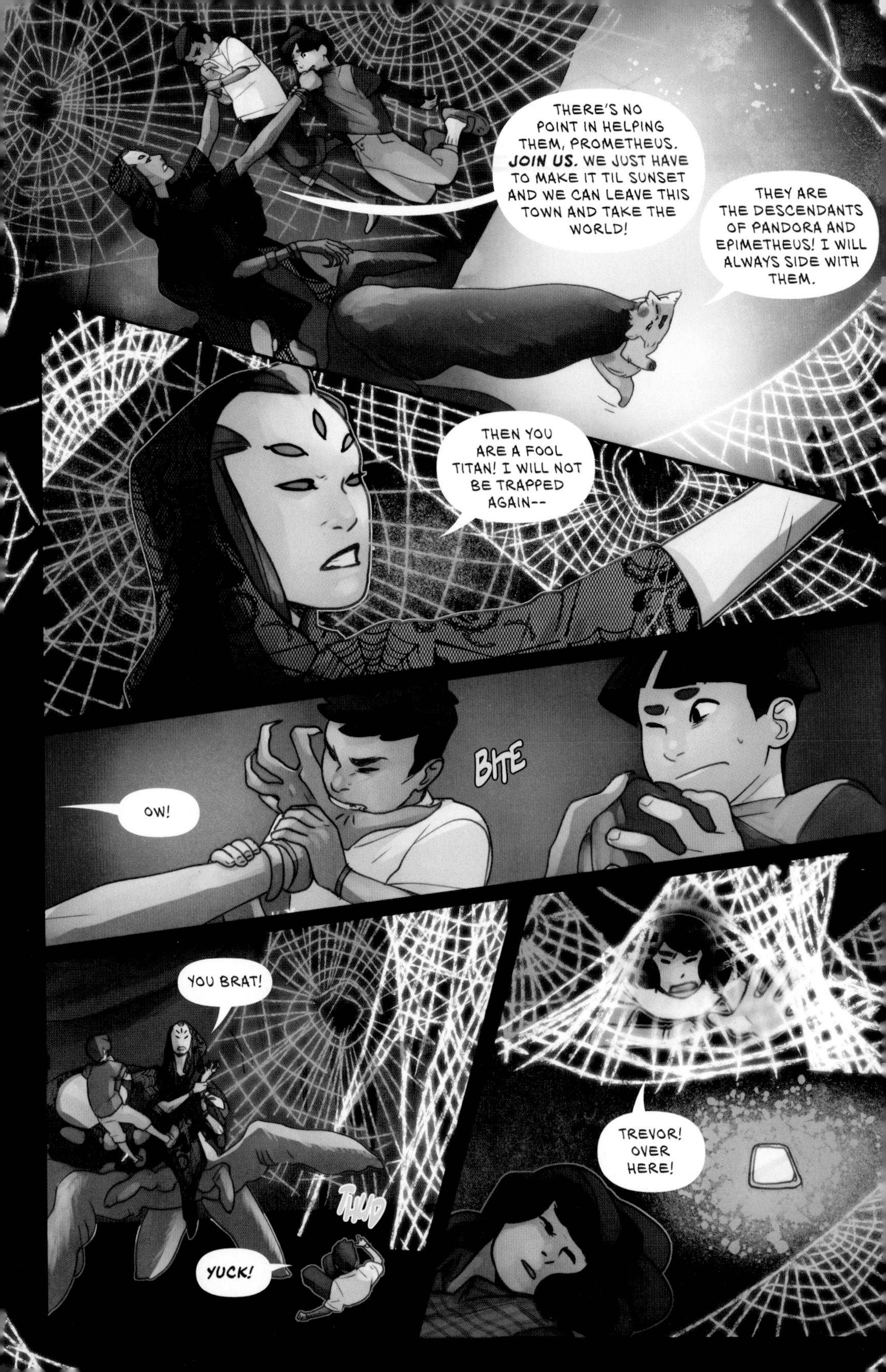
THERE'S NO POINT IN HELPING THEM, PROMETHEUS. **JOIN US.** WE JUST HAVE TO MAKE IT TIL SUNSET AND WE CAN LEAVE THIS TOWN AND TAKE THE WORLD!
THEY ARE THE DESCENDANTS OF PANDORA AND EPIMETHEUS! I WILL ALWAYS SIDE WITH THEM.
THEN YOU ARE A FOOL TITAN! I WILL NOT BE TRAPPED AGAIN--
BITE
OW!
YOU BRAT!
THUD
YUCK!
TREVOR! OVER HERE!

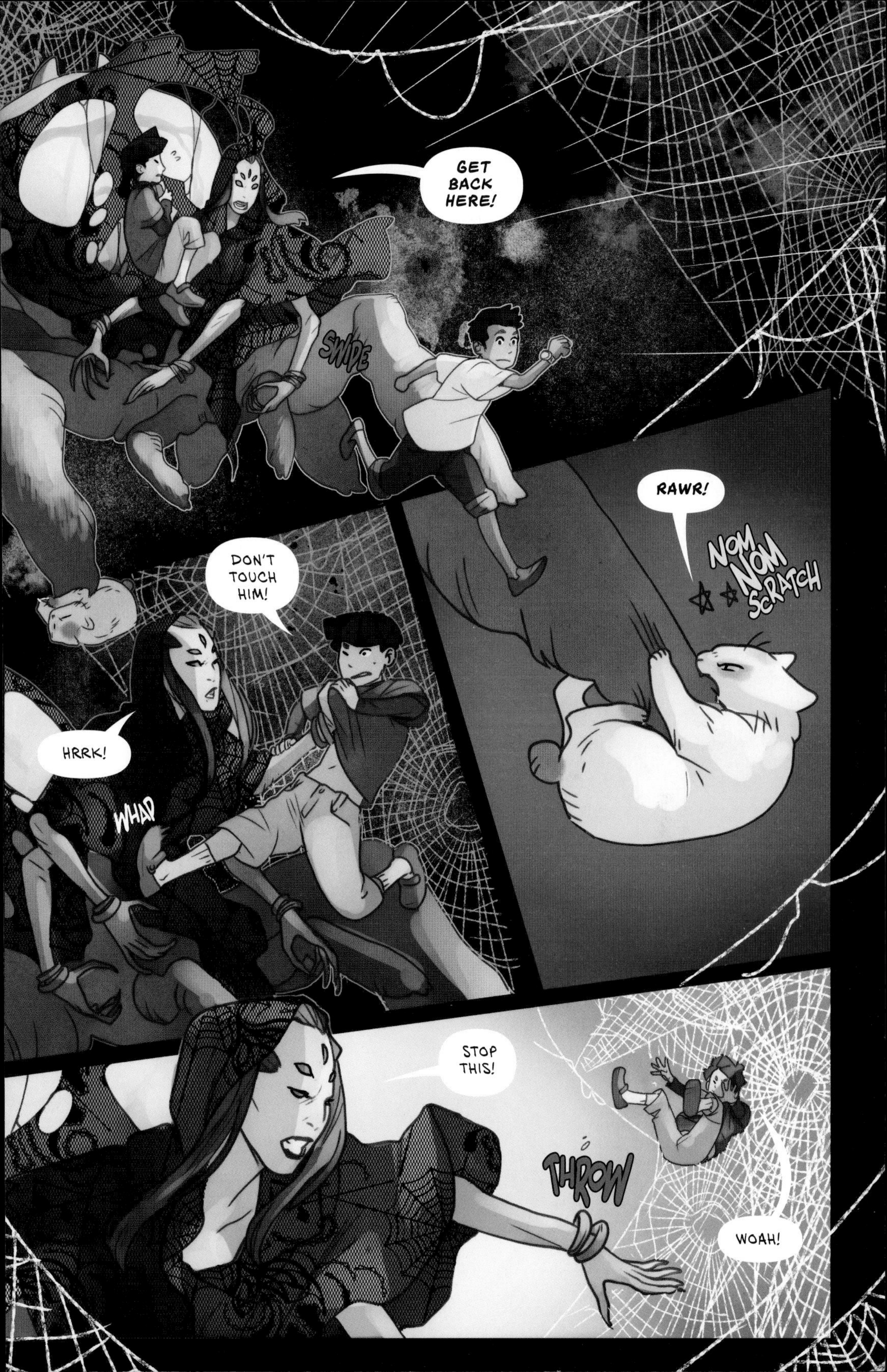
GET BACK HERE!
SWIPE
RAWR!
NOM NOM SCRATCH
DON'T TOUCH HIM!
HRRK!
WHAP
STOP THIS!
THROW
WOAH!

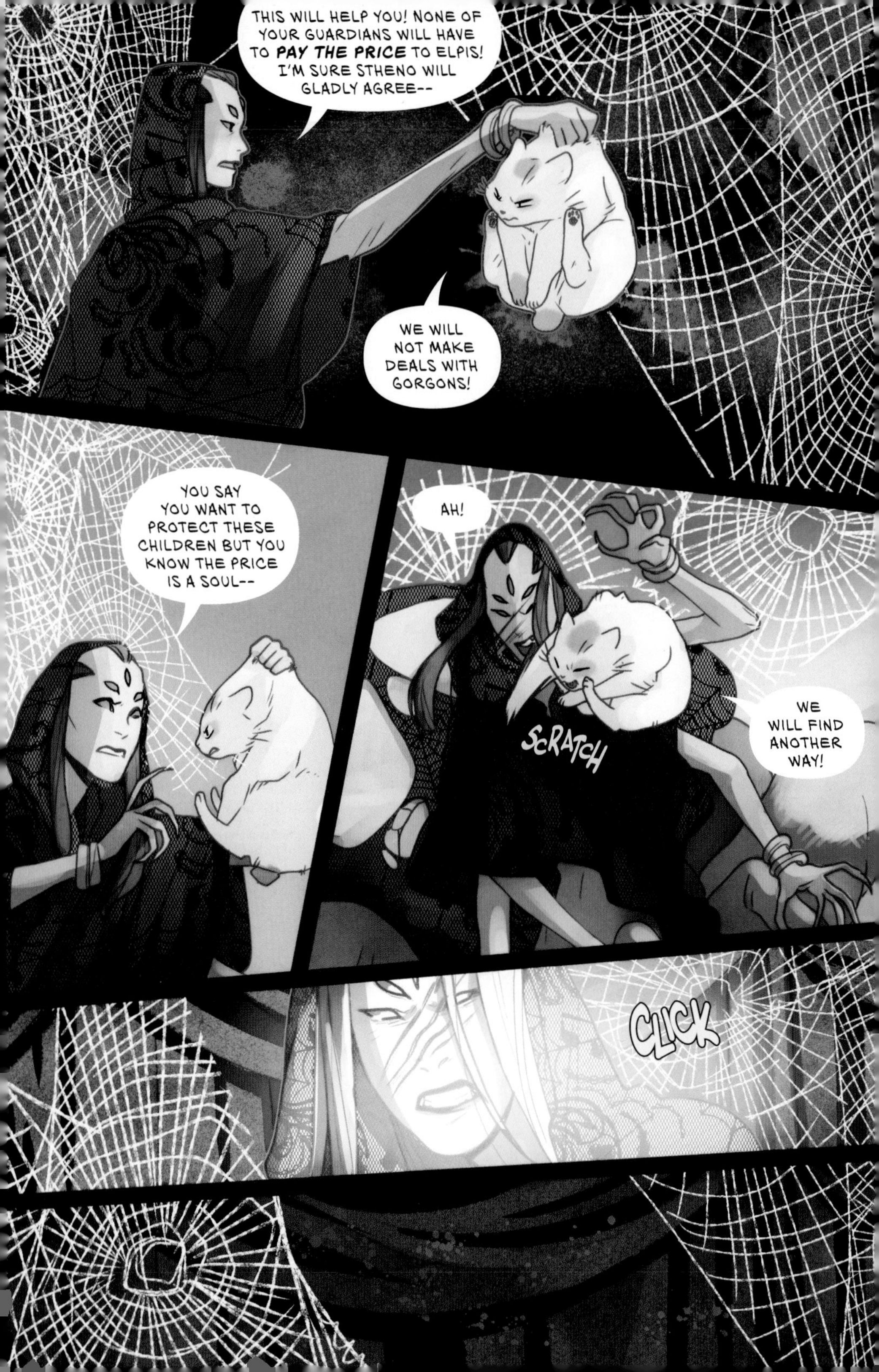
THIS WILL HELP YOU! NONE OF YOUR GUARDIANS WILL HAVE TO **PAY THE PRICE** TO ELPIS! I'M SURE STHENO WILL GLADLY AGREE--
WE WILL NOT MAKE DEALS WITH GORGONS!
YOU SAY YOU WANT TO PROTECT THESE CHILDREN BUT YOU KNOW THE PRICE IS A SOUL--
AH!
SCRATCH
WE WILL FIND ANOTHER WAY!
CLICK

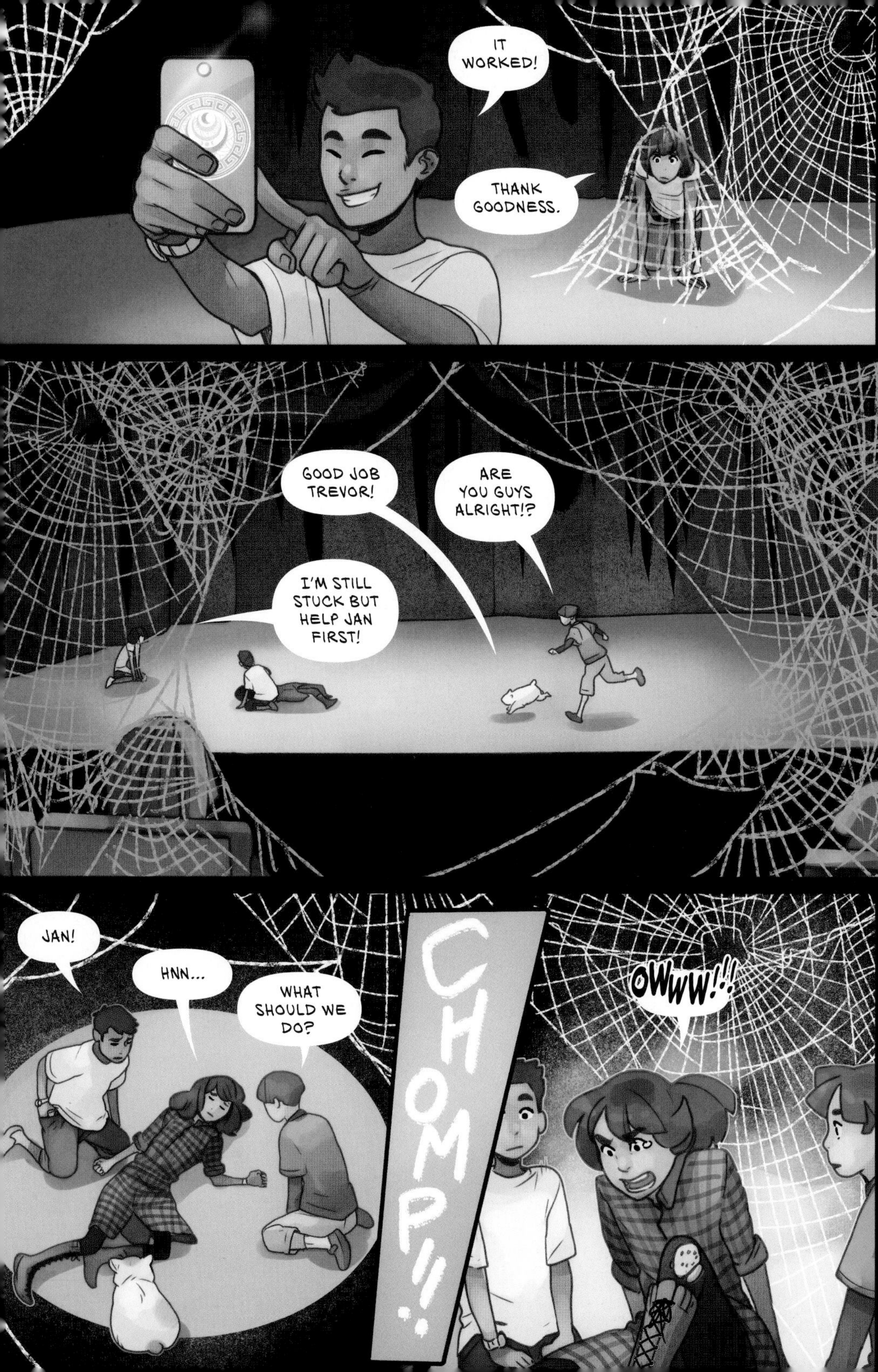
IT WORKED!
THANK GOODNESS.
GOOD JOB TREVOR!
ARE YOU GUYS ALRIGHT!?
I'M STILL STUCK BUT HELP JAN FIRST!
JAN!
HNN...
WHAT SHOULD WE DO?
CHOMP!!!
OWWW!!!

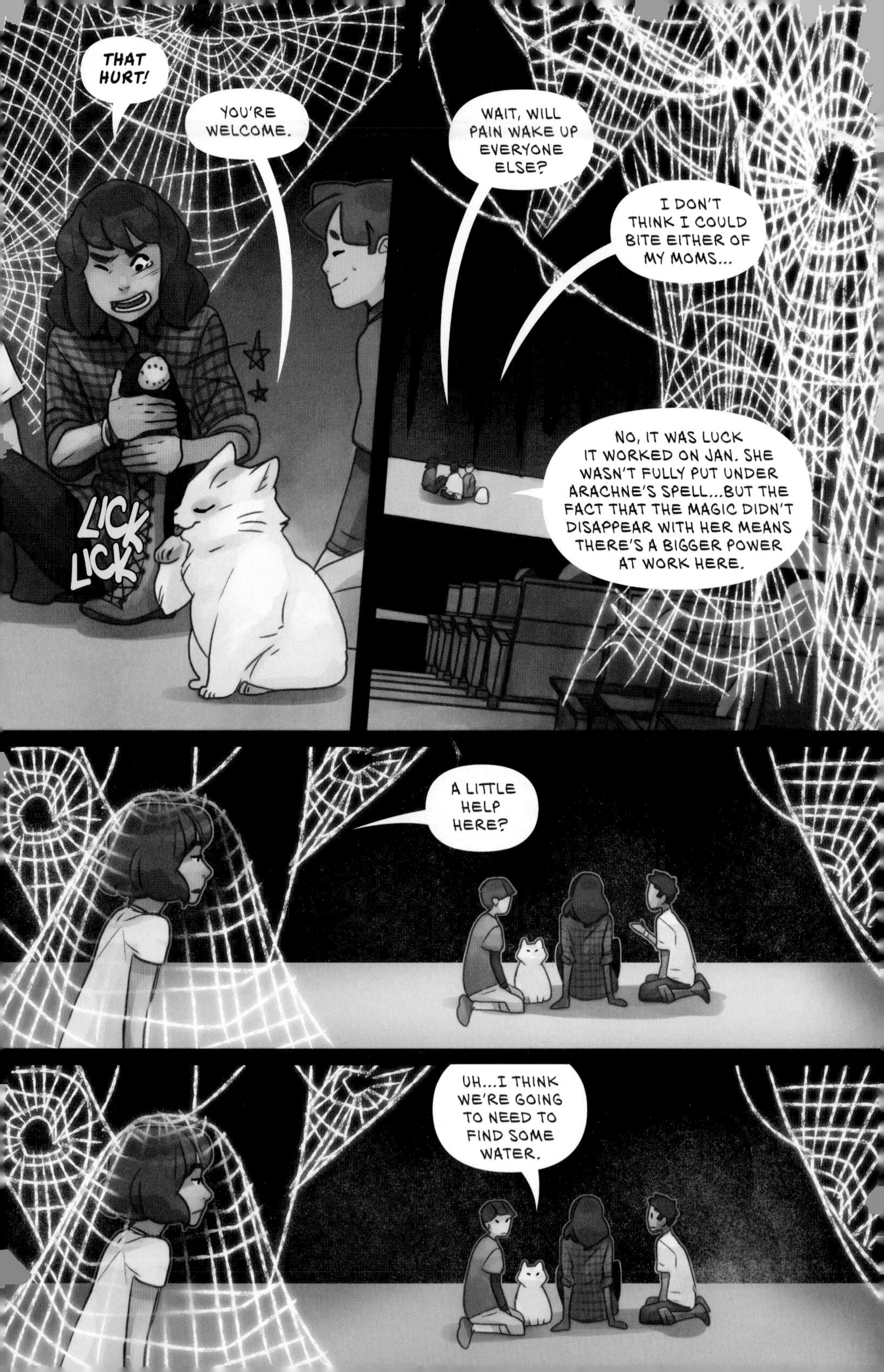
THAT HURT!
YOU'RE WELCOME.
LICK LICK
WAIT, WILL PAIN WAKE UP EVERYONE ELSE?
I DON'T THINK I COULD BITE EITHER OF MY MOMS...
NO, IT WAS LUCK IT WORKED ON JAN. SHE WASN'T FULLY PUT UNDER ARACHNE'S SPELL...BUT THE FACT THAT THE MAGIC DIDN'T DISAPPEAR WITH HER MEANS THERE'S A BIGGER POWER AT WORK HERE.
A LITTLE HELP HERE?
UH...I THINK WE'RE GOING TO NEED TO FIND SOME WATER.

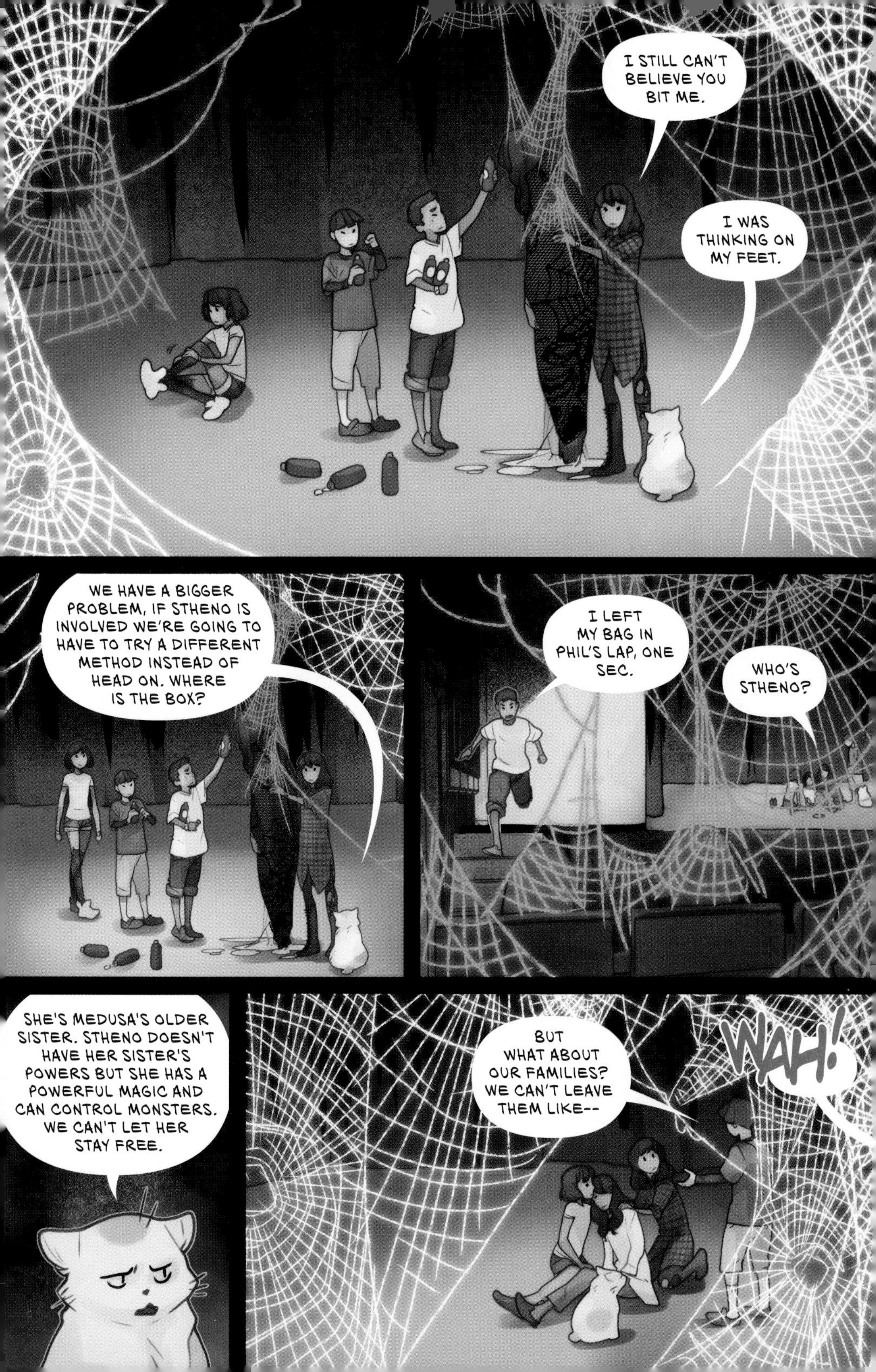
I STILL CAN'T BELIEVE YOU BIT ME.
I WAS THINKING ON MY FEET.
WE HAVE A BIGGER PROBLEM, IF STHENO IS INVOLVED WE'RE GOING TO HAVE TO TRY A DIFFERENT METHOD INSTEAD OF HEAD ON. WHERE IS THE BOX?
I LEFT MY BAG IN PHIL'S LAP, ONE SEC.
WHO'S STHENO?
SHE'S MEDUSA'S OLDER SISTER. STHENO DOESN'T HAVE HER SISTER'S POWERS BUT SHE HAS A POWERFUL MAGIC AND CAN CONTROL MONSTERS. WE CAN'T LET HER STAY FREE.
BUT WHAT ABOUT OUR FAMILIES? WE CAN'T LEAVE THEM LIKE--
WAH!

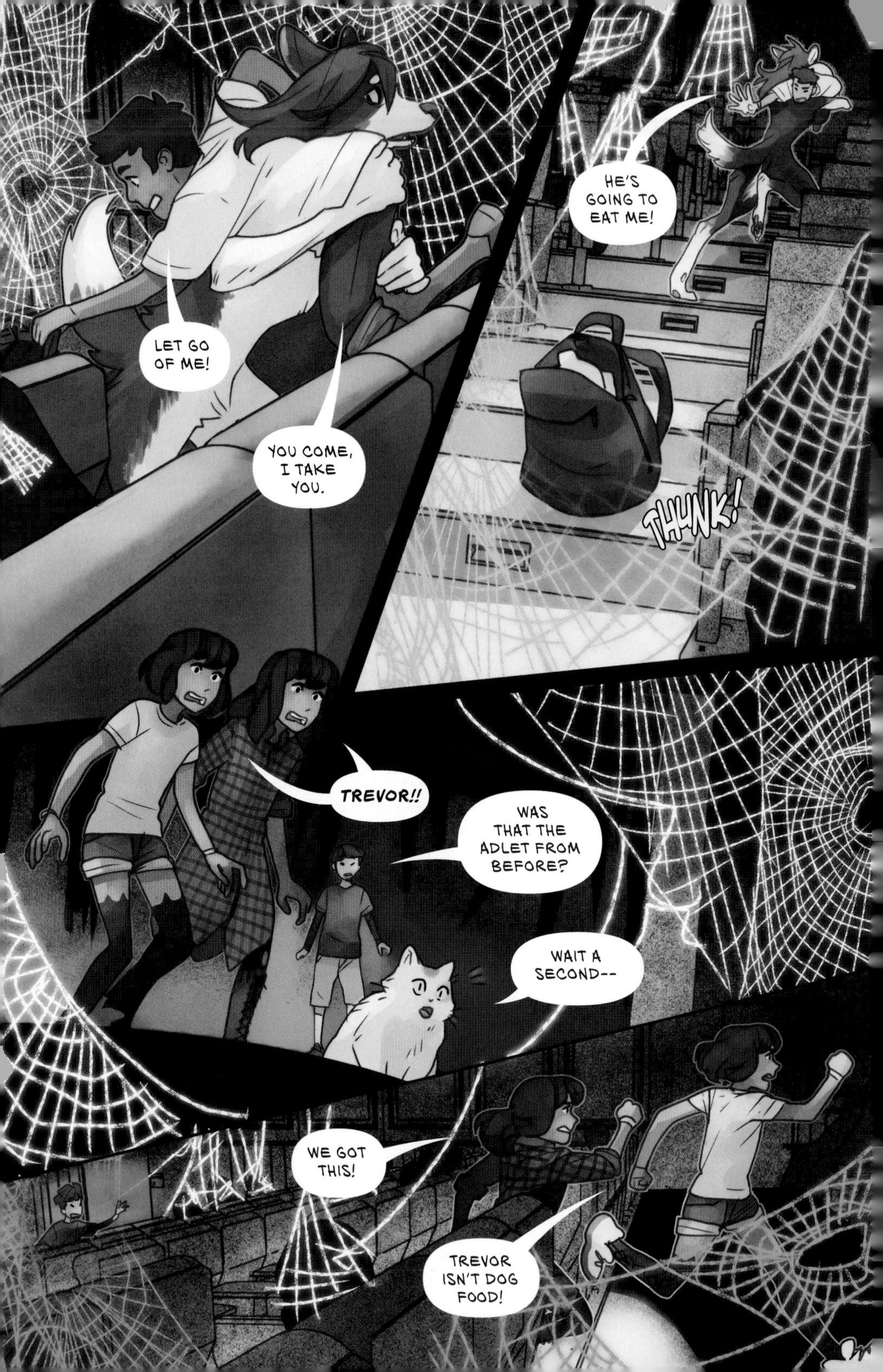
LET GO OF ME!
YOU COME, I TAKE YOU.
HE'S GOING TO EAT ME!
THUNK!
TREVOR!!
WAS THAT THE ADLET FROM BEFORE?
WAIT A SECOND--
WE GOT THIS!
TREVOR ISN'T DOG FOOD!

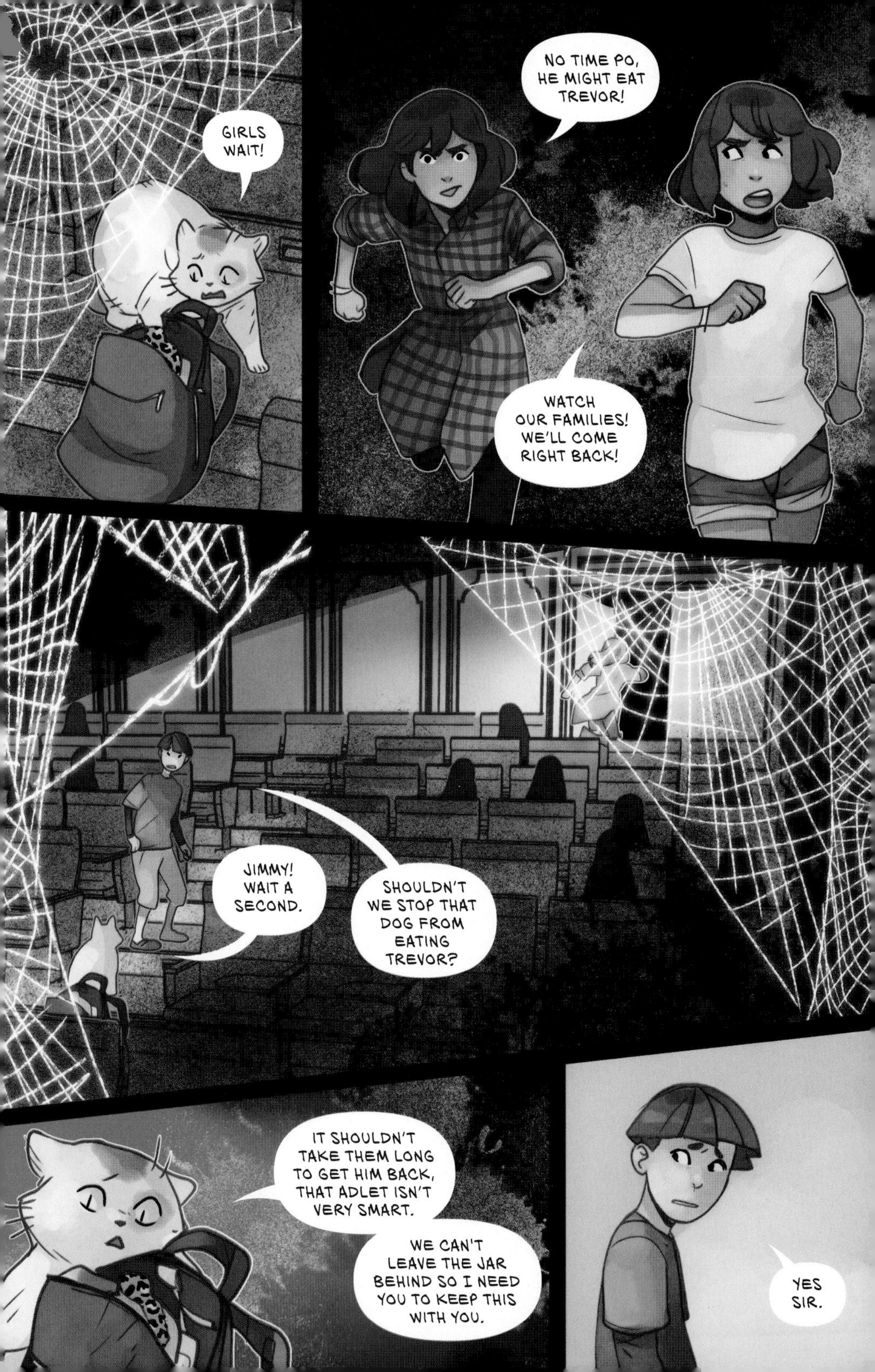
GIRLS WAIT!
NO TIME PO, HE MIGHT EAT TREVOR!
WATCH OUR FAMILIES! WE'LL COME RIGHT BACK!
JIMMY! WAIT A SECOND.
SHOULDN'T WE STOP THAT DOG FROM EATING TREVOR?
IT SHOULDN'T TAKE THEM LONG TO GET HIM BACK, THAT ADLET ISN'T VERY SMART.
WE CAN'T LEAVE THE JAR BEHIND SO I NEED YOU TO KEEP THIS WITH YOU.
YES SIR.

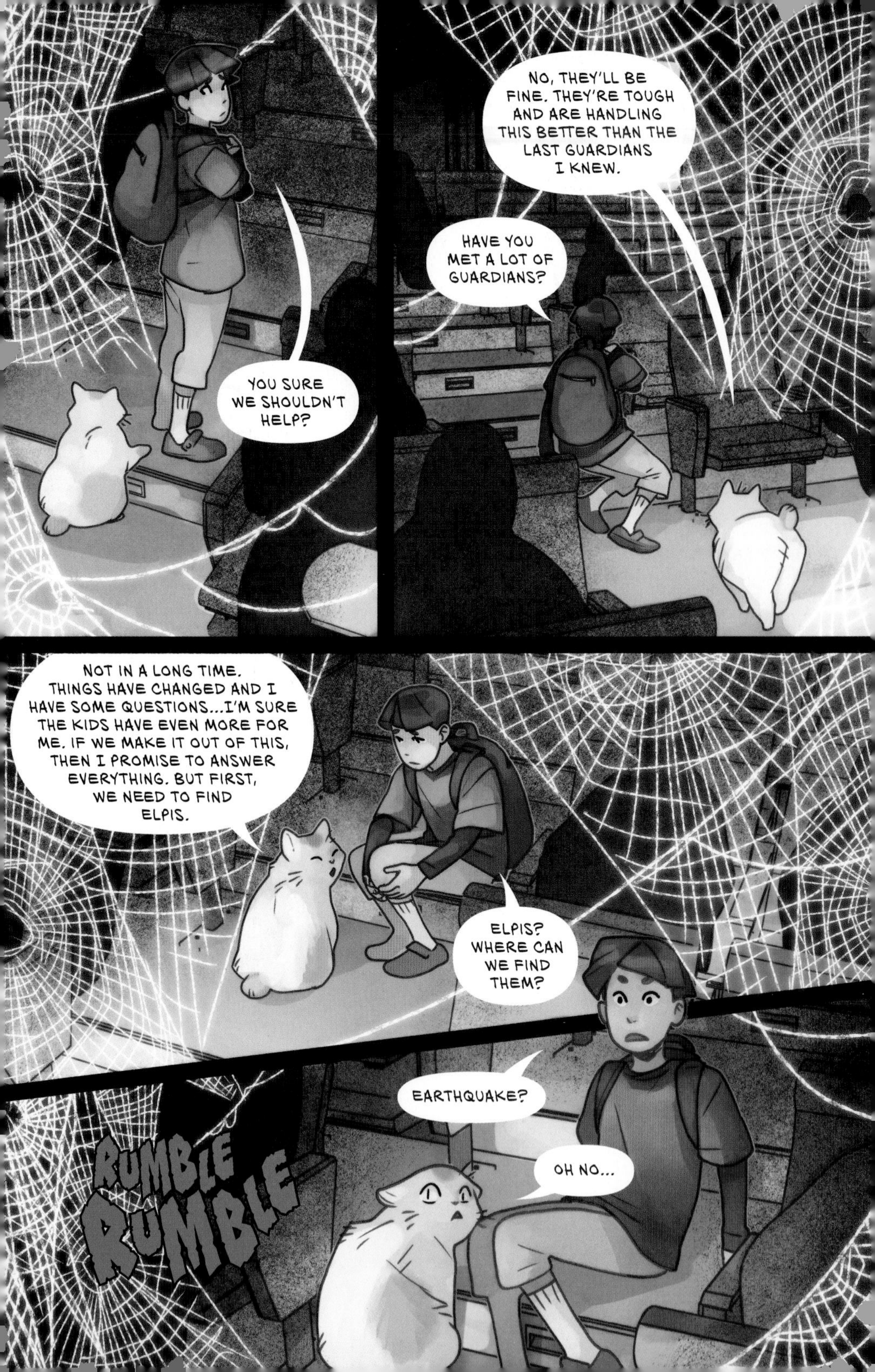
YOU SURE WE SHOULDN'T HELP?
NO, THEY'LL BE FINE. THEY'RE TOUGH AND ARE HANDLING THIS BETTER THAN THE LAST GUARDIANS I KNEW.
HAVE YOU MET A LOT OF GUARDIANS?
NOT IN A LONG TIME. THINGS HAVE CHANGED AND I HAVE SOME QUESTIONS...I'M SURE THE KIDS HAVE EVEN MORE FOR ME. IF WE MAKE IT OUT OF THIS, THEN I PROMISE TO ANSWER EVERYTHING. BUT FIRST, WE NEED TO FIND ELPIS.
ELPIS? WHERE CAN WE FIND THEM?
RUMBLE RUMBLE
EARTHQUAKE?
OH NO...

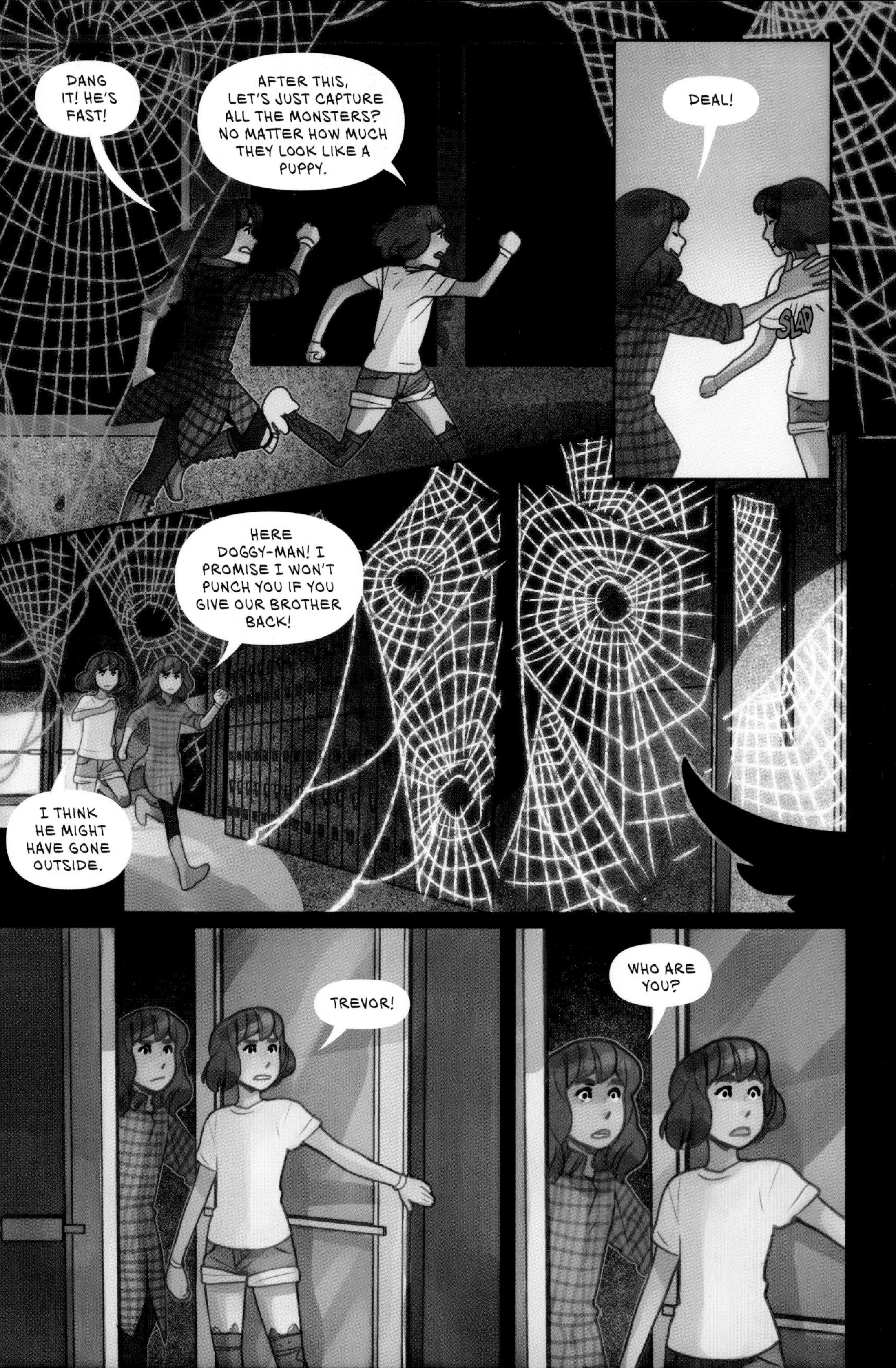
DANG IT! HE'S FAST!
AFTER THIS, LET'S JUST CAPTURE ALL THE MONSTERS? NO MATTER HOW MUCH THEY LOOK LIKE A PUPPY.
DEAL!
SLAP
HERE DOGGY-MAN! I PROMISE I WON'T PUNCH YOU IF YOU GIVE OUR BROTHER BACK!
I THINK HE MIGHT HAVE GONE OUTSIDE.
TREVOR!
WHO ARE YOU?

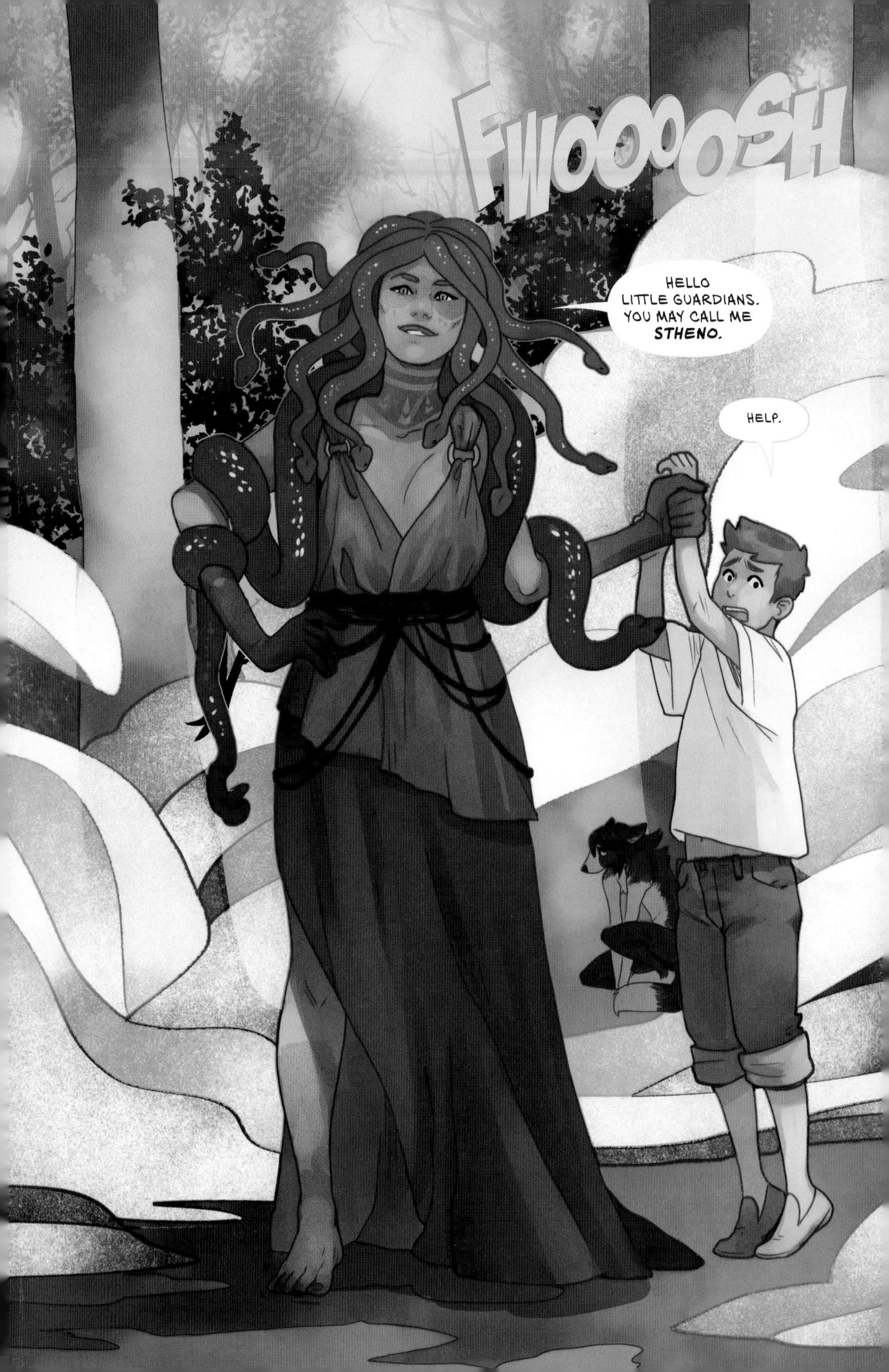
FWOOOOSH
HELLO LITTLE GUARDIANS. YOU MAY CALL ME STHENO.
HELP.

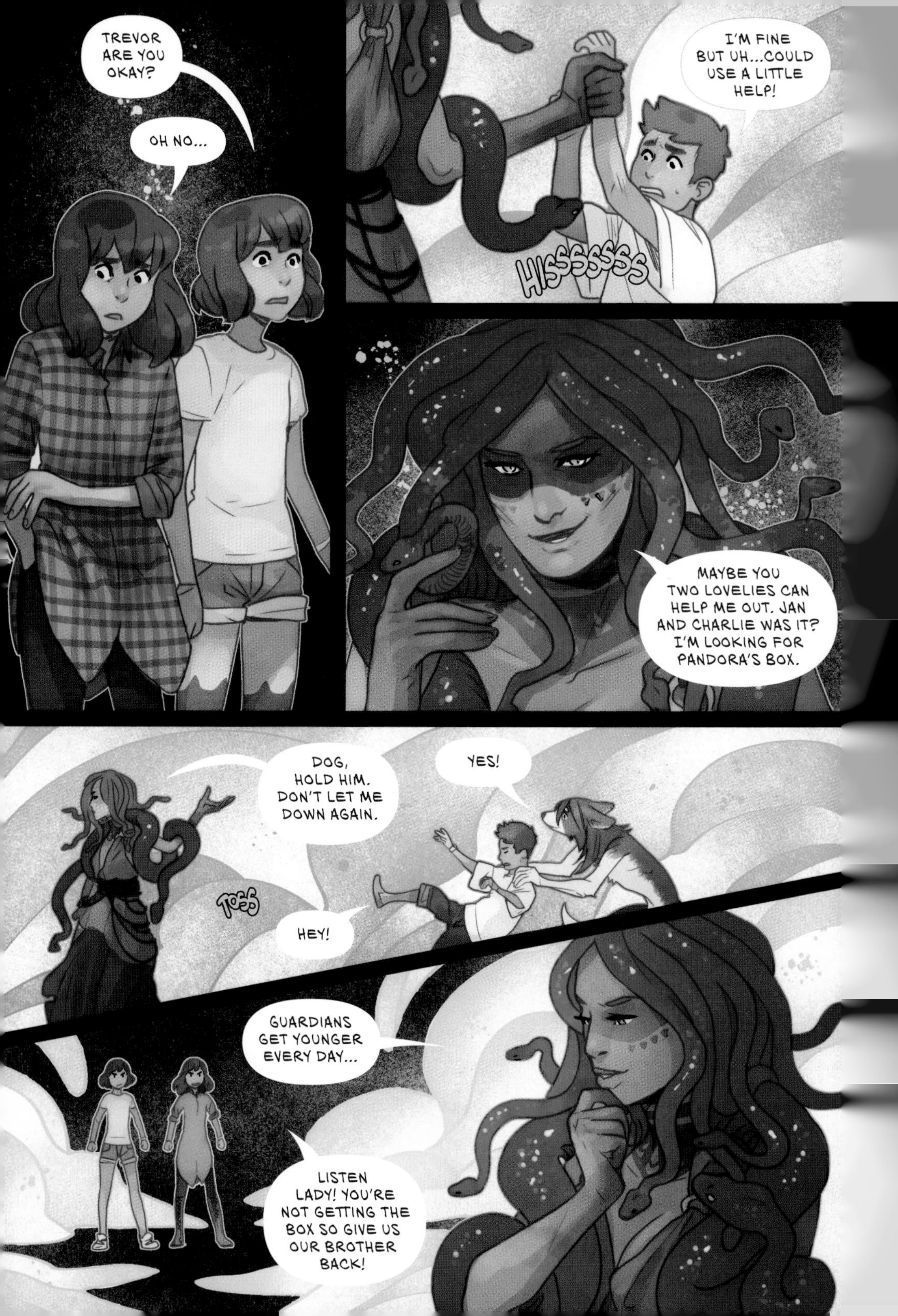
TREVOR ARE YOU OKAY?
OH NO...
I'M FINE BUT UH...COULD USE A LITTLE HELP!
HISSSSSS
MAYBE YOU TWO LOVELIES CAN HELP ME OUT. JAN AND CHARLIE WAS IT? I'M LOOKING FOR PANDORA'S BOX.
DOG, HOLD HIM. DON'T LET ME DOWN AGAIN.
YES!
TOSS
HEY!
GUARDIANS GET YOUNGER EVERY DAY...
LISTEN LADY! YOU'RE NOT GETTING THE BOX SO GIVE US OUR BROTHER BACK!

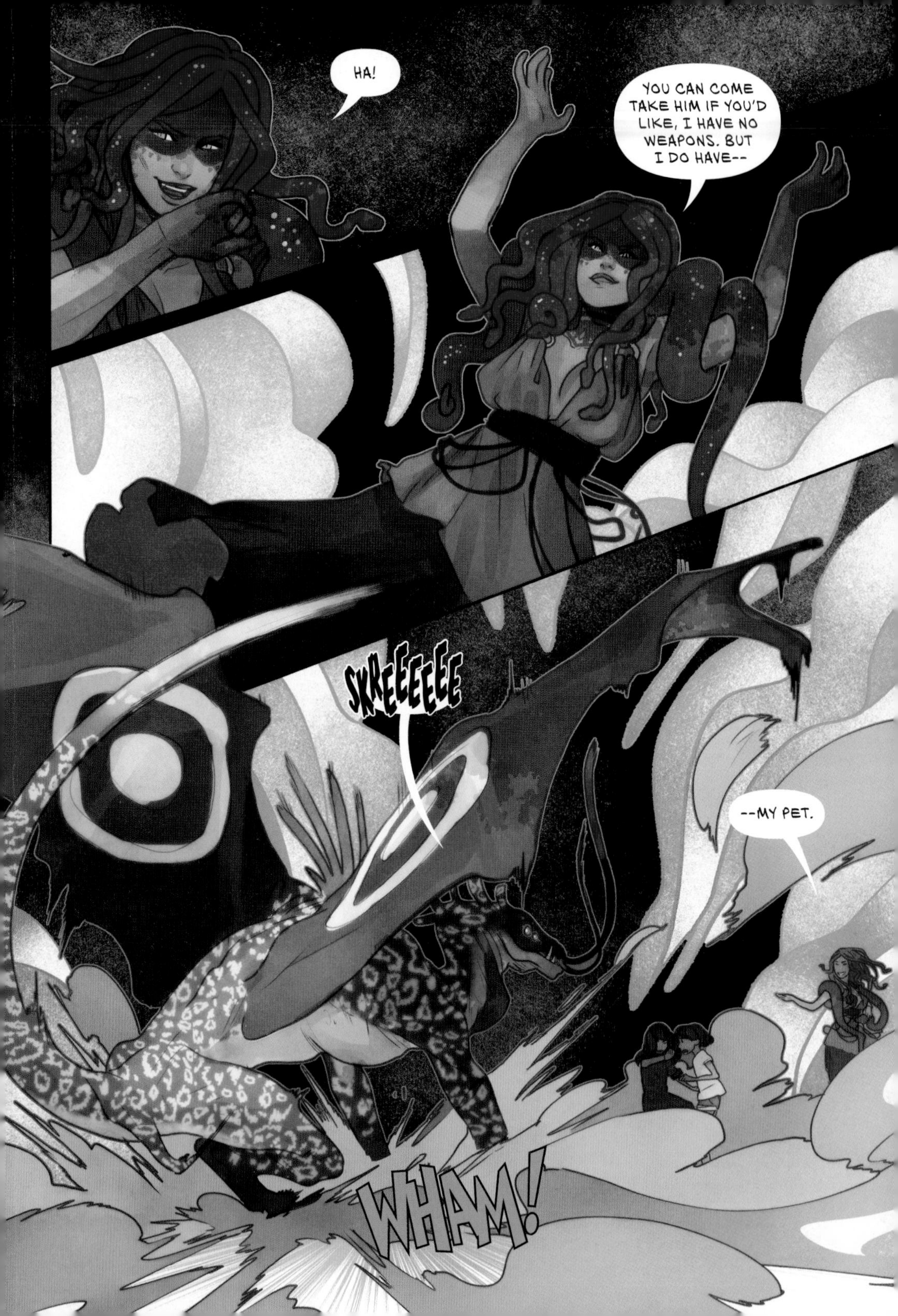
HA!
YOU CAN COME TAKE HIM IF YOU'D LIKE, I HAVE NO WEAPONS. BUT I DO HAVE--
SKREEEEEE
--MY PET.
WHAM!

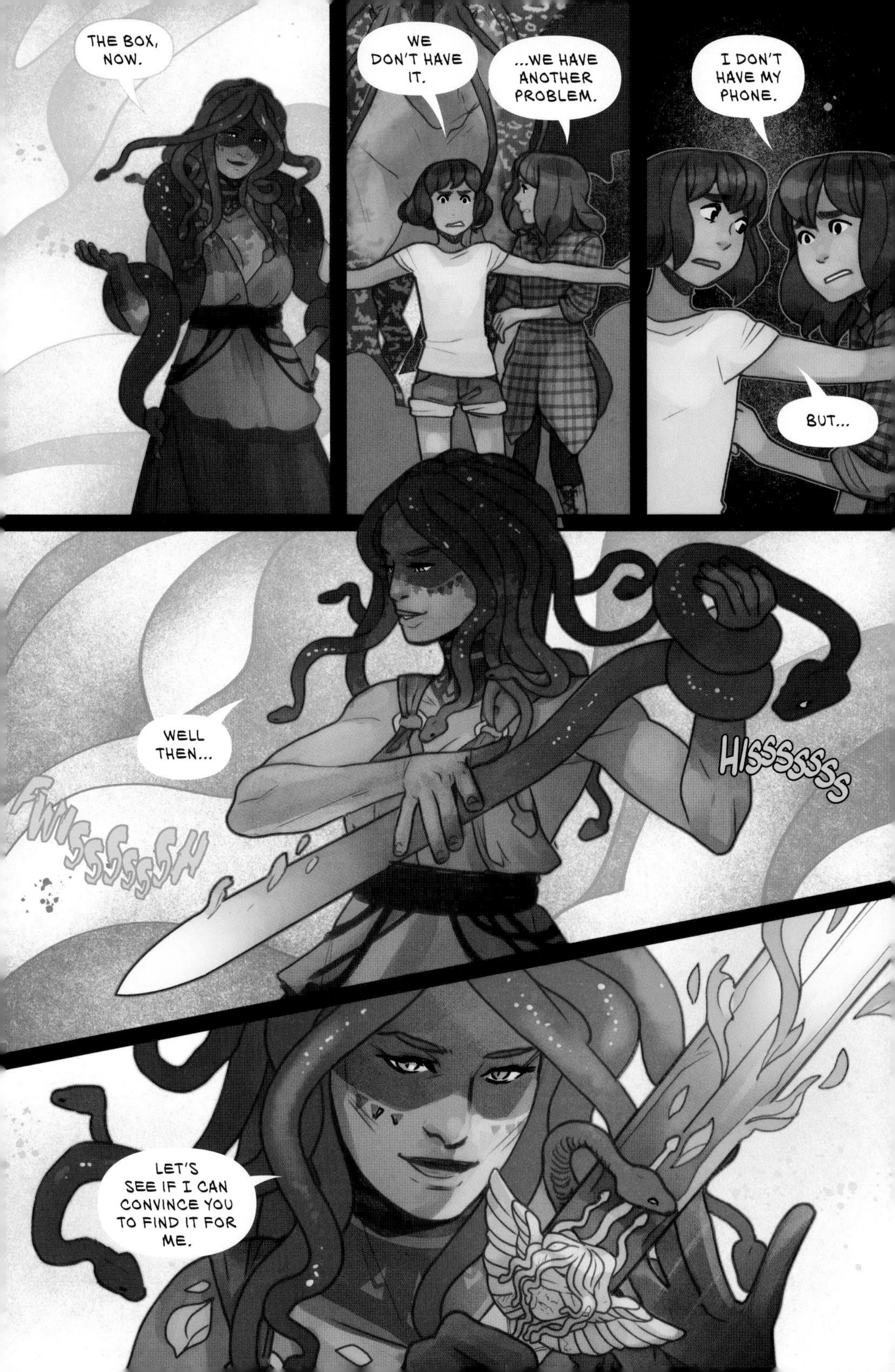
THE BOX, NOW.
WE DON'T HAVE IT.
...WE HAVE ANOTHER PROBLEM.
I DON'T HAVE MY PHONE.
BUT...
WELL THEN...
FWISSSSSSH
HISSSSSSS
LET'S SEE IF I CAN CONVINCE YOU TO FIND IT FOR ME.

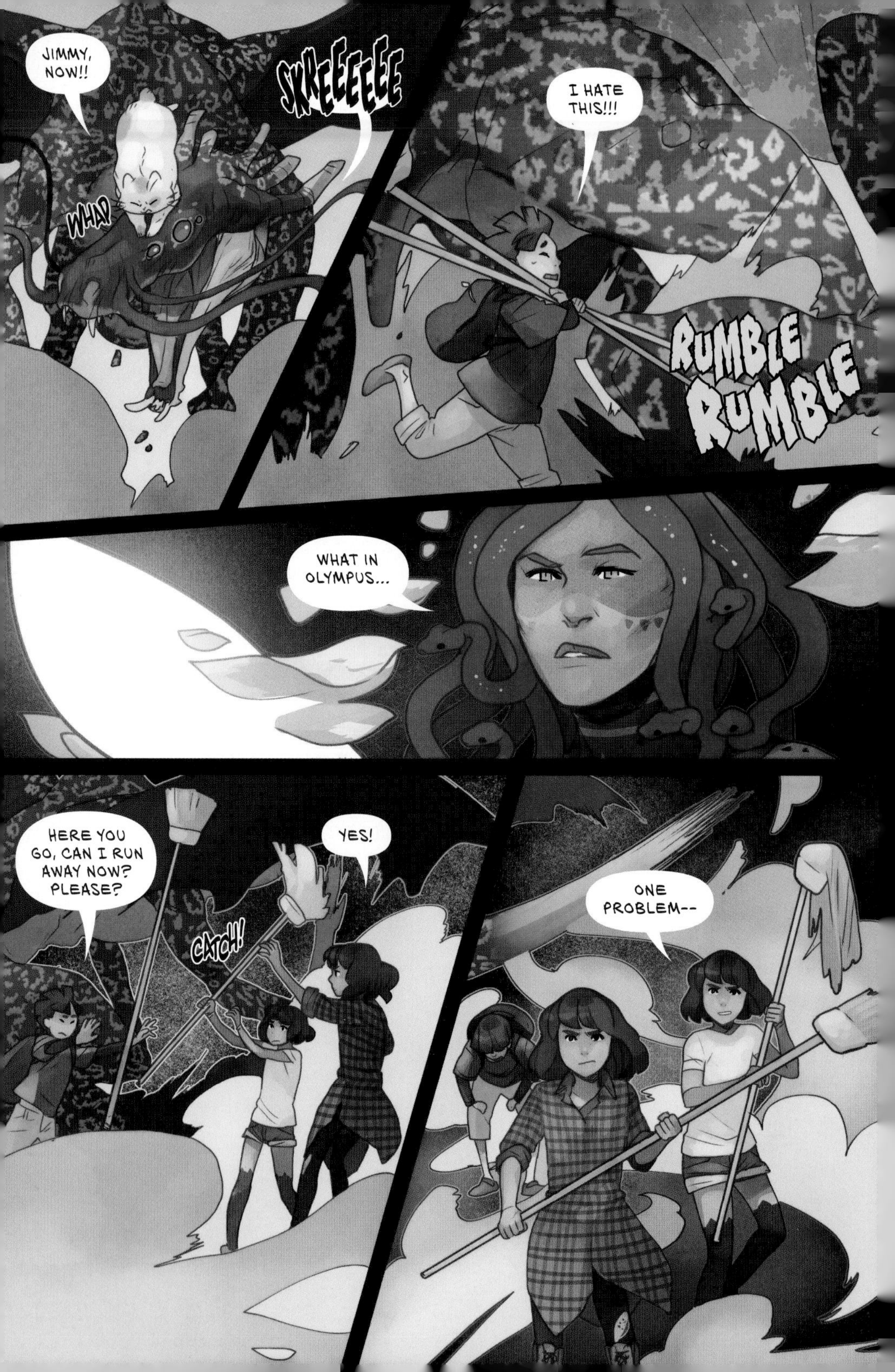
JIMMY, NOW!!
SKREEEEEE
WHAP
I HATE THIS!!!
RUMBLE RUMBLE
WHAT IN OLYMPUS...
HERE YOU GO, CAN I RUN AWAY NOW? PLEASE?
YES!
CATCH!
ONE PROBLEM--

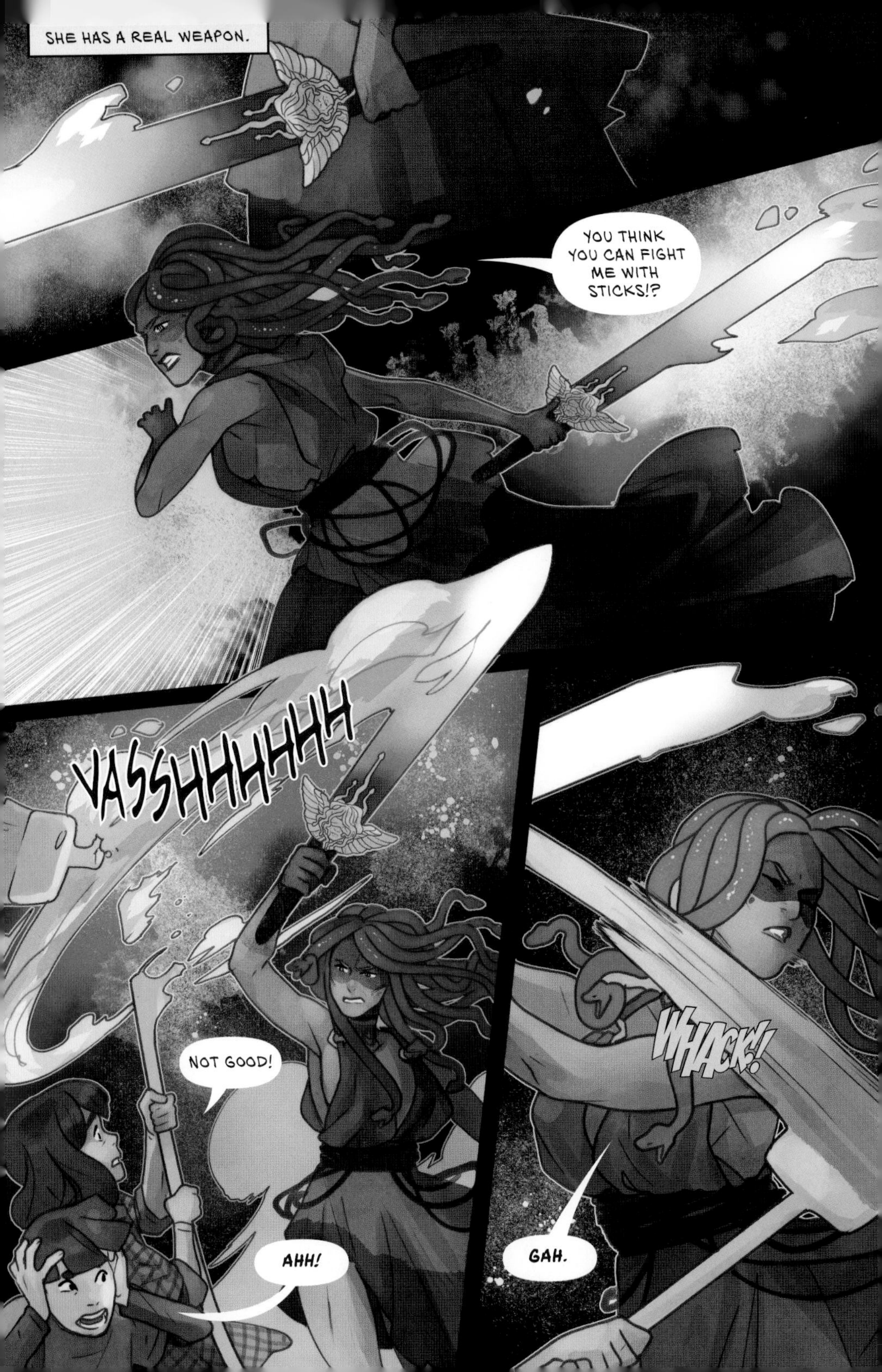

SHE HAS A REAL WEAPON.
YOU THINK YOU CAN FIGHT ME WITH STICKS!?
VASSHHHHHH
NOT GOOD!
AHH!
WHACK!
GAH.

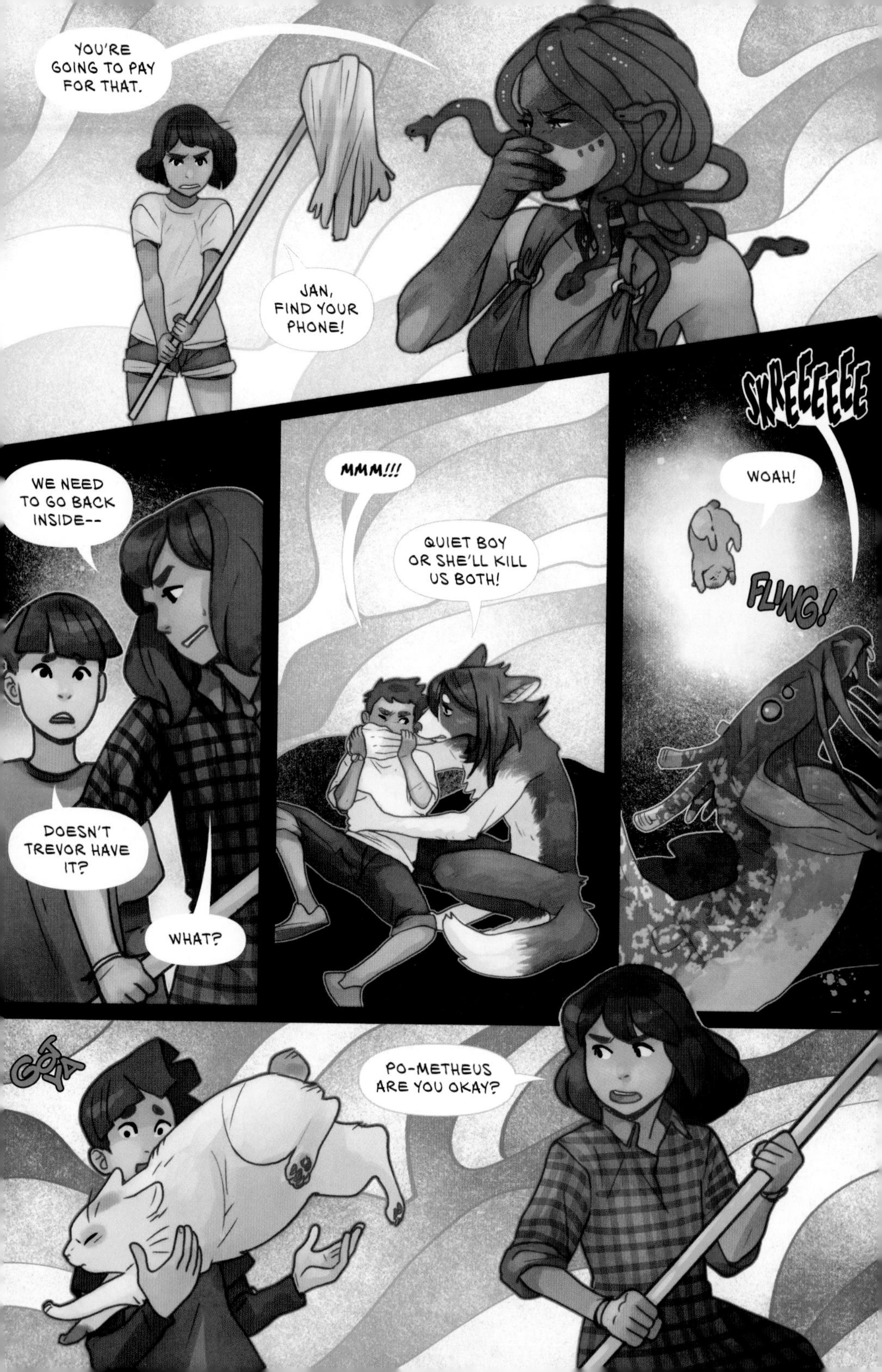
YOU'RE GOING TO PAY FOR THAT.
JAN, FIND YOUR PHONE!
WE NEED TO GO BACK INSIDE--
DOESN'T TREVOR HAVE IT?
WHAT?
MMM!!!
QUIET BOY OR SHE'LL KILL US BOTH!
SKREEEEEE
WOAH!
FLING!
PO-METHEUS ARE YOU OKAY?

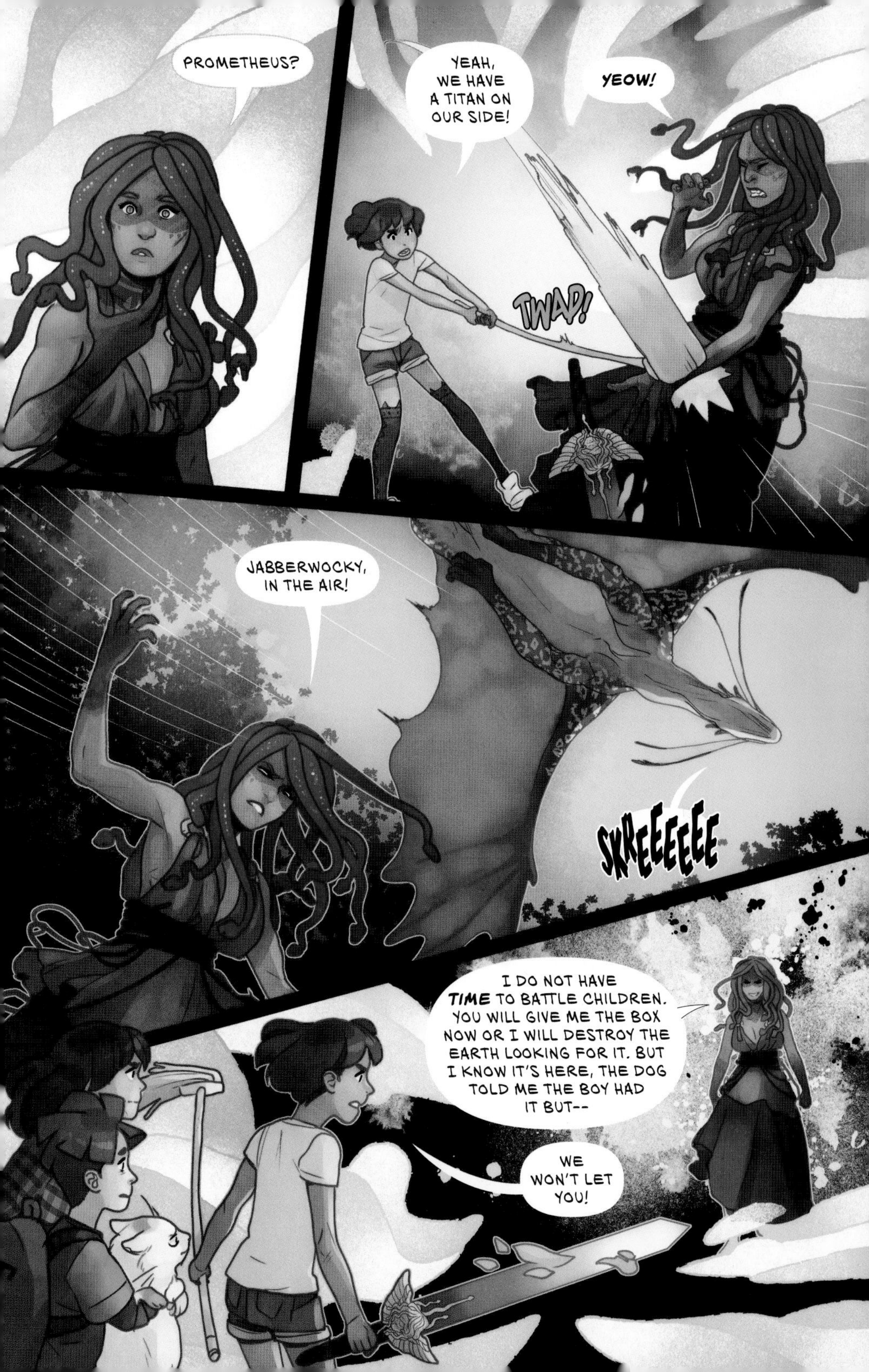
PROMETHEUS?
YEAH, WE HAVE A TITAN ON OUR SIDE!
YEOW!
TWAD!
JABBERWOCKY, IN THE AIR!
SKREEEEEE
I DO NOT HAVE TIME TO BATTLE CHILDREN. YOU WILL GIVE ME THE BOX NOW OR I WILL DESTROY THE EARTH LOOKING FOR IT. BUT I KNOW IT'S HERE, THE DOG TOLD ME THE BOY HAD IT BUT--
WE WON'T LET YOU!

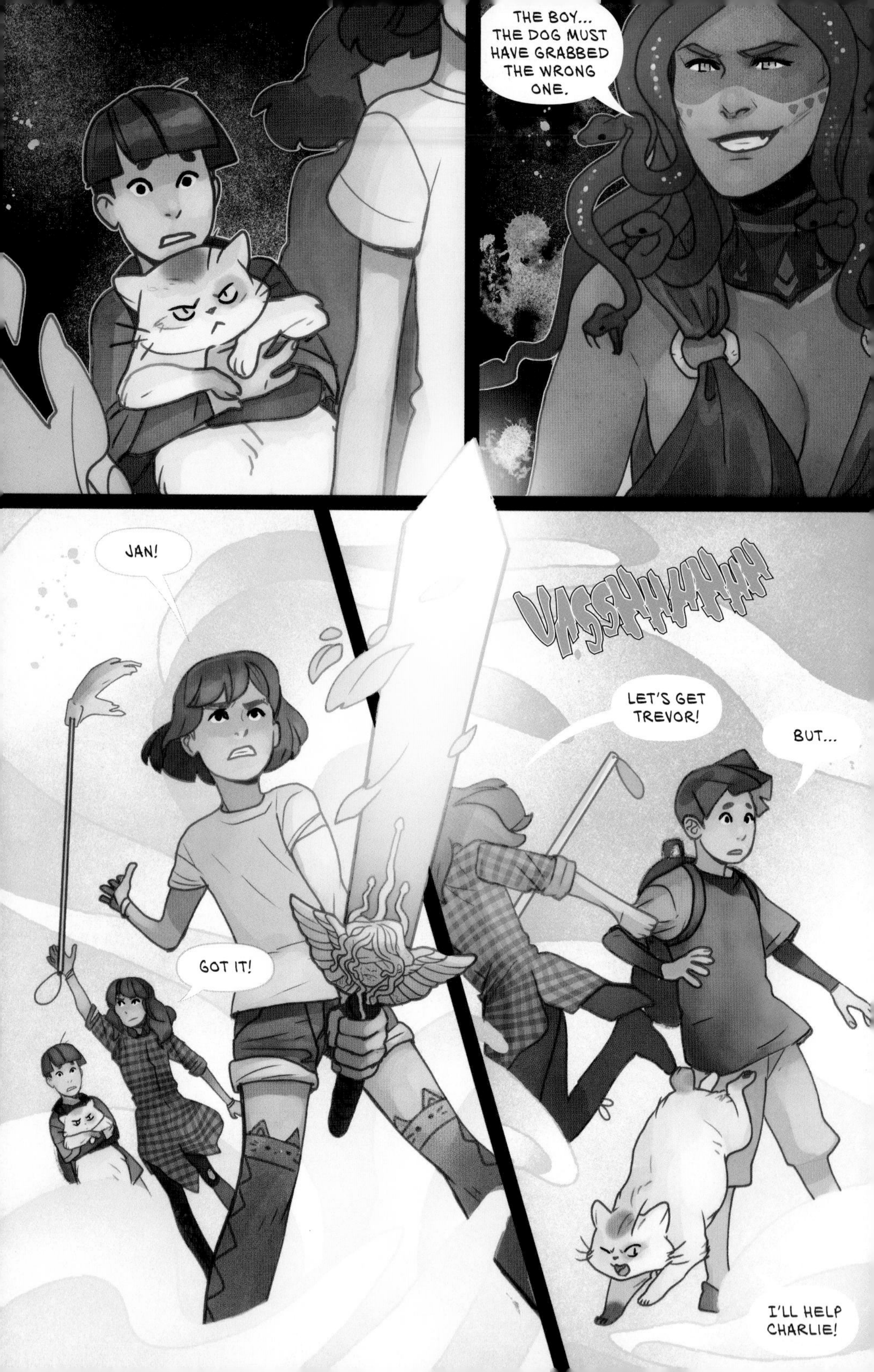
THE BOY... THE DOG MUST HAVE GRABBED THE WRONG ONE.
JAN!
GOT IT!
VASSHHHHHH
LET'S GET TREVOR!
BUT...
I'LL HELP CHARLIE!

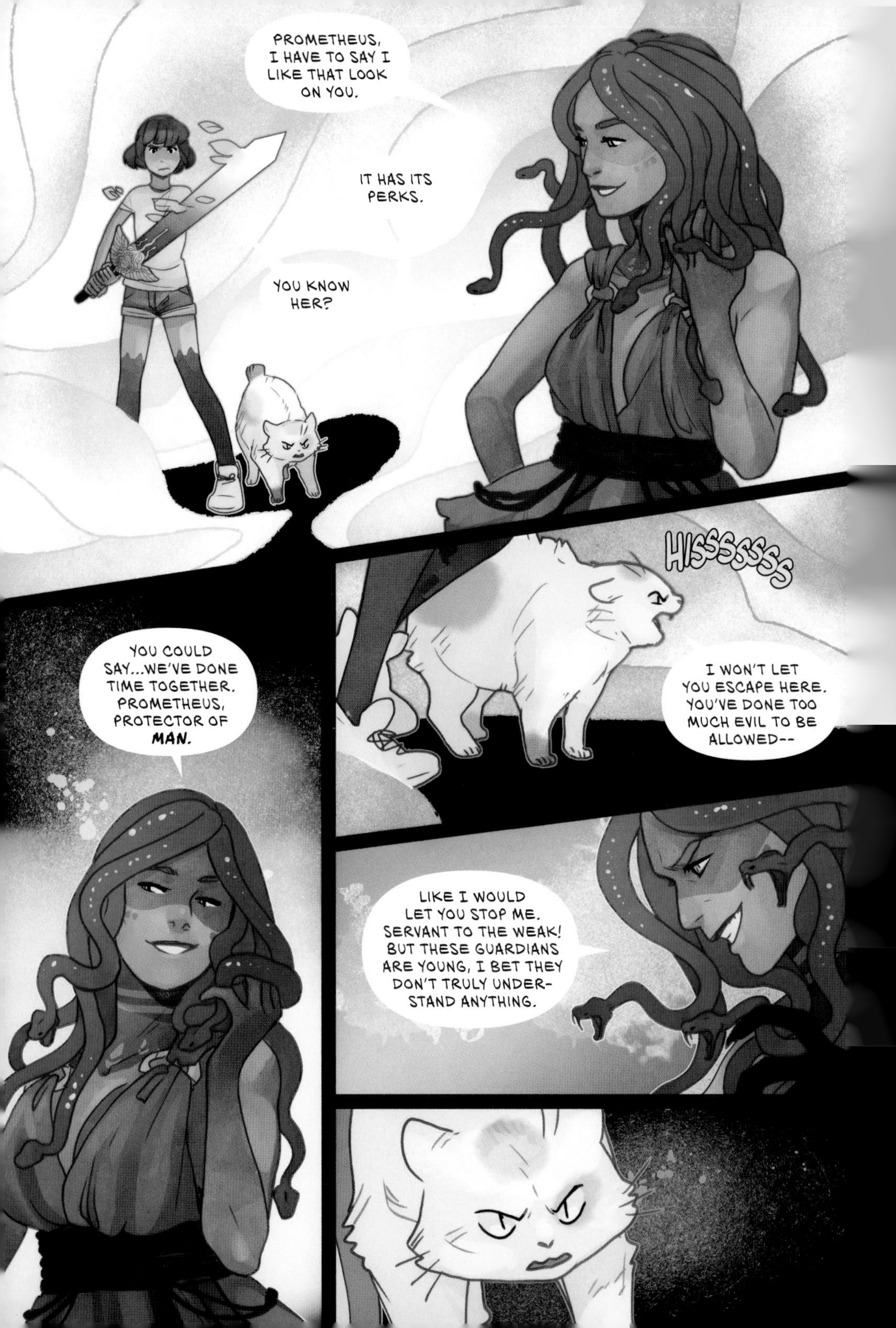
PROMETHEUS, I HAVE TO SAY I LIKE THAT LOOK ON YOU.
IT HAS ITS PERKS.
YOU KNOW HER?
HISSSSSSS
YOU COULD SAY...WE'VE DONE TIME TOGETHER. PROMETHEUS, PROTECTOR OF **MAN.**
I WON'T LET YOU ESCAPE HERE. YOU'VE DONE TOO MUCH EVIL TO BE ALLOWED--
LIKE I WOULD LET YOU STOP ME. SERVANT TO THE WEAK! BUT THESE GUARDIANS ARE YOUNG, I BET THEY DON'T TRULY UNDER-STAND ANYTHING.

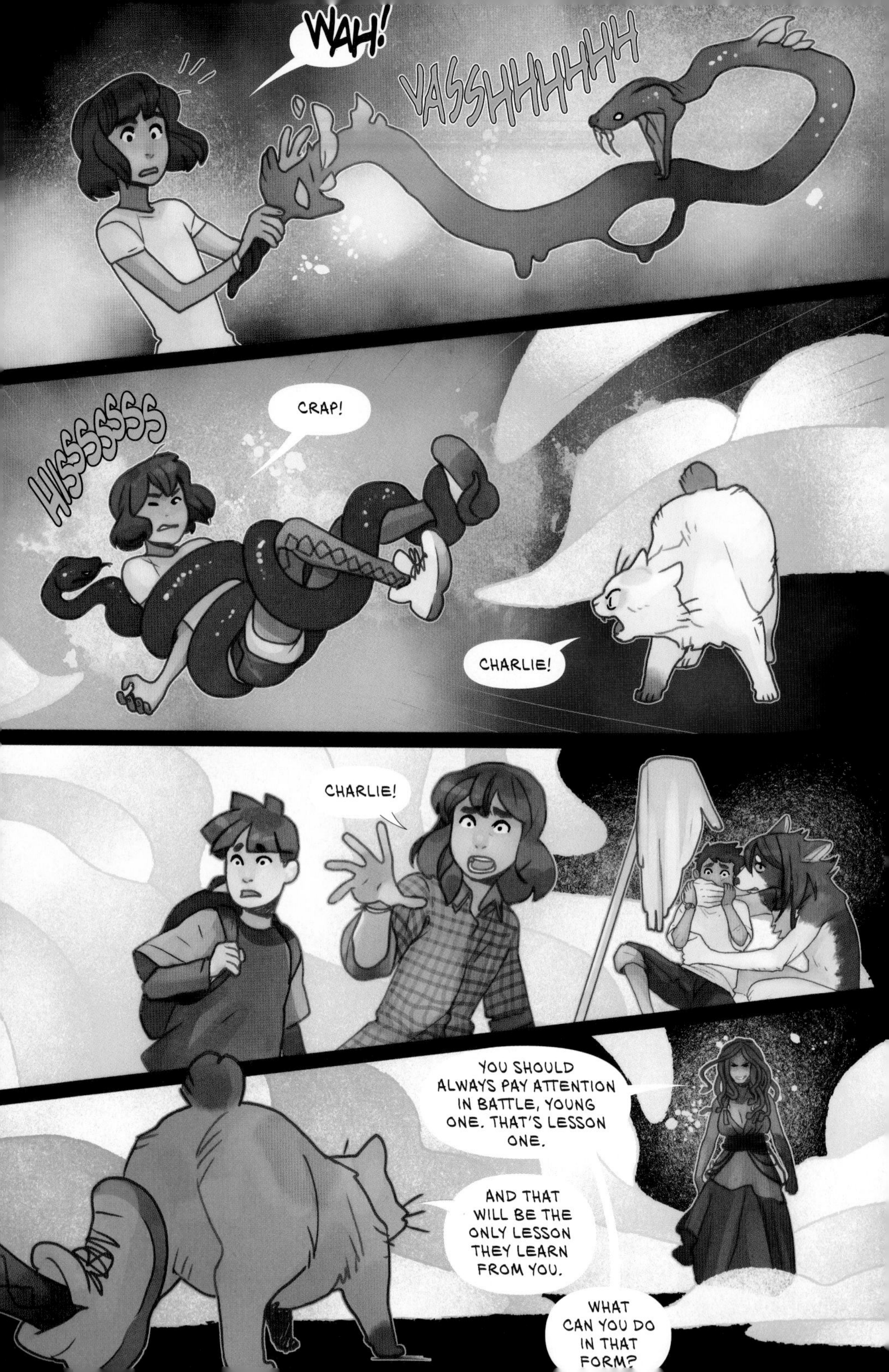
WAH!
YASSHHHHHH
HISSSSSS
CRAP!
CHARLIE!
CHARLIE!
YOU SHOULD ALWAYS PAY ATTENTION IN BATTLE, YOUNG ONE. THAT'S LESSON ONE.
AND THAT WILL BE THE ONLY LESSON THEY LEARN FROM YOU.
WHAT CAN YOU DO IN THAT FORM?

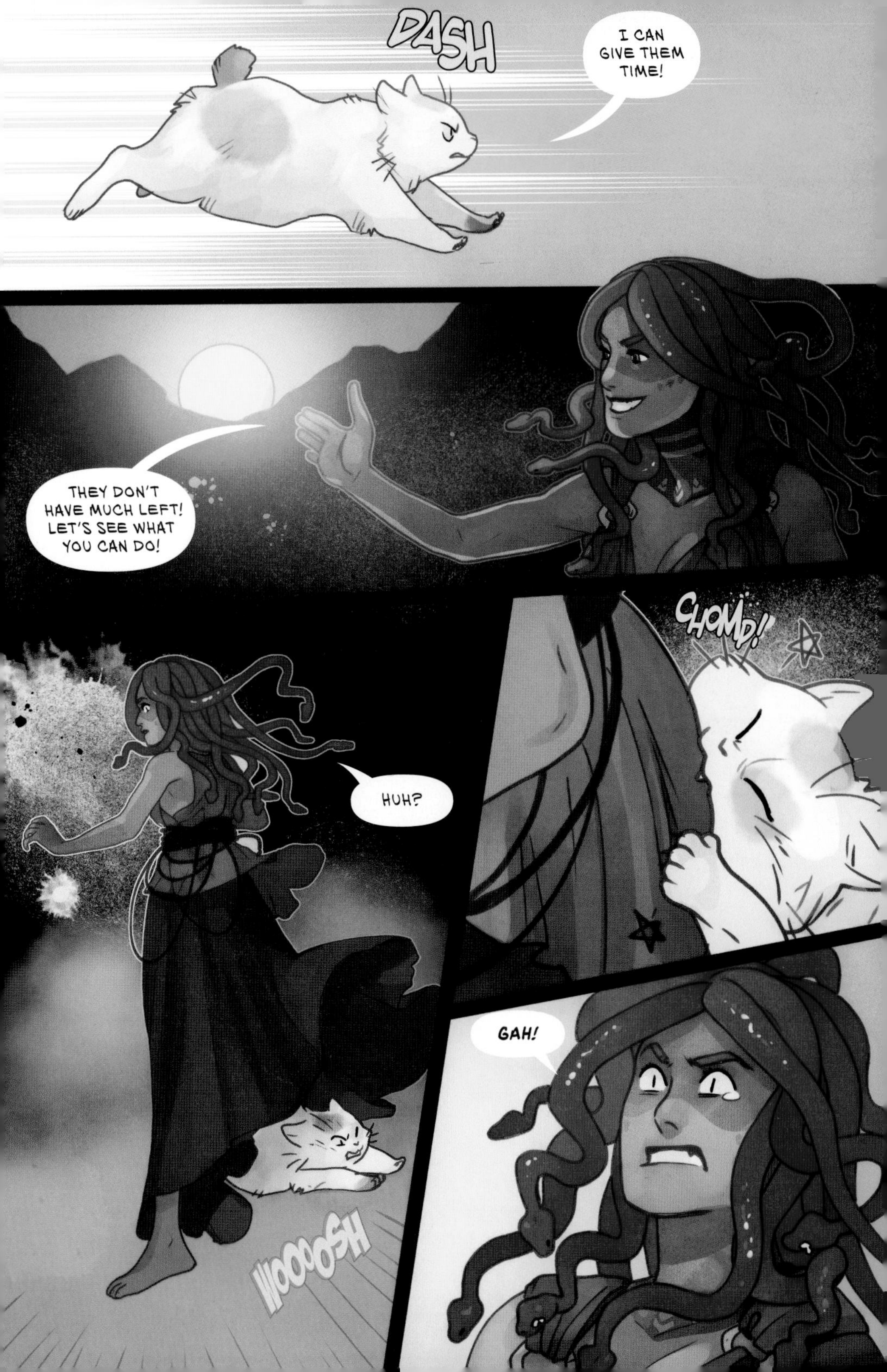
DASH
I CAN GIVE THEM TIME!
THEY DON'T HAVE MUCH LEFT! LET'S SEE WHAT YOU CAN DO!
HUH?
WOOOOSH
CHOMP!
GAH!

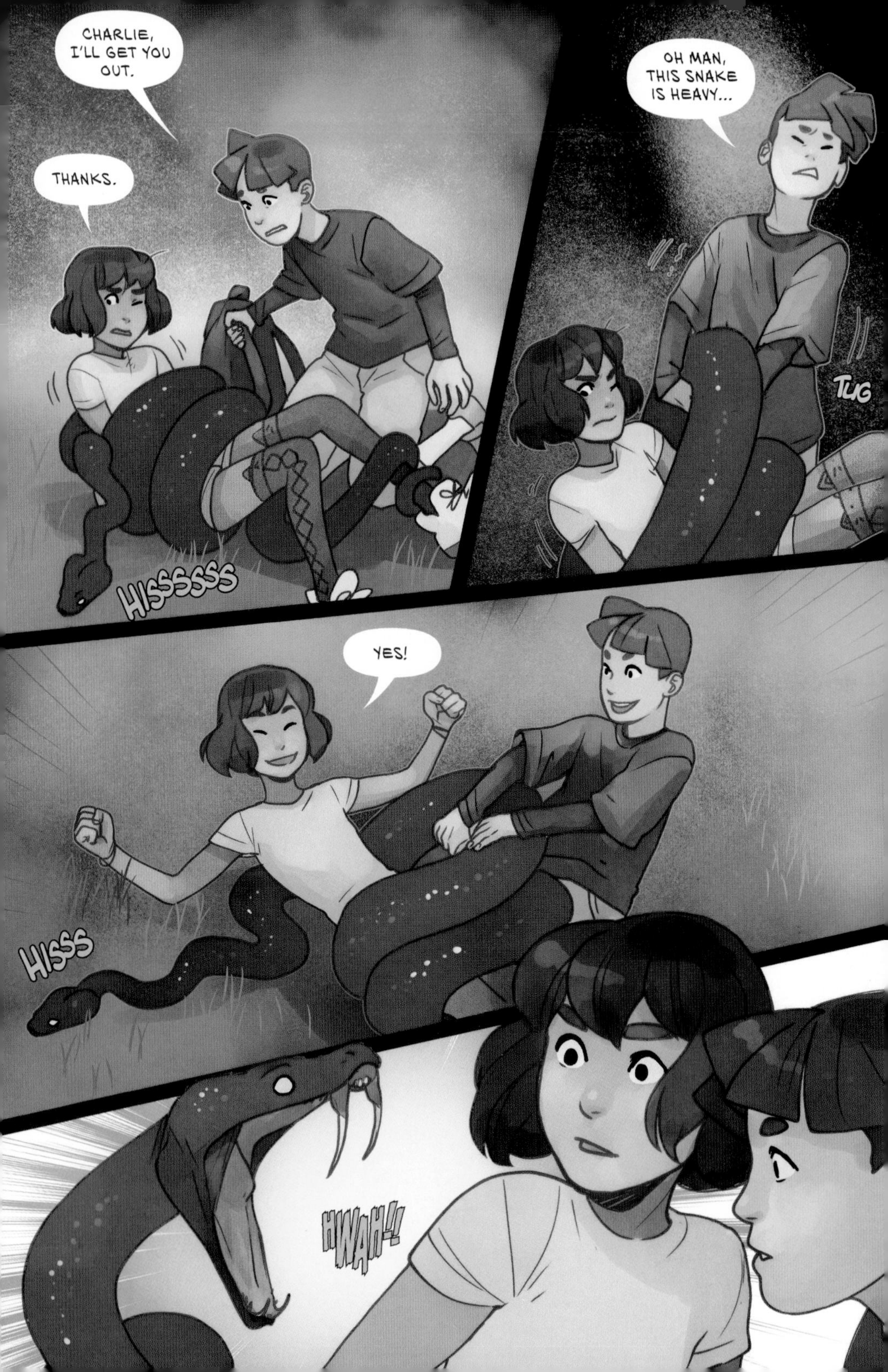
CHARLIE, I'LL GET YOU OUT.
THANKS.
HISSSSSS
OH MAN, THIS SNAKE IS HEAVY...
TUG
YES!
HISSS
HWAH!!

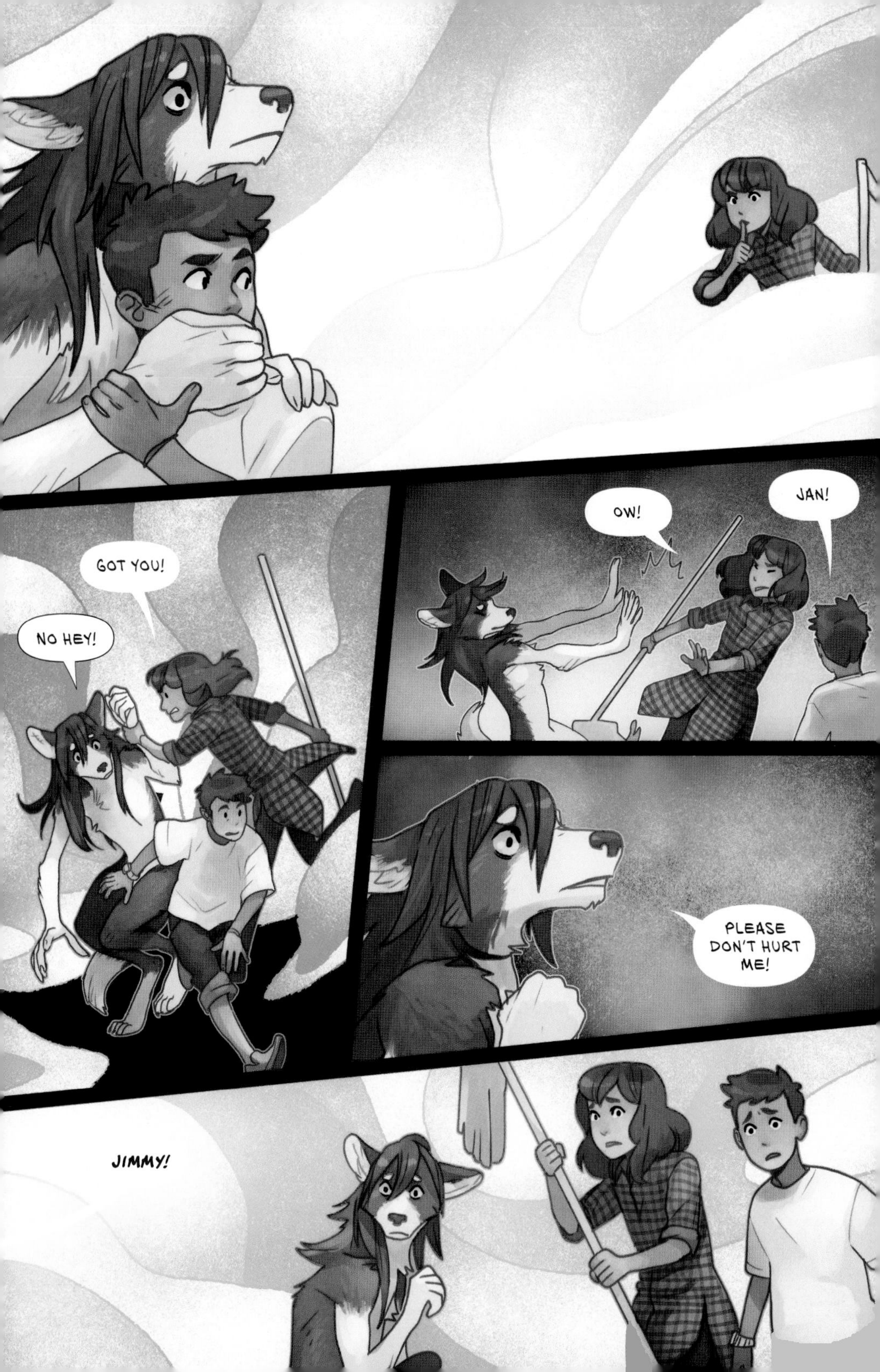
GOT YOU!
NO HEY!
OW!
JAN!
PLEASE DON'T HURT ME!
JIMMY!

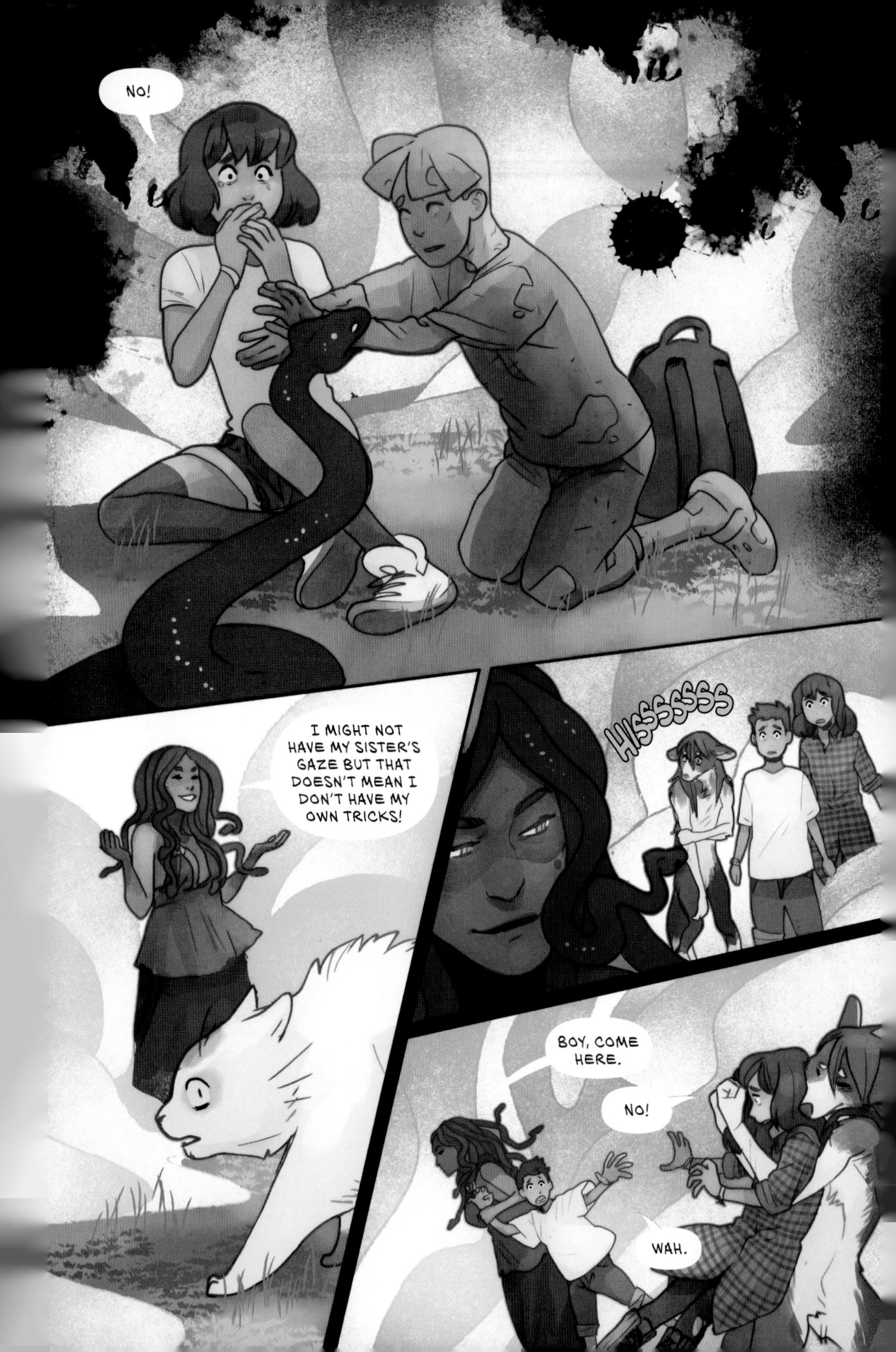
NO!
I MIGHT NOT HAVE MY SISTER'S GAZE BUT THAT DOESN'T MEAN I DON'T HAVE MY OWN TRICKS!
HISSSSSS
BOY, COME HERE.
NO!
WAH.

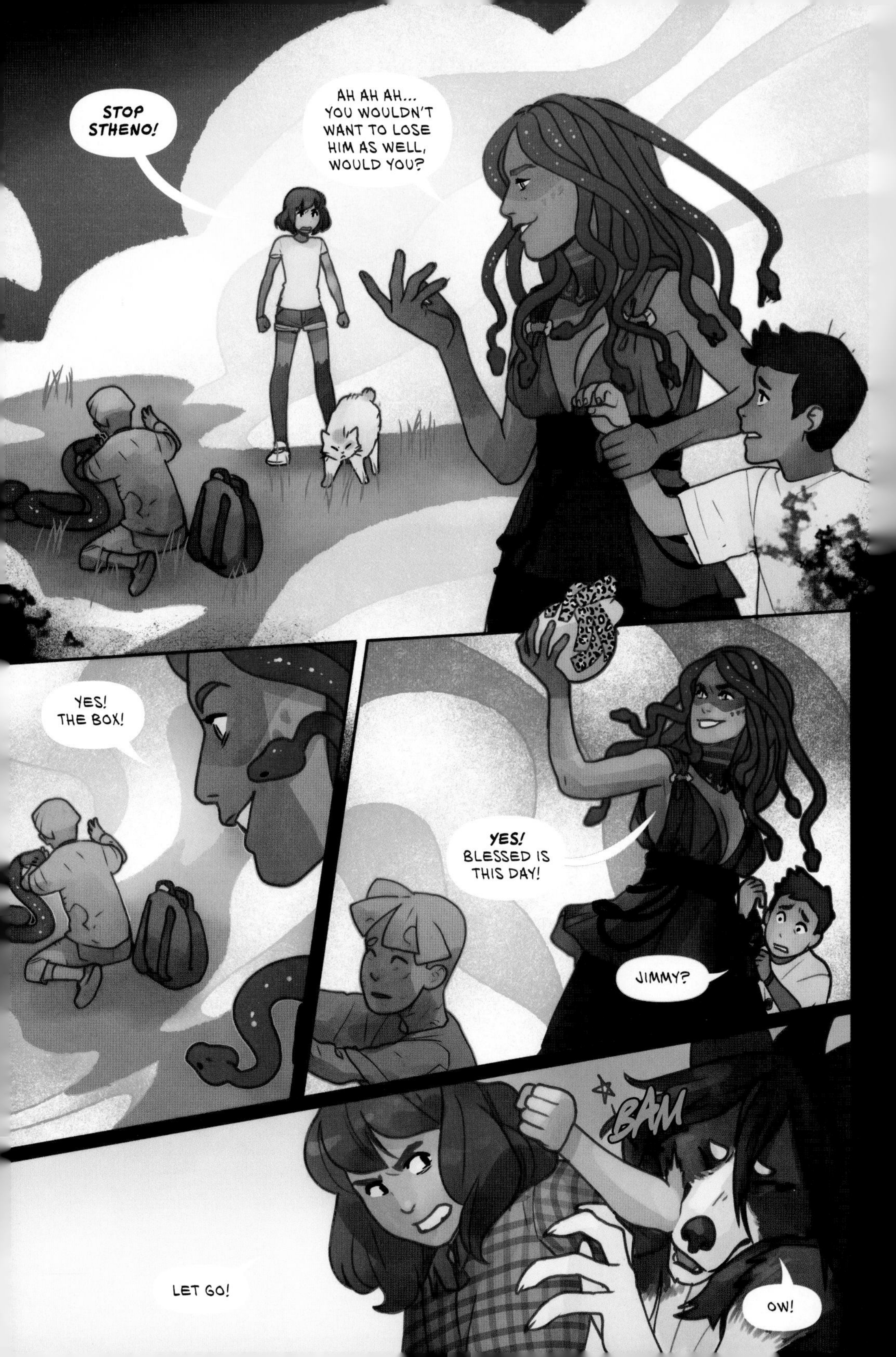
STOP STHENO!
AH AH AH... YOU WOULDN'T WANT TO LOSE HIM AS WELL, WOULD YOU?
YES! THE BOX!
YES! BLESSED IS THIS DAY!
JIMMY?
BAM
LET GO!
OW!

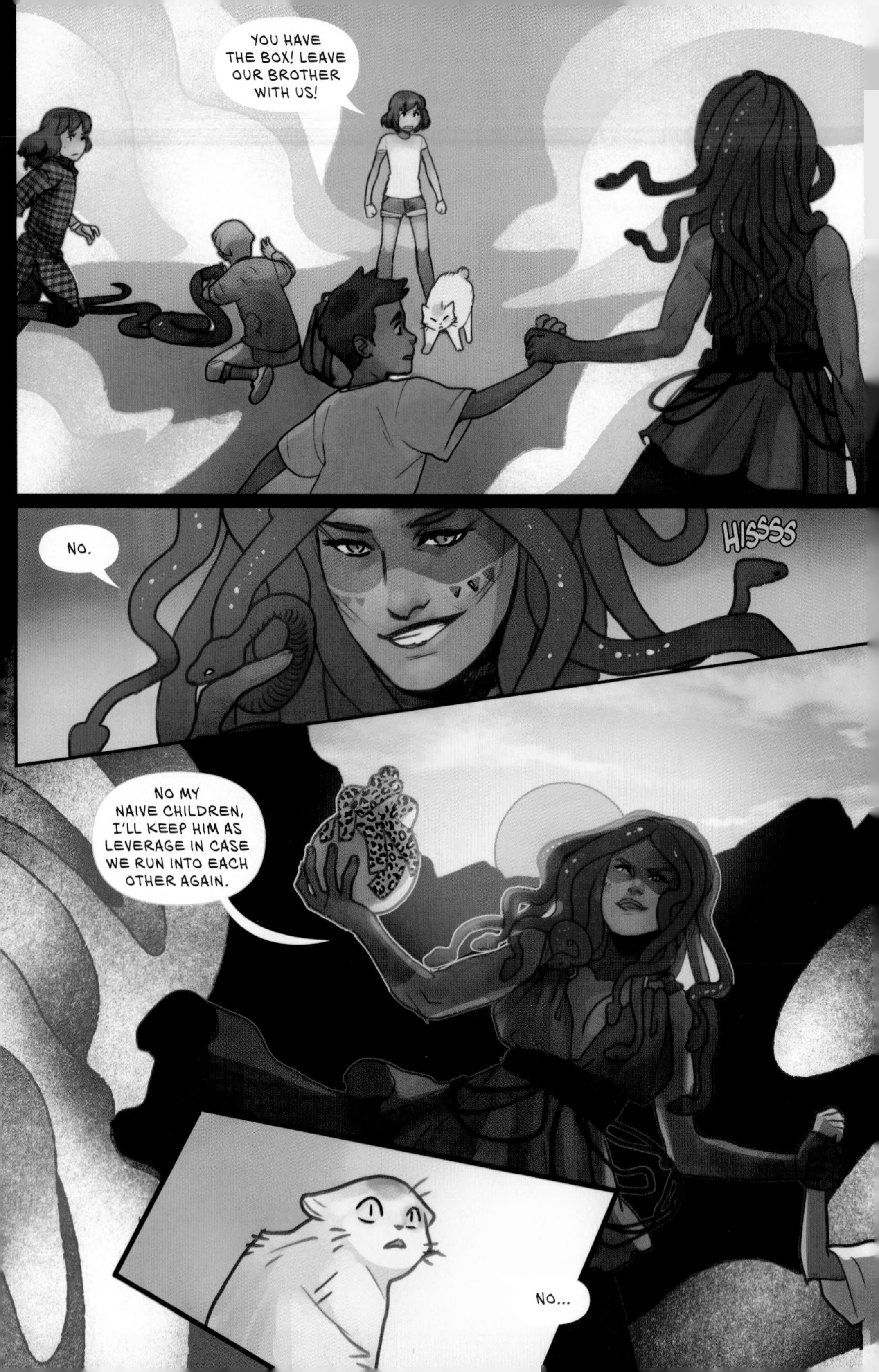
YOU HAVE THE BOX! LEAVE OUR BROTHER WITH US!
NO.
HISSSS
NO MY NAIVE CHILDREN, I'LL KEEP HIM AS LEVERAGE IN CASE WE RUN INTO EACH OTHER AGAIN.
NO...

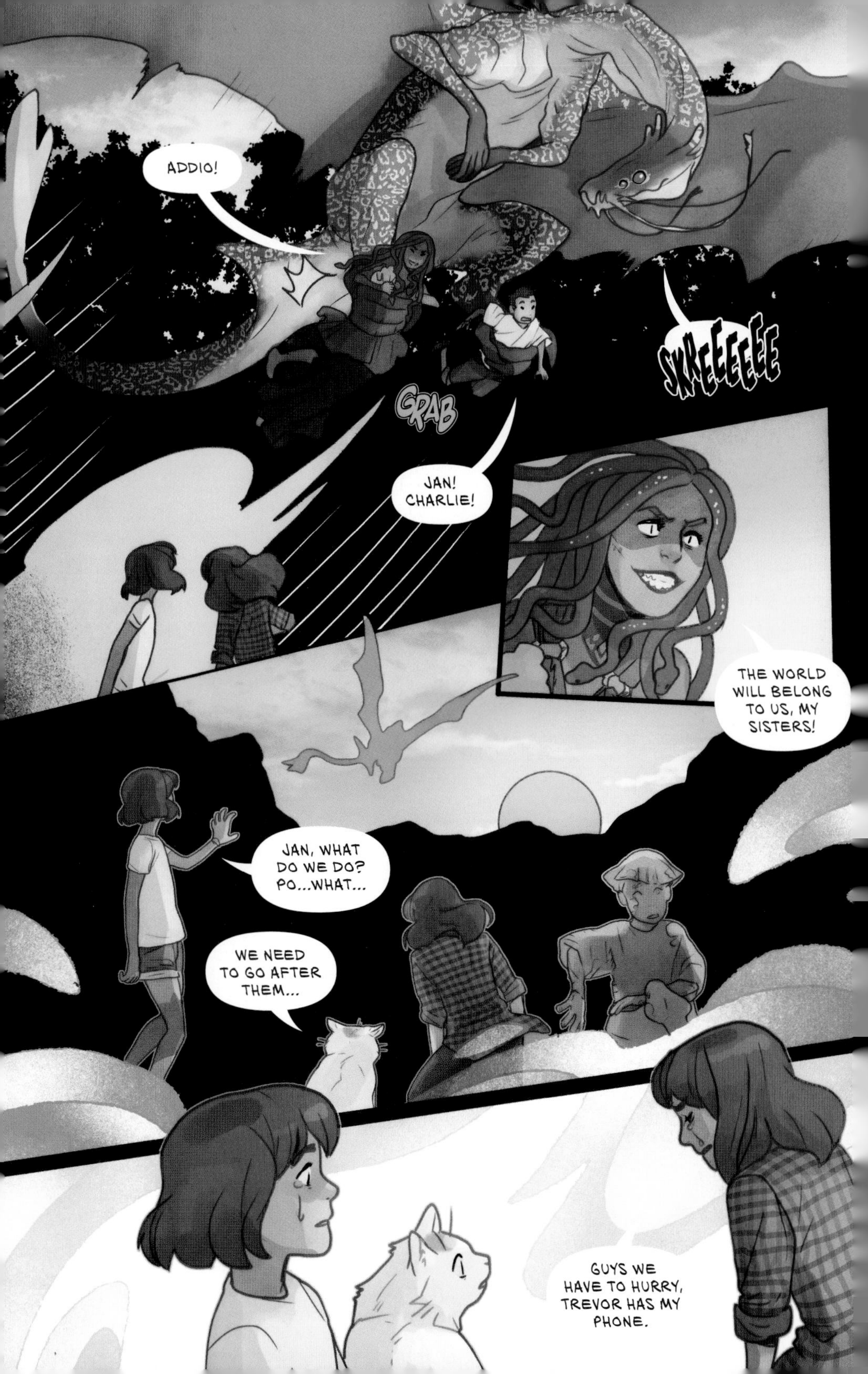
ADDIO!
SKREEEEEEE
GRAB
JAN! CHARLIE!
THE WORLD WILL BELONG TO US, MY SISTERS!
JAN, WHAT DO WE DO? PO...WHAT...
WE NEED TO GO AFTER THEM...
GUYS WE HAVE TO HURRY, TREVOR HAS MY PHONE.

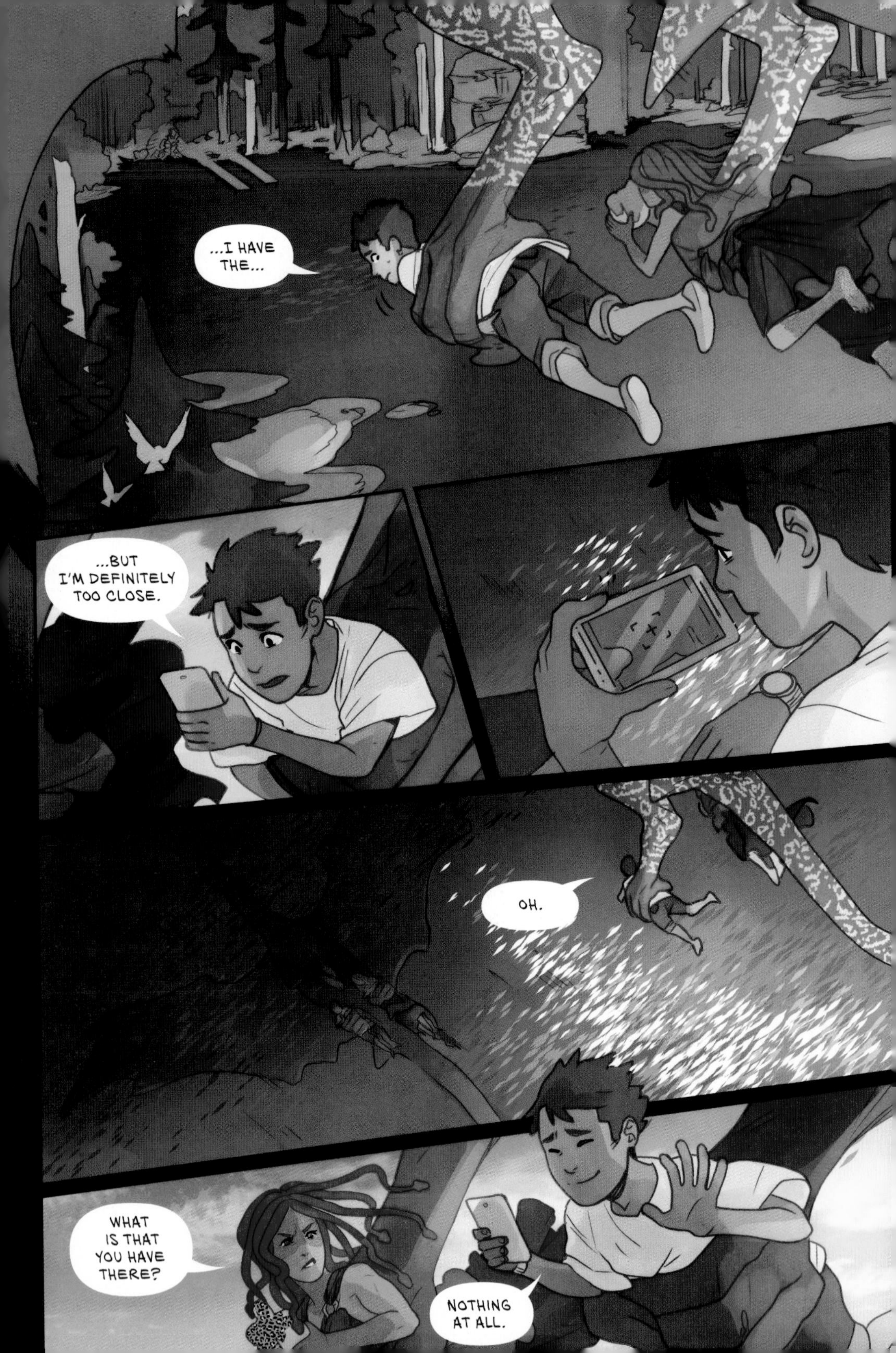
...I HAVE THE...
...BUT I'M DEFINITELY TOO CLOSE.
OH.
WHAT IS THAT YOU HAVE THERE?
NOTHING AT ALL.

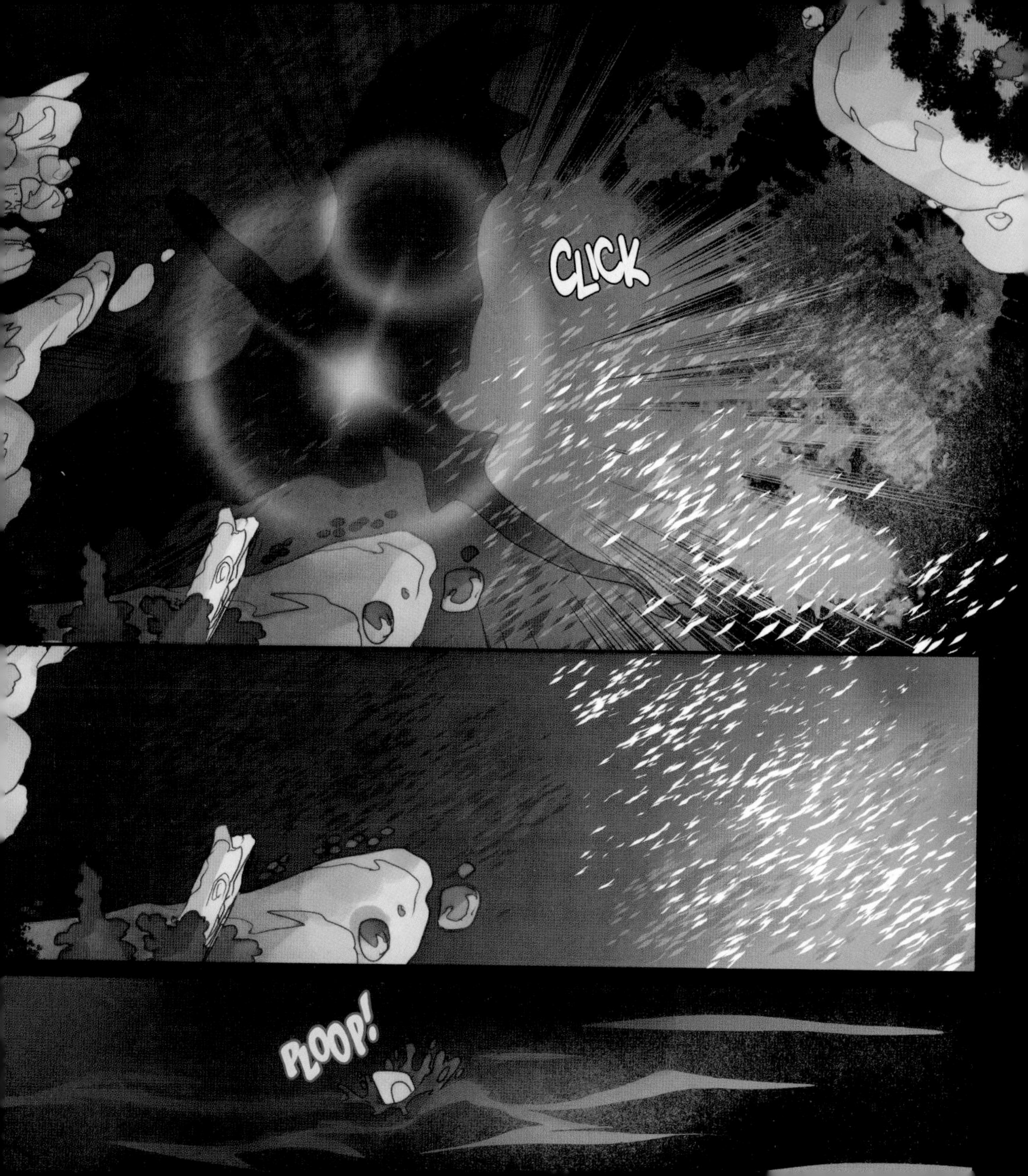
CLICK
PLOOP!

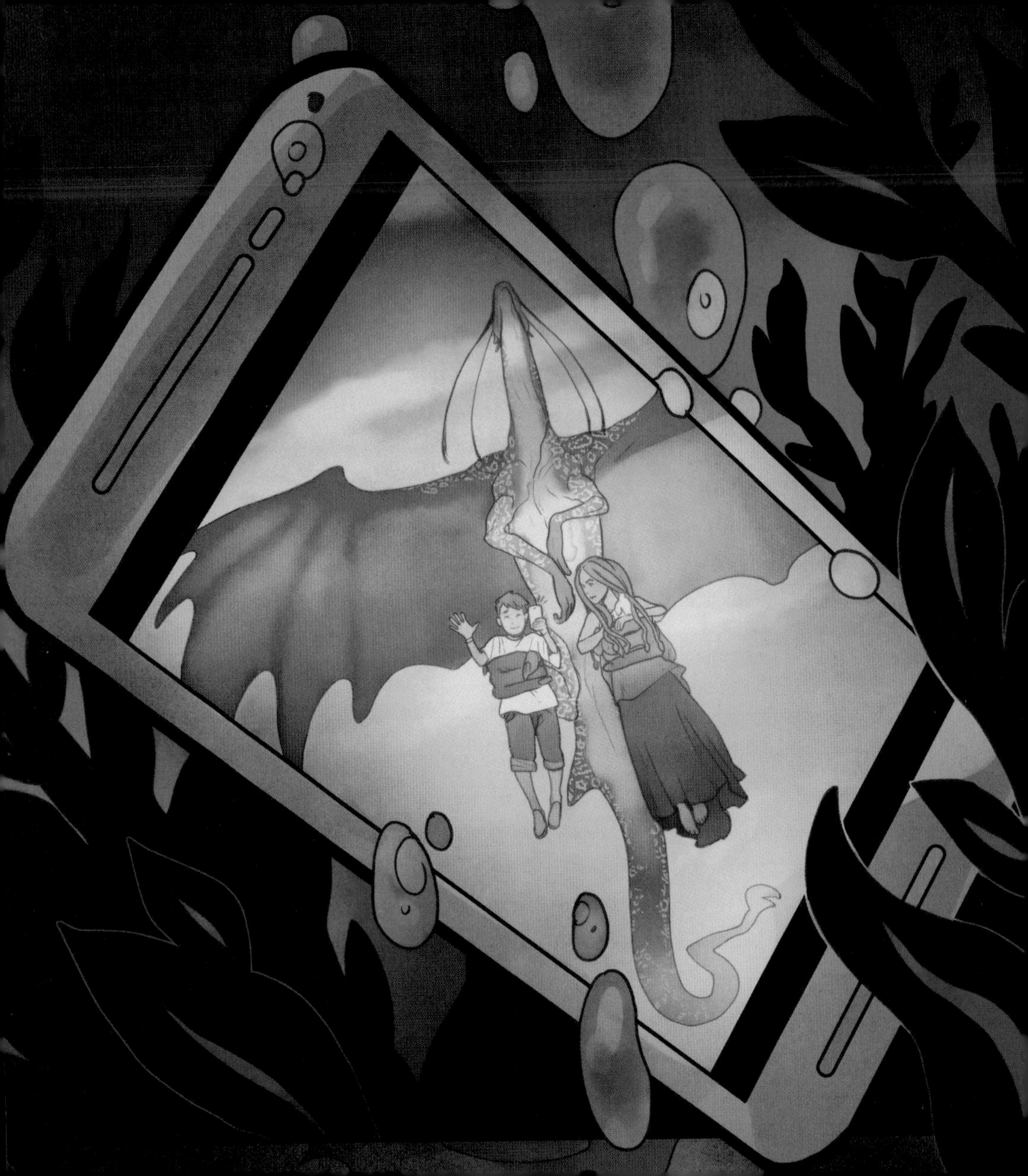

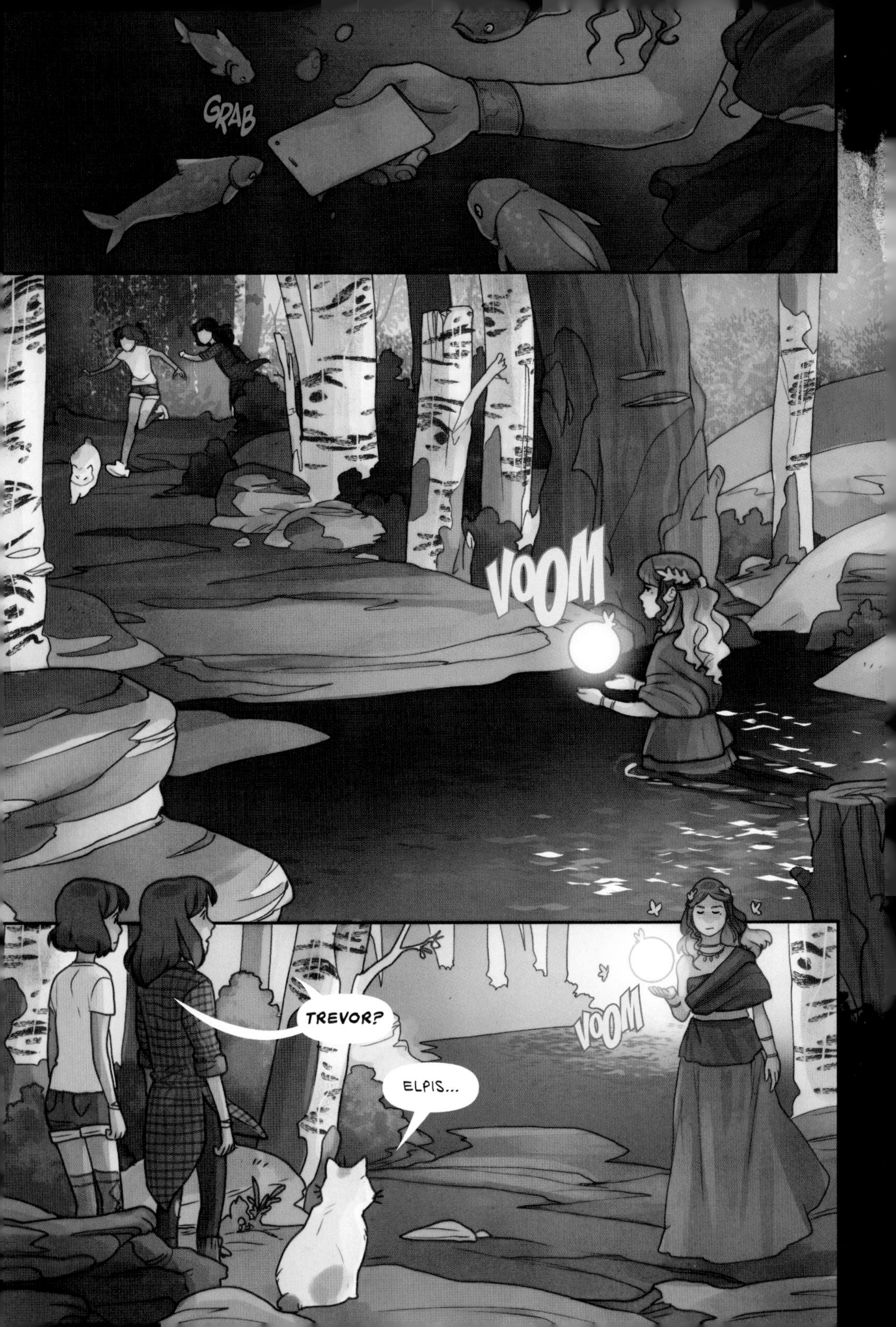
GRAB
VOOM
TREVOR?
ELPIS...
VOOM

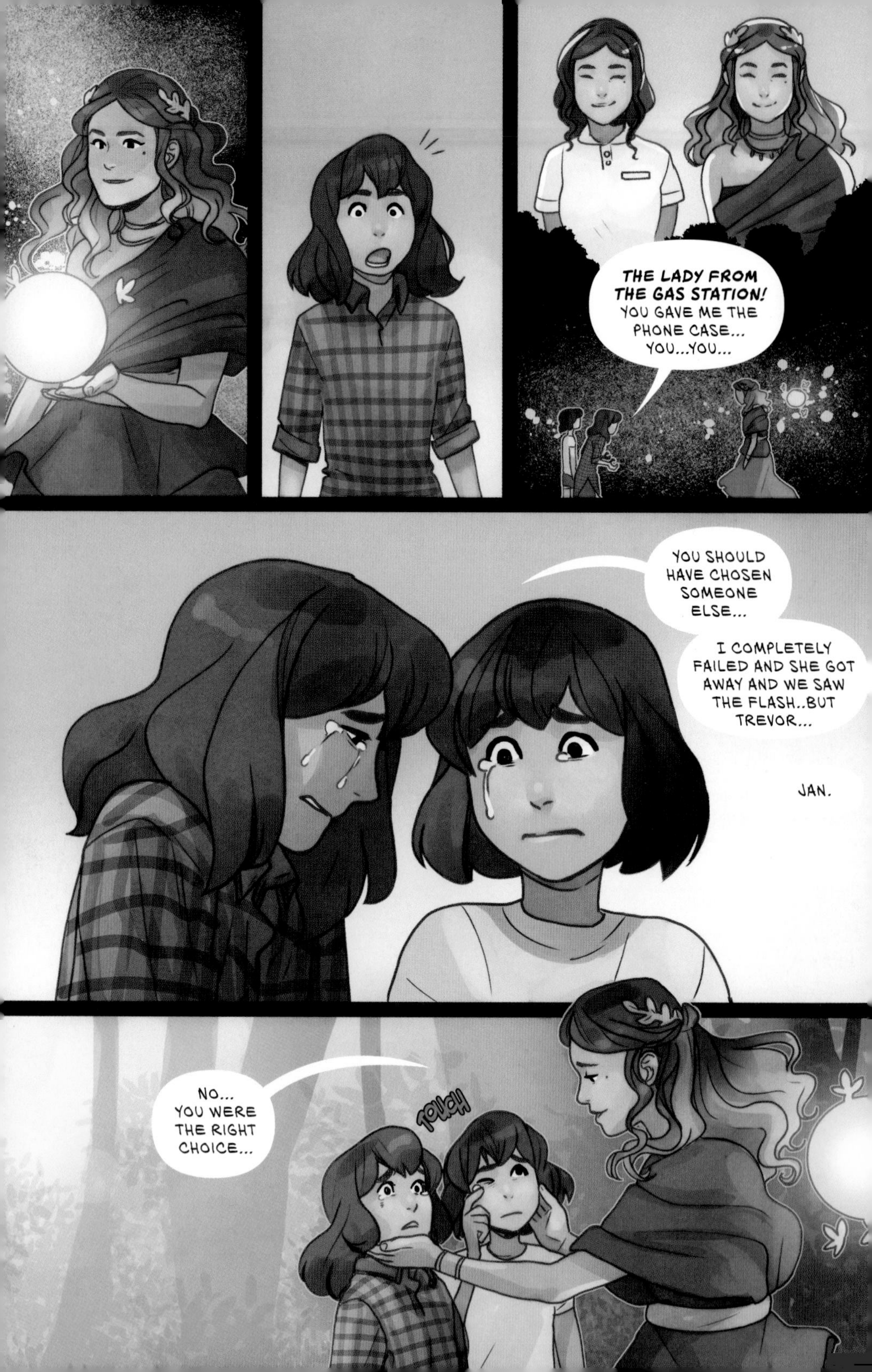
THE LADY FROM THE GAS STATION! YOU GAVE ME THE PHONE CASE... YOU...YOU...
YOU SHOULD HAVE CHOSEN SOMEONE ELSE...
I COMPLETELY FAILED AND SHE GOT AWAY AND WE SAW THE FLASH..BUT TREVOR...
JAN.
NO... YOU WERE THE RIGHT CHOICE...

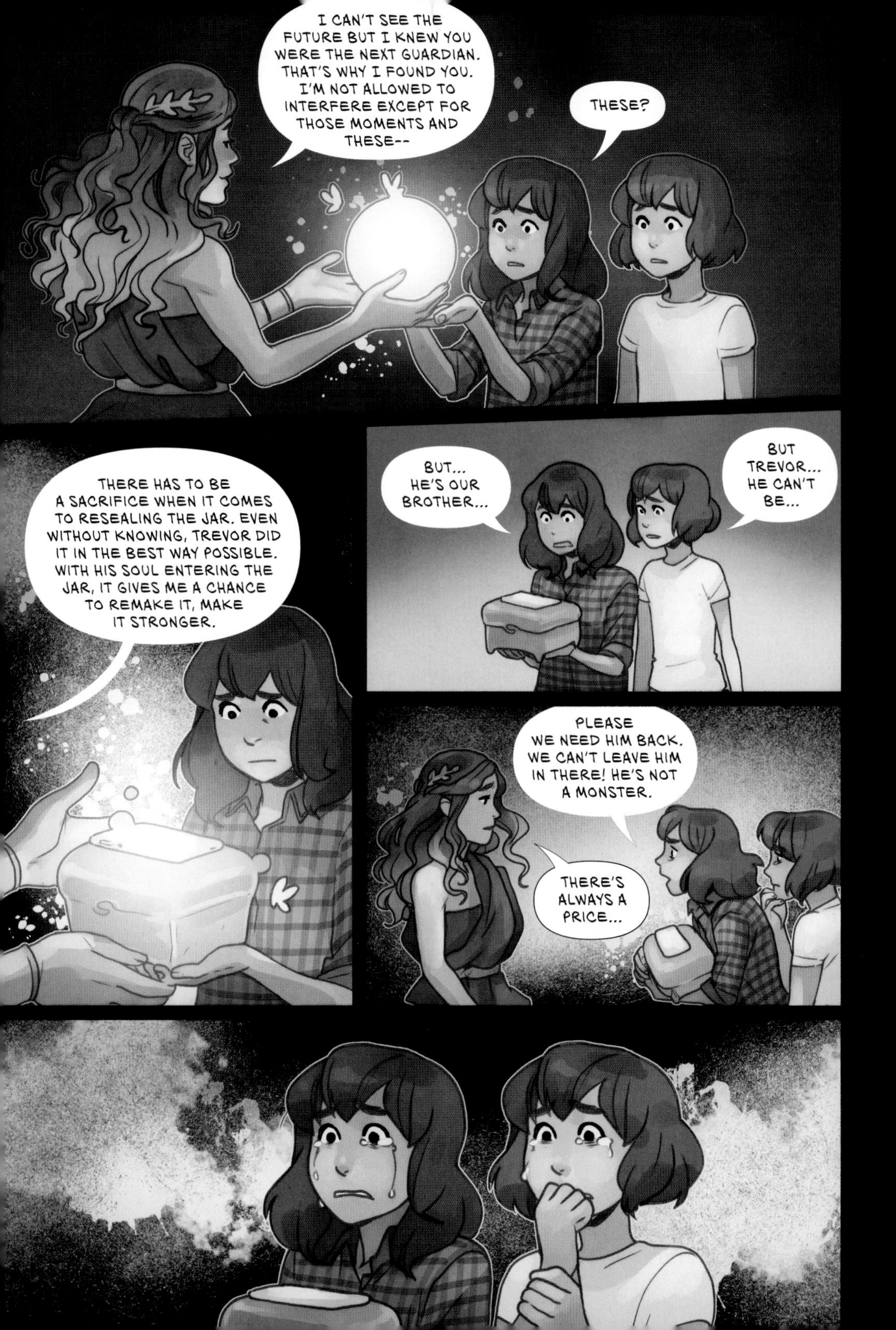

I CAN'T SEE THE FUTURE BUT I KNEW YOU WERE THE NEXT GUARDIAN. THAT'S WHY I FOUND YOU. I'M NOT ALLOWED TO INTERFERE EXCEPT FOR THOSE MOMENTS AND THESE--
THESE?
THERE HAS TO BE A SACRIFICE WHEN IT COMES TO RESEALING THE JAR. EVEN WITHOUT KNOWING, TREVOR DID IT IN THE BEST WAY POSSIBLE. WITH HIS SOUL ENTERING THE JAR, IT GIVES ME A CHANCE TO REMAKE IT, MAKE IT STRONGER.
BUT... HE'S OUR BROTHER...
BUT TREVOR... HE CAN'T BE...
PLEASE WE NEED HIM BACK. WE CAN'T LEAVE HIM IN THERE! HE'S NOT A MONSTER.
THERE'S ALWAYS A PRICE...

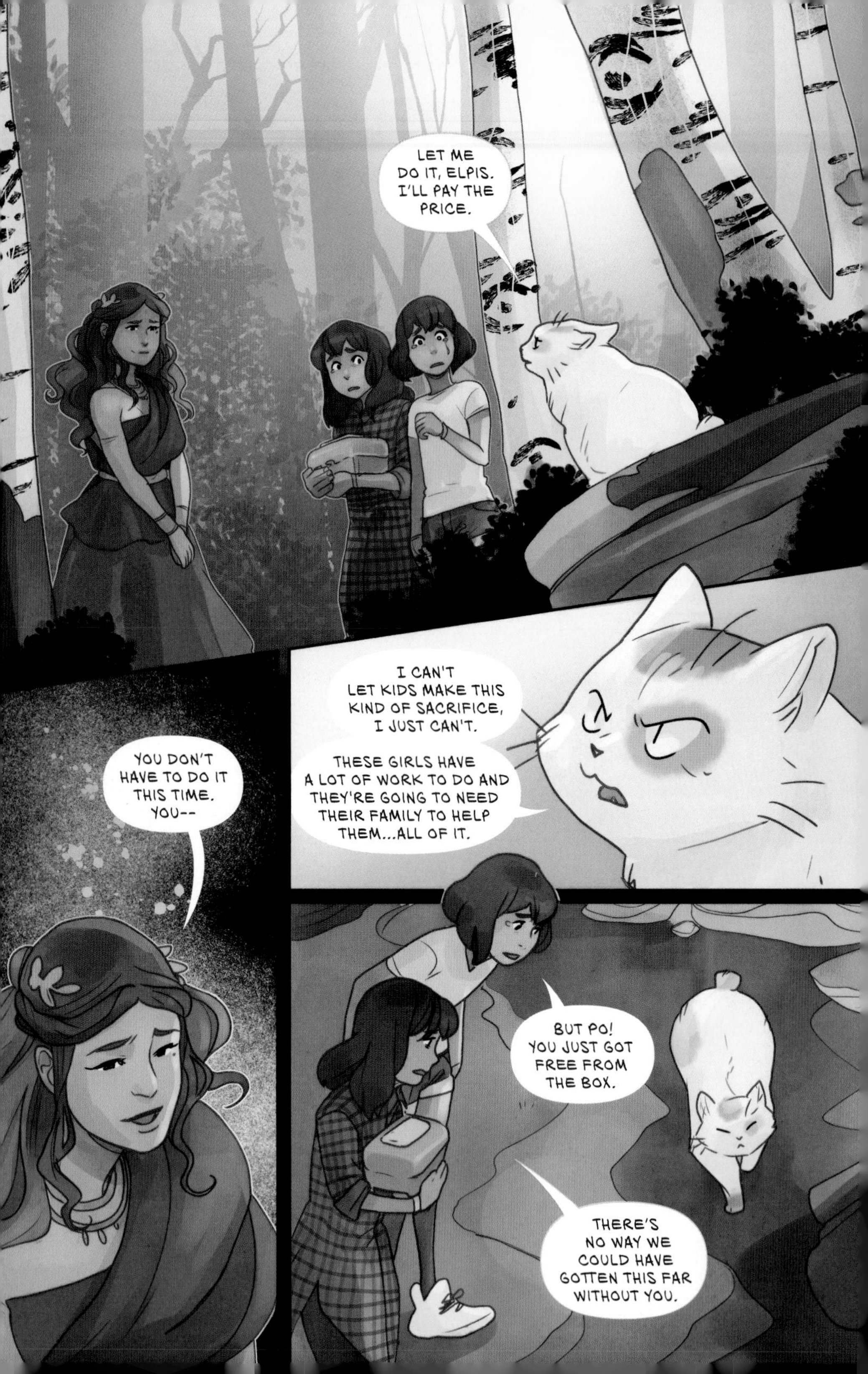
LET ME DO IT, ELPIS. I'LL PAY THE PRICE.
I CAN'T LET KIDS MAKE THIS KIND OF SACRIFICE, I JUST CAN'T.
THESE GIRLS HAVE A LOT OF WORK TO DO AND THEY'RE GOING TO NEED THEIR FAMILY TO HELP THEM...ALL OF IT.
YOU DON'T HAVE TO DO IT THIS TIME. YOU--
BUT PO! YOU JUST GOT FREE FROM THE BOX.
THERE'S NO WAY WE COULD HAVE GOTTEN THIS FAR WITHOUT YOU.

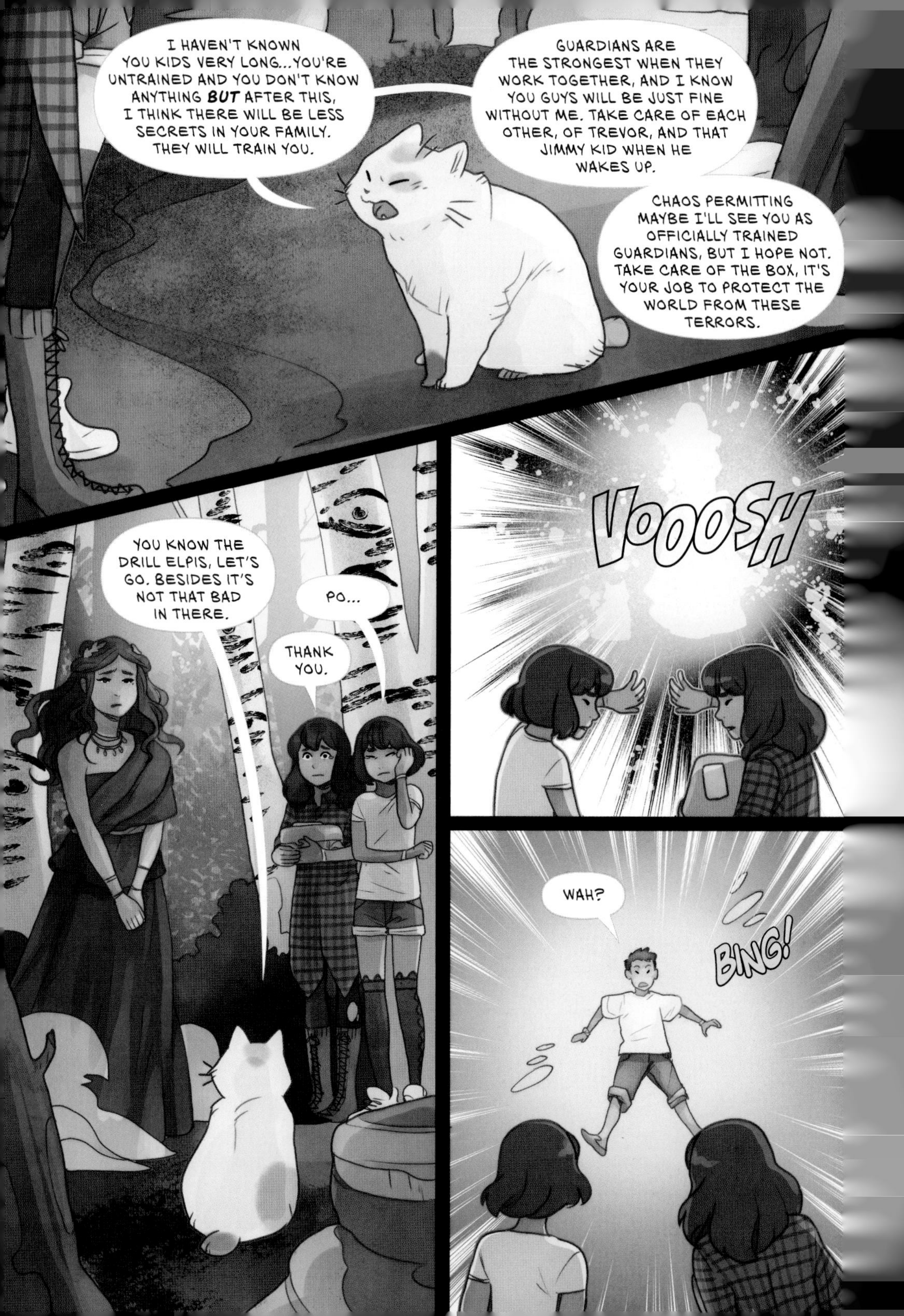
I HAVEN'T KNOWN YOU KIDS VERY LONG...YOU'RE UNTRAINED AND YOU DON'T KNOW ANYTHING **BUT** AFTER THIS, I THINK THERE WILL BE LESS SECRETS IN YOUR FAMILY. THEY WILL TRAIN YOU.
GUARDIANS ARE THE STRONGEST WHEN THEY WORK TOGETHER, AND I KNOW YOU GUYS WILL BE JUST FINE WITHOUT ME. TAKE CARE OF EACH OTHER, OF TREVOR, AND THAT JIMMY KID WHEN HE WAKES UP.
CHAOS PERMITTING MAYBE I'LL SEE YOU AS OFFICIALLY TRAINED GUARDIANS, BUT I HOPE NOT. TAKE CARE OF THE BOX, IT'S YOUR JOB TO PROTECT THE WORLD FROM THESE TERRORS.
YOU KNOW THE DRILL ELPIS, LET'S GO. BESIDES IT'S NOT THAT BAD IN THERE.
PO...
THANK YOU.
VOOOSH
WAH?
BING!

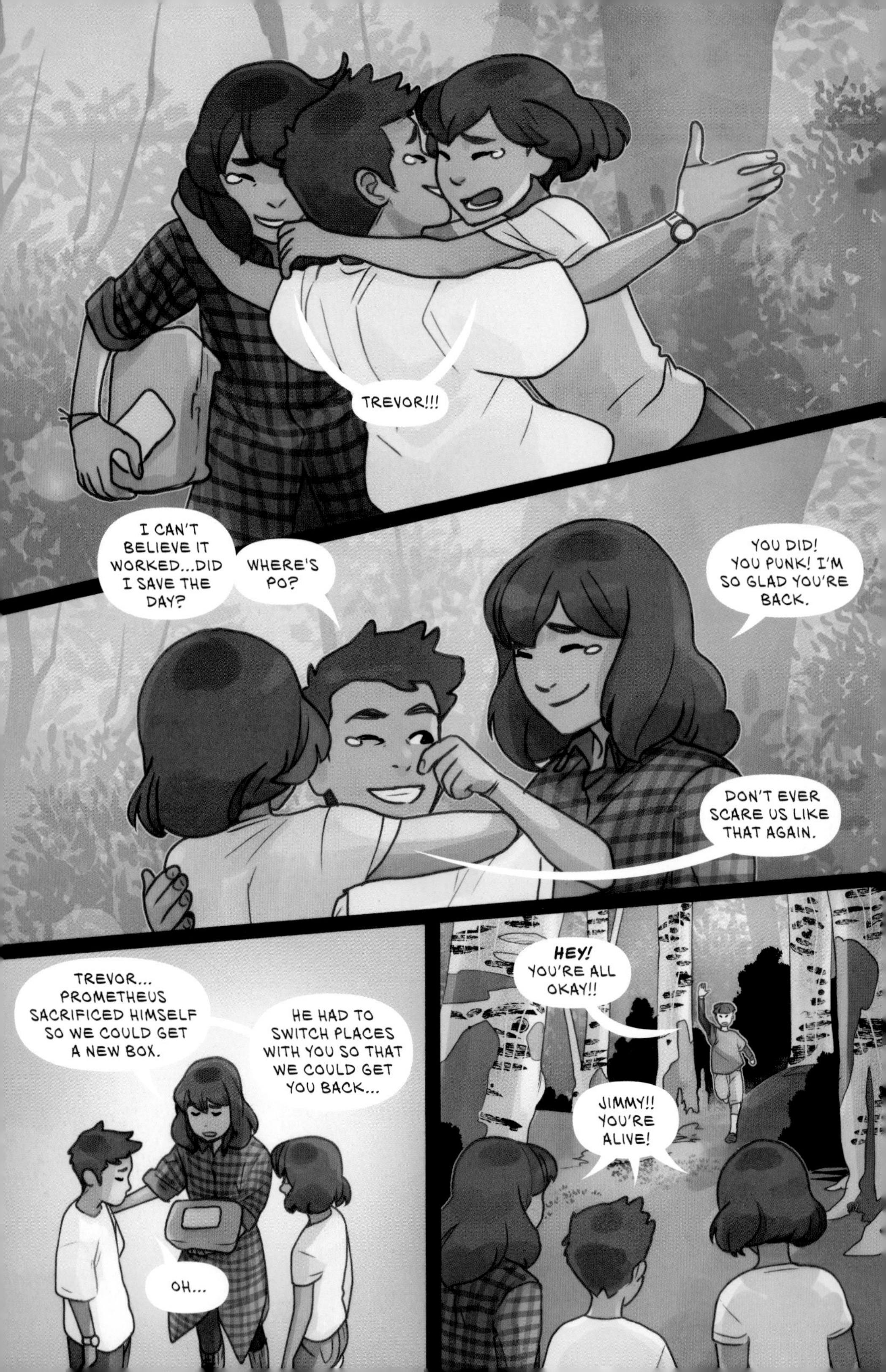
TREVOR!!!
I CAN'T BELIEVE IT WORKED...DID I SAVE THE DAY?
WHERE'S PO?
YOU DID! YOU PUNK! I'M SO GLAD YOU'RE BACK.
DON'T EVER SCARE US LIKE THAT AGAIN.
TREVOR... PROMETHEUS SACRIFICED HIMSELF SO WE COULD GET A NEW BOX.
HE HAD TO SWITCH PLACES WITH YOU SO THAT WE COULD GET YOU BACK...
OH...
HEY! YOU'RE ALL OKAY!!
JIMMY!! YOU'RE ALIVE!

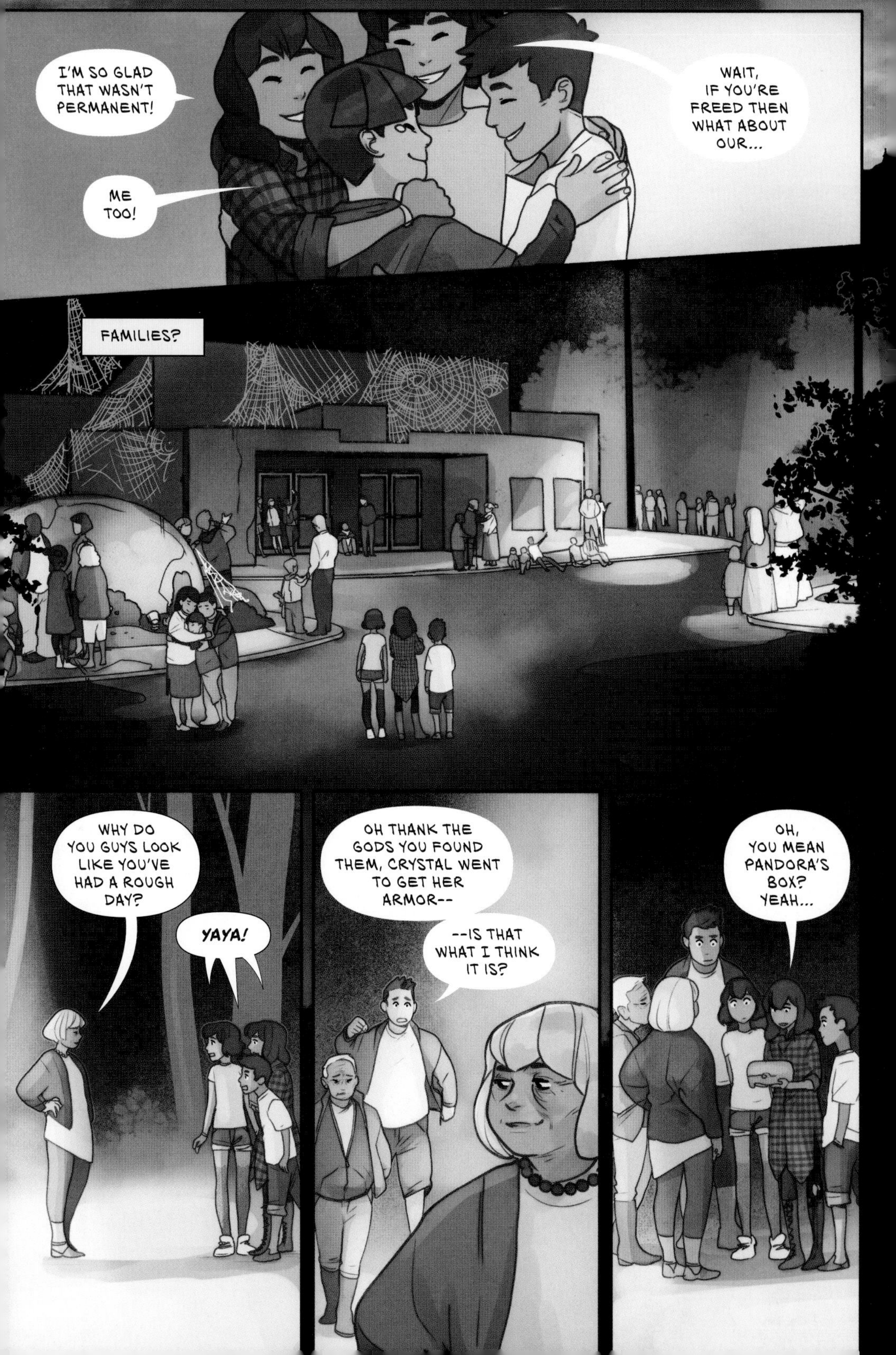
I'M SO GLAD THAT WASN'T PERMANENT!
ME TOO!
WAIT, IF YOU'RE FREED THEN WHAT ABOUT OUR...
FAMILIES?
WHY DO YOU GUYS LOOK LIKE YOU'VE HAD A ROUGH DAY?
YAYA!
OH THANK THE GODS YOU FOUND THEM, CRYSTAL WENT TO GET HER ARMOR--
--IS THAT WHAT I THINK IT IS?
OH, YOU MEAN PANDORA'S BOX? YEAH...

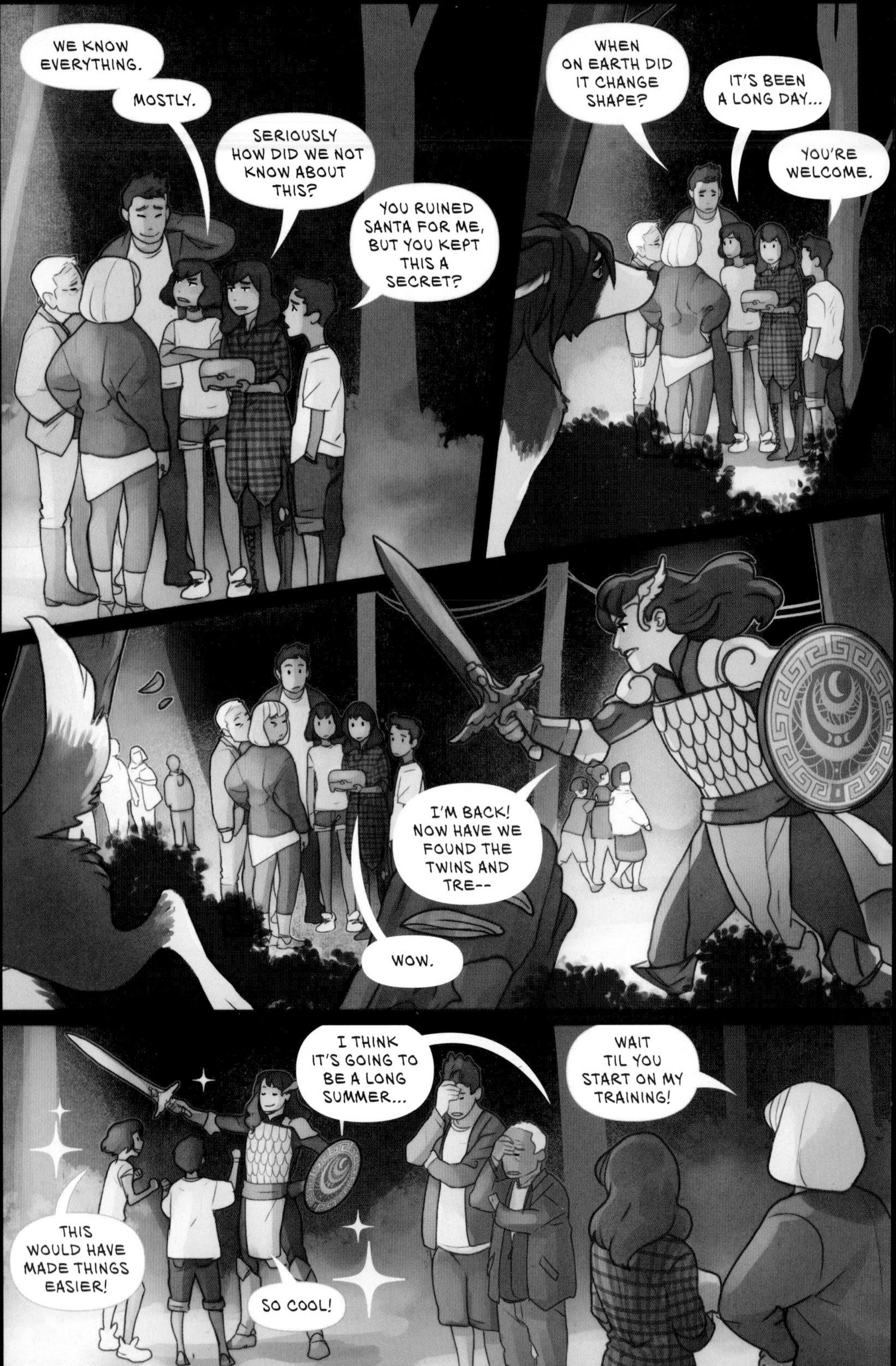
WE KNOW EVERYTHING.
MOSTLY.
SERIOUSLY HOW DID WE NOT KNOW ABOUT THIS?
YOU RUINED SANTA FOR ME, BUT YOU KEPT THIS A SECRET?
WHEN ON EARTH DID IT CHANGE SHAPE?
IT'S BEEN A LONG DAY...
YOU'RE WELCOME.
I'M BACK! NOW HAVE WE FOUND THE TWINS AND TRE--
WOW.
I THINK IT'S GOING TO BE A LONG SUMMER...
WAIT TIL YOU START ON MY TRAINING!
THIS WOULD HAVE MADE THINGS EASIER!
SO COOL!

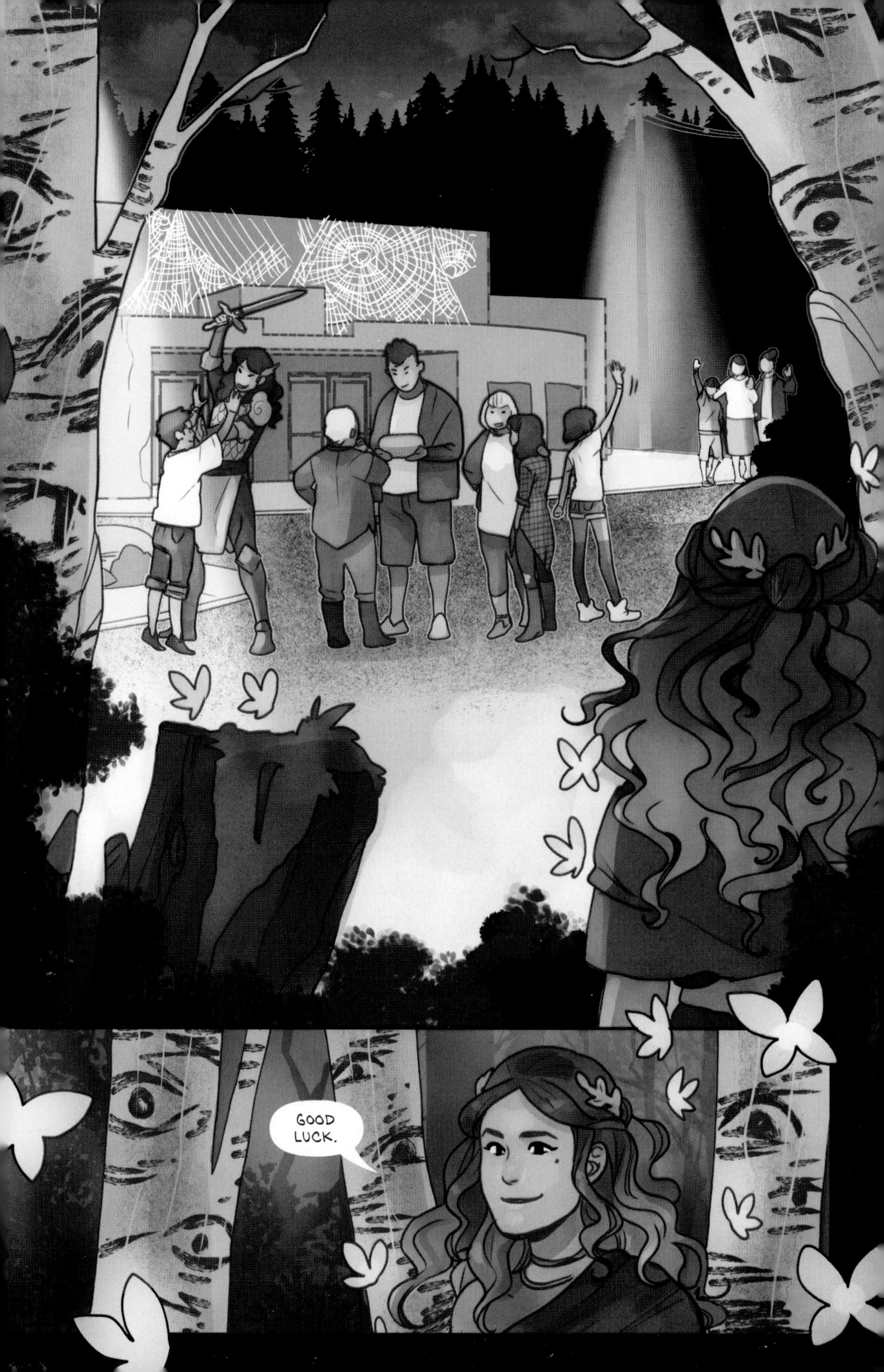
GOOD LUCK.

ABOUT THE CREATORS

KARA LEOPARD is a comics creator and designer, has a bunch of siblings, and is the younger twin by 5 minutes. They've worked on successful kickstarters like *Pandora's Book of Monsters*, *[Super]Natural Attraction* and *They Have Issues: Tales from Comic Book Stores*. They finished their first webcomic *Mr.Hare & Mr.Bear* in 2017 and plan on starting another one soon with the support of their cat Marbles.

KELLY AND NICHOLE MATTHEWS are a pair of twin sisters who were born 7 minutes apart. They combine their powers to create fantastical and imaginative comics and illustrations. They're working on R.L Stine's *Just Beyond: The Scare School* and have worked on series such as *Jim Henson's The Power of the Dark Crystal*, *Lumberjanes/Gotham Academy*, and participated in the anthologies *Beyond 2*, *Oath* and *Valor 2*.